BODY
OF
EVIDENCE

Books by Irene Hannon

Heroes of Quantico

Against All Odds

An Eye for an Eye

In Harm's Way

Guardians of Justice

Fatal Judgment

Deadly Pursuit

Lethal Legacy

Private Justice

Vanished

Trapped

Deceived

Men of Valor

Buried Secrets

Thin Ice

Tangled Webs

Code of Honor

Dangerous Illusions

Hidden Peril

Dark Ambitions

Triple Threat

Point of Danger

Labyrinth of Lies

Body of Evidence

Hope Harbor Novels

Hope Harbor

Sea Rose Lane

Sandpiper Cove

Pelican Point

Driftwood Bay

Starfish Pier

Blackberry Beach

Sea Glass Cottage

Praise for *Labyrinth of Lies*

"Hannon continues her Triple Threat series with this enjoyable second-chance romance between two undercover agents. Hannon's winning inspirational thriller will please fans and newcomers alike."

Publishers Weekly

"This is one of the best offerings by master of romantic suspense Hannon."

Library Journal

"Any Irene Hannon novel is a suspenseful delight. Ms. Hannon is very adept at crafting taut, believable characters."

Interviews and Reviews

"In addition to the mystery, Irene creates a cast of characters that you come to love."

More Than a Review

Praise for *Point of Danger*

"As a general rule, men shun romance novels, while some women turn away from suspense thrillers. But in *Point of Danger*, author Irene Hannon gives readers a thriller with a persistent romantic angle."

St. Louis Post-Dispatch

"An action-packed drama that will have you hooked, trying to piece together clues until the very end."

Best in Suspense

"A page-turner. The surprise ending has a twist readers will not guess."

Military Press

"Riveting suspense focused on controversial issues. Hannon delivers a heart-pounding novel that had me on the edge of my seat."

Relz Reviewz

TRIPLE THREAT 3

BODY OF EVIDENCE

IRENE HANNON

Revell

a division of Baker Publishing Group
Grand Rapids, Michigan

© 2022 by Irene Hannon

Published by Revell
a division of Baker Publishing Group
PO Box 6287, Grand Rapids, MI 49516-6287
www.revellbooks.com

Printed in the United States of America

Library of Congress Cataloging-in-Publication Data
Names: Hannon, Irene, author.
Title: Body of evidence / Irene Hannon.
Description: Grand Rapids, MI : Revell, a division of Baker Publishing Group,
    [2022] | Series: Triple threat ; 3
Identifiers: LCCN 2021061212 | ISBN 9780800736194 (paperback) | ISBN
    9780800742188 (cloth) | ISBN 9781493438709 (ebook)
Subjects: LCGFT: Novels.
Classification: LCC PS3558.A4793 B63 2022 | DDC 813/.54—dc23/eng/20211216
LC record available at https://lccn.loc.gov/2021061212

This book is a work of fiction. Names, characters, places, and incidents are the
product of the author's imagination or are used fictitiously. Any resemblance to
actual events, locales, or persons, living or dead, is coincidental.

Baker Publishing Group publications use paper produced from sustainable for-
estry practices and post-consumer waste whenever possible.

22 23 24 25 26 27 28   7 6 5 4 3 2 1

To the incredible team I've partnered with at Revell
for fifteen years and twenty-eight books:

Dwight Baker
Jennifer Leep
Kristin Kornoelje
Michele Misiak
Karen Steele

Thank you for your professionalism,
dedication, responsiveness,
commitment to excellence—and friendship.

It is a privilege and a pleasure to be
your publishing partner.

1

SOMEONE WAS IN THE MORTUARY PREP ROOM. Someone besides her and the body in the cooler awaiting tomorrow's autopsy.

Someone who shouldn't be here.

Forensic pathologist Grace Reilly set aside the police report on seventy-six-year-old Mavis Templeton and cocked her ear.

Silence.

She waited, straining to pick up another out-of-place sound.

Only the drip of the leaky faucet, the hum of refrigeration from the cooler, and the squeak of the desk chair as she leaned forward broke the stillness.

There was no one here.

And she shouldn't be, either.

There were better places for a thirty-year-old single woman to hang out at nine o'clock on Friday night than a funeral home in rural Missouri.

Unless you were a thirty-year-old single woman whose last hot date had been three months ago. A date that had cooled off fast after the guy asked about your day, and you'd told him in perhaps a *tad* too much detail while the two of you were chowing down on barbecue.

Grace sighed and slumped back in the chair.

As soon as the color began leaching from her companion's complexion, she'd changed the subject—but not fast enough to salvage the evening or win herself another dinner invitation. He'd dumped most of his meal into a takeout container, hustled her home as fast as he could, and never called again.

So with nothing more interesting to do on *this* Friday night, she'd swung by the mortuary to review the paperwork and medical records for tomorrow's autopsy.

Pathetic.

Huffing out a breath, she pushed the chair back and stood. She was out of here. Watching a movie by herself from her collection of oldies wasn't her first choice of activity for a Friday night, but it was preferable to—

She froze.

There it was again. A muffled, metallic tapping noise. Faint but discernible.

And it was coming from the cooler.

A shiver snaked down her spine.

The only person in there was Mavis, and she wasn't doing any tapping.

Sidling around the desk, she eyed the refrigeration unit. There had to be a logical explanation for the noise.

Of course there did.

Nevertheless, she opened her purse and pulled out the compact Beretta she'd carried ever since—

No.

She was *not* going there.

That was then, this was now—and lightning didn't often strike twice. She was overreacting.

Even so, she kept her pistol at the ready as she approached the cooler.

The faint tap sounded again. More to the right, and muffled. Like it was outside the building.

Exhaling, she lowered the gun. A noise on the other side of

the wall was nothing to worry about. For all she knew, a careful of teenagers had pulled into the parking lot of the funeral home and decided to down a few illegal beers where no one was likely to disturb them.

This out-of-proportion response to a stray noise wasn't like her.

But she *was* tired. It had been a long week, and she was stretched thin. Doing autopsies for six adjacent rural counties, not to mention the occasional private job she picked up, kept her on the move.

Add in that weird noise she'd heard outside the window of her rental house last night, and it was no surprise her usual calm was a mite wobbly.

Time to call it a night, go home, watch that old movie, and chill.

She returned to the desk, picked up her purse, and started to tuck her Beretta inside. Hesitated. Shook her head in annoyance.

This was farm country, for pity's sake. Two and a half hours away from St. Louis and the types of crime that plagued all big cities. In the three years she'd been doing autopsies for the county coroners, homicides had been few and far between.

After all, if you couldn't be safe deep in the heartland, where could you be safe?

Despite that little pep talk, she kept her weapon in hand—where it would stay until she was behind the wheel of her car and locked inside. It never hurt to be careful, as she'd learned the hard way.

She exited through the wide back door in the small foyer off the work area, filling her lungs with the warm June air as she gave the dim parking lot a swift perusal.

No beer-drinking teens in sight.

So much for that theory.

Nor was anyone else about. Whatever the source of the noise she'd heard from inside, it was gone.

More proof that letting her imagination give her a case of the shakes had been silly.

She closed the door behind her, tested it to make certain it was locked, and strode toward her Civic.

Six feet away, she came to an abrupt halt, stomach lurching.

Apparently the noise she'd heard hadn't been innocent after all.

And despite her original suspicion that it had come from inside the cooler, this had been done by someone very much alive.

Backing up, she groped in her purse for her cell. Punched in 911.

And kept her finger on the trigger of her Beretta.

Sheriff Nate Cox hung a right into the parking lot of Larktree Mortuary and circled around to the back.

First call he'd ever gotten to a funeral home—but there'd been a ton of firsts since he'd been elected to the job four months ago.

A Larktree cruiser came into sight, and Nate pulled up beside it. Thank God local police were willing to respond to 911 calls until he or one of his deputies could arrive. With only seven of them providing 24/7 coverage for more than 750 square miles of territory, it wasn't unusual to be twenty minutes away from a crime scene, even with sirens blaring and a heavy foot on the gas pedal.

But despite the courtesy response, the mortuary was beyond the town limits and therefore outside the jurisdiction of the local cops. Meaning this case was going to land on his desk.

He slid out of his patrol car as the officer walked toward him from the shadows of the protective roof that shielded the back door of the building. Over the man's shoulder, Nate squinted at the victim, who remained near the exit, purse gripped in front of her, posture taut. Though he couldn't distinguish any features in the dim light, she appeared to be on the young side.

"Matt Jackson." The fiftyish officer stuck out his hand.

Nate gave it a firm shake and returned the introduction. "Thanks for responding. I got here as fast as I could."

"No worries. It's a quiet night in town."

"What do we have?"

The man gave him a cursory overview. "I poked around after I got here, but I didn't see anything helpful."

"Thanks. I'll take another look. Two sets of eyes can't hurt. Who's the victim?"

"Grace Reilly."

It took no more than a second for her name to click into place. He'd seen it on a few autopsy reports—including one that had struck too close to home—but their paths had never crossed.

"What was she doing here at this hour?"

"Paperwork."

"On a Friday night?"

The man shrugged. "To each his own. Said she was prepping for an autopsy tomorrow."

Must be the one for Mavis Templeton. He'd responded to that call yesterday morning, and there'd been no other suspicious deaths in the past few days.

"Anyone else here?"

"No."

She'd been alone in a mortuary with a dead body after dark. By choice.

He suppressed a shudder. After all the death he'd seen during military missions overseas, the idea of spending an evening in the company of a lifeless body shouldn't spook him.

But it did.

Having death thrust upon you was one thing. Seeking it out? Not his cup of tea.

"Thanks again for swinging by and hanging out until I got here."

"Happy to do it. Good luck."

As the officer returned to his cruiser, Nate circled Grace's car, giving it a cursory scan. It had been keyed on all door panels and sported several small, deep, round dents—as if someone had hammered the end of a pipe against the frame.

Circuit complete, he walked over to her, extending his hand as a low rumble of thunder reverberated in the distance. "Nate Cox. I've read quite a few of your reports. Sorry we have to meet under these circumstances."

"Likewise."

Her fingers were cold as she returned his firm squeeze, and he gave her a quick assessment.

Early thirties, at most. Five four, give or take an inch, using his six-foot frame as reference. Wavy, longish hair the color of the spicy ginger cookies his mom used to make. A strong chin that could suggest a personality to match. Hazel eyes that were big . . . and appealing.

He frowned at that last, inappropriate thought. Cataloging a victim's features was part of the job. Reacting to them wasn't.

Switching mental gears, he refocused. "I know you told Officer Jackson what happened tonight, but I'd appreciate it if you'd run through it again."

She complied, her report straightforward, precise, and detailed. No less than he'd expect from a forensic pathologist. They were trained to tune in to the tiniest details.

"And that's what I found when I came outside." She motioned toward her car as she concluded.

"Any idea who may have done this?"

"No."

"Any known enemies?"

"No."

"Does anyone have a grudge against you?"

"Not that I'm aware of."

"Have you received any recent threatening communication?"

She hesitated—and a blip appeared on his radar.

"Not communication in the sense you mean it."

"Explain that."

She exhaled and tucked her hair behind her ear. "I'm probably being paranoid."

"Or not, considering the state of your car."

She conceded the point with a nod. "Last night, about one in the morning, I heard a noise that sounded like someone was rattling the knob on my back door."

"Did you call the police?"

"No. It was windy, and I wasn't certain anyone was out there. I also have excellent locks, a security system, and my Beretta was on the nightstand. I didn't think there was any real danger. But it was rather unnerving."

The lady kept a weapon close at hand while she slept?

The blip got bigger.

"Any particular reason you have a gun?"

She lifted one shoulder, her features flattening. "My oldest sister is a police detective in St. Louis. After all the stories I've heard, getting a concealed carry permit seemed prudent. I've had it for years."

Her response was straightforward, and he couldn't argue with her rationale. Nor was there anything in her answer to suggest she had a personal motive for carrying.

But his gut was sending a strong message that she wasn't telling him everything.

However—if she'd had the gun for as long as she claimed, it probably wasn't relevant to the current situation.

"Did you find any evidence to suggest anyone had been on your property?"

"Nothing specific."

"But you found something."

Twin grooves creased her forehead. "There are two daylilies beside the steps to the back porch. All of the buds had been snapped off. I know deer like to munch on them, but they've never bothered those plants before. Besides, the buds weren't eaten. Just broken off and scattered around."

Adding credence to her theory that someone with two legs had paid her a visit.

He gave her car another sweep. In most cases, that sort of damage could be attributed to petty vandalism. It was the type of stunt bored high school kids were known to pull.

It was also possible her nocturnal visitor last night and this evening's damage were unrelated.

But the instincts he'd honed and learned to trust on the battlefield were beeping a yellow alert.

Translation? He wasn't going to be able to write off tonight's crime as easily as he'd expected. If the two incidents *were* related, it would suggest someone was targeting Grace Reilly for unknown reasons.

A few raindrops began to fall, and he motioned toward his car. "Would you like to wait in the cruiser after you give me your contact information while I take a closer look at your vehicle?"

"No, thanks. I'm protected here."

Once she provided the information he requested, he left her under the overhang, retrieved his flashlight, and did another circuit of her red Civic. As the rain picked up, he swept his light over the asphalt, pausing to take photos of the scratches and dents with his cellphone.

By the time he rejoined her, his shirt was damp and cling-ing to his torso.

"Did you see anything helpful?" She jingled her keys in her hand, as if she was anxious to leave.

"No. The doors are all locked, and it doesn't appear anyone tried to break in. The damage is confined to the outside. As far as I can tell, whoever did this didn't leave any evidence behind. But I'll swing back by in daylight in case I missed anything. I understand you'll be here in the morning?"

"Yes. Along with the coroner and my autopsy tech."

"I'll knock on the door after I finish and give you an up-date." The comment was out before he could stop it.

Strange.

Another one-on-one visit wasn't necessary. He could file his report, including any additional findings he discovered tomorrow, and she could obtain a copy for insurance purposes from the office. He didn't have to see her again.

But he wanted to.

Another first during his tenure as sheriff.

"Are we finished for tonight?" She continued to jingle her keys.

"Yes. I'll walk you to your car." Also not necessary. And not an offer he'd ever made on past calls.

Grace maintained a white-knuckled grip on her purse as he walked beside her—a clear indication her calm demeanor was nothing more than a façade. The lady was far more shaken than she wanted to let on.

"Thanks for your help tonight and for the follow-up tomor-row." She angled toward him, the faint illumination from the inadequate overhead lights throwing the taut planes of her face into stark relief.

"All part of the job. I'll wait until you pull out."

She nodded in acknowledgment, slid behind the wheel, and started the engine.

He closed the door and stepped back, remaining in place while she drove across the lot, stopped at the entrance, and hung a left onto the dim, deserted road.

As her taillights disappeared, he walked back to his car, flexing his shoulders to loosen the damp material stuck to his skin. It was going to be uncomfortable until his shirt dried.

He'd endured far worse during his military days, however. The physical discomfort this call had produced was tolerable.

The disquiet, less so.

His radio crackled to life as he opened the door of his cruiser, summoning him to a potential burglary fifteen miles away. He shifted into drive and pulled onto the road, accelerating through the rural darkness as fields and pastures flew by.

But no matter how much distance he put between himself and the mortuary, he couldn't shake the sense that tonight's incident was more than a random act of vandalism.

2

THAT WAS ODD.

Grace lifted the large, clear measuring cup that held the contents of Mavis Templeton's stomach and scrutinized the one-half-by-one-eighth-inch flat oval on top.

It looked like a seed of some kind.

It also resembled an object she'd found in a stomach during an autopsy a few months ago.

"Come across something interesting?"

She turned toward her autopsy technician. Who knew, when she'd accepted this gig in rural America, that a tech with Max's skills, experience, and insights would come forward and make her job so much easier?

"What do you think that item on top is?" She held out the cup for his inspection.

He moved closer, the plastic apron he wore over his disposable surgical gown crinkling as he approached, and peered into the cup. "No clue." His response was slightly muffled by the splash shield covering his face.

"Best guess."

He lifted his gaze. "Why?"

"It's unusual."

"You mean beyond the fact it's intact?"

A sound observation. Gastric juices were efficient. In most cases, stomach contents became pulp within an hour or two.

"Yes."

Max inspected it again. "It could be a seed."

"That's what I thought."

He shrugged. "People do eat seeds."

"I doubt Mavis would have. Not on purpose."

"How do you know?"

"We attended the same church and often talked after services. Sometimes about food. She told me she was a picky eater."

He motioned toward the seedlike object. "Is that why this caught your attention?"

"It's one of the factors. I also saw a couple of these in an autopsy six, eight months ago. In that case, the stomach wall was hemorrhagic, thickened, and stiff—which is why I took a closer look at the contents in the first place. Mavis's stomach is in the same condition."

"So?"

"I've done more than a thousand autopsies, and I've only come across an object like this twice. Seems strange to find it within a small geographic radius mere months apart."

He squinted at her. "Strange as in suspicious?"

She cast a glance at Russ Franklin on the far side of the room. The coroner was finishing his second donut while he talked on his cell. "Maybe."

"That may be a stretch." Max plopped Mavis's liver on the scale. "There's more, isn't there?"

Her seasoned tech knew her well.

She joined him, skimmed the readout, and jotted 1,240 grams on the autopsy form. Within normal range, as almost all the findings had been.

"Call it intuition, but Mavis was healthy. She had a physical two weeks ago and got a positive report from her doctor.

Also, other than over-the-counter allergy pills, she took no medicine. She gave me a topline health history while I chatted with her last Sunday."

He removed the liver from the scale. "Physicals don't catch everything."

"I know." Yet she couldn't extinguish a smoldering ember of unease. "I want to take a larger-than-usual sample of that." Since the liver was the most valuable tissue specimen for toxicology testing, having more material on hand rather than less was prudent.

Just in case the weird vibes she was getting led to deeper investigation.

"What are you going to do with that?" He indicated the cup of stomach contents.

"Will you sieve it for me while I get my sample?"

"Not our standard protocol."

"Humor me."

"Fine." He rummaged around in her tool kit while she got her liver sample, then dumped the stomach contents into the strainer. "Another seed—or whatever they are."

She joined him, poking through the semi-solid mush with her forceps. There were a total of three oval objects.

"I want a sample of this too. Including all the seeds."

"You got it."

While Max attended to that task, she wrote a few notes on the standard autopsy form attached to her clipboard.

When he handed her the sample container for labeling, she motioned toward the table. "You can reset the head block."

As Max repositioned it from under the woman's back to behind her head, Grace picked up the saw.

So far, there was nothing to suggest foul play, even though Mavis had been found halfway up the stairs and there'd been signs of a break-in at her home. While the circumstance had prompted the coroner to request an autopsy, a robber hadn't directly caused her demise.

Max stepped back, and Grace took his place.

Unless an abnormality in the brain suggested otherwise, she'd list the cause of death as cardiac arrhythmia due to atherosclerotic coronary artery disease, assuming the toxicology report came back negative—if the coroner even ordered toxicology. The blocked arteries she'd found in Mavis weren't uncommon in older folks, and they often went undetected while people were living. In all probability, Russ would classify the manner of death as natural, and that would be the end of the story.

Officially.

That didn't mean she couldn't dig deeper, though. Try to determine whether the similarities between the other death she recalled and this one went beyond the inclusion of seed-like objects in the stomach.

A long shot, for sure, as Max had implied. She could invest a ton of effort and end up with nothing to show for it.

But like her two sisters, she was stuck with the justice gene that pushed them to seek answers often shrouded in shadows.

And danger.

His timing couldn't have been worse.

As soon as the guy in head-to-foot personal protective equipment opened the door, Nate heard the saw.

Grace Reilly was cutting off the top of the skull to examine the brain.

The autopsy wasn't winding down, as he'd hoped. It was in full swing.

"May I help you?" The man gave him a once-over, keeping a firm grip on the door with a latex-gloved hand.

Nate swallowed and introduced himself. "I told Dr. Reilly I'd stop by this morning."

"Sorry. I was expecting a uniform." He pulled the door wide.

"I'm off duty today."

"That would explain it. I'm Max, her tech. Come on in."

Nate held back. "I thought you'd be to the paperwork stage by now."

"Doc's very thorough."

He already knew that. The autopsy reports he'd seen dotted every i and crossed every t. No surprise that diligence and meticulous attention to detail were as important to Grace during exams as they were in the reports that documented her findings.

"I don't want to interrupt." The whir of the saw ceased.

"You won't be. Doc doesn't let anything or anyone interfere with her concentration while she's working." Max gave him a speculative perusal. "Unless you'd rather wait outside. Autopsies aren't for everyone."

But law enforcement types were expected to have the stomach for them.

A spurt of misplaced pride zipped through Nate, propelled by the humor glinting in the man's irises. "I'll come in."

You're being stupid, Cox. The man gave you an out. You should take it.

Too late. Max had moved aside and was waiting for him to enter.

Fine. He'd claim a spot off to the side, as far from the action as possible.

Gritting his teeth, he followed Max through the small foyer and into the mortuary prep room, which felt at least twenty degrees cooler than the mideighties temperature outside.

"Have a seat." Max motioned to a chair against the wall. "Unless you want to suit up like the coroner."

"I'll sit." He lifted a hand in greeting to Russ, who was eating a donut.

Amazing.

But maybe after thirty years on the job witnessing thousands of autopsies, you learned to overcome any squeamishness.

"Thought you might. Restroom's over there." Max waved a hand toward the far wall, at the other end of the autopsy table.

Was that a smirk behind the man's face shield?

A distinct possibility. His gut said the guy had seen right through his momentary show of bravado.

Grace Reilly spared him a quick glance as he claimed the chair. "Sorry to keep you waiting. We'll be wrapping up in a few minutes."

"Don't rush on my account."

He sat, pulled out his cell, and pretended to check email.

"No sign of a stroke or tumor." Grace's back was to him, her voice slightly muted by the face shield. "Everything looks normal."

"Are you going with cardiac arrhythmia as cause?" This from Russ, who'd finished his donut and wandered over to the table.

"Yes."

"You okay if we skip toxicology and go with manner as natural?"

In the silence that followed, the air-conditioning kicked on—and Nate's nose twitched as the dreaded scent of formalin swirled around the room.

He stifled a groan. He should *not* have eaten that fast-food sausage biscuit an hour ago.

"Yes."

Grace's belated reply registered at a peripheral level, but he was too busy trying to hold on to his breakfast to pay much attention to the conversation.

The sights of an autopsy he could handle. The cutting and

24

dissecting and blood—what little there was of it—never bothered his stomach.

It was the smells that got to him. Especially the preserving fluid. A scent so subtle no one but him ever seemed to notice it.

Despite the cool temperature in the room, he began to sweat.

Stomach churning, he gauged the distance to the restroom as the discussion near the body continued.

Too far away. And he did *not* want to add upchucking in front of an audience to his list of most embarrassing moments.

The sole potential antidote to his condition was fresh air. Lots of it.

Shoving his phone back into his pocket, he bolted for the door. Pushed through into the foyer. Dashed for the exit.

Once outside, the sun took some of the chill out of his bones. But banishing the formalin from his lungs didn't do as much to settle his stomach as he'd hoped.

In fact, in the end it merely delayed the inevitable.

Thirty seconds after his hasty escape from the mortuary's back room, he admitted defeat. He was going to lose his breakfast—or what was left of it.

But he wasn't going to do it in the middle of the parking lot, where the evidence would be splattered on the asphalt for the whole world to see.

Holding back the rumbling volcano in his stomach as long as he could, he sped toward the bushes edging the lot. Made it. Barely.

After he finished heaving, he pulled out his handkerchief, wiped his mouth, and gave the deserted lot a surreptitious sweep.

Thank heavens there had been no witnesses to his mortifying spectacle. Puking at an autopsy didn't fit the image of a county sheriff—or a former Special Forces soldier.

He couldn't avoid autopsies forever, though. One of these days he was going to have to get over his smell issues.

Today, however, hadn't been that day.

At least he'd made it outside before he humiliated himself.

Yet as he walked over to his off-duty Jeep to wait for Grace Reilly, a pungent stench dogged his heels. It was far worse than the formalin . . . and clear evidence of his Achilles' heel.

There was also no disguising it.

If fate was kind, by the time Grace finished and came in search of him, the wind would shift, and the obnoxious odor would—

The back door of the mortuary opened, and the woman in question emerged into the sunlight.

He blew out a breath.

Fate wasn't in his corner today.

She'd shed her protective garb to reveal well-broken-in jeans that hugged her slim hips and a soft, curve-enhancing T-shirt emblazoned with the words "My job requires humor, heart, and brains."

His lips quirked up.

Clever—and sort of a private joke. Most people wouldn't realize the humor part referred to the sample of eye fluid taken during autopsies.

As soon as she spotted him, she strode his direction across the asphalt, a breeze ruffling the wavy hair she'd freed from her surgical cap.

The stink was somewhat diffused now, but definitive. She had to smell it.

In the name of diplomacy, would she ignore it . . . or was she the type to confront an awkward situation, deal with it, and move on?

"Don't feel bad about what happened in there—or out here." She waved a hand in the direction of the smell. "A weak stomach doesn't equate to a weak character. One of the finest men I know gets queasy at the sight of blood. Even a cut finger can turn his stomach. That would be my dad."

Question answered.

"For the record, the visuals I can handle. It's the formalin that does me in."

"Really? I don't even notice that smell."

"Hypersensitive nose. What can I say? I'm working on it."

"If it's any consolation, you do get used to autopsy scents. But reaching that point isn't always pleasant."

"Tell me about it. Are you done in there?" He motioned toward the mortuary.

"Yes. Max is closing for me. I'll finish up the paperwork at home. The day's too pretty to spend in a funeral home. Any news on the vandalism?"

"I went over the lot again before I joined you inside, but it's clean. I'll talk with the local police, see if there's been a rash of this sort of crime recently, discuss potential suspects."

Twin furrows scored her brow. "Whoever did this is going to get away with it, aren't they?"

He studied the faint shadows beneath her lower lashes—clear evidence that last night's incident had disrupted her slumber—as he debated how to answer. Grace Reilly struck him as the kind of woman who liked the truth straight up.

But the truth wasn't going to help her sleep.

"We could get a lead from the local police. If not, we'll keep this on our radar and work it from our end."

"That didn't answer my question."

Why was he not surprised she'd called him on his hedge?

"Without a lead or two—fast—this could be difficult to solve."

She exhaled. "No one dusted the car for prints."

"I doubt anyone touched the car."

"They could have."

"If they did, odds are they were wearing gloves. Even the most inept criminals these days are smart enough to do that. And if it was teenagers out for fun and games, they wouldn't have a record that would put them in the database."

Her nostrils flared, and she propped her fists on her hips as she scanned her Civic. "I want to know who did this."

Of course she did. Anyone would be upset by a vandalism incident directed at them and would want the perpetrator found.

But there was a subtle, simmering anger in her tone that went beyond righteous indignation.

Why?

Did it have anything to do with the gun on her nightstand . . . and perhaps in her purse?

"I do too." He considered her. "I could swing by your place later today and dust around the areas of damage on the car." The odds of that resulting in any useful prints were negligible, but if the effort gave her more peace of mind, why not? Until dinner tonight, there was nothing on his agenda that couldn't wait.

She surveyed his jeans and T-shirt. "Are you on duty today?"

"Sheriffs are always on duty."

"Let me rephrase. You're not officially working today, are you?"

"No. But I wasn't supposed to be working last night, either—until one of my deputies had a family emergency. Odd hours and an unpredictable schedule go with the job."

Her frown deepened. "I hate to infringe on your day off. Besides, like you said, there's probably nothing on the car."

"I'll be happy to take a look anyway. While I'm at your place, I can also nose around for any evidence of your trespasser from two nights ago."

She caught her lower lip between her teeth. "I don't know . . ."

He made the decision for her. "I have your address. I'll swing by the office for supplies and meet you at your house. Or do you have other places to go first?"

"No. I was planning to head home and finish the autopsy paperwork."

"Expect me in forty-five minutes." Without waiting for her to respond, he unlocked his Jeep and slid behind the wheel.

She was still standing there, expression puzzled, when he pulled out. As if she couldn't figure out why he was going to all this trouble.

That made two of them.

The truth was, barring a miracle or a very careless vandal, there weren't going to be any usable prints on the car. And the chances of finding evidence of the knob-rattler's visit were also slim to none.

He'd volunteered for extra duty with one goal in mind.

To extend his time with Grace Reilly.

And that was wrong. Not just because it bordered on un-professional, but because of Becky.

A stab of self-reproach skewered him, and he clamped his jaw shut. Tightened his grip on the wheel. Dodged a pothole in the road.

Why did life always have to be complicated?

Why couldn't he have met Grace Reilly a year ago?

Why did he have to have such a finely honed conscience?

He tossed the questions to the heavens, not really expecting answers. So it was no surprise none appeared.

Since it was too late to retract his offer, he'd have to do the job at warp speed and get out of there as fast as he could.

After that, there'd be few excuses for them to interact. Near as he could recall from what Russ had told him about Grace early in his tenure, she'd been under contract with the county for three years. If this was their first encounter in his four months on the job, it was doubtful they'd run into each other often. And reading her clinical autopsy reports wasn't going to juice his libido like an in-person meeting would.

All he had to do was complete his fruitless search for fingerprints and evidence of a trespasser and make a fast escape.

Even if he'd much prefer to linger.

3

SHE WAS WASTING HIS TIME.

Grace peeked through the blinds on the kitchen window as Nate Cox nosed around her backyard after dusting for, and lifting, a few prints from her car and the knob on the back door.

The man had been spot-on back at the mortuary. Nothing he found was going to produce any leads. Unless the perpetrator—or perpetrators—were total idiots or had never seen a TV crime show, they hadn't left prints for law enforcement to discover.

He reached down to move aside the leaves on a clump of lilies, and as his T-shirt stretched across his broad shoulders, Grace's breath hitched.

Oh. My.

She leaned closer to the window.

Bulging biceps peeked below the edges of his sleeves, snug jeans molded his lean hips, and potent masculinity oozed from his pores.

Now *that* was a view.

Much more inspiring than the doe and frolicking twin

fawns who paraded through her backyard each night on their foraging trek to the woods-rimmed open field behind her house.

But it was far less calming.

As her pulse accelerated, she fanned herself. Was her blood pressure spiking, or had the finicky air-conditioning in the house decided to—

Nate straightened up and turned toward her.

Drat.

She jerked away from the blinds, letting the slat snap back into place. Getting caught ogling the man would be almost as embarrassing for her as his upchucking had been for him this morning.

Footsteps sounded on the back porch, followed by a knock.

Wiping her palms on her jeans, she crossed the room and pulled the door open.

"All done, except for elimination prints." He smiled, sending a faint fan of lines radiating from beside eyes as blue as the chicory that grew along the rural roadsides.

Focus, Grace.

"That's, uh, not necessary. I did a forensic fellowship in New Mexico, and the state required a background check complete with fingerprints for licensing. I'm in the FBI database."

"That will simplify the process."

"Would you like to, uh, come in? I have coffee or soda or tea. I also have orange juice and, uh . . . milk."

Milk? Really, Grace? You think a hot guy like this drinks milk?

She tried not to cringe.

If the sheriff thought her offerings odd, he gave no indication. "Thanks. I grabbed a soda while I was at the office picking up supplies. I had to get rid of the aftertaste from my Olympic-worthy hurling exhibition this morning." He hitched up one side of his mouth.

A man who wasn't afraid to admit his foibles—and joke about them.

Refreshing.

"I hear you. I lost my lunch at my first autopsy."

"Maybe there's hope for me yet."

"How many have you attended?"

"Too many for my personal taste, too few for a law enforcement professional. I was a local patrol officer before I got elected sheriff, and I managed to finagle my way out of autopsy duty on most occasions. When I couldn't sidestep it, the result was always the same. But now that I'm sheriff, my stomach needs to get with the program."

"It will."

"I hope so. Circling back to your situation, I did lift a few prints from the car and doorknob, but I expect most, if not all of them, are yours. I'll let you know the results. And I didn't find any evidence of your trespasser." He pulled out his keys. "Feel free to call us if anyone shows up uninvited again, though."

He seemed eager to leave.

A silly surge of disappointment swept over her. How ridiculous was that? The man had already gone above and beyond on his day off, and he doubtless had personal obligations to attend to today.

Heck, for all she knew he was married.

She flicked another quick glance at his ring finger to confirm what she'd noted earlier on the parking lot. Yep. Empty.

But he *could* be married. Not all men wore rings. Or he might be involved with someone. Most guys who'd passed thirty had a significant other—and there was no question the county sheriff fell into the thirtysomething group, given the maturity, levelheadedness, and confidence he projected.

If he did happen to be available, though, he clearly wasn't interested in getting acquainted.

Fine.

While the pickings were slim in her circle, and her last date had been months ago, she wasn't desperate enough to chase after a man who appeared to be immune to whatever charms she possessed.

No matter how hot he was.

She summoned up a smile. "If there *is* another incident, you'll hear from me. Now it's paperwork for me and fun, I hope, for you."

"Depends how you define fun. I happen to enjoy rehabbing, but that's not everyone's idea of recreation."

"It is for my sister Eve. Give her a saw and a screwdriver and she's in heaven. What are you rehabbing?"

"The house I bought a year ago. It has great bones, but it'll be a work in progress for the foreseeable future. Especially since it's a one-man show."

One-man show?

Hmm.

That must mean he was unattached. Unless he had a wife or girlfriend who didn't enjoy climbing ladders or wielding paintbrushes.

If that was the case, she could relate. Why Eve got such a kick out of refinishing floors and tearing out walls was beyond her.

Grace leaned against the doorframe and crossed her arms. *Careful how you phrase this. You don't want him to think you're being nosey—even if you are.* "Can't you recruit anyone to help you?"

"Not many people are willing to give up their free time to inhale drywall dust on someone else's behalf if they have no vested interest in the outcome."

More proof he was single and available, right?

"You could always try the Tom Sawyer fence-painting trick."

An appealing dimple dented his cheek. "I'd have to have

the gift of gab for that—and serious salesmanship skills. I was shortchanged on both when those attributes were being handed out."

"Why do I think you're selling yourself short?"

"No. I'm being honest." His grin broadened, and a twinkle appeared in his eyes. "Could I convince *you* to help me?"

At the subtle hint of flirtiness in his voice, she blinked. "Um . . ."

"No answer expected." His lips flattened as he lifted his hand palm forward, a slight ruddiness tinting his cheeks. "I was just trying to make a point." He retreated a step, and his tone morphed back to businesslike. "I'll let you get to your report. Try to fit in a little fun later."

"I will." Her brain was too busy trying to process that brief, enticing glimpse of playful roguishness to concentrate on the conversation. "But after I, um, finish the report on Mavis Templeton, I want to review an autopsy I did a few months ago."

He squinted at her, any lingering traces of levity vanishing. "Is that usual?"

Drat again.

Bringing up her afternoon plans had been foolish. As Max had implied, her conjecture that the two deaths with seedlike objects in common could be connected was a major stretch. Once she compared them, she'd probably come to the same conclusion.

If she could ditch her annoying niggle of suspicion without wasting a Saturday afternoon, she'd do it in a heartbeat.

But she did *not* need to share her propensity toward zealousness with the sheriff.

"No, it's not." Grace swatted away a fly intent on thwarting her efforts to keep it outside. "But I want to satisfy my curiosity about a question that came up today."

"During Mavis's autopsy?"

"Yes."

"Because there's a connection?"

"Possibly."

"Want to clue me in?" His discerning gaze locked on to her.

The man's ability to pick up nuances was impressive.

But until—or unless—she had concrete grounds for concern, she wasn't going to waste any more of his day.

"Let's just say I'm toying with a theory that has about as much likelihood of panning out as you have of getting through your next autopsy without emptying your stomach."

He winced. "If the odds are that low, I won't ask any more questions. Remember to call if you have any concerns."

"I will. Thanks again, Sheriff."

"Make it Nate."

Without waiting for a response, he descended the two steps from her back porch and disappeared around the side of the house. Less than a minute later, an engine revved to life . . . then slowly faded away.

Taking a long, deep breath, Grace closed the door and locked it.

What an intriguing turn of events.

For years she'd been complaining to her sisters about the lack of romance in her life. And for years Eve and Cate had been telling her that hanging out with dead people was the major contributing factor to her dilemma.

Yet thanks to those dead people, a very appealing man had entered her orbit.

Meaning there was hope for her yet.

While Nate might not be The One, the mere fact that she'd met a seemingly eligible man *because* of her profession rather than *despite* it was encouraging.

As for what the future held for her and the sheriff, who knew?

But two things for sure.

She was going to stop worrying that her career was putting a curse on her social life.

And if she and Nate ever did happen to go out on a date, she was *not* going to describe her day over dinner.

Dear God.

Another one had died.

Fighting back a wave of nausea, Dave Mullins stared at the obit that had popped up in the latest online edition of the *County Examiner*. This was the second sudden death—that he knew of—and it had to be more than coincidence.

What if there were more?

Easy to verify, Dave.

Yeah, it was. But he didn't want to know.

Yet there were two realities he couldn't escape.

First, this was out of control.

And second, he was getting in deeper and deeper.

"You want a refill, hon?" Jolene stopped beside his table and hefted the pot of coffee in her hand.

"Not today." He laid his phone screen-down on the table. "Thanks."

She tipped her head, her short ponytail bobbing behind her, the mahogany color nowhere close to any natural hue on earth. "You seem a little down in the dumps. Everything okay with Kimberly?"

Dave clenched his fingers around his mug. This was one of the downsides of small-town living. Everyone was privy to too many personal details—including his wife's problems.

"Everything's fine." He called up the amiable manner he cultivated for his job. As he'd learned, people trusted you—and bought more—if you were friendly and personable. "She's working at the library this morning. I decided to stop in for a cup of coffee before I pick her up."

"You look tired."

"Long week—and it's not over yet. Saturday is one of my busier days."

"Same here. Difference is I get to stay in one place instead of driving all over creation like you do. Although I do log a fair number of miles on these." She lifted a sport-shoe-clad foot and wiggled it. "But activity's good for the waistline. Helps me keep my girlish figure." She grinned and smoothed a hand down her ample hip. "You ready for your check?"

"Whenever you get a minute."

"I'll have it here in a jiffy. Give Kimberly my best."

"I'll do that."

As Jolene hustled off, Dave flipped the phone over. The screen had gone dark.

Kind of like his life had.

He raked his fingers through his thinning hair, more gray than brown after the past four trauma-filled years. The face reflected back at him in the mirror every morning looked far older than his fifty-five years.

No surprise, when death and illness and more death dogged your footsteps.

His cell beeped—the fifteen-minute warning to pick up Kimberly—and he pocketed it. After he took her home, she'd probably spend the rest of the afternoon gardening while he called on clients. That was a safe, healthy pastime—and he wouldn't have to worry about her doing anything dangerous while she was absorbed with her flowers.

It was hard to shake worry these days, though.

But even if some aspects of their relationship were different . . . even if *she* was different . . . they still had a good life.

And he didn't intend to put that in jeopardy.

"Here you go, hon." Jolene slapped the bill on the table.

"Thanks."

"Don't work too hard."

"Ditto."

"I learned to prioritize and pace myself years ago. It's the only way to survive in this job."

He watched as she wove among the tables to dole out coffee refills, her comment echoing in his mind.

Prioritize. Pace.

Pace was hard to regulate, especially if too many elements of your life were out of your control.

But he had his priorities straight. If he'd learned one lesson these past few years, it was the importance of putting what counted first.

And Kimberly and their marriage came first.

He drained his coffee, grimacing at the bitter dregs as he set his mug aside.

Until his dying day, he would protect his wife. Care for her. Do everything in his power to ensure no one ever hurt her. Yes, she was different—but that didn't mean he loved her any less. Life without her was unimaginable.

He couldn't lose her.

He *wouldn't* lose her.

And if that meant he had to take risks, put his own neck on the line, so be it.

Dave pulled a few bills from his wallet, set them on the table, and rose. As he zigzagged through tables toward the exit, half the people in the diner greeted him. Digging deep into his energy reserves, he managed to call up smiles in response.

But coaxing up the corners of his mouth took tremendous effort.

More so after reading about Mavis Templeton.

The coroner may have ruled her death natural, but Dave would bet his life savings—what was left of it—that there was nothing normal or routine about her passing. That it was, instead, highly suspicious.

How the deed had been accomplished without leaving a trace of evidence behind was a puzzle.

But odds were, if the coroner knew where to look, he'd find homicide.

And the police would find first-degree murder.

This was the case she'd been searching for.

Grace leaned closer to the screen of her laptop and skimmed the material on Fred Wilson from six months ago.

The eighty-one-year-old farmer in the next county had been found dead outside his barn, the only visible trauma a gash on his temple. Based on evidence at the scene, law enforcement had concluded he'd fallen and hit his head on the tractor beside him. While the death had been ruled accidental in the end, there *had* been an investigation because of complaints Wilson had lodged about petty vandalism and pressure tactics from his neighbor to sell him the farm.

Grace moved on to the autopsy results.

The head injury hadn't been the cause of death. Other than red-flagging the prescription narcotic he took for persistent back pain, the tox screen had been clean.

Most other findings had been unremarkable too. There'd been sufficient enlargement and thickening of the walls of the left ventricle to justify cause of death as cardiac arrhythmia due to ventricular hypertrophy. Chronic heart disease was often the culprit in deaths of older people.

Grace pulled up Mavis's autopsy and did a side-by-side comparison.

Except for heart issues being the cause of death for both people, there wasn't much overlap. Both had congestion of the lungs, liver, and kidneys—but that was a nonspecific finding common in most autopsies.

If there was a link between the two deaths beyond the

seedlike objects in the stomachs and the abnormalities in the gastric wall, she was missing it.

Leaning back in her chair, she sipped her daily splurge of Tazo mango iced tea and glanced out the kitchen window. The late-afternoon light had painted the distant woods a golden hue—which meant she'd once again worked most of a Saturday.

But it beat removing wallpaper or patching drywall or whatever Nate Cox was doing.

Truth be told, though, DIY projects might be palatable if they were done with a guy like that. And it would be a small price to pay for company on a Saturday night if the alternative was working or watching a chick flick alone.

She took another sip of her iced tea.

On a brighter note, she had tomorrow with her sisters to look forward to. With Eve just back from her Tuscan honeymoon and Cate finalizing the plans for her wedding next month, their get-together should be even more lively than usual.

It was also sweet of them to carve out time for her in the midst of their busy lives. While they'd characterized tomorrow's lunch as a catch-up session, it was more than that. They wanted her to know that despite the new men in their lives, she—and the sisterly bond they shared—would always be important to them.

Grace finished off the iced tea and watched through the window as the deer and two fawns began their daily trek across the field, toward the woods.

Funny how life had played out. Eve and Cate had always been ambivalent about a walk down the aisle. Open to it but perfectly happy being single and focusing their energies on fulfilling careers. She'd been the one with stars in her eyes about finding a happily-ever-after.

Go figure.

If nothing else, Nate Cox's sudden entrance into her orbit had proven her career wasn't to blame for the lack of appealing men in her world.

Someday, that special man could appear.

Until then, she loved her job as much as her sisters loved theirs—and there was more to be done with Fred and Mavis.

Grace leaned toward the computer screen again. While a comparison of the autopsies and police reports hadn't identified any commonalities, there were other areas that could overlap. It was possible the two of them shared traits or circumstances or pieces of background that would establish a link.

And with nothing more pleasant to do on the long Saturday evening stretching ahead, why not dive in and see what treasures she could unearth on Google?

Two hours later, stomach rumbling in protest and eyes bleary, Grace sat back and scanned the information she'd gleaned from a variety of sources, circling items common to Fred and Mavis.

Both had lived in the country—alone.

Neither had any close family. Fred had never married, and Mavis's husband had died a decade ago after a marriage that produced no children.

Both were members of a church, and both had left the bulk of their estates to various charities. Fred's contributions had been noted in his church bulletin, and Mavis had mentioned not long ago that what money she had would go to make the world a better place after she was gone.

Unless the two of them were part of the millionaire-next-door crowd, neither appeared to have amassed great wealth. There were no tantalizing fortunes that could make them targets for someone with nefarious purposes.

She sighed and set down her pen.

Bottom line, the dissimilarities between the two of them

were more pronounced than their commonalities. Frank appeared to have been hermit-like, while Mavis was friendly and outgoing—though by her own admission, her arthritis had slowed down her socializing and kept her closer to home. They lived in two different counties, separated by dozens of miles, making it unlikely they'd ever met, shared the same acquaintances, or frequented the same stores or restaurants.

Yet they'd both had gastric wall abnormalities and odd, seedlike objects in their stomachs.

It shouldn't be difficult to identify the seeds. A botanist at the state university ought to be able to help her with that.

But was it worth the effort?

Grace rose and wandered over to the fridge. Poked through the sparse contents. An omelet and fruit would have to suffice, since her weekly trek to the grocery store had been bumped off her schedule by back-to-back, miles-apart autopsies at the end of the week.

During the drive home tomorrow, after the lunch and gabfest with her sisters, she'd stock up.

Until then, she'd noodle on whether sending one of the seed samples from yesterday's autopsy to a botanist was due diligence or overkill.

After all, what were the odds that the deaths of two older residents of rural Missouri who didn't appear linked in any way and who had no fortune worth stealing could be anything but natural?

4

MORNING, YOU TWO. Your regular table's ready and waiting. You're lookin' mighty fine today, Becky."

As the woman beside him exchanged pleasantries with Jolene, Nate surveyed the diner. All the usual suspects were here, all in their usual seats. The table he and Becky always sat at in the corner was set as usual—two mugs, with a Lipton tea bag beside Becky's, and a pitcher of syrup for the Belgian waffles they ordered every Sunday. The usual clatter came from the kitchen as the two cooks on duty hustled to satisfy the palates of the after-church crowd.

Everything was the same as usual.

A wave of discontent swept over him, and he exhaled.

Why did the predictable routine he'd once found comforting suddenly feel confining—and boring?

A vision of Grace Reilly flashed across his mind, and he frowned. It was the same image that had kept him tossing most of the night. The one in which her wavy hair was blowing in the breeze, the gold flecks in her hazel eyes glinting with humor while her oh-so-appealing lips were—

". . . think we lost him."

At the slight chuckle from Jolene, he tuned back into reality.

The two women were watching him, the waitress's expression indulgent, Becky's not so much. His companion appeared to be more pensive than amused.

No wonder, after their stilted conversation last night at her place during their usual Saturday dinner and the quick, simple kiss that had ended their evening.

His it's-been-a-long-week-and-I'm-tired excuse had been met with puzzlement, and Becky seemed even more perplexed today.

"Yep. We lost him." Jolene grinned.

"No, you didn't. I'm with you 100 percent."

"That's true now—but you were gone for a minute." She patted him on the arm. "Not to worry. I'm sure you've got a hot case or two on your mind. We'll cut you some slack as long as you keep our fair county safe. Right, Becky?"

"Sure."

He glanced at her and called up a smile. She had enough to worry about without adding concerns about him to her list.

"Are Kathleen and Luke joining you today?" Jolene's hand hovered over the stack of menus.

"No. It's a working Sunday for them."

"I hear you. With all the rain we had earlier in the spring, every farmer in the county is behind schedule." She tapped the menus into a neat stack and started to retract her hand. "I don't expect you'll need these."

"Actually, I may try something different today."

The two women did a double take, but Jolene recovered fast and picked up two menus. "More power to you. We all have a tendency to get stuck in a rut. Nothing wrong with expanding our horizons. Let me show you to your table."

She led them through the crowded diner, and Nate kept a firm, protective grip on Becky's arm as he returned greetings from many of the patrons.

Once they were seated, Becky waved aside the menu Jolene

held out. "I'll have my usual waffle. Why switch if you've found what you like?"

The quick look she darted at him suggested she wasn't talking about food.

He stifled a groan.

This was *not* going to be their usual pleasant, low-key, no-pressure breakfast.

Nate took the menu Jolene offered and braced as the waitress walked away.

Becky didn't keep him waiting long.

"You want to tell me what's up?" She unfolded her napkin, draped it across her lap, and fiddled with her tea bag.

The lack of eye contact was no surprise. Becky hated confrontation. Just bringing up difficult subjects was a stretch for her.

Meaning his uncharacteristic behavior was bothering her—big time.

It was bothering him too.

Why on earth would he want to jeopardize an eight-month relationship that was easy, stress-free, and comfortable? Did he really want to let a sudden surge of unruly hormones undermine the groundwork they'd laid for a potential long-term commitment?

No. Not without careful thought.

Becky was smart, kind, caring, and pretty, with solid values and a generous heart. They were a good fit in many respects—a fact Kathleen had emphasized before he'd agreed to let her set them up. And as his sister-in-law had also reminded him, he wasn't getting any younger. If he wanted a family, it would behoove him to get serious about it and find a woman to share his future.

Trouble was, other than their first few dates, when newness had added a touch of spice, his relationship with Becky lacked zing. In all honesty, he'd probably have broken up with her six months ago if it hadn't been for—

"Nate." At a touch on his arm, he lifted his gaze from the dark depths of the coffee Jolene had poured him. Becky was watching him now, her features taut. "Is everything okay?"

He had no idea.

And until he figured out the answer to that question and dealt with the sudden, unsettling restlessness swirling through him, it would be a mistake to change anything. One wrong word could cause irreparable damage.

He took a deep breath and wove his fingers through hers. "I have a lot on my mind. Adjusting to the new job has been challenging. I'm still learning the territory and the personalities. There have also been a few cases that deserve more attention than my deputies have time to give them, and I'm trying to pick up the slack. I'm sorry if I've been preoccupied."

Her brow crinkled as she extracted her tea bag from the mug. "The preoccupation is a recent phenomenon."

Yeah, it was. As of last night—and today.

But Becky wouldn't be that specific. It would be too in-your-face, and she never created waves or initiated arguments.

Nevertheless, she deserved a response—if he could phrase it without hurting her.

"To tell you the truth, I'm feeling a bit overwhelmed." He spoke slowly, cherry-picking his words. "I'm not suggesting we change anything, but I could use a little breathing room."

"So you're okay if we stick with our usual schedule?"

That would be Wednesday dinner out, Saturday dinner at her house, and church together on Sunday with breakfast afterward.

He'd been fine with that routine until Friday.

Now it felt predictable. Stale.

Because he'd met Grace—and in the handful of minutes he'd spent in her presence, there'd been more zing than he'd experienced in eight months with Becky.

But relationships weren't built on zing. All that angst and

electricity and raging hormone stuff was for teenagers in the throes of their first crush. It was immature. Juvenile.

So maybe, once he got past this adolescent testosterone surge, the status quo would be fine again.

Nice try, Cox.

He throttled that little naysaying inner voice and squeezed Becky's hand. "If that works for you."

"Yes. It does." She smiled, and the tension in her features eased. "I do understand about the pressures of adjusting to a new job—especially one in law enforcement."

No, she didn't. He'd tried to talk with her about the challenges he was facing and the cases that had come across his desk during his first few weeks as sheriff, but those discussions had upset her.

Odds were they wouldn't upset a woman who cut up bodies for a living, though—and who saw man's inhumanity to man up close and personal in her forensic work.

"You two ready to order?" Jolene rejoined them. "Of course, I already know what you want." She winked at Becky.

Nate picked up the menu. "I haven't had a chance to read this yet."

"Too busy with sweet talk, I imagine." She grinned and waggled her eyebrows. "I saw you two over here with your heads close together."

Nate opened the menu and hid behind it. "I forgot how many choices there are."

"True in life, true in the Spotted Hen Café. If you want my recommendation, I'd go with today's special—the sunrise skillet. It's got eggs, sausage, cheddar cheese, potatoes, mushrooms, green peppers—"

"Sold." He closed his menu and passed it to her.

"I'll get these orders in the queue and let you two get back to whatever you were discussing."

Not if he could help it.

Instead, Nate put the spotlight on Becky, asking the kinds of questions that always kept their Saturday night dinners moving at a jaunty pace.

She followed his lead, as usual.

And by the time they left the diner, everything seemed back to normal.

Except his equilibrium.

That, unfortunately, was out of whack. Thanks to a forensic pathologist who was playing havoc with his assumption that his future would be business—and relationships—as usual.

"What on earth happened to your car?"

Grace closed the door and locked the Civic as Cate tossed the question over the roof and moved closer to inspect the damage.

So much for her plan to arrive late and defer the inquisition from her oldest sister as long as possible.

"Petty vandalism."

Cate squinted at the damage. "This isn't petty. I hope you have a small deductible."

"Not small enough." She circled the car toward the sidewalk. "How come you're late?"

"I was stuck at a homicide." She straightened up and flipped her long auburn ponytail over her shoulder.

"Not as stuck as the victim."

"Very funny." She swept a hand over the Civic. "When did this happen?"

"Friday night."

"Where?"

"A funeral home. I was reviewing paperwork for an autopsy I did yesterday."

Cate stared at her. "Please tell me you didn't spend your Friday night at a funeral home."

"I'm dead serious. Pardon the pun."

Her sister held up a hand. "Don't start with the dead jokes. And no details about any gruesome cases, either." She suppressed a shudder.

"You know, I can understand why Eve's freaked out by dead people. A radio talk show host doesn't encounter bodies every day. But you're a police detective. Dead bodies are your business."

"Correction. Solving crimes is my business. I don't touch dead bodies—or cut them open." She waved toward the car. "I assume the local police are investigating this."

"They are, but I doubt they'll find the culprit. There weren't any witnesses to the crime. Not live ones, anyway."

Cate fisted her hands on her hips and pinned Grace with the intimidating big-sister look that had scared away more than one suitor during Grace's high school years. Even back then, Cate had been a master at the third degree.

"You're carrying, right?"

Grace patted her purse. "Always. I'm not the sister you have to worry about. Eve's the one who should get with the program, especially after what happened last year."

"I agree—although I don't fret about her as much as I used to now that she's married to one of my colleagues."

"Hey." They turned in unison as the sister under discussion stuck her head out the front door, the midafternoon sun burnishing her copper hair. "Are you two coming in, or are you going to stand out there all day gabbing without me? If you're talking about the wedding, you're going to have to repeat everything, you know."

Grace linked her arm with Cate's. "Let's go, bride-to-be."

Her sister's features softened. "I like the sound of that—and I have a ton of info to share with you two."

"Then let's get this party rolling."

Eve met them at the door with hugs. "I'm so happy to see you both. Come on in."

"Where's the groom?" Cate entered first and tossed her purse on a convenient chair.

"Running errands and meeting a friend for dinner to give us sister time."

"Good man."

"Trust me, I know."

Grace inspected Eve. "You're glowing. I take it the honeymoon was fantas—" She sniffed. "Is that Mom's moussaka?"

"The very same." Eve closed the door.

"Don't tell me you also baked a carrot cake." Grace's salivary glands went into overdrive.

"I did. But I'd rather have your baklava."

She waved aside the comment. "You both know that's a special occasion dessert. It takes more time to make than I have to spare on an everyday basis. But I promise to bring it for dessert on Christmas."

"We'll hold you to that." Eve led them toward the kitchen. "Let's get drinks and settle in for a long chat. I stocked up on Diet Sprite for you"—she motioned toward Cate—"and high-end froufrou iced tea for my other sibling."

"You can buy a cheaper brand." Grace crossed to the oven.

"Nope. Nothing but the best for my baby sister."

Grace leaned closer to the oven and sniffed the aroma that always said home. "Are we eating soon?"

"Forty minutes. By the way, Dad's back in Cambridge after detouring to that dig in Jordan after the wedding—and with big news. They've extended his visiting professorship through next June."

"I bet he was over the moon about that." Cate filched a tortilla chip from the bowl on the island and swirled it in salsa.

"They're lucky to get an archaeologist with his credentials, if you ask me." Grace joined Cate at the island and helped herself to a loaded chip too.

Eve handed them their drinks. "Where do you want to sit?"

"On the deck?" Cate's tone was hopeful.

"Forget it." Grace took another chip. "You're the only one who inherited Mom's Mediterranean, heat-loving blood. I vote we stay inside. It's pushing ninety out there."

"I have to side with Grace on this one." Eve peeked at the moussaka. "Besides, I want to keep an eye on our entrée. We could go out later, after the sun dips behind the trees."

"That'll work. Why don't you show us your honeymoon photos?" Cate brushed off her fingers.

"As long as we save a chunk of the evening to talk about *your* wedding." Eve topped off her glass of lemonade.

"Naturally. I have to bring my maid and matron of honor up to speed."

"In that case, let's take our snacks into the living room and get comfortable. We hooked the computer up to the TV for large-screen viewing."

Grace followed her sisters to the front of the house, sat on the couch, and for the next four hours oohed and aahed over Eve's honeymoon photos from Tuscany, ate moussaka and carrot cake, discussed the details for Cate's big day and the plans for *her* honeymoon in Provence, and played a killer game of Scrabble.

It was the perfect antidote to the bad vibes she'd been battling since the lily-bud episode and the vandalism of her car. By the end of the evening, they'd all but disappeared.

Until Cate shared the news about the incident at the funeral home with Eve as she walked them to the front door.

"You waited until now to tell me this?" Eve didn't try to hide her exasperation.

"I figured Grace would be mad if I brought it up sooner." Cate fished her keys out of her purse.

"That's true. It would have cast a pointless pall over the evening. Vandalism happens. My car had the bad luck to be in the wrong place at the wrong time. I have an appointment with a garage tomorrow to get the damage fixed, and law enforcement is working on the case. End of story."

Not counting the midnight caller who'd broken off all the buds on her lily plants.

But no way was she bringing *that* up. Her sisters were both worrywarts and already too overprotective of their little sister. She'd keep that incident to herself, just as she'd kept them in the dark about—

"Who in law enforcement is on this?" Cate stopped at the front door, blocking the exit. "The cops in the local town?"

"No. The county sheriff."

"A deputy?"

"No. The sheriff himself. He happened to be on duty Friday night. A local cop responded until he got there, but the funeral home was outside of the town limits and—"

"Whoa." Eve held up a hand. "What were you doing at a funeral home on a Friday night?"

"Reviewing paperwork for an autopsy." As Cate responded, she and Eve exchanged a look that was all too transparent.

"No date, huh?" Eve assessed her.

"Not last Friday—but there are possibilities on the horizon."

"Yeah?" Cate gave her a skeptical perusal. "Did you meet someone new?"

Whoops.

"New people cross my path every week."

Eve dismissed that with a flip of her hand. "We're talking about living, breathing people."

Leave it to the hard-hitting talk-radio host to cut to the chase.

"I am too. In fact, I met someone new this weekend."

"Someone new as in male and eligible?"

She expelled a disgruntled sigh. "I'm not trolling for men to date."

"You should be." Cate jumped back into the fray, morphing

into the deductive-reasoning mode that made her a stellar detective. "You worked Friday night and Saturday. I'm guessing the only new people you met were the cop and the sheriff. How old were they?"

"I have no idea."

"Ballpark."

"What is this, an interrogation?"

Cate nudged Eve. "She's avoiding the question."

"I noticed."

"Fine. The cop was at least fifty. The sheriff . . . thirtysomething."

"Married?"

"I don't know."

"You did a ring check."

Refuting Cate's statement would be foolish. Single women in the market for a relationship did ring checks.

"No ring—which doesn't mean anything. I'm sure he's involved with someone."

"Aha. That must mean he's hot." Eve smirked at her.

"Aren't you jumping to conclusions?" Grace scowled back.

"Am I wrong?"

Grace eyed the door. Could she push past Cate, make a run for it?

"I think she's seriously interested in this guy." Eve gave Cate a fist bump.

Oh, for heaven's sake. She needed to put a stop to this.

"Doesn't matter if I am. It's not mutual."

Both heads swiveled toward her.

"How do you know?" Cate folded her arms, still barring the door.

She was *not* going to tell them about his visit to her house and the invitation he'd declined.

"Trust me, I know." She tapped her watch. "I hate to break this up, but I have to stop for groceries on the drive home."

"If she doesn't want to talk about him, this guy must have really tickled her fancy." Eve arched an eyebrow at Cate.

There was only one way out of this, and it wouldn't be pretty. But desperate predicaments called for desperate measures.

Grace pulled out her keys. "Why don't I tell you about the bizarre case I got two weeks ago. This guy was herding cattle with an ATV, and he hit a soggy spot on a slope. The ATV tipped over and crushed his leg. He managed to pull himself free, but a storm rolled in, and the cattle got spooked by the lightning and thunder. They stampeded right over—"

"Stop!" Eve clapped her hands over her ears.

"Clever diversionary tactic, Grace." Cate's reaction was less emotional, but she'd lost a shade or two of color too. "We won't ask any more questions about your sheriff—today."

Grace ignored the caveat, as well as the temptation to correct her sister's "your sheriff" comment.

"Hey, I listen when you guys talk about *your* work." She gave them an innocent shrug. "What do you do if Brent wants to tell you about *his* day?" Grace nudged Eve with her elbow.

She removed her hands from her ears. "I listen. But unlike you, he spares me the gory details."

"You'll keep us apprised of developments with the sheriff?" Cate didn't budge from the door.

"He didn't think the odds of solving the case were super high."

"I meant personal developments."

"You two are becoming annoying."

"Just answer this question." Eve leaned in. "If he asked you out, would you go?"

Go on a date with Nate Cox? Was Eve kidding? She'd accept faster than—

As her sisters suddenly grinned, she narrowed her eyes. "What's so funny?"

"You. And good luck." Cate pivoted and opened the door.

Sheesh. Was her attraction to the man that obvious?

"One piece of advice. If you flash that starry-eyed expression at your sheriff, he'll be begging you for a date. Guys find women who are attracted to them irresistible." Eve leaned over and gave her a hug.

She must be more transparent than she thought.

Better work on her poker face in case she and Nate bumped into each other again. She wouldn't want him to think she was *too* interested. There was merit in playing hard to get.

Wasn't there?

After Cate hugged Eve, Grace walked out to the street with her oldest sister.

"Call me if your guy finds out anything about the vandals—and be careful."

"I will."

They paused beside her Civic. "I hope you find someone wonderful someday, Grace." Cate's usual take-charge manner softened as she switched into the mother-substitute role she'd taken on after their mom died far too young. "I know love and romance were always more important to you than to me and Eve, but now that I have Zeke—well, I want that for you too."

This kinder, gentler side of Cate never failed to choke her up. Her oldest sister rarely showed her sensitive, sentimental streak.

"Thank you. If it's meant to be, it will happen. I'm just happy both of you found terrific guys."

"There's someone out there for you too. I know it. Someone who won't care in the least that you cut up dead bodies for a living." A teasing glint sparked in Cate's eyes.

"Thanks for the pep talk." She leaned over and gave her a hug.

"That's what big sisters are for. Drive safe."

"Always."

"I don't envy you the long trip."

"I'm used to it, after working for coroners in six counties." With a wave, she circled the car and slid into the driver's seat.

As she tooled toward home, she considered her entertainment options. Music always helped pass the extended hours she spent behind the wheel. Or she could listen to one of the audiobooks she kept in the car.

Or maybe she'd spend the next two hours daydreaming about being swept off her feet by a handsome sheriff.

Even if such fantasies had no more basis in reality than the futuristic sci-fi novel on her nightstand.

5

"HAPPY MONDAY, ELEANOR." Nate set a lidded paper cup from the local coffee shop on the department administrator's desk.

The fiftyish woman looked up from her computer screen. Faint furrows etched her brow despite the spark of interest in her eyes. "You don't have to bring me mochas."

"I thought you liked them."

"I do—but it doesn't seem right."

"Why not?" He already knew the answer. Her previous boss of twenty-plus years had been old school. No personal involvement with staff. Formalities and rank were strictly observed. He'd called her Eleanor, but she'd called him Sheriff. Fetching or making coffee hadn't been part of his routine.

She remained wary about the relaxed code her new boss had initiated and his "we're a team" mentality, but his mocha Mondays campaign should eventually win her over.

He hoped.

"A sheriff has more important things to do."

"Thanking people who do excellent work is important." He lifted his java in salute. "Like you and Deke. You two made my transition into this job about as smooth as it could be."

That was the truth. Eleanor knew the ins and outs of the office politics and all the key county players, and his chief deputy knew the ins and outs of the territory as well as the trouble spots. With input from them, he'd been up to speed much faster than he'd expected.

"I was just doing my job." She eyed the mocha.

"Are you going to drink that?" They went through the same routine every Monday.

"I suppose so. I don't want it to go to waste." She picked up the cup. "Thank you."

"You're welcome. Anything I need to know about before the day gets rolling?"

"Yes. Dispatch called." She picked up one of the old-school pink message slips she favored and held it out. "A man says he has information on the Mavis Templeton case."

Nate glanced at the unfamiliar name. "Do you happen to know this Jack Carson?" A reasonable question, since Eleanor appeared to be acquainted with half the citizens in the county.

"No."

Too bad. She'd been a font of information about many of the people he'd dealt with over the past four months.

"I'll call him." He started toward his office.

"I saw the report you filed yesterday on the car vandalism at the mortuary. You were supposed to be off."

Yeah, he was. But after his breakfast with Becky, he'd been as antsy as he used to be before a dicey mission in the Middle East, when the situation was volatile and he had no idea how it would play out. Going to the office had given him an outlet for his nervous energy.

He swiveled back toward her. "I decided to come in for a couple of hours to catch up on paperwork. You must have gotten here extra early today if you're up to speed on the weekend cases already."

"I like to stay on top of things."

He already knew that. While her job description limited her duties to handling court papers that had to be served, processing concealed carry permits, and attending to miscellaneous secretarial duties, she kept a finger on the pulse of everything that happened in the department.

"I appreciate your diligence. Employees who go above and beyond are gold."

A faint flush tinted her cheeks. "That's how I'm programmed. Any new leads on that case?"

"Not yet. I'm going to talk to the chief in Larktree this morning, see if there's been other vandalism in the area."

"I expect Dr. Reilly was upset."

He cocked his head. "You know her?"

"Not well—but she's had a few meetings here with Sheriff Blake and Russ during the past three years. We've chatted. She's a very nice woman."

"Seems to be. I hope the Larktree chief can shed some light on the situation." He wasn't holding his breath, however. Without witnesses or evidence, it would be tough to nail the perpetrator. "But first, I'll call Jack Carson." He lifted the piece of paper she'd handed him.

"You think someone actually robbed Mavis?"

"I didn't find any evidence to suggest anything was taken, but it's possible."

"The robber didn't hurt her, did he?"

"No. The autopsy listed cause of death as heart issues. Russ ruled it natural."

She exhaled. "I'm glad to hear there wasn't any violence. You never know these days, with the world we live in. Nowhere is safe anymore. Even our quiet little county."

True enough, as Grace Reilly had learned Friday night.

"That will get cold if you don't dive in." He motioned toward the mocha.

"I plan to. Thank you again, Sheriff."

"Enjoy."

He continued toward his office, sipping his coffee as he

fingered the message slip she'd handed him. Who was Jack Carson, and what did he know about Mavis Templeton?

Only one way to find out.

He circled behind his desk and got to work.

With the man's address and phone number in hand, it didn't take long to find the answer to the first question. How had his colleagues from years ago operated without databases and search engines?

Turns out Mr. Carson was actually Reverend Carson, pastor of a church not far from Mavis's house. That raised his credibility factor—always important with unsolicited tips.

After pulling out a pad of paper and a pen, he tapped in the man's number.

The minister answered on the second ring, and Nate introduced himself. "I understand you have information about Mavis Templeton that you think will interest us."

"I don't know for certain it will, but I'll let you decide. At a church gathering last evening, the woman who called the police about Ms. Templeton mentioned her. As you know from your report, she tried without success to reach her Wednesday evening and went over to check on her Thursday morning. She told us last night there were signs of a break-in at the house, which is what prompted my call."

"Could you tell me the name of this woman?"

The man gave the correct answer and continued. "I don't know the exact timing of the events that occurred, but my wife and I were driving by Ms. Templeton's property Wednesday night a bit later than we're usually out and about, and we saw a car pulling out of her drive. It caught our attention because the headlights weren't on."

Suspicious.

Nate picked up his pen. "What time was this, and did you notice the make of the car?"

"Around eleven thirty. I couldn't identify the make, but as

it pulled in front of us, I could tell it was a dark sedan. I got as close behind it as I could and my wife was able to read the last part of the license plate." He recited four letters and digits. "It was a Missouri plate."

Nate jotted down the information. "How did you know that was Mavis Templeton's house?"

"I didn't on Wednesday, but we noted the location in case we learned anything more that prompted us to report what we saw. I realized the connection after the woman from my congregation told her story and I asked where Ms. Templeton lived."

This could be a lucky break—or a wild goose chase.

And it might not matter, since the woman's death had been ruled natural.

But something about her death had piqued Grace's interest, so a follow-up on the license plate and a call to the county's forensic pathologist for details were warranted.

"I appreciate you taking the time to report this, Reverend Carson. Concerned citizens like you make our job easier."

"I hope the information is helpful. I hate to see crime in our fair community. The charm and security of small-town living are why my wife and I relocated here from the city twenty years ago."

"We'll do our best to keep it safe for you. Thank you again for passing on this tip."

Nate ended the call and swiveled toward his computer. With only a partial license plate, MULES wouldn't help him. The Missouri Uniform Law Enforcement System portal required the complete alphanumeric sequence. However, the Missouri Information Analysis Center was often a godsend in situations like this. Not only would the center cross-reference the number and letters he had with a variety of databases, they'd manually try to match those results with whatever other information was provided.

In this case, there wasn't anything else to match to other than a dark sedan. But it ought to be fairly simple to cull through the results and single out the vehicles located in this vicinity, come up with a name or two he could—and would— contact and question. While the presence of that car at Mavis Templeton's house on the night in question could be innocent, it was too coincidental for his tastes.

Nate initiated the search in the MIAC, entering all the information he had. In twenty-four to seventy-two hours, he should have names to go with the letters and digits the minister had provided.

In the meantime, he'd touch base with the police chief in Larktree on the vandalism situation and give Grace Reilly a call to find out what had raised a red flag in the Mavis Templeton case.

Because this new tip suggested that whatever she was concerned about had a greater probability of being valid than she'd assumed on Saturday.

Call me.

Stomach twisting, Dave read the text displayed on the burner phone that had shown up three long years ago, left at his office in a box with his name on it, a note inside with a chilling message and an instruction to answer it in privacy when it rang the next afternoon.

That had been the beginning of his descent into a second hell.

One from which there appeared to be no escape.

He weighed the cell in his hand as he tried to psych himself up for the meeting scheduled to begin in fifteen minutes. Insurance and investments weren't top of mind this Monday afternoon. He'd reschedule if he could—but his clients were already on the road, the thirty-mile trip to his office prompted by a stellar recommendation from a former neighbor.

Fred Wilson.

God rest his soul.

Dave fought back a wave of nausea and squeezed the cell, fingers trembling. If there was a way out of this, he'd take it in a heartbeat. But his nemesis held all the cards.

Sucking in air, he punched in the number.

The voice that answered was muffled, as always. It was impossible to tell if the person on the other end was male or female, and the name he'd been told to call his nemesis didn't help, either. BK was genderless.

"I have a new client for you."

Bile rose in his throat. "You said when we started this it would only be one a year."

"That was the original plan."

"This is the fourth one in the past two years—and the gap between them is getting shorter and shorter."

"I don't have to spread them out as much as I anticipated in the beginning. The scheme has been running smoothly, for the most part. And the window of opportunity with this new one is closing fast. She's considering other investments."

He tightened his grip on the phone. Sticking his head in the sand wasn't going to make the situation go away. He had to address the suspicion that had been churning in his gut since Saturday at the diner.

"I saw Mavis Templeton's death notice in the paper over the weekend."

A millisecond ticked by.

"So? Old people die."

"Fred died too."

Another tiny pause.

"What are you suggesting?"

"You know very well what I'm suggesting." He rose and began to pace. "Our agreement was supposed to be about money. You never said anyone would get hurt."

"They were all old. It wasn't as if they had many years left anyway. People that age die every day."

His stomach bottomed out.

That response more or less confirmed his suspicion that all of the people he'd been instructed to see hadn't just died.

They'd been murdered.

He massaged his forehead as he paced. "Why are you doing this? You already had their money."

"The monthly payments are burdensome—and they drain my capital."

"You mean *their* capital."

"Semantics."

"What if someone gets suspicious?"

"Why would they?"

"I don't know—but we do have a new sheriff in my county."

"I'm aware of that. But without evidence, there's no case. And there isn't any. Besides, barring extenuating circumstances, elder deaths are rarely investigated. No one raises an eyebrow when old people die—except maybe the county pathologist. But that annoyance can be dealt with. Now let me give you the contact information for your new client."

As BK recited the particulars, he circled back around his desk and jotted them down, hoping he could read his shaky chicken scratching later. "How do you know about these people, anyway?"

"I have my sources. Trust me, every prospect I send you is ripe for the picking. Dangling an investment that pays high dividends in front of them will get you in the door."

"You know, not everyone is receptive to cold calls."

"You have an excellent reputation and first-class client references. Plus, I have every confidence in that smooth delivery and dazzling charm of yours. Just think, Dave—without those attributes, we'd never have met."

At the mocking tone, anger began to percolate deep inside him. "You know, I could always choose not to play your little game anymore."

"I think not. Even if you decided at this late date to tell your wife the sordid tale, you're in too deep with this scheme. You couldn't get out without implicating yourself. And I don't think you want to spend the rest of your life in jail."

His tormentor had recognized his empty threat for what it was and called his bluff.

"How much longer is this going to go on?" He slumped into his desk chair and dropped his head into his hand.

"I haven't decided yet."

"You said three or four people, tops. This is number six."

"I changed my mind."

Meaning this could continue forever.

"That wasn't part of our agreement."

"So sue me. Call your new client, Dave—and let me know as soon as she signs on the dotted line and the paperwork is in order for the transfer of funds."

The line went dead.

Dave hit the end button and lowered the phone to his desk.

This was a disaster.

His *life* was a disaster.

All because of a stupid mistake. A lapse in judgment that should have stayed in the dark corner he'd swept it into and never seen the light of day again.

Until someone had decided to make him pay for his error. Forever, if today's conversation was any indication.

Swindling people out of money was bad enough.

But now those people were dying.

And he was as much to blame for their deaths as the person who was doing the actual deed.

A knock sounded on the door, and he wiped a hand down his face. It had to be the clients Fred had sent him after he'd sweet-talked the man into taking advantage of the once-in-a-lifetime investment he'd offered, thereby signing his own death warrant.

At least these clients had nothing to fear on that score. His special investment was reserved for a select, unfortunate few chosen by the person who had turned his life into a living hell.

And there was no escape from his miserable fate unless he was willing to abandon the wife who needed him and spend the rest of his life behind bars.

That wasn't an option.

So barring a lightning strike from the heavens that took out the person who made the dreaded calls on the burner phone, what choice did he have except to do as he was told—and pray for the poor souls who signed on for an offer that really was too good to be true?

6

AS NATE COX'S NAME FLASHED ON HER CELL, Grace killed the contemporary romance audiobook from one of her favorite authors and put the phone on speaker. Talking to a handsome real-life guy was far more enjoyable than listening to the escapades of a fictional one.

"Good afternoon, Sheriff."

"Afternoon. And can we make it Nate? I'm not into titles or formalities."

Nice that he'd repeated the first-name request.

"Sure. Do you have news on the vandalism incident?" Why else would he be calling?

"I actually have two pieces of business to discuss. Are you anywhere close to the courthouse?"

"No." *Dang it.* "I'm on my way to the morgue in the next county." Far preferable to a funeral home for autopsies, but since most rural counties didn't have a morgue and didn't want to haul bodies halfway across the state to the closest one, mortuaries were her second home—much to the chagrin of her sisters.

"In that case, why don't we talk by phone?"

Was there a touch of disappointment in his inflection? Or was that wishful thinking?

Put away the rose-colored glasses, Grace.

Check.

"That works for me."

"I'll start with the vandalism. I wish I had better news to report, but the Larktree chief didn't have anything to offer in terms of suspects, and the prints I lifted at your house and from your car didn't generate any hits in the database."

She sighed. "Discouraging but not unexpected. At least my car should be almost good as new by the end of the week. I dropped it at a body shop yesterday. I'm in a loaner car as we speak."

"I'll continue to keep my ear to the ground. It's possible we'll get a lead on the vandalism."

"I appreciate that."

"The other piece of business relates to the Mavis Templeton case. We've had a tip from someone who saw a suspicious car leaving her property late on the night before her body was discovered. There's a high probability it was the person who broke her window. I wanted to follow up on your comment from Saturday about a connection between her case and a previous autopsy. If my tip pans out, it could raise the odds your hunch has credibility."

Grace tapped a finger against the steering wheel. "I don't think a robbery—or attempted robbery—would have any relationship to the theory I'm playing with. There wasn't any evidence of that sort of crime in the other case I researched."

"So what made you connect the two?"

She pulled around a slow-moving tractor on the rural road and explained the unusual item she'd found in both stomachs, plus the further research she'd done over the weekend, trying to find other similarities. "Honestly, in the end I couldn't see why anyone would want to harm these two people. Mavis had no apparent enemies, and I doubt Fred's neighbor would kill him just to have a chance to acquire his property. Other than age, lack of family, and a rural address, there was no overlap between them."

"The seedlike thing is strange, though—especially since there were also stomach irregularities."

"I know. Whatever it is, it's hard to imagine an older, Midwest bachelor farmer like Fred Wilson would venture far from a meat-and-potatoes menu in his cooking or eating. Not to stereotype anyone, you understand. I know many men are wonderful chefs."

"Not any in my circle—including me. I do grill a decent burger, but I'm a one-dish wonder. If I want a home-cooked meal or homemade dessert, I go to someone else's home. In terms of the seedlike items, I'm curious what they are."

"I am too. I debated over the weekend whether I should follow up on that question, and finally decided to close the loop by asking a botanist at the state university to see if he could identify them. I dropped one off there this morning as I passed by." She pulled around a car tooling along at thirty miles an hour. Did no one but her have places to go on this Tuesday afternoon?

"Let me know what you find out. If my lead pans out, I may dig deeper on both cases. It couldn't hurt to review the Fred Wilson file. I'm sure my counterpart in his county would share it."

"I hate for you to waste your time on what could turn out to be nothing more than a weird coincidence."

"I don't put much stock in coincidences, and your rationale for being suspicious is sound." A few seconds passed. "Well . . . I won't distract you any further from your driving. Let's talk again as soon as one of us has any new information. If you want to reach me, this is the best number."

"Got it. The botanist thought he could get to this in the

next few days, so you may hear from me by the end of the week. Early next week at the latest."

"I'll look forward to it. Take care."

As he ended the call, a few drops of rain splattered on her windshield. Leaning forward, she scanned the horizon, where dark clouds had gathered. The thunderstorms the meteorologists had predicted appeared to be brewing.

Too bad she couldn't hole up somewhere with a cup of coffee and a handsome man until the tempest blew over.

But duty called—so she was headed into the thick of it.

If her luck held, though, perhaps she'd be home safe and sound before the worst of the storms erupted and made the road ahead slippery . . . and dangerous.

Nate pulled into the feed and farm-equipment company lot, cruiser tires crunching on the gravel.

The MIAC had outdone itself.

Not only had the information analysis center narrowed down the list of possible matches from the partial license plate the reverend had provided, it had completed the task in record time.

End result? Four plates were connected to a dark sedan, and one of them was based in this county.

It belonged to nineteen-year-old Tyler Holmes—who was about to be visited by the county sheriff.

Nate set the brake and skimmed through the notes he'd taken after running the man's plate and doing a background check.

Holmes lived in a small town not far from Mavis's house and drove an older-model Mazda. He had a high school education, a spotty credit history, and a couple of speeding tickets. There were no outstanding warrants, but he'd had a few run-ins with the law as a juvenile.

While his presence at the scene didn't make him a murderer, it did put him in the hot seat to explain why he'd been there the night Mavis died.

Considering his history, it wasn't a stretch to assume he'd been up to no good.

Nate closed his notebook, slipped it back in his pocket, and slid out of the car. Showing up at a suspect's place of business wasn't always his modus operandi, but sometimes the strategy worked to his advantage. It made people uncomfortable, and nervous subjects often let important information slip.

Assuming Holmes's boss hadn't alerted him the cops were en route—and the man *had* promised to keep that information to himself—the element of surprise could also work in his favor.

The owner met him as he entered the building and introduced himself. "I've been watching for you. Tyler's out back, loading bags of feed with two other guys. You're welcome to use my office if you'd like to talk with him in private."

"Thanks. I'd appreciate that."

The man's forehead wrinkled. "He's not in trouble, is he? I run a straight-arrow business here, and my customers trust me. I don't want anything to jeopardize that."

"At the moment, I just want to ask him a few questions in connection with an investigation. He's not being charged with a crime."

"Glad to hear it." But the indentations on the man's brow didn't diminish much. "You want to walk outside with me, or shall I send him in?"

"I'll walk out with you." Holmes's expression when he realized the sheriff had come to see him could be telling.

Nate followed the owner out to the loading dock, where three young men in T-shirts were hefting large sacks from a pallet and depositing them into two different trucks backed up to the dock.

"Tyler!"

At the summons from his boss, a lanky guy with well-developed biceps turned.

As the uniform registered, his eyes widened and his mouth opened slightly. Then he frowned and set down the bag of feed he was holding.

He was surprised—and worried.

The owner motioned him over, and Holmes wiped his palms on his jeans as he approached.

"Tyler, this is Sheriff Cox. He wants to talk to you for a few minutes. I told him he could use my office."

"Mr. Holmes." Nate held out his hand.

The man swiped his palm again and gave him a lackluster shake. "What about the loading? The customer's waiting." He aimed the question at the owner.

"I won't keep you long." Nate motioned toward the door.

Left with no choice, the man preceded him, spine rigid, shoulders stiff.

Being surprised and a bit nervous about a visit from law enforcement wasn't all that unusual, but based on the subtle behavioral signs Nate had learned to read in the military, this guy was transmitting powerful distress signals.

However, any number of factors could make people anxious. While body language was a helpful indicator of a person's emotional state, in his experience it was most useful in determining which questions provoked discomfort—and thus merited further investigation.

As Holmes entered the small, cluttered office, Nate indicated a chair. "Have a seat." He perched on the edge of the desk as the man complied, keeping his posture relaxed. "Sorry to interrupt your work."

"No problem." Holmes wove his fingers together, avoiding eye contact.

"Could you tell me where you were last Wednesday night around eleven thirty?"

The man's gaze flew to his. Skittered away.

But not before Nate caught the flash of fear in his eyes.

"I was, uh, at home."

"Is that right?" Nate crossed his arms, keeping his tone conversational. "Then who was driving your car?"

The man's Adam's apple bobbed. "What are you talking about?"

He was delaying. Trying to figure out how much the cops knew so he could fabricate a plausible story.

Wasn't going to work.

"Someone was driving your car at eleven thirty that night. It was seen coming out of Mavis Templeton's driveway."

A muscle ticced in the man's cheek. "I don't know a Mavis Templeton."

"You won't have the opportunity to meet her, either. She's dead."

Holmes looked at him. "What does that have to do with me?"

No reaction to the woman's death—suggesting that piece of information wasn't news to him.

"Why don't you tell me?"

"I don't know what you're talking about." He straightened his interlaced fingers and began to rub them back and forth. "Do I need a lawyer?"

"Do you?"

"Listen, I know my rights. I don't have to talk to you." The man glared at him—but behind the defiance was fear. So strong Nate could smell it.

"Okay. I'll talk to you." He rested one hand on the desk, the other on his holster. A little subtle intimidation never hurt. "Your car was seen coming out of Mavis Templeton's driveway at eleven thirty Wednesday night by a credible witness. The next morning, Mavis was discovered dead halfway up the stairs to the second floor. We found evidence of a break-in, including a print of a sport shoe by the back door. Now that you're a person of interest, we shouldn't have any difficulty getting the judge to issue a warrant to let us search your apartment for a matching shoe."

Why tell Holmes that the cast they'd made of the single print they'd found hadn't been all that clear or useful? If it had been, he'd have executed the search warrant before confronting the man.

Some of the color leached from Holmes's face. "What would that prove? Lots of people wear the same brand of shoes."

"But every wear pattern is different."

Sweat beaded on the man's forehead. "Are you gonna arrest me?"

"Not today—but your cooperation would be viewed favorably by a judge."

"I didn't do anything wrong."

"Mavis is dead."

"I didn't kill her!"

"What about Fred Wilson?"

The man sucked in a breath. Recoiled. "I didn't have anything to do with Fred dying. He fell and hit his head on a tractor."

It took every ounce of Nate's self-control to maintain a neutral façade.

Throwing out Fred's name had been a longshot. At this stage, other than Grace's hunch, he had no proof the two deaths were connected.

But it appeared he'd hit pay dirt. If Holmes and Wilson had been on a first-name basis, they'd had a relationship.

"Tell me how you knew Fred."

He shrugged. "Everyone knows their next-door neighbor." What?

Holmes lived in town, according to his intel.

Nate held on to his placid expression. "That's not your

76

official address." He pulled out his notebook and recited it. "Are you telling me you don't live there?"

"No. I do. But my dad owns the farm next to Fred's, where I grew up."

Nate's brain began to process at warp speed.

Could this guy's father be the neighbor Grace had told him about this morning? The one who had been pressuring Wilson to sell? The one Wilson had told law enforcement he believed was responsible for the vandalism occurring on his property?

This wasn't the direction he'd expected his conversation with Holmes to take—but Nate went with the flow.

"I understand your father wanted to buy Mr. Wilson's farm."

Holmes shifted. "Yeah."

"Where does that stand?"

The younger man continued to fidget. "I, uh, think my dad is working with the bank on that."

So the elder Holmes was still after the farm.

"I'm going to back up to my earlier question. What do you know about Fred's death?"

"I already told you." He swiped away a bead of sweat trickling down his cheek. "What does all this have to do with the Mavis woman, anyway?"

"Again, you tell me."

"I don't know."

"Two people are dead."

"I don't know anything about that."

"A footprint I suspect will match yours was found under the broken window at Mavis's house . . . and there are different types, and degrees, of homicide. You don't have to pull a trigger to be charged with murder."

Holmes sat up straighter, panic flaring in his eyes. "Wait a minute. I didn't go there to—" He stopped abruptly. Spat out an expletive.

Bingo.

That slip of the tongue confirmed he'd been at Mavis's house the night she died.

"Why *did* you go there?"

The nineteen-year-old slammed his arms across his chest and jerked up his chin. "I'm not saying anything else until I have a lawyer."

Nate waited a few beats. Stood. "Fine. But remember what I said. Judges are much more disposed to look kindly on co-operative subjects than on ones who thwart the efforts of law enforcement to do its job." He pulled out a card and passed it over. "My cell number's on there. Anytime you want to talk, day or night, give me a call. If I don't hear from you, you'll hear from me."

He left Holmes in the office, tracked down the owner to thank him for his cooperation, and returned to his cruiser.

First order of business, get Fred Wilson's file from his colleague in the adjacent county and go over it with a fine-tooth comb. Repeat the exercise Grace had already done with a side-by-side comparison of the files for Fred and Mavis.

How the seed business related to the puzzle that was becoming more curious by the hour remained to be seen.

But if he was a betting man, he'd wager the two deaths were somehow connected, as Grace suspected—and that there was a decent probability the manner of death on the official death certificates was wrong.

Because there was nothing natural about homicide.

1

THIS COULD BE A HUGE MISTAKE.

But desperation was a powerful motivator.

Stomach clenching, Dave set the brake in the parking lot of the high-end hair salon and rested a hand on the brief-case beside him. Inside was all the paperwork for his newest client—aka the next victim. Lorraine Meyers had signed on the dotted line for the exclusive, once-in-a-lifetime offer less than an hour ago.

And when he stopped by tomorrow to pick up her cashier's check for $110,000, all she had to do was endorse it to the shell company and trust him with a chunk of her nest egg for a minimum of five years, with the expectation of monthly interest more than triple what she could get in any other "safe" investment.

But her interest wouldn't roll in for long, given the lethal turn this scheme had taken.

Dave fought back a wave of nausea.

He couldn't keep doing this.

Hence today's visit to the salon.

He scanned the parking lot, half empty on this hot Thursday afternoon.

Perfect.

The last-minute appointment he'd booked under an assumed

name with Lee had verified she was working today. And meeting her in a public setting, at her place of business, wouldn't raise any eyebrows or cause any problems.

Except with Lee. She was *not* going to be happy to see him.

But he had to find out what, if anything, she knew that could help him figure out who was pulling the strings that kept him dancing like a marionette.

His next step if he *did* manage to identify his tormentor? Unknown. But having BK's real name would give him a tiny bit of leverage and perhaps a fighting chance to pull out of the tailspin he was in.

He slid from the car and approached the front door, his mood not unlike it had been on his first visit almost four years ago. He'd been seriously in the dumps as he drove home that day. In need of a pick-me-up. Of pampering. A high-end haircut had never been part of his routine, but the sign had caught his attention—along with the "you deserve to indulge" tagline—and he'd pulled in.

A decision he'd rue for the rest of his life.

He paused at the front door, his pulse picking up as another wave of doubts crashed over him. It wasn't too late to abort this dicey mission.

Yet if there was even a remote possibility Lee could link a potential name or two to the voice on the other end of the burner phone, it was worth a conversation.

Assuming she'd talk to him.

Not that she'd cause a scene, put her job at risk. She was too smart to endanger her livelihood. But that didn't mean she'd tell him anything helpful.

As long as he was here, though, he ought to go through with this.

Ramping up his courage, he pushed through the door.

The receptionist was unfamiliar, as he'd expected. Lee had told him they rotated through the job on a regular basis.

"Good afternoon." The woman offered him a cheery smile. "Do you have an appointment?"

"Yes. With Lee." He gave her the name he'd used.

"I see it. I'll let her know you're here. Make yourself comfortable." She motioned toward the seating area and disappeared behind the wall that hid the working part of the salon from the view of passersby.

Dave remained standing. The waiting area was empty midafternoon—no surprise, since the salon catered to a male, working-age clientele. Evenings and weekends were their busiest periods, according to Lee.

The receptionist reappeared.

"She's ready for you. Fourth station down."

Same place she'd been on his first visit.

A sense of déjà vu overwhelmed him as he circled behind the wall. Very little had changed. New lighting fixtures, a subtle shift in color scheme—but the discreet glass partitions that muted conversation still stood between the amply spaced stations, allowing clients privacy as they chatted with their stylist.

Thank goodness.

Lee swiveled toward him as he approached.

Froze.

Recoiled.

His heart stumbled, but he kept moving.

She narrowed her eyes as he drew close, animosity oozing from her. "Why are you here?" As she spat out the low-pitched question, she flicked a glance at the stylist two stations down who was chatting with her customer as she snipped and clipped.

"For a cut—and information."

"I have nothing to say to you."

"If I leave, your boss will want to know why you turned away a customer."

"I could say you were hitting on me." Venom wove through her words.

"I have a witness who'll confirm that isn't true." He motioned to her coworker.

Her eyelid twitched. "Fine. Sit."

He eased into the chair, and she draped a black cape around him. Scissors appeared in his field of vision, not far from his jugular.

Maybe this was a bigger mistake than he'd thought.

But she wouldn't do anything to injure him. Not on the job, anyway.

"I have to ask you something."

Silence.

She wasn't going to make this easy.

May as well cut to the chase. "I'm being blackmailed. Someone has photos."

The scissors stopped. Started again.

More silence.

"Lee, I'm sorry about what happened." He angled his head away from the other duo farther down, keeping his tone subdued. "I've told you that. I never meant to hurt you."

"Right." A loud snip sounded close to his ear.

Too close.

He tried not to cringe.

"I'm telling you the truth. If you choose not to believe me, I can't help that. But for years I've been paying a steep price for my indiscretion. I have to find out who's behind this. I thought you might have an idea or two."

She continued to cut.

He waited.

"How much are they soaking you for?"

"They're not after *my* money. I don't have any to spare. They're bilking older folks of *their* money—and it's escalated beyond theft. These people are . . . they're dying." His voice rasped.

Once again, the scissors stopped and she moved into his field of vision. Appraised him. "You're *killing* people?"

"No! Of course not. Not directly. But I suspect the person who's blackmailing me is."

"How many people have died?"

"Two that I know of."

"What are their names?"

"Why?"

"I have a large clientele. It's possible I know them."

"They aren't in your demographic."

She tapped her scissors against her palm. "Is there a reason you won't tell me who they are?"

None he could pinpoint, though the request seemed odd.

Still, if he wanted her to provide information he would be wise to reciprocate.

"Fred Wilson and Mavis Templeton."

She went back to cutting. "I don't know them. Why don't you contact the police?"

"I'm in too deep. I'd go to jail. What would happen to Kimberly?"

Her features hardened. "You should have thought of that before you decided to cheat on her."

"I know." Regret hounded him like a collection agency on a mission.

"You men are all alike. Users and abusers, one and all." She retreated behind the chair and continued cutting.

He didn't attempt to refute that assessment. After her experience with the male species, she had more than sufficient grounds for her opinion.

"I'm just asking if you have any idea who may have known about us and who could have had the opportunity to shoot photos."

"Where were they taken?"

"Some at the reservoir. Others in the gazebo during our trip to that small inn on the lake."

"Those were both secluded spots."

"Not secluded enough."

"Sorry, Dave." *Snip, snip, snip.* "I don't have a clue who could be behind this."

Panic began to gurgle in his gut.

"Did you tell anyone we were going to either of those places?" A thread of desperation he couldn't hide wove through the question. She was his last hope of getting a handle on this.

"I don't think so, but I do talk to my clients about personal stuff on occasion. However, I would never have mentioned your name."

This was going nowhere. Lee wasn't able—or willing—to help him.

No surprise, in light of her almost palpable bitterness.

She finished the cut in silence, whipped off the cape, and stepped back. "You can pay up front as usual. I'd walk you out, but I need to visit the ladies' room."

With that, she pivoted and hurried toward the back of the shop.

Shoulders drooping, Dave trudged to the front, paid his bill, and returned to his car . . . and Lorraine Meyers's paperwork.

If only the scheme he'd been sucked into had remained about money.

Taking the hard-earned savings of trusting seniors struggling to make ends meet on small Social Security checks and pathetic bank account interest sickened him, but they were supposed to receive monthly payments for the duration of the scheme, and half of their cash assets had been left untouched. None had ended up destitute.

As for setting up a hard-to-trace offshore account—that

had been simple. Heck, they were offered on the internet like vacation packages. Pay your money, and voilà, you were incorporated in Seychelles, given a business address and bank account in Cyprus and Panama, and provided with a Manhattan address for mail forwarding to imbue a company with the ring of legitimacy.

But no one was supposed to die.

That was a game-changer.

Dave pulled out his handkerchief, mopped his brow, and turned on the engine, cranking up the air.

For the thousandth time, he asked the question that had haunted him since the first world-shattering call had come in on the burner phone.

Who could be behind this?

Lee had been his best hope of identifying BK. The leak had to be on her end. *He* certainly hadn't told anyone about their trysts.

Yet she didn't appear to have the faintest notion who could have taken the compromising photos that were ruining his life.

But she may not have told him even if she did. From the get-go, she'd made no secret of her animosity toward men, thanks to the philandering husband she'd divorced and a subsequent abusive ex-boyfriend.

Why she'd warmed to him remained a mystery. Perhaps she'd recognized a kindred emotionally broken spirit in search of comfort and consolation. Realized he was a decent, caring, honorable man.

Or had been, in a previous life.

The invectives she'd hurled at him when he'd broken off their relationship, however, suggested her simmering resentment toward men had never been far below the surface. And the final curse she'd flung at him before she'd stormed out of their breakup scene—the one he'd tried to banish from his memory—suddenly replayed in his mind.

"I hope you rot in hell, Dave Mullins. You're scum. I had a feeling all along you'd end up being like—"

He sucked in a breath.

Wait.

All along?

Did that mean she hadn't trusted him from the beginning? That throughout their brief but intense relationship, she'd laid the groundwork to extract revenge to ensure he *did* rot in hell if he deserted her?

Was *she* BK?

As the air-conditioning chilled the car, a shiver raced through him.

Maybe she'd paid someone to take those photos and kept them in reserve in case he proved to be as much of a scumbag as the previous men in her life.

Maybe Lee and an unknown cohort were behind the scheme he'd come here today to discuss.

If so, was she even now leering malevolently into the bathroom mirror, like the wicked queen in *Sleeping Beauty*, certain she was the smartest in the land? Relishing the fact that at least one deceitful male was getting his comeuppance?

Massaging his forehead, he leaned back against the headrest and closed his eyes.

A few years ago, such a suspicion would have seemed preposterous. Back then, he'd been an eternal optimist, always believing the best of people. Always trusting that tomorrow would be brighter than today. Always certain God was in his heaven and all was right with the world.

But he wasn't that optimistic, faith-filled man anymore. Recent history had given him up-close-and-personal experience with the callous, heartless, greedy side of human nature.

So yes, in the darker world he now inhabited, it was possible this woman—whose sympathetic ear, gentle touch, and flirty smile had undermined his wobbly self-control at that bleak point in his life—was, indeed, the cause of his current misery. Revenge could be a potent force. And if she could also use him to build up her shaky financial reserves, why not?

Dave straightened up and surveyed the salon that had gone from haven to hell in a heartbeat after he'd made a choice that would haunt him to his dying day.

And his return had accomplished nothing.

If Lee *was* running the show, she knew he was stuck. There was no way out without implicating himself.

If she wasn't involved, he'd given her an opportunity to gloat about his misfortune.

Dave lowered the AC and aimed the vents away from him as another shudder snaked down his spine.

While it was impossible to determine beyond the shadow of a doubt whether she was BK, only the two of them had known about the trysts that were photographed, and the leak hadn't come from him.

That left three possibilities.

Her assertion that she'd never told anyone about them was a lie.

She'd arranged the photography herself as an insurance policy. One she was now cashing in on.

Or someone else had discovered his secret and was using that knowledge to manipulate him—and put innocent people to death.

Lee watched Dave drive away, raining silent curses on him. The man had a boatload of nerve, showing up here after all this time.

The receptionist hung up the phone. "Sorry, Lee. He didn't leave a tip—which surprised me. I would have pegged him as the generous type."

"Just goes to show how wrong you can be about people."

"Yeah. He didn't say much, either. He was out of here in a flash as soon as he paid. Oh, that was your next appointment on the phone. He's running about ten minutes late."

"No worries." She forced up the corners of her mouth. "I'll clean up my station and try to resist those brownies in the break room that are calling my name."

"As if you have to worry about weight. Me, I inhale the scent of a potato chip, and ounces latch on to my hips. I gained a few pounds for sure during finals—and my boyfriend noticed."

Lee's lips flattened. "Don't let anyone define you by externals."

"Oh, he doesn't do that. I mean, it was just a few innocent comments."

"That's how it always starts."

The young woman wrinkled her brow. "How what starts?"

"Never mind." This wasn't the place to climb on a soapbox or reveal anything about her past. Only the shop manager knew a few scant details of her history. "Let me know when my next customer arrives."

"Will do."

Lee returned to her station, did the cleanup by rote, then sat in her chair and took a deep breath.

The shock of seeing Dave walk toward her station today could have registered as a major quake on the Richter scale. The day he'd told her he was never coming back, he'd meant it. Not once in all these years had he sought her out.

She'd sought *him* out, though—on the sly. Watched him from afar. Followed him. Knew his habits. It paid to be thoroughly briefed on your adversaries. To do your best to understand those who betrayed you.

And now Dave was worried. Up to his neck in a very messy business with criminal repercussions.

The question was, had he told anyone else about his dilemma?

Not Kimberly, certainly. And unless his pattern had changed, he didn't have any close friends. Only clients. His wife had always been the center of his world.

Had he perhaps sought guidance from his pastor?

She studied her reflection as she pondered that question.

No. That wasn't his style—and it would be too dangerous.

But if law enforcement had any suspicions about a death, they'd be looking into it. Had Dave found out that the death of one of the people he'd help bilk was under investigation? Was that what had prompted his visit?

Hmm.

It would be helpful to know if the cops had any concerns about Mavis or Fred.

She crossed her legs and jiggled her foot. Russ Franklin was one of her customers, and he was about due for a cut. And the sheriff in the next county came in on a regular basis. Both of them loved talking about their work, and while funeral homes and autopsies and crime scenes weren't of much interest to her in general, it wouldn't hurt to see if she could ferret out a few nuggets about investigations that involved Mavis or Fred.

Because forewarned was forearmed—not that she intended to share anything she discovered with Dave.

Oh no.

He deserved whatever he got.

Making him pay for his betrayal in every way she could think of without calling attention to herself or exposing her own secrets was her right.

It was called sweet revenge.

8

"SO WHAT'S UP BETWEEN YOU AND BECKY?" Kathleen flipped the dish towel over her shoulder and skewered Nate with a don't-try-to-snow-me stare.

Smothering a groan, he stowed the salt and pepper shakers, watching through the window as his sister-in-law's fiancé drove away from the farm in a cloud of dust.

Too bad *he* couldn't conjure up an excuse to escape too—like Luke's dubious explanation about promising to help a neighbor mend a fence on this Sunday evening.

But his predicament was his own fault. He should have read the clues, realized there was an ulterior motive to Kathleen's last-minute invitation after breakfast this morning at the Spotted Hen. His sister-in-law planned every social occasion in advance, and she always included Becky if he was involved. Her flimsy excuse about having farm business to discuss wouldn't have precluded Becky from joining them.

Rather than jump to conclusions, though, why not see where she was headed?

"What do you mean?" He swept up a few wayward grains of salt with his finger, keeping his tone nonchalant.

She waited until he gave her his full attention to respond. "There were strange vibes at breakfast today. I asked Becky about them in the ladies' room. She blew me off—after she teared up."

His stomach twisted.

The last thing in the world he wanted to do was hurt her.

Nate propped one hand on his hip and raked the other through his hair. "I don't know what to say."

Kathleen appraised him. "Is that your subtle way of telling me to mind my own business?"

"No." He met her gaze. "If I wanted to say that, I'd say it."

"That's what I thought." She leaned back against the sink. Folded her arms. Waited.

Blast.

He'd rather face off against a hardened, armed criminal than get the third degree from Kathleen.

As far as he could see, however, there was no escape unless he wanted to be rude—and hurt *more* feelings.

Not in his plans on this Sabbath day.

"I told you the truth." He paced over to the window. Scanned the scene he'd looked at every day until he left for college. The same scene his brother had looked at every day of his entire, too-short life. Sighed. "I honestly don't know what to say."

"Did you meet someone else?"

At Kathleen's quiet question, he swung around. How on God's green earth had his sister-in-law discerned the core of his dilemma so quickly?

She held up a hand, palm forward. "You don't have to say anything. The answer is written all over your face." She picked up her mug of tea and moved to the table. "Let's sit."

After a brief hesitation, he topped off his coffee and joined her.

"You want to tell me about her?" Kathleen sipped her tea.

Denying her assumption would be stupid. Besides, he could use a female perspective, and Kathleen wasn't only the sister he'd never had, she was also blessed with keen insights into human nature.

Nate wrapped his fingers around his mug. "There isn't much to tell, which is why this is bizarre. I just met her nine days ago. All of our conversations have been about work." He blew out a breath. "It doesn't make sense. I don't know anything about her."

"Except she revs your engine."

His brother's wife had never been one to beat around the bush.

"I don't know if I'd use that exact expression, but she does trigger a big-time attraction reaction."

His sister-in-law regarded him. "You've been dating Becky for eight months."

"I know."

"She thought you had serious intentions."

"I thought I did too. But when I met this woman, I . . ." He faltered.

She filled in the blanks. "Was bowled over? Blown away? Had your socks knocked off? Pardon the clichés, but they catch the spirit of what I'm suggesting."

"Basically, yeah. But I don't want to hurt Becky. She's a great gal, and she's had a lot to deal with."

"May I be blunt?"

He arched an eyebrow. "Have you ever been otherwise?"

"Very funny. So here's my take. When I set you up with Becky, I was convinced there was potential. But I've watched you over these past few months, and something's missing." She took a sip of tea. "Did Jeff ever tell you I was seriously dating someone when I met him?"

He blinked at the non sequitur. "No." What little he'd known about their courtship had been shared through spotty emails over very long distances. His brother hadn't been the type to write lengthy messages.

"Well, I was. Had been for close to six months. Then one night, at a party, Jeff walked in and I short-circuited. I tried to fight the attraction. Told myself I already had a good man who'd make a fine husband and father. Asked myself if I wanted to let that almost-guaranteed future slip through my fingers because I had the hots for this new guy."

"Since you and Jeff got married, the answer is obvious."

"It wasn't at the time. I agonized over the decision. And Jeff didn't try to sway me. After he realized I was involved with someone else, he backed off. He may have had his faults, but poaching another man's girl wasn't one of them."

Her features contorted, and Nate covered one of her hands with his. Repeated what he'd told her too often to count. "I'm sorry, Kathleen. If I could change what happened, I would."

"I know that, Nate, and no apology is necessary. It wasn't your fault. It wasn't anyone's fault . . . except Jeff's."

"Yeah." He wanted to believe that, but it was impossible to shake the guilt, however misplaced it might be. If he'd mustered out a few months earlier, been around more, he may have been able to—

"Don't do that to yourself." Kathleen's expression grew fierce. "I know what you're thinking. I've battled the same what-ifs. If anyone was responsible, it was me, not you. I was here. I knew there was an issue."

"There was always an issue."

"I knew that too. I just never imagined it would have deadly consequences." Her voice hitched. "I loved him, Nate. With all my heart."

"I never doubted that. I don't doubt it now."

"Despite my engagement to Luke?"

"I'm glad he came along."

"Do you mean that?" She searched his face.

"Yes."

"I want you to know I never expected to meet anyone else." Her words shook.

"You're too young to spend the rest of your life alone, Kathleen." He squeezed her hand. "And I wouldn't want you to let the past dictate your future."

"I appreciate that." She squeezed back. "And if you decide you want the farm to stay in the family, Luke and I—"

"It *is* in the family, Kathleen. We've been over this already. I never wanted to be a farmer. You know that. I was glad to sell my share to Jeff, and I'm glad you and Luke will be the stewards going forward." He retracted his hand. "We're way off the subject."

"Yeah." She sniffled and pulled a tissue out of her pocket. "Where were we?"

"You were talking about the sparks between you and Jeff."

"Right. In the end, I was the one who took the initiative— and the plunge." She linked her fingers and leaned forward. "Here's the conclusion I came to, for whatever it's worth. I knew Jeff could end up not being The One, but the electricity between us told me the guy I was dating, safe and nice as he was, wasn't the man I wanted to spend the rest of my life with. If I stayed with him, I'd be settling. And I didn't want to do that. You shouldn't either. It wouldn't be fair to you *or* Becky."

"But is it fair to her to add a breakup to all the trauma she's been through these past twelve months—some of it thanks to me?"

"The accident wasn't your fault."

"It was, in a roundabout way."

"That's misplaced guilt talking, and guilt won't sustain a marriage over the long term. In fact, it could lead to resentment." Kathleen leaned closer. "Let me ask you this. Do you feel the same about her as you do about this new woman you've met?"

He shifted in his seat. "That's not a fair question. I don't even know this new woman."

"Do you want to know her?"

Oh yeah.

"That's what I thought." She dropped back in her chair. "Staying with Becky would be safe, but I don't think that's how you're wired. And you'll hurt her worse if you continue down a road that seems like a dead end."

He took a sip of his coffee. "Dead end is strong language."

"But accurate, based on the evidence."

"What evidence?"

"You're the cop. Figure it out." She rose. "You want more coffee?"

"No." He drained his mug and stood too. "I'm going to go home and finish sanding the kitchen cabinets."

"Not a very exciting conclusion to the weekend." She took his mug and set it in the dishwasher.

"I had enough excitement overseas to last a lifetime, and I get more than my share every day as sheriff. Sanding cabinets will be a perfect end to my weekend."

"If you say so. But maybe you could spice up your rehabbing in the future with some company—of the female variety."

"I'll take that under advisement."

She rolled her eyes. "Go home. And work on the situation with Becky. She already senses the relationship is on shaky ground. If I were in her position, I'd prefer a clean break. And it wouldn't hurt to throw a few prayers into the mix, either, as you straighten this out." She walked toward the door, and he followed.

"Thanks for the dinner—and the advice." He stopped on the threshold.

"That's what sisters-in-law are for. Call me with an update."

"I will." He gave her a hug, walked to his Jeep, and lifted his hand in farewell.

And as he drove down the long, dusty drive that led from the home of his youth to the main road, he made a resolution.

Before this week was out, he'd mull over everything Kathleen had said, try to determine whether the electricity he felt in Grace's presence was a permanent increase in wattage or a temporary power surge, and decide what to do about Becky—and the appealing forensic pathologist he hadn't known a mere ten days ago.

"What's the matter with you tonight, boy? You're jumpy as a hog on butchering day."

As his big brother cackled at their father's question, Tyler looked over from the TV to find his old man watching him. "What do you mean?"

His father aimed a pointed glance at his jiggling foot.

Tyler put the brakes on his leg.

"You having trouble at work?"

"No. Job's fine." Even if the rest of his life was a mess. The sheriff hadn't bothered him anymore, but that didn't mean the problem had gone away. The man had said he'd be in touch if Tyler didn't call him. Cox was probably trying to dig up more dirt on him.

And there was plenty to find if he got lucky again, like he had with Mavis Templeton.

Talk about a rotten break.

Who could have predicted someone would be driving by at such a late hour on that quiet country road?

And how on earth had the sheriff connected her with Fred?

". . . off in la-la land." At his brother's taunt, Tyler tuned back into the conversation. "Or maybe he's found a new source for weed."

Tyler glared at his older sibling. "I don't do drugs. But if I wanted to, marijuana's legal in a bunch of states."

"Not Missouri."

"Tyler, what aren't you telling us?" His father squinted at him, ruddy-faced from hours in the fields—and from the combination of suspicion and displeasure Carl Holmes always reserved for his younger, screwup son.

Joining him and the favored heir for the duo's usual Sunday sports and pizza night had been a mistake. But he was probably going to need a lawyer, and his father was the only source of funds for that.

Unless he wanted to dig himself deeper into the hole he was already in.

"Tyler." His father's tone darkened.

"I'm tired, okay? We were busy at the feedstore this week. It's hard work."

"Hard work never hurt anybody. It builds character. I worked hard all my life, turned this broken-down farm into a money-making operation. I'm not putting it in the hands of anyone who isn't willing to work up a sweat to keep it going."

Irritation pricked his composure. "I busted my butt for years on this farm."

"I'm not saying you don't have it in you to work hard, but I want to see you keep your nose clean and show some responsibility. Prove you can stick to a job and pay your bills."

"How come Wayne never had to prove himself?"

"Your brother has never given me a lick of trouble."

Tyler glanced at him, and Wayne raised his can of beer with a smirk.

Anger began to simmer deep in his gut. Too bad Mom wasn't still around. She'd take his side in a discussion like this.

But despite her loyalty, she would have been hard-pressed to stand by him after the stupid stunts he'd pulled in high school. Nor would she have been able to change the old man's mind about cutting him loose after that minor fender bender on graduation night thirteen long months ago. Or stop the ultimatum he'd issued to get his act together or forget about taking his place at the farm.

Like that was ever going to happen now anyway, with the sheriff on his tail.

He glared at his gloating brother and righteous father, a harsh rebuttal hovering on the tip of his tongue.

Keep your mouth shut, Holmes. Anything you say will backfire. Talk to the old man when Wayne's not around.

For once, Tyler listened to the silent voice of reason he'd too often ignored.

"I'm going home." He rose. "Thanks for the pizza."

His father stood too. "I'll walk you out."

"I know where the door is."

"I said I'll walk you out."

Fine.

He strode toward the door, brushing past his sibling's chair.

"Enjoy the rest of your evening, Ty. Stay out of trouble."

"Wayne." His father frowned at the favored son. "There's no call to bait your brother."

His father was coming to his defense?

That was out of pattern.

The old man followed him into the hall and out the door. On the front porch, he paused. "I have news. All of the paperwork on the Wilson place is finally finished. It's mine."

"I'm glad you got it."

That wasn't a lie. His dad *had* worked hard his whole life. The sun-weathered skin, deep crevices on either side of his mouth, and fan of lines beside his eyes aged him a decade beyond his fifty-one years.

He and his dad may have had their disagreements, but his

father had done his best to provide for the family—and had bailed him out whenever he'd strayed from the straight and narrow.

That's why he'd tried to help him get Fred's land.

But like too many of his schemes, that one had gone awry.

Now he'd messed up again with Mavis Templeton.

"I'm sure Wilson's turning over in his grave to know the land ended up in my hands. Never met such an ornery cuss in all my life." His father shook his head and scratched the shiny bald spot on top. "Anyway, there'll be more work to do now, with two places to manage. I could use your help here."

His spirits took an uptick. "You want me to come back?"

"Not yet. I told you to take a couple of years to get your act together, hold down a steady job, keep your nose clean. Far as I can see, you've been doing that. If you keep it up, I'd like you to come back next spring." He clapped a hand on his arm. "I always told your mom I wanted to leave each of you boys your own spread. Now I can do that. But you have to earn it first. You understand where I'm coming from, son?"

After all his mess-ups? Yeah, he did. He couldn't fault his father for wanting to ensure his hard work wouldn't be squandered.

"Yes sir."

"Good. You hang in. I like what I've been seeing. Drive safe going home." He squeezed his arm and left him on the porch.

As the door shut behind him, Tyler muttered a word that would have shocked his mother.

Why, oh why, had he caved? What he'd done at Wilson's place may have been wrong, but he'd only been trying to help his father. However, he had no such selfless excuses for Mavis Templeton or his other lapses. Those had been about supplementing his income at the feedstore, pure and simple.

Shoving his hands in his pockets, he descended the steps and trudged toward his car.

His father was going to find out about the Templeton woman. Guaranteed. The sheriff wasn't finished with him yet.

And once his father discovered his son was in the middle of what appeared to be a murder investigation, any hope he had of returning to the man's good graces would vanish as fast as a spooked rabbit in the sights of a coyote on the hunt.

9

GRACE STOPPED in front of the county courthouse and huffed out a breath, hoisting her tote into a more comfortable position.

This was crazy.

She had absolutely no justification for dropping by the sheriff's office on this Monday afternoon. A quick phone call would have sufficed. She could pass on the information she had in a few short sentences.

Except she'd wanted to see him.

That was the truth of it, and a woman in a truth-seeking profession ought to face facts.

But she didn't have to follow through on her impulse to stop in. It would be much safer to talk to him by phone. From the other end of the line, he wouldn't be able to see any of the telltale blushes that were the bane of redheads and could clue him in to the real motivation for her visit.

Namely, that she was attracted to him. Big time.

Yep. Much more prudent to make a fast exit.

Pivoting, she hustled down the stone steps toward her car.

"Dr. Reilly!"

At the greeting, she halted and peered down the sidewalk, shading her eyes against the glare of the one o'clock sun.

Eleanor Duncan waved at her.

Well, shoot. Could her timing have been worse?

The sheriff's department admin hurried over to join her. "I haven't seen you in a while."

"Hello, Eleanor. I don't have much cause to swing by here unless I'm working on a tricky case."

"Thank the Lord we don't have many of those. Unless a new one popped up?"

"No. The past week has been routine."

"Routine is underrated. Normal days are a blessing." The woman motioned toward the courthouse. "If nothing thorny has come up, what brought you here today?"

"I, uh, had a small matter to discuss with the sheriff. But I know he's busy, so I decided to handle it with a text or email."

"Nonsense." The woman waved aside her comment. "As long as you're here, why not pass on the message in person? There isn't enough face-to-face communication these days. Everyone's always glued to their cellphones."

"Really . . . I don't want to bother him." She edged away.

"Don't you worry about that. I expect he can spare a few minutes for a brief meeting after working through lunch—again." She shook her head. "He insists I take *my* lunch break. Says getting away from the office in the middle of the day refreshes the mind. But does the man follow his own advice? No. It will do him good to talk to someone who's not complaining or reporting a crime."

Grace watched the woman march up the steps.

She was stuck.

But truth be told, it was hard to feel bad about being railroaded into a meeting she wanted to have.

Eleanor waited for her at the door as Grace ascended. "I sure was sorry to hear about the vandalism to your car. And at a funeral home, of all places." She tut-tutted as she pulled

104

the door open and the blessedly cool inside air enveloped them. "I know the sheriff is trying his best to find a lead or two, but those kinds of cases are hard to solve."

"I don't expect miracles. I'm chalking the whole experience up to having the bad luck of being in the wrong place at the wrong time."

"Well, you be careful." The woman patted her arm as they walked toward the sheriff's department offices. "I've seen my share of crazies in this job. From afar, of course. I expect your situation was an isolated incident, but it never hurts to be extra cautious after an experience like that."

A niggle of unease snaked through Grace as she accompanied the woman down the hall.

There *were* crazies out there, as she knew firsthand.

And the vandalism *wasn't* an isolated incident, coming on the heels of the late-night visitor who'd snapped off all her lily buds. An innocuous exercise that hadn't harmed anyone—but two back-to-back incidents could suggest someone had her in their sights.

Or perhaps it was nothing more than an odd coincidence. As the seeds could be.

Except Nate didn't put much stock in happenstance, and neither did she.

"Give me one minute to ditch my purse, and I'll let the sheriff know you're here, Dr. Reilly."

"Thanks. And please, call me Grace."

Eleanor waved off that request. "You worked hard for that title. You deserve to be called by it. I have great respect for accomplished people. Using titles is the least I can do to recognize their success."

An old-fashioned attitude, but also endearing.

"I appreciate that."

"See if you can convince the sheriff to leave me be on that score while you're in there, if you get an opening." She leaned closer and lowered her voice. "He's been after me to use his first name too."

"If an opportunity comes up, I'll pass along our discussion."

"Thank you." She stowed her purse and trotted down the short hall that led to the sheriff's office.

Half a minute later, she reappeared. "Go on down. He's waiting for you."

"Thanks."

As she walked toward his office, Grace smoothed out a wrinkle in the black slacks designed more for utility than style. If she'd thought ahead, she'd have worn a more chic outfit for her visit.

But perhaps this would work in her favor. She could legitimately claim it was an impromptu call.

Nate stood when she appeared in his doorway, and the welcome in his smile warmed her from head to toe. "This is a pleasant surprise." He came out from behind his desk and motioned to a small round conference table off to the side. "Please, have a seat."

She crossed the room, scanning the pristine space that was devoid of clutter, the walls bare save for a framed photo of a two-story farmhouse flanked by towering oak trees.

"This decor is quite a change from your predecessor's."

Nate hitched up one side of his mouth as he claimed a chair at a right angle to hers. "I know. It took Eleanor and me a week to dig the place out. I don't think Sheriff Blake ever threw out a document, book, binder, American Legion flyer—you name it. But as a weekend rehabber, I could see the potential. And a fresh coat of paint can work wonders."

"Considering how you've transformed this place, I imagine your house will be a showplace after it's finished." *Just get to the point, Grace. You didn't come here to chitchat.* "So I happened to be in the area"—sort of—"and decided to drop in and give you an update from the botanist at the university."

"Was he able to identify the object?"

"Yes. It's a sunflower seed."

"So your seed theory was correct. Did he say if there was anything unusual about it?"

Amazing how their brains seemed to track in parallel directions.

"I wondered that too, and asked the same question. The answer was no. It's an ordinary sunflower seed."

"But not necessarily an ordinary food ingredient for the two people in question, in light of what you told me about them."

"I agree—and that bothers me."

"Don't discount intuition." He leaned back. "I have a piece of news too. That lead I mentioned in the Mavis Templeton case? It panned out. I was able to identify a suspect in the possible robbery."

"Did you arrest him?"

"No. Insufficient evidence. But we've talked—and he knows more than he's sharing."

"He didn't hurt Mavis, though. There was no indication of trauma. However, it's possible the panic of a break-in triggered a heart attack."

"Wouldn't that have shown up in the autopsy?"

"Not if she died less than four hours afterward. My cause of death allowed for the possibility of an acute myocardial infarction, but I can't say for certain it happened."

"Then we couldn't use that to pursue a felony murder charge, even though the late-night car sighting does fall within the window for time of death." He tapped the tip of his pen against his palm. "I do have one other piece of news. My suspect also knew Fred Wilson."

Grace did a double take. "Another connection between the two of them in addition to the seeds."

"Yes."

"And Fred's death also appeared to be natural." She exhaled. "I'm not getting positive vibes about this."

"Me neither. I went over Wilson's file, but other than the few similarities you noted, I didn't see any other commonalities. The link with my suspect is curious, but I can't figure out the significance of the seeds in this scenario."

"Maybe there isn't any." She frowned and caught her lower lip between her teeth. "Maybe there's no connection between *any* of these disparate facts."

He studied her. "You're not ready to accept that, are you?"

How was this man she barely knew able to read her so well?

"No. Not until I do more digging."

"What did you have in mind?"

"I think I'll take a look at deaths of older residents classified as natural in the counties in this area over the past couple of years, especially ones where the deceased shared characteristics with Fred and Mavis. See if anything jumps out at me."

"That could be time consuming."

She smiled. "Unlike you, I don't have a house to rehab. I can devote a few evenings to this." Even if her sisters would be all over her about spending time with the dead rather than the living—*if* she shared her plans with them. Which she had no intention of doing.

"I admire your dedication."

A surge of pleasure swept through her at the compliment. "What can I say? Like my sisters, I was born with the truth-seeking gene."

"Now I'm intrigued." He leaned forward, laced his fingers on the table, and gave her his full attention. As if her impromptu visit hadn't disrupted what was no doubt a packed schedule. "What do they do?"

"My oldest sister is a police detective in St. Louis. My middle sister is the host of an issues-oriented radio show, also in St. Louis."

"Impressive family."

"Yeah. As the baby, I had hard acts to follow."

"I was including *all* the Reilly sisters in my comment."

Oh.

Her pulse picked up, and her fingertips began to tingle.

If she didn't get out of here fast, the blush she'd managed to contain thus far was going to break free.

"Although I am curious about one thing." He studied her. "You seem awfully young to be a board-certified forensic pathologist."

"Not really. I'm thirty."

"But you have three years tenure with the county. From what I know about the schooling required for your job, the math isn't adding up. Were you a child prodigy?"

"Hardly. But I did skip a couple of grades and I finished college in three years. I came here straight from my fellowship work."

"I stick by my original assessment. Impressive."

"More like driven. What can I say?" She gave a self-deprecating shrug. If they talked any more about her fast-track achievements, the faint flush on her cheeks would turn crimson. "And now I'll let you get back to work." She picked up her tote from the floor and stood. "Besides, I have another autopsy this afternoon in the next county."

He stood too. "Thanks for stopping by. Let me know if you stumble across anything helpful as you dig into the death records."

"I will." She walked toward the door, pausing in front of the photo of the farmhouse. "I like this picture. It has a feel-good vibe."

He stopped beside her, close enough for her to catch the subtle hint of a distinctive, very masculine aftershave. "That's the house where I grew up. There used to be an awesome tire swing on that tree." He indicated the oak on the left. "I remember the day my dad climbed up to secure it, and how all of us—me, my brother, my mom, and my dad—took turns trying it out and celebrated with fresh-squeezed lemonade."

She peeked at him.

His lips were bowed, softening the angular planes of his face, and his wistful expression tugged at her heart.

"Is it in Missouri?"

"Yes. Not far from here."

"Do your parents still live there?"

An echo of sadness replaced the joy of remembrance in his eyes. "No. They're both gone."

"I'm sorry."

"Me too. We were blessed to have a charmed family circle for a lot of years. But I have the photo—and enough happy memories to last a lifetime. Let me walk you out." He opened the door to his office.

"No need. I've already taken up too much of your day." She slipped past him. "I'll let you know if my scavenger hunt unearths anything."

Without waiting for a response, she strode down the hall.

But as she reached the corner, she couldn't resist the temptation to glance back.

Nate lifted a hand in farewell and disappeared into his office, closing the door behind him.

In other words, he'd watched her walk away. Kept her in sight as long as possible.

Spirits ticking up, she waved at Eleanor as she passed the woman's desk and continued toward the outside door.

Too bad she couldn't have been impulsive for once, invited him to join her for a quick lunch. That would have given her an opportunity to pick his brain about the farmhouse he loved but didn't occupy. What was the story there? Who owned the farm now? Had he and his brother remained close? What had prompted him to go into law enforcement rather than stick with the family business and live in the house that held such fond memories?

Unfortunately, those questions would have to wait for another day.

But unless she was misreading every cue he was sending, that day would come. The man was as interested in her as she was in him.

In the interim, a shift in gears was in order. The autopsy scheduled for this afternoon deserved her full attention.

However . . . if the lingering hint of a certain sheriff's tantalizing aftershave prevailed over the usual smells of an autopsy, she wasn't going to fight it.

———————

The burner phone vibrated in his hand with the return call he'd been waiting for, and Dave put it to his ear, scanning the parking lot of the filling station convenience store as he spoke. "We have a problem."

"It better be a big one." BK's annoyance came through loud and clear. "I told you never to initiate a call unless it was an emergency. It's difficult for me to talk on the fly. Make it fast."

"Lorraine Meyers is getting cold feet."

One second ticked by.

Two.

Three.

Dave started to sweat.

"Give me the details."

He swallowed. "You know as much as I do. She called ten minutes ago and said she may want to pull out."

"Why?"

"I don't know."

Silence.

"You obviously didn't do your usual confidence-building sell job."

"I gave her the same spiel I gave everyone else."

That was true—but it was possible the woman had picked up on his growing discomfort. That any unease he'd unwittingly transmitted had taken root and mushroomed after he'd left.

"You got her check, correct?"

"Yes. I mailed it to the account Saturday."

"Then she's in."

"You know we give everyone a thirty-day grace period to change their mind. It helps with the sell-in."

"The opt-out clause was your idea."

"Nevertheless, it's in there."

"In that case, I suggest you get over to her place and do some fast-talking and serious hand-holding."

"We could always return the money."

"Not happening."

"Why not? There will be other people to soak down the line. It wouldn't hurt to leave more space between the deals, like you intended at the beginning."

And a gap would buy him time to continue searching for an escape, despite the long odds against finding one.

"I run this show." BK's voice hardened. "We do this my way, and on my timetable. You know what the repercussions will be if you don't follow through. Let's not add to Kimberly's problems." His tormentor gave him a few seconds to absorb that threat. "Are we clear on next steps?"

"Yes." His wife was always the trump card that would ensure compliance, and the person on the other end of the line knew that. "I'll go see Lorraine again in the next day or two."

"I'm sure you'll convince her to stick with the program, considering what's at stake on your end. I'll check back with you Thursday." BK severed the connection.

Dave lowered the cell from his ear.

He had two days to snuff out the protests from his conscience and persuade the older widow to trust him.

A hard task, when that trust was undeserved.

But what choice did he have? It was either follow orders or hurt Kimberly—and his wife came first.

So sometime tomorrow, he'd sit down with Lorraine, use every ounce of his sales skills to convince her to leave her money where it was . . . and try to figure out how to save her life before the ax fell.

10

KATHLEEN WAS RIGHT. It was time to talk to Becky. Past time.

Patching compound in one hand, putty knife in the other, Nate surveyed the bedroom the previous owner of the house must have used as a kennel, if the claw marks marring the walls from waist-high down were any indication.

Tackle this massive patching job and put off the unpleasant task for another day, or suck it up, call Becky, and get the job done?

Don't procrastinate, Cox. Just do it.

Sensible advice.

Especially since those few minutes he'd spent with Grace in his office yesterday had confirmed everything his sister-in-law had said. The forensic pathologist with the ginger hair and animated hazel eyes might not be The One, to borrow Kathleen's term, but if she wasn't, she'd given him a preview of the sizzle to expect when the right woman did come along.

And Becky wasn't her.

If he didn't take care of this before this day ended, their usual Wednesday dinner out tomorrow would be worse than awkward. Tell her up front, the meal would be a bust. Wait until the end, the evening would be interminable—and nerve-wracking.

Tonight was the optimal choice.

He set down the compound and knife, sent a silent plea for courage heavenward, and pressed her number.

After four rings, it rolled to voicemail.

Odd.

Nate ended the call without leaving a message.

She always answered her phone. And on a Tuesday night at this hour she'd be with her mom, cell in her pocket. His call shouldn't roll. Unless she'd sensed this conversation was coming and—

His phone began to vibrate in his hand, and Becky's name appeared on the screen.

He punched the talk button. "Did I catch you at a bad time?"

"Sort of." She sounded winded. "There was an incident with Mom, and we were trying to calm her down."

"Is she okay?"

"For the moment. What's up? I don't usually hear from you on Tuesdays."

"I know." He walked over to the window and propped a shoulder against the frame, surveying the bucolic field backed by woodland. Unfortunately, the peaceful scene didn't work its usual soothing magic. "I wanted to ask if I could drop by your place for a few minutes later, after you get home from visiting your mom."

Silence.

"Um . . . it could be late. I may have to hang around here longer than usual. I'll see you tomorrow, won't I?" The hint of apprehension in her voice suggested she already had an inkling about the topic he had in mind.

And she didn't want to face it tonight.

Waiting wasn't going to make the break any easier, but

giving her the requested twenty-four hours to adjust to the idea and mentally prepare for the hard conversation ahead was the least he could do.

Even if he'd be on edge until this was over.

"Yes. I'll pick you up at—"

"Why don't I meet you instead? The, uh, seminar I'm taking this week has been running late."

"No problem." In fact, that would be less awkward. They could go their separate ways after dinner—literally *and* figuratively.

"Nate, could we eat at the Spotted Hen?"

That was different. But it *was* her favorite place. Truth be told, she'd have been content to give the diner all their business if he hadn't suggested they venture farther afield for their Wednesday night dinners.

However, the noisy, crowded place wasn't an ideal location to terminate a relationship.

"I was going to suggest somewhere a little quieter." And more private.

"I like the Spotted Hen. It's homey."

And comforting.

Got it.

He could always call ahead, ask for the one secluded booth in the back corner that offered a modicum of privacy.

"The Spotted Hen it is. I'll see you tomorrow. Take care of yourself."

"I'll try." Not her usual cheery response to his standard sign-off. "Good night, Nate."

The line went dead, but the hint of tears lingered.

He gritted his teeth. Filled his lungs.

Tomorrow was going to be traumatic, and sleep tonight would be elusive.

He picked up the patching compound and putty knife again. May as well put the long night ahead to productive use.

And use the dark hours ahead to pray for courage—and fortitude.

"I'm home, hon. Whatever you're cooking smells delicious." Dave set his briefcase on the kitchen counter, dropped his keys beside it, and went in search of his wife.

He found her in the darkened bedroom, eyes closed, lying flat on the bed, a washcloth draped across her forehead.

His spirits nose-dived. When he'd left this morning, she'd been chipper, alert, and energetic.

But as he'd learned, her condition could change in a heartbeat.

He crossed the room and sat on the edge of the bed, careful not to jostle the mattress. "Kimberly?" He touched her hand.

It was ice cold.

Panic clawed at his windpipe until the slight rise and fall of her chest registered.

Thank God!

Her eyelids fluttered open, and she peered up at him. "Dave? What time is it?"

"Noon. How are you?" He smoothed back a few strands of damp hair that were clinging to the tepid washcloth.

"Fine now. I . . . I got a headache and thought I'd . . . rest for a while. You must be hungry."

She started to rise, but he pressed her back. "Don't get up. Stay here if you're not feeling well."

"No. The headache . . . it's gone." She removed the washcloth from her forehead, sat up, and gave him a shaky smile. "I made your favorite casserole."

"I smelled it the minute I walked in the house."

"What time is it again?"

"Noon."

"It should be ready."

"Are you certain you don't want to stay in bed?"

"No. Would you hand me my cane?"

He rose and retrieved it as she swung her legs to the floor, then helped her up after she slipped on her shoes. Held tight until she was steady. Stayed close as she slowly walked down the hall, his heart aching anew.

Some days it was hard to believe the woman who'd once loved to swing dance, whipped up gourmet meals with aplomb, handled the books for his business, and given articulate presentations that showcased her expertise in gardening now shuffled along with a cane, had difficulty scrambling eggs, couldn't balance a checkbook, and spoke in halting, hesitant sentences.

But she was here.

That was all that mattered.

And day by day, God willing, she would continue to improve.

"Could you take the casserole out of the oven while I . . . get the water, Dave? I already set the table."

"I'll be happy to."

He pulled out two potholders, removed the baking dish, and set it on the table. "You didn't have to go to all this trouble." He joined her at the refrigerator, taking the glasses as she filled them.

"I wanted to. I used to cook. I remember that. I've been wanting to . . . make you a real meal. I know you must be tired of all the . . . the bring-out . . . we eat." Her forehead puckered. "Is that the right word?"

"I think you mean takeout—but you were close." He helped her into her chair and took his place beside her. "Shall I dish this up?"

"Please."

He scooped out a generous portion for himself, a smaller one for her. Her appetite had been another casualty of the accident that had changed both their lives. "I can't wait to dig into this."

"I hope it's good." She picked up her fork.

"It looks delicious."

But it wasn't.

As he chewed his first bite, it was obvious a vital ingredient . . . or two . . . or three . . . were missing.

"Oh, Dave!" Tears brimmed on her lower lashes. "It's terrible."

He set his fork on the table and moved beside her, dropping down on one knee to gather her into his arms. "Don't be upset, Kimberly. It was a wonderful effort. A big step forward. Six months ago you wouldn't have tackled a dish like this. I bet your next try will be perfect."

"But I copied the recipe out, and I . . . crossed off the ingredients after I added them. How could it turn out . . . so bad?"

"Mistakes happen. Don't worry about it."

She eased back, tears trailing down her cheeks. "Sometimes I don't think . . . I'll ever get . . . better."

"You *are* getting better. I see improvements every day."

That wasn't a lie. While the bulk of her recovery had happened in the first few months after she'd come out of the coma, and while progress had slowed, she continued to make incremental gains.

Would she ever be back to the way she'd been before the car had slammed into her as she'd hurried across the street to meet him for lunch at the Spotted Hen?

Unlikely.

But compared to her condition four years ago as she lay unconscious in intensive care while the doctors monitored her brain function and warned she could end up in a vegetative state, her level of function was miraculous.

"My boss at the library says . . . I'm improving . . . too."

"There you go. The opinion of an impartial third party."

Thank God they'd been willing to let her come back in a part-time capacity doing simple tasks as she recovered. That, along with her gardening, gave her an incentive to get out of bed every day.

But she couldn't drive. Needed help with many daily tasks. Depended on him to manage her life, protect her independence.

And he wasn't going to let her down.

That's why his meeting with Lorraine this afternoon was critical. If she asked for her funds back, his blackmailer would follow through and tell Kimberly his terrible secret.

While it was possible his wife would forgive him, she'd never trust him again. Their relationship would be irreparably damaged.

Besides, even if he could summon up the courage to go to the authorities, confess his part in the scheme, what would be the point? All BK had to do was change the login and password on the account, and law enforcement would be locked out of the records for the shell company. An offshore bank had no incentive to cooperate with US officials. If they did, and word got out, current clients would disappear, and recruiting new ones would be next to impossible.

And what could he tell the cops, anyway, beyond admitting he'd cheated on his wife and was being blackmailed? He had no proof the shell company clients were being murdered, and the police and coroners hadn't noticed anything amiss with their deaths. Whatever method BK was using appeared to be undetectable. The authorities could think he was a nutcase.

Bottom line, he was stuck.

"Dave?"

At Kimberly's tentative touch on his arm, he forced up the corners of his mouth. "Sorry. I zoned out for a minute. Did you ask me a question?"

"Is everything all right?"

"Right as rain." The blatant lie burned his tongue. "I'll tell you what. Why don't I run out and get us a pizza from that new place in town? I hear it's great. And I'll pick up a couple of those turtle brownies you like from the bakery."

Her eyes began to shimmer, and she leaned forward to press a kiss to his lips. "You're the best, you know that? What would I do without you?" Her breath was warm on his cheek as she nestled against him.

"Don't ever worry about that. I'm here for you, sweetheart. You can count on me."

Given the circumstances, that promise could be hard to keep.

Especially now that he was on to BK's murderous scheme and his conscience was imploring him to find a way out.

Grace knuckled her eyes, took another swig of coffee, and leaned back in her chair at the kitchen table as she stared at her laptop screen.

After culling through old death reports and autopsies for the past two nights and this autopsy-free Wednesday afternoon, what did she have?

Eight people who fit the loose parameters she'd used to winnow through the documents—over age seventy-five, no next of kin or distant NOK, lived alone in the country, and died of natural causes that were most often cardiac related. Three of them had been autopsied, including Fred and Mavis, and the rest had been buried or cremated after the coroner ruled on both cause and manner of death, sometimes in consultation with the deceased's doctor.

The question was, what else—if anything—did all these people have in common?

Had any of them ingested sunflower seeds shortly before their death?

Had they known Nate's robbery suspect?

Would an autopsy have provided clues that could have suggested there was more to their deaths than natural causes?

Important questions, but difficult, if not impossible, to answer in hindsight.

Meaning all the hours she'd spent reviewing the records from the past two years had provided very little new information other than a few additional names that fit her sketchy profile.

She finished off the lukewarm coffee that had helped keep her eyes from glazing over during the long afternoon. It had been a valiant effort, but as far as she could see it had also been a colossal waste of time. Whatever secrets Mavis and Fred had taken to their graves appeared destined to remain—

Her phone began to vibrate on the table, and she snatched it up, pulse surging.

How silly was that?

Of course it wasn't Nate. Why would he call her? She was the one who'd told *him* she'd be in touch if her records search yielded anything worthwhile.

Nevertheless, her respiration continued to misbehave until she read the name on the screen.

Cate.

She fought back a wave of foolish disappointment and summoned up her perkiest voice. "Hey, bride-to-be."

"What's wrong?"

Grace furrowed her brow. "What do you mean?" Her greeting couldn't have been any more chipper if she'd downed a gallon of happy juice.

"You sound like you did the day after the cheerleader calls went out in high school and you didn't get one. Trying to act like you didn't care but crying inside."

Sheesh.

With her abilities to see straight through pretense, no wonder Cate was such a stellar detective.

Didn't mean she had to admit anything to her sister, though.

"You're nuts." She adopted a breezy, dismissive tone. "I only cared about being a cheerleader because the guy I had the hots for was on the football team. In the end I was glad I didn't have to go to all those practices."

"Yeah?"

"Yeah." She tapped a few keys on the laptop and began scrolling through autopsies older than two years. Not that she was going to continue to pursue this line of investigation, but it couldn't hurt to eyeball the names while she talked to Cate. "I happen to be in an especially upbeat mood today." Sort of. Thanks to the sugar rush she'd gotten from the ice cream cone she'd treated herself to at lunch.

"Why? Did you meet someone new—or has your sheriff picked up the pace?"

"There's no pace to pick up. And no, I didn't meet anyone new unless you count the autopsy I did this morning. An interesting gentleman, according to the coroner. He gave me the guy's history while I was dissecting the liver and—"

"Stop. I did not call to get a blow-by-blow account of your day."

"Why *did* you call?"

"To double-check on your date status for the wedding. I'm working on the final seating arrangements for the reception."

"I'm coming solo. I already told you that."

"Hope burns eternal, as they say. I don't have to turn in the head count to the caterer for two weeks, if you want to make any changes."

An image of Nate flashed across her mind.

She erased it.

It wouldn't be fair to ask a man she barely knew to the wedding and subject him to the third degree from her sisters, their husbands, her father, and any other relatives who managed to corner him.

Even if she was certain he could hold his own.

"Does your silence mean you have someone in mind?" Cate sounded hopeful.

"No. But if the situation changes, I'll let you know." She stopped her idle tapping and frowned. Leaned closer to the screen.

Her heart hiccupped as the name from one of the first autopsies she'd performed after being hired for this rural forensic pathology job registered.

There had to be a connection.

Why hadn't she remembered this? Yes, it had happened three years ago, and no, there'd been nothing special to take note of, but recent events should have triggered a—

"Hey. Are you still with me?"

With an effort she refocused on the conversation. "Yes. Sorry. I was working when you called, and I got distracted by a piece of information I spotted on my laptop."

"Why are you working instead of eating dinner?"

"I'm shutting down now." Or soon. After she refreshed her memory on the details of this report.

"In that case, I'll let you go. I don't want to delay your meal. If you decide to bring someone to the wedding, give me a call."

"Uh-huh." She clicked on the entry.

"You're as bad as I am while I'm tracking down a lead. Don't work too hard."

"Says the pot to the kettle." Grace began to scan the report.

"Cute. And with that, I'll bid you good night."

As Cate severed the connection, Grace speed-read the document.

After she finished, she sat back again.

Maybe the meager results from her hours of searching didn't require a lengthy discussion with the sheriff, but this report merited a conversation.

An in-person conversation.

First thing tomorrow.

11

IT HAD BEEN AS BAD AS HE'D EXPECTED.

No. Worse.

Nate set his napkin on the table at the Spotted Hen and signaled Jolene for the check, surveying Becky's barely touched plate.

Neither of them had eaten more than a few bites, and the soothing ambiance of the familiar setting hadn't been as comforting for his companion as she'd hoped, based on the sheen in her eyes.

Jolene hustled over, inspected the two of them, and frowned. "Did the cook mess up?"

"No. We aren't very hungry tonight. Could I have the check?"

"Sure thing, honey." She gave Becky a worried glance. "You want takeout boxes?"

Becky dipped her chin and rummaged through her purse. "Not for me."

"Me neither." Nate extracted his wallet and handed Jolene his credit card. "I'll tell you what. Don't worry about the check. Just ring us up and add my usual tip."

"I'll take care of it and bring your receipt right over."

Giving them another troubled assessment, the waitress hurried back toward the register.

Becky pulled out her keys. "Would you like me to pay for my dinner?"

"Come on, Becky. You know me better than that."

"I thought I did." Her lower lip began to quiver. "You've met someone else, haven't you?"

The question wasn't unexpected. Most women would have asked it at once. But knowing Becky's distaste for confrontation, he hadn't been certain she'd bring it up—and he hadn't volunteered the information.

At least he'd prepared an answer, in case she asked.

"I *have* met a woman who interests me." He wasn't going to lie or try to dance around the question. He'd always been honest with her. "But I think I'd have ultimately gotten to this place even without that. As much as I care for you, there should be a spark between people who are falling in love."

"There is on my end."

Ouch.

"I'm sorry." Lame, but what else could he do except repeat what he'd already said twice? "I hope someday you'll meet a man who can return all the love you have to offer."

Mashing her lips together, she zipped up her purse.

"Here you go, hon." Jolene set his card and receipt on the table. "God bless you both."

Usually the waitress lingered to exchange a few pleasantries before they left, but she didn't attempt to engage them in conversation tonight. Jolene could be a bit rough around the edges, but she had excellent intuitive skills.

Thank goodness.

Nate signed the receipt, slid from the booth, and waited for Becky to follow.

"You don't have to walk me out." She scooched across the vinyl-covered bench on her side of the table and stood.

"A gentleman always escorts a lady to her car, and you're a lady through and through."

She didn't respond.

Nevertheless, he took her arm as he always did and walked her to the parking lot.

At her car, she tossed her purse on the passenger seat. As she turned toward him, a tear trailed down her cheek.

Man.

He felt like a heel.

Leaning forward, he pulled her into a hug. "Take care of yourself—and if you ever need anything, call me. Just because we're not a couple anymore doesn't mean I don't care about you."

She clung to him for a few moments, then eased out of his embrace and slipped into her car. "I appreciate the offer, but it doesn't work that way. If one person has strong feelings, a clean break is best." Her voice choked, and she twisted the key in the ignition. "I hope you find what you're looking for."

He did too.

In fact, while it didn't seem very honorable to be thinking about another woman before Becky had driven out of sight, the little zing in his nerve endings as an image of Grace flashed through his mind gave him hope that Becky's parting wish for him may have already come true.

Well, shoot.

From her tiny table for one wedged against the window in the far corner of the Spotted Hen, Grace took a sip of water and watched Nate give the attractive, dark-haired woman in the parking lot a hug. The kind that came naturally between people who were well acquainted.

Very well acquainted.

So much for all her romantic fantasies.

Propping her chin in her palm, she continued to observe

them as the two disengaged, the woman drove away, and Nate remained in place, watching until she disappeared.

As if he wished she hadn't left.

Grace sighed, spirits plummeting as the tough-talking, buck-up internal drill sergeant that had gotten her through other difficult situations kicked in.

Get over it, girl. Chalk it up to a major lapse in your usually reliable signal-reading skills. You'll live. Someone else will come along.

Yeah, but when? She wasn't getting any younger. The big three-oh had come and gone last winter. If she wanted a family someday, the clock was ticking.

"Have you decided what to order?"

As Jolene spoke, Grace redirected her attention to the menu. "No. I was, uh, distracted."

Jolene squinted out the window. "Oh. Nate's still here."

"Uh-huh."

"Great guy. Do you work with him often?"

"No." Grace took a sip of water. "As a matter of fact, we only met a couple of weeks ago."

"No kidding?" Jolene pulled out her order pad. "I'd think in your line of work you two would be bosom buddies."

If only.

"I have more contact with the coroner."

"Makes sense, I suppose." Jolene peered out the window again as Nate crossed the lot and slid behind the wheel of his Jeep. "I hope everything's okay with him."

"Why wouldn't it be, after having dinner with a very pretty woman?"

Jolene pulled the pencil from behind her ear. "Appearances can be deceiving."

"What does that mean?"

"Don't know that I should say. A body hears—and over-hears—all sorts of conversations in this job. We waitresses

130

are invisible to customers, you know. It's like being a fly on the wall. You have to learn to stay mum and be discreet."

"I see what you mean." Even if she wished the woman would bend her rules tonight.

"Are you ready to order, or do you need a few more minutes?"

"No." Grace skimmed the menu and handed it to the waitress. "I'll have the meat loaf special that's on the board."

"Can't go wrong with that." She jotted the order on her pad. "So how goes the job?"

"No complaints."

"You're a rare one. Most people find a ton of stuff to whine about. But I'm with you. I like my job. An interesting cast of characters crosses my path every day."

"Mine too."

"But mine talk to me." She gave her a wink and an elbow nudge, then grew more serious. "I sure was sorry to hear about your car. They ever track down the culprits?"

Grace arched an eyebrow. "How did you know about that?"

"Like I said, fly on the wall. You wouldn't believe all the juicy tidbits I hear."

"I can imagine. Sad to say, there haven't been any leads. At this stage, I doubt there will be, either. The sheriff said he'd keep his ear to the ground, but I'm not holding my breath."

"I wouldn't give up yet. If there's a lead to be found, I expect Nate will dig it up. That man is a dynamo." Jolene stuck the pencil back behind her ear. "I'll get your order in the queue."

As the waitress trotted toward the kitchen, Grace scanned the parking lot. Nate was gone. Perhaps headed back to the office to log a few more hours, if Jolene's take on his work ethic was accurate.

No doubt it was. She'd come to the same conclusion. The man radiated tenacity and dedication. If *she* was on the wrong side of the law, she wouldn't want to come up against the county sheriff. Nor would it be wise to count him out with any investigation, no matter how long the odds. Including the vandalism incident.

But after the affectionate parting she'd witnessed a few minutes ago, it would be prudent to count him out on the romance front.

Nate Cox was taken.

That didn't mean she should change her plans for tomorrow, though.

No, she'd swing by his office, do what she had to do—even if her motives now were more professional than personal.

And after that, she'd walk a wide circle around the handsome sheriff and talk to Russ about any concerns she had on the work front.

———

Clamping his teeth together, Tyler slid from behind the wheel of his car in front of the house where he'd grown up.

He did *not* want to be here.

Waiting around for the other shoe to drop, however, was stupid. In the end, it would serve him better to be up-front with his father and take the consequences rather than stick his head in the sand and hope the problem went away.

Tyler surveyed the drive. As expected, Wayne's truck was gone. His brother never missed his Wednesday night bowling-and-beer outing with his friends.

That meant his dad was home alone, probably in the barn repairing whatever piece of equipment had given him fits today.

Tyler forced his feet to carry him behind the house and across the small field that separated the living quarters from the outbuildings.

As he approached, the sharp clang of hammer against metal

drifted across the humid air that hadn't cooled off much despite the waning sunlight.

At the door to the barn, he stopped.

His father was standing beside the tractor that was long past its prime. The one Wayne always said his dad kept running with spit and luck. Hopefully that magic mix would continue to work, because after the purchase of the Wilson place, there wouldn't be much money to spare for repairs.

And there might not be *any* to spare for high-priced-lawyer bills.

Tyler fisted his hands at his sides.

Asking his dad to pay for his latest screwup wasn't fair. He'd dug himself into this hole. He should dig himself out.

Or go to jail.

Either way, the mess he was in wasn't his old man's fault, and he shouldn't expect his father to bail him out.

Coming here tonight had been a mistake.

He pivoted and strode away.

"Tyler?"

Three steps into his retreat, he halted. Slowly turned back.

His father scrutinized him. "What are you doing here in the middle of the week?"

"I, uh, wanted to talk to you. But I can come back when you're not busy."

The Holmes patriarch snorted. "Like that'll ever happen." He wiped his hands on a rag and walked toward him. "Must be important if you made a special trip out here."

"Yeah, but it can wait."

His dad assessed him. "You certain about that? Putting off hard stuff doesn't make it any easier."

No, it didn't.

But making a confession that could destroy your future was harder.

"Let's take the load off." His father motioned to the log

bench against the outside wall that had been there for as long as Tyler could remember. The one where he'd sat as a kid whenever his dad wanted to have a private talk with him.

It was a fitting place to spill his guts—if he could muster up the courage.

Shoulders drooping, he trudged over to it and sank down. Leaning forward, he clasped his hands between his knees and watched an overloaded ant struggle across the rough dirt, weighed down by its burden.

He could relate.

His father sat beside him and pulled off his work gloves. "Must be serious."

"Yeah."

"You in trouble with the law?"

His dad's uncanny knack to see straight into his soul was as unnerving now as it had been when he was a mischievous kid.

But his current transgressions were far worse than trespassing on Fred Wilson's property to steal apples off their neighbor's tree.

"Maybe."

"Thought something was up on Sunday night. You want to tell me about it?"

"No." He swallowed. "But I reckon you're gonna find out anyway, and I'd rather you hear it from me."

"Okay. Let's have it."

His father didn't appear to be all that upset. Didn't push. Didn't ask a single question.

He just waited.

Tyler squeezed his linked fingers together until his knuckles whitened. "You're not gonna like it."

"Don't expect I will. But if you're willing to talk to me, I'm willing to listen. And two heads are better than one at working through a problem."

Did that mean his dad would help him? Stand by him?

Not much chance of that.

But carrying the burden alone, waiting for the sheriff to swoop in for the kill, was turning him inside out. He had to talk to somebody, and despite their constant clashes, his dad had the clearest-thinking mind of anyone he'd ever met.

At this point, he could use all the brainpower he could marshal to get out of the corner he'd backed himself into.

So he told his dad everything, starting with Fred. He didn't try to whitewash anything he'd done, didn't manufacture excuses. He simply laid it all out there.

After he finished, only the hoot of an owl and the loud, droning buzz of cicadas drifted through the silence of the deepening twilight.

Tyler kept his head down as he waited for the verdict, heart pounding as hard as it had that night at Mavis Templeton's as he'd stared death in the face.

"Sit up and look at me, son." His father's tone was tough, as it always was when his younger son messed up, but he didn't sound angry.

Tyler leaned back against the wall and forced himself to face his dad.

The sadness and disappointment in the man's demeanor shredded his insides.

"I'm sorry, Dad." The apology scratched past his tight throat. All he'd ever wanted to do his whole life was win his dad's approval. Now he'd blown that hope forever.

"I thought you'd straightened yourself out. That come spring, you'd be back here, where you belong."

"That's what I still want." His voice rasped. "More than ever."

"I can't have lawbreakers in my house."

He knew that.

But he also knew something else, at the deepest core of his being—and his dad needed to know it too.

Tyler gripped the edge of the bench and wrapped his fingers tight around the edge. "I understand why it's hard for you to believe me after all the dumb stunts I've pulled, but I swear to you, if I can straighten this mess out, I'll never cause any trouble for anyone again."

His dad studied him for several seconds. "You realize there will be consequences for what you've done."

"Yes, sir. I'll pay them. But after that, I want a fresh start. I want to be a son you can be proud of—like Wayne. I'll do my best from now on to be like him."

His father's forehead knotted. "I don't want you to be like Wayne. I want you to be like *you*. To be the best you that you can be. That's all I ever wanted."

Tyler tried to wrap his mind around that. "But . . . Wayne's always been . . . he's the one you favored and wanted me to live up to. To be like. You were always comparing me to him."

His father gave a slow blink. Massaged the bridge of his nose. Resettled his ball cap as he watched a swallow sail into the barn rafters to roost for the night. "It appears you aren't the only one in this family who's made mistakes." He looked over at him. "You know you were born early, right?"

"Yeah." His mom had told him the whole story. About the weeks he'd spent in neonatal intensive care, hovering between life and death. About the hours she'd camped out there, holding him, willing him to live.

"Well, after we brought you home from the hospital, your mom worried and fussed over you no end. For the rest of her life, she hovered, took your side, protected you. I saw how that affected Wayne, and I tried to give him extra attention. I guess I carried that too far, especially after your mom passed. But I don't have favorites, son. Never did. I love you both the same."

Tyler examined the weathered face of the man whose affection and esteem he'd sought his whole life.

Apparently he'd had it all along.

His vision misted, and he swiped the back of his hand across his eyes. So many mistakes, so many misguided attempts to win approval, to be noticed.

Instead, all he'd ever done was shoot himself in the foot. After his recent offenses, he didn't deserve this hard-working, honest, ethical man's help. He was a stupid, ungrateful no-account who—

"Hey." His father gripped his arm, his sad, disappointed expression replaced by one of steely resolve. "Will you give me your word you've told me the truth—all of it—and that you'll accept the punishment for what you've done?"

"Yes, sir." He didn't hesitate.

His dad gave a sharp, decisive nod. "In that case, let's talk about next steps."

As his father laid out his thoughts about how to proceed, Tyler's spirits lifted. The road ahead wouldn't be easy. That was a given. But if his father was willing to stick with him . . . if his dad trusted him to keep his promise . . . he'd suck it up and deal with whatever the future held.

Because when people believed in you, they gave you a gift all the ill-gotten money in the world couldn't buy.

It was called confidence. And hope.

12

"SHERIFF? Sorry to disturb you, but Dr. Reilly stopped by again. Do you have a few minutes?"

At Eleanor's question, Nate swiveled away from the DUI incident report he'd been reviewing on his computer. After last night's painful interlude with Becky, he could use a pick-me-up. A chat with Grace Reilly should do the trick.

"Yes. Go ahead and send her back."

"Will do. Would you like a refill on your coffee?"

"I can take care of my own refills, but thank you for offering."

"I always got Sheriff Blake's coffee."

"And I'm sure he appreciated it."

"It was expected."

"Not anymore."

"Well . . ." The department admin adjusted the collar on her crisp blouse. "I'll tell Dr. Reilly to come back."

As Eleanor disappeared, Nate leaned back in his chair, rested his elbows on the arms, and steepled his fingers, lips curving up. No matter what crises the rest of his day brought, at least he could launch it with a few pleasant minutes in Grace's company.

But the instant she appeared in the doorway, it was clear

from the faint furrows on her brow and her taut posture that the purpose of today's visit wasn't pleasant.

Holding on to his smile, he rose. "Good morning."

"Morning. I won't keep you long."

"No need to rush. Would you like to sit?" He motioned to the table.

After a fraction of a second, she nodded. "For a few minutes."

She wanted out of here fast.

Why?

"I didn't expect to see you again so soon—not that I'm complaining." He joined her at the table, striving for a welcoming tone.

She ignored his personal inference and laced her fingers on the polished surface in front of her. "I have two reasons for stopping by."

Man, she was all business today.

"You have my full attention."

"First, I've spent hours combing through the death records and autopsies from the past two years for this county and the adjacent ones. I found a handful of people who fit my parameters. An autopsy was ordered for one of them, but after reviewing my notes, I didn't spot anything suspicious. Bottom line, I'm no closer to figuring out the link between Fred and Mavis."

"It was a worthy effort, though. I applaud your diligence."

She dismissed his compliment with a flick of her wrist. "I don't like trails that lead nowhere—and I sense we're missing crucial information. Here's what I'd like to propose. I'm going to talk to the sheriffs in the counties where the people I've identified lived. If there's another death that fits my parameters—and I'll email those to everyone—I'd like to be called before the body is removed."

"You want to come to the scene?"

"Yes."

"In a rural area like this, very few deaths are suspicious enough to warrant an on-site visit by the pathologist—unless the pathologist is a medical examiner." A rare occurrence in less-populated counties, where elected coroners like funeral director Russ determined the manner of death when they weren't doing their day jobs.

"I realize that. I'm not saying I'll spot anything anyone else wouldn't, but another pair of eyes can't hurt."

"Those calls can come in at all hours."

"I was a medical student once." She flashed him the hint of a dimple. "Trust me, I'm used to weird hours."

"In that case, I'm fine with your request. I doubt Russ will have any objections, either."

"Thanks." Her knuckles whitened, and the tension in the room ratcheted up. "That brings me to the second reason for my visit. I only looked closely at documents for the past twenty-four months, but I did scan the ones in this county further back—and I came across your brother's autopsy report." Distress clouded her hazel irises. "I want to apologize for not remembering the name, making the connection, and offering my condolences."

He stared at her.

She was upset because she hadn't linked him to an autopsy she'd done three years ago?

Good grief.

What impossible standards did this woman hold herself to?

He leaned forward, locking on to her gaze. "With all the autopsies you've done in your job, Grace, I never expected you to remember the name."

"But meeting you should have reminded me." She caught her lower lip between her teeth. "His autopsy was one of the first ones I did here, and it was tragic. I remember it clearly, even if the name didn't stick."

A wave of sorrow lapped at Nate's heart, as it always did

when he thought about Jeff's senseless death, though it was far milder than the tsunami of grief and anger that had engulfed him after the news reached him overseas. If either of them had to die, it should have been him—a man who put himself in deadly situations every day, taking enemy fire, at the mercy of IEDs and ambushes.

Instead, Jeff was the one whose life had been cut short. And the loss continued to send out ripples of grief, disturbing the placid surface of his world.

Perhaps it always would.

Swallowing past the tightness in his throat, he forced himself to focus on Grace's last comment. "Yes, it was tragic. But it was also avoidable. Farm equipment and alcohol don't mix. He knew that."

"He wasn't over the legal limit."

"No, but he was close. And I have to believe that was why he forgot to activate all the safety switches before investigating why the header on the combine wouldn't turn. If he *had* remembered to follow protocol, he would have realized the combine hadn't finished its last cycle and was still under pressure—and he wouldn't have gotten sucked in."

Or lost both his legs.

Or bled to death in the field before anyone could respond to his frantic 911 call.

Even three years later, the whole scenario sickened him.

She touched his hand, a mere whisper-soft contact, but it was a balm on his soul. "I'm very sorry for your loss, Nate."

"I appreciate that." He hesitated—then covered her hand with his, sending a clear, intentional signal.

Her breath hitched, and sparks began pinging off the walls. Message received.

But all at once she pulled her fingers free and stood. "I, uh, have to go." She snatched up her tote from the floor and fled toward the door, like a spooked deer trying to elude a hunter.

What on earth?

He hadn't imagined the electricity between them moments ago, or during their previous encounters. It was as real as a summer lightning storm in Missouri. And until today, he'd gotten the distinct impression she was receptive to the high-voltage current that energized the air whenever they were together.

Yet the dynamics had changed since their last visit, and he had to find out why before she bolted. Before the roadblocks she was erecting sent them spinning off course.

"Grace."

She hesitated as he murmured her name, her hand on the knob. Slowly turned. Every angle of her taut body said she was poised for flight. "Yes?"

He stood. "Tell me what's going on."

She clasped the handle of her tote with both hands, squeezing it tight. "What do you mean?"

If she wouldn't offer up the answers he wanted, he'd have to play twenty questions.

"Have I offended you somehow?"

"No. Absolutely not."

Good to know.

Rather than invade her personal space and perhaps reactivate her flee instincts, he kept his distance, maintaining an open, approachable posture. "I thought we were establishing not only a professional rapport but a friendship. Now you're backing off. Shutting me out. Why?"

She evaded his gaze and rummaged through her purse. Extracted her keys. "I just have a busy schedule today. I imagine you do too. I should go."

A partial truth, at best.

That left him two choices.

He could let her walk away—or lay it on the line and possibly set himself up for a fall.

But if he'd misread her signals, if the attraction was one-sided, may as well find out now, before any of the romantic fantasies he was harboring sent down deeper roots.

"I do have a full plate today, but I can make time for you. Always." He offered her his warmest smile.

She didn't return it. In fact, the creases on her forehead deepened. "May I ask you a question?"

"Sure."

"Are you flirting with me?"

At the unexpected query, a red alert began beeping in his brain. With all the harassment charges being filed these days against people in public positions, he couldn't afford to have any female colleague misunderstand his intentions.

"I was being honest." He phrased his response with care. "You're an interesting, appealing woman, and I've enjoyed our conversations. I hoped you felt the same, and that we could continue to get acquainted. But I'm not trying to force you to do anything you don't want to do. Nor would a rejection by you have any bearing on your position with the county."

Short of a direct harassment reference, he couldn't be any more transparent about his concerns.

But to emphasize his point, he stepped back and put the table between them while he waited for her to respond. A new sheriff couldn't afford to give anyone the wrong impression.

Even a woman who didn't strike him as the type to over-react and interpret a straightforward expression of attraction as slimy manipulation.

———

As Nate retreated, barricading himself behind the table, Grace's stomach dropped to her toes.

He was worried she thought he was hitting on her and was going to report him for unwanted advances.

Mercy.

Concerns about harassment had nothing to do with her decision to leave. She simply needed space to try to figure out why a man she'd judged to be true blue, with a boatload of integrity, would flirt with her if he had a girlfriend.

Somehow there'd been a major breakdown in communication between them.

First order of business? Clear up his legal concerns.

"Let me put your mind at ease. Your behavior has been well within the bounds of propriety, based on signals I'm sure I sent. I'm not planning to report any sort of inappropriate advances."

"I'm glad to hear that." Nevertheless, he stayed behind the table, fingers gripping the back of a chair.

His wariness was no surprise after her attempt to make a fast escape and the revolting charges splashed all over the media every day.

Since he'd been honest with her, why not broach the subject that was top of mind?

She crimped the handle of her tote in her fingers. "I *am* confused, though."

"About what?"

She took a deep breath. "I don't understand why you're interested in me if you're already involved with someone."

His forehead bunched. "I *was* dating someone on a steady basis. I'm not anymore."

"You were as of last night."

"Ah." His brow smoothed. "You were at the Spotted Hen."

"Yes. I didn't notice you until you left. I had a table by the window."

"And saw us in the parking lot."

"Yes. I wasn't spying on you, but you were standing in the middle of the pavement, in plain sight."

"Yes, we were. And what you witnessed was a goodbye scene. One that was too long in coming."

145

All at once, Jolene's comments about not judging by appearances fell into place.

Relief coursed through her—but on its heels came guilt.

"Was I why you broke up?"

"As I told Becky, meeting you did prompt me to reexamine our relationship, but the breakup was inevitable. I stayed with her for all the wrong reasons." He swept a hand over the table. "If you want to sit again for a few minutes, I can fill you in."

"You don't have to explain anything to me."

"I'd like to."

Well, if he was *willing* to share details . . .

She returned to the table and reclaimed her chair.

A faint hint of his distinctive aftershave tickled her nostrils as he moved past her and retook his seat. "Can I ask you a question before I launch into this?"

"Sure."

"Have I been misreading your signals?"

That was direct.

And it deserved a direct answer.

"No."

One side of his mouth quirked up. "That's the best news I've had all day. Maybe all year."

A delicious tingle raced through her. "Now you're flirting."

"No. Being honest again." He leaned back and crossed an ankle over a knee, as if he had all the time in the world. "Let me back my story up, since we've talked a little about Jeff already and you asked about the house on a prior visit." He motioned toward the photo on the wall.

"I assume he ran the farm."

"Yes. I sold him my share. Much as I loved the place, I had no interest in being a farmer."

"Were you always drawn to law enforcement?"

"Not the uniformed variety. I had law school in my sights. I was all set to go after I got my undergraduate degree—and then my best friend was killed in Iraq." A shadow of grief once again darkened his eyes. "I decided to defer law school and serve my country."

"Admirable."

He waved aside that comment. "Don't give me too much credit. My motive was equal parts patriotism, Don Quixote, and guilt. My friend appreciated the freedom and opportunities in America more than I did, and he died trying to safeguard what I took for granted. I decided the least I could do was put in a stint in the Army and defend the values I believe in."

"How long did you serve?"

"Eight years."

She arched her eyebrows. "That's more than a stint."

"The work was worthwhile."

"What did you do?"

He shifted in his seat. "I was in Special Forces."

Nate Cox had been a Green Beret? A member of one of the most elite fighting units in the world, peopled by intelligent, brave, motivated, and relentless warriors?

Whoa.

"I'm impressed." To say the least.

He shrugged. "That's just where I ended up. I'd have been willing to serve wherever they put me."

The man was modest too.

Also impressive.

"Why did you leave?"

He exhaled. "Jeff died, and Kathleen needed help on the farm. At that point in my service, I was facing a decision, anyway—leave, or make the military a career. I was on the fence until the accident. After that, the choice was clear."

"Or a very unselfish act."

"No." He dismissed that suggestion with a definitive shake of his head. "It was the right choice. And it wasn't a sacrifice to come back here after living in war zones. While I didn't want to be a farmer, I did appreciate the peace and slower pace of country living."

"Did you live on the farm?"

"Yes. In the apartment over the barn, for propriety's sake. I helped her with the day-to-day operation of the place."

"What happened to law school?"

"I lost interest. After my experience in the Middle East, I didn't want a desk job. I was still interested in law enforcement and justice but at the field level. After I was back in the States for a while, I signed up for the Missouri Sheriff's Association satellite training academy, taking classes at night and on weekends. Once I completed that, I was hired as a part-time police officer in a small town nearby. When the sheriff announced his retirement, my boss convinced me to run for the job. The rest is history."

That could be true career-wise, but he hadn't given her any insights into his romance.

Maybe he didn't intend to. After all, a gentleman wouldn't tell tales out of school. Nor would she expect him to. But a few pertinent details would be helpful.

Could she probe a bit without sounding nosey?

"Why did you buy a house and leave the farm?" Perhaps that move was related to his ex-girlfriend.

"Eighteen months ago, Kathleen met someone new. After they got serious, I bought my house and moved off the property. She and Luke are engaged now, and he's stepped into my shoes at the farm."

So the house purchase hadn't been precipitated by his girlfriend but by his sister-in-law's boyfriend.

"You okay with that?"

"More than. Luke's a good guy, and Jeff wouldn't have wanted Kathleen to spend the rest of her life alone. She's the type of woman who should be married with a houseful of kids—and who thinks everyone else should be too. Including me. That's why she introduced me to Becky eight months ago."

The conversation had worked its way back to the ex-girlfriend.

Excellent.

And since he'd brought her up, that opened the door to a few questions.

"You mentioned that you stayed in the relationship for the wrong reasons."

"Yeah." He rubbed the back of his neck. "A few months before I met her, her father had died suddenly. She took it hard. A month after we met, I convinced her to go bicycling with me. She fell and broke her leg, requiring months of rehab and a ton of assistance—which I provided. She didn't finish with physical therapy until April. Ten weeks after we started dating, her mother was diagnosed with rapidly progressive dementia. Within four months, she had to be put into an extended care facility. Every time I thought about breaking up, I backed off. I didn't want to add to her stress."

"I can understand that. But guilt isn't the best basis for a relationship."

"Kathleen told me that too. I don't disagree. So I sucked it up and did what had to be done."

He'd shared a great deal, but she did have another question that was very important to her—if she could phrase it delicately.

"Eight months is a long time to date in today's world without getting . . . serious." She kept her tone conversational, positioning it as a comment rather than a question.

Nate had no difficulty hearing the query underneath, though, and nailing her concern. The man's ability to read her was both intriguing and disconcerting.

"You're wondering if we lived together."

Now it was her turn to squirm. "I wouldn't ask such a personal—"

"The answer is no. Nor did we sleep together."

If he was willing to be candid, why not ask the next critical question?

"May I ask why not?"

"I don't believe in casual intimacy. I was raised with traditional Midwestern values. We attended church every Sunday as a family, and the moral principles my parents and my pastor instilled in me stuck. I took more than a little flak for that in college and in the service, but my values have deep roots and can withstand storms. Becky shared them. Common moral ground has always been important to me in any dating relationship."

He stopped there, but *his* implied question was also clear. And she had no problem answering it.

"Since you've been frank with me, I'll return the favor. I didn't grow up on a farm, but I did grow up in the Midwest with the same values you did, backed by family and faith. I not only respect your beliefs about casual intimacy, I share them."

"I'd say that's good news all around—and an excellent omen for the future. I just have one other question." He leaned forward and folded his hands on the table. "Are there any dark secrets or significant others lurking in the shadows of *your* world that I should know about?"

Despite his teasing inflection, a shiver rippled through her at his reference to dark secrets.

But that topic could wait for another day.

"I've never had a serious relationship. Or any that came close to yours in terms of length."

"Are you in the market for one?"

"Yes, as my sisters would happily confirm. Of the three of us, I always had the most interest in romance. Yet the two of them are the ones who found someone to love. Eve got married last month, and Cate is tying the knot next month. They always kid me that if I continue to put all my energies into dead people, I'll never meet any eligible men."

"I'm not dead. And I'm very eligible." His eyes began to twinkle.

Heat surged through her, and she had to restrain the urge to fan herself. Had someone shut down the air-conditioning in here?

"Can I say I'm glad—that you're eligible, I mean?"

"If I can return the sentiment." His voice warmed, ratcheting up her temperature again. "I think we should celebrate our agreement on that subject."

The man was definitely flirting now.

"What did you have in mind?"

"Dinner. There's a restaurant out by the lake with a deck that extends over the water. I'm told it has excellent ambiance and great food."

So he hadn't been there with Becky.

Perfect.

"That sounds amazing."

"Why don't we—"

At a knock on his door, he leaned back in his chair. "Come in."

Eleanor poked her head into the office. "Sorry to disturb you, Sheriff, but your nine thirty appointment is here."

Shoot. If only they'd had another five minutes.

However, Nate's office wasn't the place for a romantic tryst—or the planning of one.

"I'm leaving, Eleanor." She stood. "My business is finished." The professional kind, anyway.

Nate rose too and accompanied her to the door.

"Shall I send the gentleman back?" Eleanor directed the question to Nate.

"Yes. Thanks."

He waited until the department assistant began her trek down the hall to lean close and lower his voice. "Sorry about that."

"No worries. Work takes priority during working hours. And mixing business and pleasure isn't wise—during working hours."

"Yeah." He sighed and pulled a card out of his pocket, jotted a number on the back, and gave it to her. "I'll call you about dinner. Until then, if you want to get in touch, that's my private cell number."

"I'll keep it close at hand—and I'll look forward to hearing from you."

A banked fire began to burn in his eyes, and for a tiny moment she half expected him to lean down and sweep his lips over hers.

But after eight years in the military, and with Green Beret credentials, his self-discipline had to be well-honed. Besides, he was too much of a pro to break protocol with a kiss on the job.

She was too.

Or she'd always thought she was.

Nate Cox, however, was a temptation that could be hard to resist.

He made do with a wink, which sent her hormones spiraling out of control again as she walked down the hall, passing his next appointment en route.

As she turned the corner toward the exit and peeked back, his door was closed again. Unlike her last visit, he hadn't lingered to watch her leave. Not that he could have even if he'd wanted to today.

Didn't matter, though. They had a pending dinner date. She'd see him again soon.

Even better?

Unless he had a prior commitment, she now had a date for Cate's wedding.

13

LORRAINE MEYERS HADN'T BUDGED.

Sweat beading on his forehead, Dave crossed the gravel drive in front of her house, slid behind the wheel of his car, and cranked up the air-conditioning to full blast. On the cusp of July, it would take a while for the heat to dissipate in the stifling vehicle.

The heat in his life, however, wasn't going away anytime soon, no matter how high he set the air. As soon as he told BK he'd failed to convince Lorraine to stay the course, his nemesis was going to go ballistic.

All he could do was promise to try again. Per the clause in the agreement Lorraine had signed, her refund check wasn't due for three weeks. He'd promised to prepare the paperwork, but that didn't mean he couldn't continue his attempts to convince her to stick with the investment. When he brought the documents back for her to sign tomorrow, he could conjure up more arguments, bring more fake charts, assure her all would be fine if she trusted him.

That's what he'd tell BK too.

As soon as he summoned up the courage to report on today's meeting.

He put the car in gear, backed around on the drive, and crunched along on the gravel toward the main road.

Halfway there, his burner phone began to vibrate.

BK hadn't waited for him to call.

Pulse escalating, he stopped the car and pulled the phone from his pocket. Ignoring the summons would only postpone the inevitable.

Steeling himself, he pressed the talk button.

"How did it go?" The androgynous voice was sharp. Impatient. Irritated.

"She hasn't changed her mind yet. But I'll keep working on her."

"I'm not happy about this."

"I didn't think you would be."

"Do I have to give you an incentive to try harder?"

His heart stumbled. "No."

"A few hints to Kimberly may be in order. Just sufficient to ruffle her feathers."

"No!" He squeezed the wheel. "I'll fix this."

"You could always repay Lorraine with your own money."

"You know I don't have those kinds of reserves."

"Then convince her fast, or I'll have to take action you may not like."

"I have three weeks."

"By *your* calculation. I don't like pushing deadlines—and I don't like loose ends."

"Look, I'm doing the best I can."

"Are you?"

"Yes."

"I'm not certain of that. You know, for a man who has a great deal to lose, you're not making much effort to get with the program. One of these days I may decide you're not even necessary to the plan anymore. And if that happens, all bets are off. Enjoy the rest of your day."

As BK severed the connection, Dave closed his eyes.

Colossal mess didn't begin to describe the state of his life.

Much as he wished he could ignore BK's demands, that wasn't realistic. At this stage, all he could do was try again with Lorraine tomorrow.

But her attitude and comments today suggested she wasn't going to change her mind. She wanted her money back as soon as possible.

Dave took his foot off the brake and accelerated toward the main road. If only he could push the gas pedal to the floor and speed away into oblivion, where BK could never find him.

Unfortunately, that wasn't an option. Kimberly needed him.

So tonight he'd put together a new presentation, polish his sales pitch, and give it another go with Lorraine.

If she didn't change her mind?

Who knew what BK would do?

One thing for sure.

It wouldn't be good.

"Sheriff?" Eleanor gave a single rap and opened his office door. "Can I disturb you for a minute? I think this may require your immediate attention."

Tamping down a sigh, Nate set his cell back on the desk. What *hadn't* needed his immediate attention in the past twenty-four hours? Since Grace's visit yesterday, he'd been going nonstop, the promised call to set up their dinner date still on his to-do list. And now, just when it seemed he had two minutes to squeeze it in, Eleanor was on his threshold with yet another urgent matter.

Perhaps he could quickly dispense with whatever business she had, send her on to lunch, close his door, and have five minutes of blessed peace to call Grace.

"Of course. Come in."

She entered, carrying a pink message slip. "A rather strange call came in to dispatch, and I thought you'd want to handle it yourself."

If Eleanor, with all her experience and common sense, had reached that conclusion, he wasn't about to dispute it.

"All right. What do we have?"

"The caller's voice was muffled, and he or she wouldn't leave a name or number, but they did provide contact information for a person they suggested you talk to regarding the deaths of Mavis Templeton and Fred Wilson."

His antennas went up.

Could this be confirmation that Grace's suspicions were legit?

He skimmed the name on the slip of paper Eleanor handed him. It didn't ring any bells.

"Do you happen to know this Dave Mullins?"

"Yes, I do. He sells investments and insurance. Has for many years. He's a very respected member of the community. But he's had his share of tribulations. Four years ago, his only son was killed in the Middle East. Three months later, his wife was hit by a car and suffered a traumatic brain injury. She was in a coma for weeks. The poor thing recovered, but she needs assistance with daily living. Dave has been her knight in shining armor. A wonderful example of the 'in sickness and in health' wedding vow. He's stuck by her every step of the way."

As usual, Eleanor's knowledge of the locals astounded him. "How do you know all that?"

She brushed a stray strand of hair back into the upsweep she favored. "His wife, Kimberly, and I are in the same garden club. But Dave is well known in this county and the surrounding area, thanks to his business. I believe he has clients in a fairly large radius."

"What could he know about Mavis and Fred?"

"I haven't a clue. It's possible they did business with him,

I suppose. But why would he have information about their deaths? Besides, weren't both ruled natural?"

"Yes—although Grace Reilly has suspicions. Those haven't amounted to anything yet, but she strikes me as a sharp woman with excellent insights. Also a go-getter. She hasn't let go of her theory, and this"—he lifted the sheet of paper— "may give it legs."

"My." The woman's eyes widened. "What is this world coming to if a person can't be safe in their own home in a quiet place like this?"

"Nowhere is safe these days." He set the paper on his desk. "I believe a bit of research on Mr. Mullins is in order, along with a visit."

"That will be quite upsetting for him—and Kimberly. Do you think this could be a crank tip? From someone who doesn't like him?"

"I'm not ruling that out. If it is, he doesn't have anything to worry about, and a chat with law enforcement shouldn't upset him too much. I'll visit him at his office rather than home to avoid disturbing his wife."

"That would be considerate. Now I'll let you get back to whatever you were doing."

As she exited and closed the door, Nate tapped the slip of paper. Grace would be interested in this unexpected turn of events.

Before he told her about the latest development, though, he'd do his homework. As Eleanor had noted, the tip could be a dead end. No sense getting her hopes up if this didn't pan out.

But maybe he could finally squeeze in a call to her and set up their dinner date.

He swiveled his chair to his computer, answered the two emails that had come in while he talked to Eleanor, and picked up his cell again. As he lifted his finger to dial her number, his landline rang. An internal call from Eleanor.

Blast.

If this was any indication how the rest of his Friday was going to play out, he'd be doing a juggling act all afternoon.

He picked up the landline and set down the cell. "Yes?"

"Sheriff, sorry to bother you again. I have a Roger Atwood on the line. He's an attorney, and he says he has a client with information that's relevant to several of the cases on your desk."

"Did he say which ones?"

"No."

Nate eyed the cellphone. Much as he wanted to talk to Grace, that conversation would have to wait.

"Go ahead and put him through."

"Would you mind if I run over to the Spotted Hen for a quick lunch?"

"Not at all. I meant to mention that while you were in here."

"Thanks. I'm putting the call through."

Five seconds later, Nate greeted the attorney. "I understand you have a client with information that may be of interest to law enforcement."

"Yes, I do. Tyler Holmes."

Nate sat up straighter. Hard as he'd tried to put together a strategy to get the nineteen-year-old to talk, he'd come up blank. The mere sighting of his car coming out of Mavis's driveway the night she died was nothing more than circumstantial evidence.

But apparently he'd put the fear of God into the kid, if he'd hired a lawyer. Holmes must be willing to bargain—and talk.

"When would you like to meet?"

"Monday. My client gets off work at three. We could be at your office by four."

"I'll put you on my calendar."

"My client, his father, and I will be in the meeting. We'll see you next week."

The attorney severed the connection, and Nate returned the handset to the cradle.

Two back-to-back possible breaks in the Templeton and Wilson cases on this last Friday in June.

Not a bad way to close out the month.

Whether they led anywhere remained to be seen, but his instincts said they were getting closer to the answers Grace was searching for in both deaths.

His phone began to ring again, and he huffed out a breath.

As soon as he got a spare minute, he'd share the news with her. Two separate but related leads lent credence to each other. Meaning it wouldn't be premature to alert her to today's developments. He'd also get a dinner date on the books. Not for tomorrow night, since he was on Saturday evening patrol, but as soon as he could manage it.

Because while the outcome of the seed-related cases remained fuzzy, he was very clear on one high-priority personal goal.

Namely, getting to know the forensic pathologist who'd entered his orbit a whole lot better.

ASAP.

―――――――――

Grace Reilly was a thorn in the side.

BK slammed the empty scotch glass on the counter, rattling the ice, and began to pace.

The woman's doggedness was aggravating—but on the positive side, forewarned was forearmed. Fortunately, credible contacts and a sympathetic ear were excellent assets if a person was on the hunt for information. It was astonishing how loose-lipped many people could be around those they dismissed as harmless. Safe. Not important enough to worry about.

Well, the surprise was on them.

Appearances weren't always what they seemed.

The question now was what, if anything, to do about the tenacious pathologist.

BK stopped beside the window and watched the comings and goings of the neighbors, all caught up in the drudgery of daily living. Working day after day to pay the bills and put food on the table, finding occasional respite in fleeting moments of pleasure, content to let those with more clout push them around.

Pathetic.

At some point, you had to take control of your life, outwit the powers that be, prove you were in charge of your destiny. That you deserved to be treated with dignity, and that your contributions should be recognized and rewarded.

Once you developed a plan to obtain both respect and a comfortable financial cushion, life became much more enjoyable—and exciting.

It was also far easier to outwit the people who thought they were smart if you were smarter. Especially if they didn't *expect* you to be smarter. Fooling them was fun *and* gratifying.

The past few years had been satisfying on many levels as the brilliant scheme Dave had helped implement ran like clockwork.

Until Grace Reilly began stirring the pot.

BK snapped the blinds closed. Pivoted. Scowled into the shadowy living room.

It didn't help that fortune appeared to be conspiring against the master plan, either. It was pure bad luck that Fred's death had been suspect. Who knew why the man had been out wandering among the farm equipment that night? If he hadn't fallen and cut his head, Grace Reilly wouldn't have been involved.

The timing of the attempted burglary at Mavis's had been another bad break. Without that weird twist of fate, no one would have taken a second look at her death.

If all had gone as expected—as it had with the previous victims—neither Fred nor Mavis would have been autopsied.

And a third suspicious death would complicate the situation. Improbable as it was that the county pathologist would ever discover the true cause of death, it was unnerving to have her poking around in the matter. Worse, it sounded as if the sheriff was beginning to listen to her suspicions.

The risk had to be contained.

BK began to pace.

It was too bad the woman hadn't been more spooked by the lily buds and vandalism after Mavis died. Started second-guessing whether she wanted to live in the sticks, where law enforcement was often far away and she could be at the mercy of someone who was out to get her.

Since those warnings hadn't worked, it appeared a stronger message was in order. Soon, given the possibility of an accelerated schedule with Lorraine. It would have to be upsetting enough to send Grace Reilly running. Or at the very least distract her until the dust settled with Lorraine.

It would also be more complicated to pull off in light of the latest developments, but a disturbing incident could still be arranged with very little risk. In fact, an idea was already beginning to percolate.

And if the message again fell on deaf ears? If the pathologist continued to persevere with Fred and Mavis?

Perhaps stronger action would have to be taken.

Much stronger.

With consequences that could end up being fatal.

14

FINALLY!

Grace smiled at the name on the screen of her cell. After two missed calls and a brief but intriguing text that hinted he had case-related news, she was going to get to talk to Nate.

A perfect end to a Friday evening.

Well, almost perfect. An in-person exchange would be preferable. But that was coming.

Hallelujah!

She pressed the talk button halfway into the second ring. "I thought we were never going to connect."

"You underestimate my perseverance. I did try to call twice, by the way."

"I know, but it's hard to answer the phone in the middle of an autopsy."

"I can imagine, even if I'd rather not." A hint of humor tickled his voice. "I'd have called earlier in the day if I could, but it's been crazy—and it hasn't slowed down yet."

She twisted her wrist to display the face of her watch. Seven ten. "Are you still at the office?"

"Yes, and I won't be leaving anytime soon."

"Because of the new leads you alluded to in your text?"

"Partly. But with a deputy on vacation this week, I'm also picking up fill-in duties."

"Bummer."

"Goes with the territory, especially in the summer. I do have news."

"Tell me." She sat on the breakfast nook window seat and tucked her bare feet under her.

"It appears the driver of the car seen at Mavis's house is ready to talk."

She listened as he filled her in. "That's encouraging."

"I agree. An anonymous lead also came in, suggesting we contact someone the caller says has information about both deaths."

"Wow. Two breaks in one day. Seems too good to be true." She leaned back, into the corner of the bay window. "You think the second one's for real?"

"Hard to tell. The guy appears to be a model citizen. Well known in the community, according to Eleanor. The background I dug up on him supports that."

"If he's well known, can you share his name? It's possible I've run into him."

There was a slight hesitation. "Usually I keep identities of suspects close to my vest, but you're a key part of this investigation. And I assume I can trust your discretion."

"You may. Dead people don't talk—and neither do the pathologists who work on them."

"His name is Dave Mullins."

Grace blinked. "You're kidding."

"You know him?"

"Yes. Both him and his wife. We go to the same church."

"Now it's my turn to say you're kidding."

"No. I joined not long after I moved here. I guess it shouldn't be all that surprising. The small population in this county can't sustain too many congregations."

"True. Tell me what you know about him."

"I've seen more of his wife, Kimberly. Sweet woman. You know about her accident?"

"Yes, but I'm more interested in him."

"I met Dave at church not long after Kimberly came home from a long-term rehab facility. From what I heard, the man had been run ragged, making the long commute to see her every day while trying to juggle his business. She has lingering problems from the accident, but I've seen steady progress over the three years I've known her. Dave, on the other hand, looks more haggard than ever."

"I imagine caring for a semi-invalid wife is stressful."

"Yes, but in light of your tip I wonder if there are other stressors in his life. I assume he earns a decent living, but he could be dealing with massive medical bills. Insurance doesn't cover everything. Particularly long-term-care expenses."

"You're thinking there could be a financial motive in this case."

"Except neither Fred nor Mavis had a great deal of money."

"That we know of."

He had a point.

"Excellent caveat."

"I'm planning to talk to Dave early next week. Stop by his office unannounced."

Frowning, she picked at a loose thread on the cushion in the window seat. "Much as I want to solve this, I hope he's not involved. I can't imagine what that would do to his wife."

"Innocent parties always get hurt when crimes are committed."

"I know." She sighed. "Depressing, isn't it?"

"Yes. So let's switch gears and talk about a more upbeat subject—like our dinner date. I'd ask you out for tomorrow, but aside from the fact it's short notice, I'm on evening shift. Could we make it a week from Saturday?"

"I'll pencil it in."

"Write it in ink. In the meantime, would you be free for lunch tomorrow?"

Dang.

"I wish I was, but I volunteer to help prepare meals one Saturday a month for the meal delivery program sponsored by several area churches. We provide dinner three nights a week for older adults. I'll be tied up from eleven to three."

"That shoots tomorrow." He sounded as frustrated as she felt. "Let's see if we can work in a coffee date one evening next week."

"I'd like that. Will you keep me in the loop on the two new developments?"

"Count on it." In the background, a phone began to ring.

"I'll let you get that. But I have an invitation for you too. You can think about it and let me know. I'm in the market for a date for my sister's wedding on July 27, and I wondered—"

"Yes."

Despite the long shadows on the field behind her backyard cast by the setting sun, the day suddenly got brighter. "Are you sure you don't want to check your calendar and—"

"No. If there's anything on it for that day, I'll cancel it." A muffled noise came over the line as the other phone continued to ring. "I have to take this call."

"No worries. Talk to you soon." She pressed the end button, lips bowing as she weighed the cell in her hand. Telling her sisters about this would be fun.

She tapped in a text to Cate.

> Add 1 to guest list. I have a date for the wedding.

Twenty seconds later, her sister's response pinged.

Details!

Forthcoming.

Is it the sheriff?

Yep.

Does he have a name?

Nate Cox—and don't run any intel.

Would I do that?

Is the pope Catholic?

Ha ha. Okay, he's on the guest list. When do I get details?

Soon. Night.

No response.

But more questions would be coming. From Eve too, as soon as Cate passed on the news. Assuming she hadn't already sent a—

Her phone pinged again, and she rolled her eyes at the name that appeared on the screen.

Eve.

Cate hadn't wasted any time.

She skimmed the text.

I hear you have a date.

Correct.

Cate didn't have details.

I didn't give her any.

Can't wait to meet him.

You mean vet him?

Ha ha.

Not meant to be funny.

You know Cate will check him out.

He'll pass.

Now I really want to meet him.

Soon. Night.

Eve left her alone after that.

But her older siblings' silence wouldn't last long. They'd both be chomping at the bit to take a gander at the guy who'd caught their baby sister's fancy.

The wedding was soon enough for introductions, however. That would let her get a few dates under her belt, confirm her impression that Nate Cox was the real deal.

And once she did, no one would be able to convince her otherwise—including her buttinski sisters—even if they happened to be so inclined.

Lorraine wanted out, and no amount of cajoling had convinced her otherwise.

After setting the investment cancellation paperwork on the seat beside him, Dave started the car, his stomach twisting into a pretzel.

BK would have to be told, and the money would have to be returned.

If it wasn't . . . if Lorraine didn't have it in hand within the thirty days specified in her original paperwork . . . she could go to the police.

BK wouldn't want that.

Neither did he.

What a disaster.

He pulled out the burner phone. No doubt BK was waiting impatiently for the cell to vibrate.

But it wasn't going to vibrate any more than his insides already were.

He punched in the number, his sweaty finger leaving damp spots on the keys.

BK answered on the first ring. "What's the word?"

"The word is no."

Despite the physical distance separating them, the anger crackling through the line was almost tangible.

"I had a feeling you wouldn't convince her."

"I tried."

"Not hard enough."

"We have to return the money."

"There are other ways to deal with this complication."

"Like what?"

"Nothing you have to worry about. I'll take over from here."

Did that mean what he thought it did? Would BK close in for the kill before the ink was even dry on the original paperwork?

"You're moving too fast." Pressure built in his chest, squeezing the air from his lungs. "We have three weeks."

"I set the pace and call the shots, Dave."

"It would be safer if you just let me return the money. We'll find someone else."

"I already told you. I'm taking over on this one. Too bad you couldn't live up to your side of the bargain. I don't think you'll like the consequences."

The line went dead.

Slowly he lowered the phone from his ear, struggling to suck in air.

Dear God, what was he going to do?

If he stayed mum, Lorraine would die. If he went to the

police, his world would collapse and Kimberly would have to fend for herself.

It was an impossible choice.

But . . . maybe he wouldn't have to choose if he pulled Lorraine's investment out of the offshore account and returned it to her despite BK's orders.

BK would be furious, but it could save Lorraine's life. And despite BK's threat, his tormentor did need him. He had the connections and credibility to sell the phony investment.

So if he bought himself a small window of time, perhaps he could come up with a plan to foil any future plans BK had to bilk seniors of both their money and their lives—without destroying his own life in the process.

———

This wasn't the sort of call he'd expected to get during his Saturday evening shift. Nor were these the circumstances under which he'd next expected to see Grace.

As he pulled into her driveway and set the brake, a crack of light spilled through the slit in the blinds covering her front window.

She was watching for him.

In her shoes, he would be too.

He slid out of the patrol car, locked it, and strode toward her front door.

She opened it as he approached. "Thanks for getting here so f-fast."

The hitch in her voice was telling, as was her pallor and the tremor in her fingers.

"All part of the job." Even if he didn't always race through the night at speeds that pushed the boundaries of safety for calls that weren't life-threatening. "Is it on the back porch?"

"Yes. I didn't touch it."

"Good. Stay inside while I take a look."

With a dip of her head, she retreated while he returned to the car to get an evidence bag, latex gloves, and flashlight. Then he circled the house to her back door.

The "gift" that had been left was exactly as she'd described it. A red-haired doll wearing a white lab coat, with a tiny gold charm that spelled out "Grace" pinned to the lapel—and a knife stuck through the chest.

Seeing it in person was like a punch in the gut.

If this had been an isolated incident, he might have been able to write it off as a vicious prank. But after the lily buds and car vandalism, there was a clear pattern.

Someone was targeting Grace.

Why?

That was a question he was going to have to pursue, no matter how many other questions he had to ask first to get to the answer.

After photographing the doll, he snapped on the gloves and examined it. No note, but the message it was intended to send came through loud and clear.

He put the doll in the evidence bag, sealed it, and jotted the time and date on the chain of custody form.

Once he deposited the bag in the cruiser and did a full circuit of the house, he returned to her front door.

Again, it opened before he could knock.

"May I come in?"

"Of course." She backed up, pulling the door wide.

He crossed the threshold, giving her an assessing scan as he passed.

Grace was fair to begin with, but her pallor tonight was alarming. Not a speck of color remained in her cheeks. And the tremble in her fingers as she fumbled her attempt to lock the door ratcheted up his own tension.

"Here." He urged her aside. "Let me."

She capitulated without protest, stepping back as he secured both of the industrial-strength locks that were far beyond what would be expected for this sort of house in a rural area.

Which raised more questions. Especially in view of the fact she also kept a Beretta close at hand.

But before he asked any of them, he had to calm her down.

"Let's sit for a few minutes. Where's a comfortable spot?"

She glanced toward the back of the house. "The window seat in the kitchen is my favorite place to chill, but I don't think that would be the best choice tonight. I can see the porch from there. Let's stay in the living room."

"That works." He motioned toward the half-empty mug of tea on the coffee table. "Why don't I nuke that for you?"

"I can do it."

He forced up the corners of his mouth as he bent to pick it up. "This is a full-service sheriff's department. Have a seat. I'll be back in a minute."

"Thanks. Help yourself to a soda or a mango iced tea from the fridge."

He paused. "Mango iced tea?"

A tiny flex relaxed the taut line of her lips a hair. "What can I say? My sisters, who prefer Diet Sprite and water, like to tease me about my fancy tastes."

"Maybe you have a more discerning palate."

"I like your take."

"I usually stick to plain old iced tea, but I may have to give your favorite a try. Sit tight."

While he nuked her tea—comforting peppermint, based on the aroma—he pulled a bottle of the mango version from the fridge. An unopened pizza box sat on the counter, emitting appetizing aromas. Must be the dinner she'd never eaten.

When he returned, Grace was sitting on the couch, feet curled under her, an afghan draped over her lap despite the sizzling temperature outside.

She was seriously spooked.

He handed her the tea, twisted open the cap on his bottle, and took a swig as he mulled over her reaction to tonight's incident.

Bottom line, it didn't fit the image he'd formed of her as the strong, no-one's-going-to-intimidate-me type. Yes, anyone would be upset after receiving a doll like the one she'd found on her back porch. And no, he didn't like it any more than she did.

But there'd been no physical attack. If the three incidents were related—and at this point, that wasn't a far-fetched conclusion—the intent hadn't been to cause bodily harm but to induce psychological stress. While that could escalate, at the moment they appeared to be dealing with either a very sick jokester or someone who'd taken a strong dislike to Grace.

"What's your verdict?"

At her question, he sat on an upholstered side chair angled toward the couch. "I don't like the pattern I'm seeing, but I haven't a clue in terms of the motive for the harassment."

"I meant about that." She indicated the iced tea.

"Oh." He took another swig. "Different, but good. I'd order it again." He set the frosty bottle on the coffee table and pulled out his notebook. "Tell me what happened tonight."

Her features stiffened, and once more tension thrummed through the air. "I got home about seven from an autopsy, changed clothes, and finished up the paperwork for the day. After I was done, I poked through the fridge and realized I didn't have anything appealing for dinner. About eight thirty, I ran into town and picked up a pizza from the new restaurant."

"How long were you gone?"

"Forty-five minutes. Tops."

"A short window."

She narrowed her eyes. "What does that mean?"

"It would suggest the person responsible for the delivery either hit it lucky or they were watching you, waiting for an opportunity to drop the doll without the risk of being seen."

"You think someone could be stalking me?" She swallowed.

"I'm not ruling that out."

"But why?" She massaged her forehead. "None of this makes any sense."

"Unless you have an enemy out there."

"I don't."

"Are you certain about that?"

"Yes." She gave him a wary look. "Why?"

He took another drink of iced tea, composing his reply. "Two reasons." He set the bottle back down. "If we were dealing with a single incident, it could be someone out for fun and games who has no personal agenda and targets you because you're convenient. Three in a row, on the other hand, is a pattern. It's not random. You have an enemy, whether you know it or not, and this person wants to scare you."

"It's working." She sipped her tea, the tremble back in her fingers despite her obvious efforts to maintain a calm, rational tone. "But what could be the motive?"

"Spite. Hate. They want to send you running. Those are the first three that come to mind."

She shook her head. "There's no one in my life who would have those kinds of motives."

"The evidence would indicate otherwise. And that brings me to the other reason I asked about enemies. You have an elaborate security system—and a Beretta. Most people around here don't have either. Those are excessive safety measures for a rural county like this."

Though he hadn't phrased his comment as a question, it was clearly implied.

The tiny bit of color that had seeped back into her complexion evaporated, and she stood abruptly, tossing her reply over her shoulder as she scurried toward the hall. "Give me a minute for a quick detour to the ladies' room."

Then she disappeared.

A few moments later, a door clicked shut.

Nate picked up his tea, rotating the icy bottle in his fingers. He couldn't force her to talk to him about her history or any traumas in her past, but if there was an incident that could have a bearing on the current situation, he needed to know about it. And in case she shut down after she returned, he'd have to pull out all the stops to convince her of that.

Because if she was harboring a secret about someone who could have sent her a doll with a knife stuck in it, there was a very real possibility that person's next prank might aim to do physical rather than psychological damage.

And if that happened, Grace could find herself in the sights of someone whose intentions had shifted from freaking her out to moving in for the kill.

15

G RACE LOCKED THE BATHROOM DOOR, sank onto the toilet seat, and dropped her head into her hands.

What was going on?

After five years, she should be past this verging-on-meltdown reaction.

In truth, she'd thought she *was* past it. That she'd put the incident behind her and moved on.

Yes, the experience had affected her life. The Beretta and her investment in security were proof of that. But both were prudent insurance in this day and age. Any smart woman would take similar precautions. Her setup wasn't over the top, as Nate had suggested.

Are you certain about that?

At the prod from her subconscious, she massaged her temples.

Okay. So maybe she was more cautious than most, but the measures she'd taken gave her a modicum of comfort and a sense of safety.

Or they had, until someone broke off her lily buds, vandalized her car, and left a doll with a knife stuck in the chest at her back door.

A shiver snaked through as she fought down a wave of panic and forced the left side of her brain to engage.

Logically, current events couldn't have anything to do with the traumatic episode that had ruined her sleep for two long years and left her edgy in dark places and tight spaces. Despite Nate's obvious concern that an enemy from her past may have reappeared, he was wrong. Sharing her history wouldn't help him figure out who was behind the recent incidents. She could keep it locked inside, as she had since that awful night in Albuquerque.

Except being thrust into the role of victim again had reawakened the angst and fears that had plagued her for years, and talking to someone about those could help. Unfortunately, her overprotective sisters were no better candidates for confidantes than they'd ever been. Their little sister might be all grown up, but they'd react the same as they always had whenever she was in trouble.

They'd freak. They'd hover. They'd worry.

Nate, however, was a different matter. Even if he couldn't banish her reawakened anxieties, it would be comforting to have him confirm her conclusion that there couldn't be a connection between what was happening now and what had happened then.

Plus, if she asked him to keep her secret confidential, he would. The man appeared to be integrity personified. She wouldn't have to worry about him spilling it to her sisters.

So stop dithering, Grace. Just tell him.

Fine. She would.

As soon as she summoned up her courage.

Sixty seconds later, she stood, squared her shoulders, unlocked the door—and prayed she wasn't making a mistake.

Nate started to rise as she entered the living room, but she waved him back into his chair. "Don't waste the effort. I'll be sitting before you're up."

To illustrate that, she picked up her pace and took her seat on the couch, resettling the afghan over her legs.

"I reheated your tea again." He slid the cup toward her.

"Thanks." She picked up her mug and wrapped her cold fingers around the warm ceramic. "Where were we?" As if she didn't know.

"We were talking about why you have an elaborate security system and a gun. In addition to the hard-core locks, I've spotted motion sensors, window and door alarms, and glass-break detectors."

She raised her eyebrows. "You were busy while I was gone."

"Yes, but I confined my assessment to the living room and kitchen. I didn't spot any surveillance cameras."

"I considered adding a few after the lily incident. I'll definitely do that now."

He drained the bottle of iced tea and set it on the coffee table. "We've talked about what you have. You want to tell me *why* you have it?"

She inhaled the soothing peppermint scent, but it didn't work its usual calming magic. "There's almost no chance my security fetish is connected to what's going on here."

"So seeing the results of violence up close and personal in your work isn't what made you more skittish than normal."

"No. Not to this extent, anyway." She waved a hand toward the door and motion detectors. "But you knew that, didn't you?" It was clear from his decisive tone he'd already toyed with that possibility and dismissed it.

"I was pretty certain."

She played with the fringe on the afghan. "I haven't told this story in almost four years. It has to stay between us."

"Goes without saying."

Exactly the response she'd expected.

You can do this, Grace—and you've picked the right man to tell. Trust your heart.

Taking a deep breath, she dived in. "I'm going to give you the condensed version. During my fellowship in New Mexico, I met a group of colleagues at a bar after a long, late shift. They'd asked me to join them on multiple occasions, and I'd run out of excuses for saying no. I was getting a reputation as an all-work-and-no-play kind of woman, which was deserved. Since that's not who I wanted to be, I decided to go for half an hour."

She took a drink of tea, letting the minty flavor chase the bitterness from her tongue.

"I stayed my allotted thirty minutes, but none of my colleagues were ready to leave yet. Two of the guys offered to walk me to my car, but I didn't want to interrupt their party."

Nate frowned and leaned forward, clasping his hands between his knees. "I don't like where this is heading."

Neither did she.

Bunching the edge of the afghan in her fists, she forced herself to continue. "The bar was a weekend hot spot for young professionals in an older, marginal part of the city, but on the Wednesday night I was there, the area was on the quiet side. To get to my car, I had to cut through an alley between two buildings. Halfway down, a guy appeared at the far end and began walking toward me. I did *not* get positive vibes."

"Did you run?"

"Not at first. I thought I might be overreacting. I mean, not everyone in the world is up to no good."

"But this guy was." A muscle in Nate's cheek clenched, and his eyes hardened.

"Yes. I should have listened to my instincts. The closer I got to him, the more my sense of danger ratcheted up. Finally I decided to bolt. But it was too late. He was on me in three steps. The next thing I knew, I was flat on the ground, he was straddling my back, and the tip of a knife was pressed against my jugular. Before I could scream, he leaned down and said, 'Make one sound—you're dead.'"

You're dead.

As the terrifying threat reverberated in the cozy living room, a wave of nausea rolled through Nate.

Yes, Grace was sitting within touching distance, safe and sound and far removed from that traumatic night, but the outcome could have been very different.

Very fatal.

And she knew that as well as he did, if her death grip on the mug and her renewed pallor were any indication.

This woman who cut up bodies for a living, who'd seen more than her share of blood and gore, was struggling to keep it together. Wrapped in a tattered afghan perhaps from happier childhood days when she'd viewed the world as a safe and welcoming place, she seemed in desperate need of comforting.

While their relationship was too new to assume she'd welcome physical consolation, the temptation to take her in his arms, wrap her in a protective embrace, hold her close, and never let go was hard to resist.

And the tenuous control he had over that impulse dissolved as she pressed her knuckle against her mouth in a vain attempt to stop a small, choked sob from escaping.

He rose and moved beside her, took the mug, and enfolded her cold fingers in his. "It's okay to cry, Grace."

"No." She shook her head, her voice tear-laced but adamant. "I won't give that piece of dirt the satisfaction."

"He'll never know."

"I will. I don't need to cry."

Yes, she did. If she'd been holding the horror of that night inside all this time, if it still had the power to reduce her to a quivering mess, tears could be cathartic.

But that was a conclusion she'd have to reach on her own.

"Did this guy . . . hurt you?" He couldn't bring himself to be more specific. The thought of someone violating this caring, compassionate woman sent red-hot rage coursing through his veins.

Of course she read between the lines. Understood what he was really asking.

"Not in the way you mean. He did feel me up, though. After I started to squirm, he covered my mouth with his hand and pressed the knife h-harder. I have a small s-scar as a souvenir. I don't know what would have happened if a group of people hadn't left the bar then. I could hear them laughing and talking, and the guy froze. The instant it became obvious they were heading for the alley, he grabbed my purse and took off."

So no physical harm had been done, other than a slight injury from the knife.

Thank you, God!

Yet a horrifying episode like that was more than sufficient to leave emotional scars for life.

No wonder she carried a gun and had a beefed-up security system.

"Did the police find him?"

"No."

Not surprising. Those kinds of hit-and-run assaults often went unsolved.

The scenario she'd outlined also suggested the attack had been a crime of opportunity. That the guy who'd jumped her hadn't known who she was or been targeting her specifically. He'd just been waiting for the next potential victim to walk down that alley. Yes, he'd learned her identity from the documents in her purse, but she'd never had any further trouble—and New Mexico was a thousand miles from rural Missouri.

Grace's assessment was spot-on. The odds of that incident being related to what was happening here were minuscule.

"Was your older sister already a cop?"

"Yes."

"What was her take on the incident?"

Grace shifted and traced the pattern in the afghan with an unsteady finger. "I never told her or Eve."

Major disconnect, but he did his best to mask his surprise. "I got the impression the three of you were close."

"We are. Too close sometimes." She exhaled. "After my mom died when I was fifteen, Cate and Eve took charge of me. Especially Cate. She was like a mother hen. If I'd told either of them about that night, they'd worry and fuss more than they already do. Besides, they couldn't change what had happened. So I decided to put it behind me and get on with my life—with a few modifications."

"Like getting a concealed carry permit and investing in top-notch security." The answers to other questions began to fall into place too. "Were safety considerations why you took a job here rather than in a big city? Because from what I understand, forensic pathologists are in short supply. Someone with your credentials could get a plum position in a place far more exciting than rural Missouri."

"Safety was a factor, although I do like the county. But rural Missouri is proving to be plenty exciting. *Too* exciting."

"That could be what the person who left the doll wants you to conclude."

"You're thinking they're trying to scare me off? Force me to leave?"

"That would be a logical conclusion."

"Which brings us full circle. Why?"

"I don't have that answer yet. I'm going to send the doll to the state police lab for analysis. There could be trace evidence on it."

"Why do I think whoever is doing this is too careful to leave a clue behind?"

He couldn't disagree.

"Criminals do make mistakes, but I won't discourage you from adding a few exterior security cameras to your setup here."

"First item on my list for Monday."

"What's on your schedule for tomorrow?"

"Church and another cooking session for the meal program. We didn't quite finish today."

He stroked his thumb over the back of her hand. "Where does fun fit into your schedule?"

"I've written it in ink for a week from tonight. That lakeside restaurant sounds fantastic. And the company won't be too shabby, either."

"I hope you feel the same after the evening's over."

"I have every confidence I will." She squeezed his hand, and as a surge of testosterone rocketed through him, a warning began to beep in his mind.

Get out of here, Cox. You're on duty, dealing with a crime report—and mixing business and pleasure is unprofessional.

That was true.

Yet with Grace's fingers tucked in his, with the warmth of her hazel eyes seeping into his soul, with her face blessedly free of tension and her appealing mouth inches from his, walking away without doing more than holding her hand would tax the formidable self-control he'd developed as a Green Beret.

As if sensing his inclinations, Grace leaned a tad closer. Her lips parted slightly in invitation. A pulse began to throb in the delicate hollow of her throat.

Oh man.

He wasn't made of steel. And if the lady was willing to send him off with a—

His phone began to vibrate on his belt.

Tempted as he was to ignore it, he wasn't wired that way. Duty came first.

"I have a call coming in." He cleared the huskiness from his voice. "Could be dispatch."

Disappointment flickered for an instant in her eyes, but she eased back. "Go ahead and answer. You *are* the sheriff, and you *are* on duty tonight."

"I wish I wasn't. And I wish I could ignore this call." Yet already he was reaching for the phone.

"But you're a man who takes his responsibilities seriously." She offered him a reassuring smile. "That's a plus in my book. And we'll have next Saturday night all to ourselves."

"Count on it." He pulled out the phone and put it to his ear.

As he jotted down the location of the three-car pileup ten miles away and asked the appropriate questions, he continued to focus on Grace.

She looked more relaxed now. More like her usual spunky self. Telling him her story may not have banished all her demons, but perhaps sharing the trauma she'd carried alone all these years had helped diminish their power.

As soon as the call ended, he stood. With three carloads of people waiting for him, he couldn't linger.

"Walk me to the door?" He took her hand again.

She kept a tight grip on it as they crossed the room. "Be careful out there."

"Likewise. Arm your system, stay inside, and call me if anything else spooks you. But I don't think your visitor will return tonight. They accomplished their mission."

"Only part of it. I got the present—but if the intent was to scare me off, the mission was a failure. I'm not a quitter."

That sounded like the Grace he was coming to know.

"Remember you're not in this alone."

"I will—and I appreciate that."

"Do me one other favor?"

"Name it."

"Eat some of that pizza you ordered."

She wrinkled her nose. "I'm not hungry anymore."

"Let's see if I can perk up your appetite." Before she could anticipate his intent, he leaned down and brushed his lips across her forehead. "Hungrier now?" He hoped his slow smile and intimate tone made it clear his question was about more than pizza.

She gripped the edge of the door as color flooded her cheeks. "Uh . . . yeah. But I'm not certain pizza's going to satisfy me."

"We'll have dessert next Saturday. Lock up." With a wink, he left her at the door—and didn't dare look back until he was behind the wheel and the car was in gear.

The door was shut now, but light once more spilled through a crack in the blinds.

She was watching him.

Leaving her alone stunk, but what he'd told her was true. Based on the pattern to date, it wasn't likely that whoever had her in his sights would return tonight.

Tomorrow was a different story.

And as he sped through the dark countryside toward what promised to be a messy and contentious accident, he couldn't shake the feeling that the harassment situation with Grace was even messier—and far more liable to explode.

The word Dave uttered would have made Kimberly blush, if she wasn't already in bed. So different from Saturday nights in the past, when they'd sought out new bands every weekend and danced the night away.

He should have gone directly to his office after meeting with Lorraine and pulled her money from the offshore account.

Instead, he'd taken care of Kimberly's errands, then coaxed her out to dinner to lift her flagging spirits—giving BK the opportunity to change the login and password and lock him out.

Translation? Lorraine wasn't going to get her money back, and her days were numbered.

Unless he took action.

Leaning back in the desk chair in his home office, he massaged his temple, where a headache was beginning to throb.

Could he go to the police, bargain with them, agree to cooperate in exchange for leniency? It wasn't as if he'd known BK was going to kill people, after all. Nothing had been said about that in the beginning. Nor had Fred's death set off too many alarms. The man *had* been older.

After stumbling across Mavis's death notice, however, the niggling suspicion that Fred's death may not have been as innocent as it seemed had become certainty, especially in light of BK's responses to his comments about their demise. If he had the stomach to check on the other clients who'd signed up for the investment he'd offered them for BK, he'd no doubt find they too had died . . . of natural causes.

But if he did go to the police, what could he use as a bargaining chip? He had no idea who BK was and no guesses about who was behind the blackmail scheme, other than Lee. But if she wasn't involved, siccing the cops on her would add insult to injury, and she'd already had more than her share of trouble.

Visiting the police would do nothing but ruin his marriage and incriminate him in a scheme they might not be able to stop, since the money was held in an offshore account he could no longer access. And if BK decided to follow through on the threat to cut him out of the loop entirely, he couldn't help much with any sting operation. His only contact with BK was via an untraceable cellphone.

"Dave?"

At Kimberly's drowsy voice, he swiveled toward the door. "Can't you sleep, sweetheart?" He stood and crossed to her.

"It's lonely in there without you."

"I'm getting ready to shut down." He pulled her close and kissed the top of her head. "I'll join you in five minutes."

"I'll be waiting. Love you."

"Love you back."

She hobbled back down the hall, cane in hand, the sleep-shirt she'd always loved hanging on her too-thin frame.

As always, his heart ached for her. For them. For what once was and would never be again.

Yet the accident hadn't damaged her sweet spirit and loving soul, and together they were coping with her physical limitations. All would have been well if he hadn't let loneliness and despair and grief short-circuit his common sense and unravel his moral fiber.

Some people emerged stronger from trials, like steel forged in fire. He'd weakened and melted.

But when you thought you were about to lose the center of your world . . . when the wife you adored slipped deeper and deeper into the abyss each day . . . when your future darkened with every passing hour . . . when you were still grieving the death of your beloved son . . . you sought solace where you could find it.

At least he had.

And he'd been paying the price ever since.

He returned to the computer, shut it down, flipped off the light, and trudged down the hall, praying for mercy, guidance, and deliverance.

Even if they were all undeserved.

16

THAT'S A WRAP FOR TODAY, LADIES. Thank you for coming back to finish up the meals for the week, and I apologize again for the skeleton crew yesterday. The summer flu that's going around is hitting hard. I know all of our neighbors in need of a hot meal and a bit of company appreciate your efforts. God bless you, and be safe going home. It appears we're in for a storm."

Even as the woman who coordinated the meal prep program for area churches spoke, an ominous rumble of thunder reverberated in the distance.

Grace ditched her apron, grabbed her purse, and took off for the exit. Running Sunday errands in a downpour wouldn't be fun. The sooner she got rolling, the less apt she'd be to arrive home waterlogged.

"I'm fine, Dave. Don't worry about it. I can wait for you here."

Kimberly Mullins's voice floated over the bustle of departing volunteers, and Grace scanned the room. The woman was sitting off to the side, brow knitted, four-legged cane standing beside her.

"No, I can take . . . my nap later, honey. Don't rush on my account. I'm not . . . that tired."

That was a lie.

Her shoulders were sagging, and even from a distance the lines of strain etched in her face were evident.

Much as Grace wanted to hit the road and avoid any contact with Dave's wife, now that she knew the man was in Nate's sights, how could she ignore the lesson of the Good Samaritan story?

She couldn't. That would be wrong. Besides, the Mullins home wasn't far out of her way, if she was correctly remembering the address she'd noticed in the new church directory a few weeks ago.

Detouring toward Kimberly, she lifted a hand as she approached and mouthed "I *can take you home.*"

"Honey . . . hang on a minute. I may have a . . . ride." Kimberly lowered the cell as Grace joined her.

"I wasn't trying to eavesdrop, but I couldn't help overhearing your conversation. I'd be happy to give you a lift home."

"I hate to put you to any . . . trouble." Indecision flickered in her eyes.

"It's no trouble. I can have you home in fifteen minutes."

Gratitude and relief smoothed the tension from her features. "Thank you." She put the phone back to her ear. "Dave? Grace Reilly is going to take me home. Don't rush with your client . . . All right, I promise . . . Love you too." She ended the call and reached for her cane.

"Can I help you?" Grace moved closer.

"I appreciate the offer, but I'm supposed to do . . . as much as I can myself. I'll be glad when I can . . . drive again, though. I hate to bother . . . anyone."

"Think of it as giving people an opportunity to practice the Golden Rule."

"I'll keep that in mind—but I miss . . . being independent." She started toward the door, and Grace fell in beside her, shortening her stride to accommodate the other woman's slower pace. "I probably shouldn't have . . . come today. Dave said I was pushing myself . . . too hard. But it's a worthwhile effort."

"I agree." She opened the outside door and motioned toward her Civic. "I'm over there. Shall I pull the car up?"

"Not unless you're in a hurry. My doctors recommend . . . walking as much as possible. But I do tend to . . . slow people down."

"No need to rush." If she had to skip one of her errands, no big deal. The only critical stop was the grocery store.

"That's what . . . Dave always says too. I don't know what I did to deserve . . . such a wonderful husband."

Not a subject Grace wanted to dwell on, thanks to the tip Nate would be following up on—perhaps as soon as tomorrow.

"I'm glad he's been there for you." She depressed the auto-lock button on her keychain and opened the door for Kimberly.

Once the woman was buckled in, she circled the car, slid behind the wheel, and shifted the conversation to more innocuous subjects during the short drive.

As she swung onto the street Kimberly directed her to, she slowed. It was a modest neighborhood of small, older, tidy houses, where children played in the yards and the smell of grilling meat permeated the air on this Sunday afternoon.

Not the type of place a man who was quietly amassing an illegal nest egg would live—*if* money was the motive in the deaths of Fred and Mavis.

"It's the house at the end of the cul-de-sac. The white one with green shutters."

Grace pulled into the driveway of the ranch home, built in the same basic design as the rest of the houses on the block.

But the lush, English-style cutting garden along the front set it apart.

"Your flowers are gorgeous." She gave the colorful blooms filling the beds on either side of the front door an appreciative sweep. "I feel like I'm at the botanical garden in St. Louis."

"Thank you. It's a labor of love."

"This is *your* handiwork?"

"Yes. The maintenance takes me longer than it used to, but I . . . enjoy every minute. My doctors say all the . . . bending and stooping is beneficial. Do you like flowers?"

"Love them, but I don't have your green thumb. I also live in a rental house. There isn't much incentive to beautify the yard. I always swing by the floral department during my grocery shopping each week, though. I like having fresh flowers on my table."

"Let me cut you a bouquet before you go, as a thank-you for the ride."

"I appreciate the thought, but I have several errands to run on the way home. I'm afraid the flowers would wilt in the car." As she spoke, the wind picked up and a few drops of rain splashed on the windshield.

"With the storm coming in, it's cooling off. They should be fine in the car. Let me give you . . . a small bouquet. Please."

If repaying the favor placated Kimberly, why not acquiesce? "If you're certain you can spare them, I accept. Your flowers are head-and-shoulders above store-bought stems."

"I have plenty, as you can see." Kimberly swept a hand over the garden. "I often take a bouquet to someone who could use a little . . . cheering up. Let me go inside and get my clippers."

Grace followed her to the porch but waited outside while Kimberly retrieved the cutters, several damp paper towels, and a plastic bag.

Five minutes later, she was pulling out of the driveway with a magnificent bouquet of summer flowers on the seat beside her.

As the woman lifted a hand in farewell, Grace smiled and waved out the window, praying Nate's tip was wrong.

Kimberly Mullins didn't deserve any more heartache or pain in her life.

But if her husband *was* somehow involved in the deaths of Mavis and Fred, another wave of trauma was about to crash over his wife, leaving destruction in its wake.

Tyler Holmes was nervous.

In addition to his sweaty-palmed handshake, the nineteen-year-old's respiration was shallow and his lips were stiff.

Nate closed his office door behind his three visitors.

This should be an interesting meeting.

"I'm sure you're a busy man, Sheriff." Roger Atwood took the seat Nate indicated, set his briefcase on the floor beside him, and folded his manicured hands on top of the conference table. "We won't keep you from your duties for too long."

As Nate took his own seat, and Tyler and his father settled in on either side of the attorney, he assessed the lawyer. While farming and serving in the military hadn't given him much grounding in fashion, he'd wager that wasn't an off-the-rack suit—and the guy's silk tie probably cost more than he made in a full day of work.

Carl Holmes was spending big bucks for the luxury of being represented by a prestigious St. Louis law firm.

Meaning his son was either guilty of a serious crime, and high-priced expertise was required for bargaining power, or Tyler's offenses were small, and his father wanted a smooth talker to negotiate the best deal possible for him.

"I always have time for people who are willing to share information that could help us solve a case." Nate picked up his pen. If Atwood was hoping to intimidate or outwit a small-town sheriff, he was in for a surprise.

193

"We may, in fact, have information that will help you solve more than one case. But let's be clear up front. We're not here to discuss murder, which you implied to my client was on your radar."

"Murder is always on my radar with suspicious deaths."

"Let me cut to the chase, Sheriff." The man gave him a daunting look designed to unnerve a witness on the stand in court. Didn't faze him in the least. "My client wishes to make a clean start. In order to do that, he's willing to atone for past indiscretions and cooperate with you on any cases about which he has knowledge. We want to handle this here, in your office, without the involvement of the prosecuting attorney—unless a victim objects. However, that won't be an issue in most of the cases we plan to discuss."

"I can't promise how this will be handled until I know the severity of Tyler's crimes."

"They're relatively minor offenses. That's not an opinion. It's a fact, based on statutes."

Nate turned his pen end-to-end as he surveyed the three people sitting across from him. Other than a greeting during the handshake, neither Holmes had said a word. But Carl, who'd left his farm behind to don church clothes and be part of this meeting, and Tyler both wore serious expressions. They'd also initiated this get-together.

In light of their willingness to come forward, cooperation could be the best strategy if he wanted to get as much information as possible. Especially since he had no grounds at this stage to pursue charges against Tyler.

"If the offenses are minor, I can promise to do my best to deal with the matter in this office—assuming the victims are willing to let Tyler make restitution and agree not to press charges. However, I can't speak for them."

"In exchange for Tyler's cooperation, you could recommend restitution as the simplest course."

If the guy was hoping for an ironclad commitment, he was out of luck. "I'm willing to consider that if the information Tyler has is as useful as you've inferred—and to do my best to help him get a clean start." But he wasn't about to be backed into a corner by a high-priced lawyer or make promises he might not be able to keep if the man was misrepresenting the gravity of the offenses.

After a few moments of silence, the attorney spoke to the two men beside him. "I believe that's an acceptable commitment. Shall we proceed?"

Tyler exchanged a glance with his father. The older Holmes gave a curt nod, and Tyler swallowed. "Yes."

The attorney pulled a thin file folder from his briefcase and laid it on the table. "I can fill you in on the basics. Tyler will answer your questions as we go along. Is that agreeable?"

"Yes." Nate positioned his tablet in front of him.

Atwood opened the file. "My client has been involved in four illegal incidents. First, he's responsible for the petty vandalism at Fred Wilson's farm. That mischief was a misguided attempt to help convince Mr. Wilson to sell the property to his father. Carl Holmes was not aware of his son's activities. Now that Mr. Holmes owns the land, he does not wish to prosecute for any of the damages."

"You're saying there was no malicious intent, nor was there any attempt to cause Mr. Wilson bodily harm."

"Correct."

"I'd like to hear that from Tyler." Nate transferred his attention to him.

The attorney motioned toward the younger man, giving him the floor.

"I just wanted to aggravate him so he'd sell the place." Tyler's Adam's apple bobbed. "All of the stuff I did was minor, and I never saw him during any of my visits. The night he died, I was at home. I don't have any witnesses to that, but it's the truth."

Nothing in the younger man's demeanor suggested he was lying.

"Shall we move on?" The attorney indicated the file folder.

Nate dipped his head.

"Second illegal incident. My client overheard Mavis Templeton tell a friend at the Spotted Hen Café that she kept a tidy sum of cash in a whipped-topping tub in her freezer. My client decided to steal it. He went to Ms. Templeton's house the night she died and broke a kitchen window to gain entry. Once inside, he walked through the downstairs to be certain she'd gone to bed. He found her on the steps to the second level, already dead. He left immediately, without taking the cash. He's prepared to pay her estate for the cost of the window replacement."

Nate scribbled notes, processing the story. It was feasible, and as far as he knew, nothing had yet been done about disposing of the woman's assets. The money should still be in the freezer if Tyler was telling the truth. Easy to verify as soon as this meeting ended.

"Did you see anything suspicious while you were at the house?" He directed his question to Tyler. "Any evidence someone else had been there?"

"No." He offered nothing more.

The lawyer had schooled him well.

"The third and fourth incidents are related. They concern vandalism aimed at Dr. Grace Reilly."

What?

Tyler was targeting Grace?

But why? He had no reason to terrorize her.

This wasn't computing.

However, since Tyler wasn't in the hot seat for the vandalism incidents connected to Grace, his willingness to confess to those offenses added credibility to his story—and to his professed fresh-start motive for coming here.

"I'm listening."

The attorney consulted a sheet of paper in his hands. "My client was contacted twice by phone by an unknown party. During the first call, he was offered 250 dollars to break plants at Ms. Reilly's home. In the second call, he was offered 500 dollars to scratch and dent her car. He's prepared to reimburse her for the damages to her car."

So Tyler had no vendetta or score to settle against Grace. He was simply a hired gun.

That made more sense.

Nate sorted through the new information as fast as he could. "First of all, tampering with a motor vehicle isn't a minor offense. It's a felony."

"Not if the victim agrees to let Tyler pay for the cost of the repair."

"I can ask." He focused on Tyler again. "Was the person who called you male or female?"

Once again, the younger Holmes checked with the lawyer, who nodded. "I couldn't tell. The voice was strange. Almost like it wasn't human."

The caller must have used a voice-changer app.

"Do you have the phone number?"

"Yes. We had to get it from my service provider. When the calls came in, my screen said 'blocked number.'"

The caller had hit *67 before dialing.

"Let me give you the number." The attorney consulted his file and recited it. "However, I assume it's a burner phone."

That was probably true, which rendered the number useless. Burners were next to impossible to trace.

Nate wrote the number down anyway.

"How were you paid?" He directed the question to Tyler.

"Both times, I got half the money upfront and half after the job was done. It was always in a plain white envelope. Under a trash can at a park, in a book at the library. Places like that."

"Give me specific locations." Nate jotted them down as Tyler complied, but the odds of finding witnesses at any of the sites were close to zero. "Did you keep the envelopes?"

"No."

"Why did you agree to do this?"

Tyler shrugged. "I wanted extra cash. Seemed like an easy way to get it."

"Does it still seem easy?" Nate lasered him with a look.

A flush crept across Tyler's cheeks. "No."

"Tell me what you know about the doll."

The kid's face went blank. "What?"

If he was acting, he deserved an Academy Award.

The attorney rejoined the conversation, homing in on Tyler. "Are we missing a piece of information?"

"No! I don't know anything about a doll." Panic flickered in his eyes.

"Where were you on Saturday night?" Nate asked.

"At my house." Carl spoke for the first time. "He was there all evening. My oldest son, Wayne, was also there. We ate dinner about seven, watched TV, and Tyler left around ten."

So the younger Holmes had a solid alibi.

"What is this about, Sheriff?" The attorney frowned at him.

"There's been another harassment incident with Dr. Reilly."

"I didn't have anything to do with that." Beads of sweat popped out on Tyler's forehead. "I swear."

"Why wouldn't the person who paid you to do the first two jobs call you again?"

"I don't know." The knuckles of his clasped hands whitened.

"Sheriff, we've given you all the information we have, and we've done so in good faith. Do you have any additional questions for my client?" The attorney tapped the papers into a neat stack and closed the file.

"Not today."

"Please call me if you wish to have another discussion with him. Otherwise, we'll wait to hear from you regarding restitution for Dr. Reilly and the Templeton estate." Atwood slipped the folder back into his briefcase, snapped it shut, and stood.

The Holmeses followed his lead.

Nate rose too. Unless his instincts were failing him, Tyler *had* come here in good faith, and he'd told the truth. That took guts—and suggested the troubled delinquent could at last be growing up.

He extended his hand to the younger man. "I commend you for coming forward, and for your willingness to take the consequences for what you've done. I'll speak to Dr. Reilly and the firm handling Mavis Templeton's estate and let your attorney know what they say."

"Thank you." He returned the handshake.

Nate showed them to the door, closed it behind them, and returned to his desk.

An intriguing meeting.

But while some questions had been answered, others had arisen.

Like . . . now that Tyler was more or less off the suspect list in the deaths of Mavis and Fred, were Grace's suspicions unfounded? Could the sunflower seeds have been a weird fluke after all?

Who had paid Tyler to vandalize Grace's property, and why was that person intent on frightening her?

Why hadn't that person paid Tyler to leave the doll on her property instead of hiring someone else or doing the job themselves?

Nate skimmed his meeting notes. The cell number Tyler had provided would likely be a dead end, and it was doubtful the state police would find any helpful trace evidence on the doll.

So where did he go from here?

A knock sounded on his door, and he leaned back in his chair. "Come in."

"Sorry to bother you, Sheriff." Eleanor entered, bearing two pink message slips. "These came in from dispatch while you were in your meeting. Both incidents are being covered, but I thought you'd want to know about them."

"Thanks." He gave the two sheets a quick read. Another car accident, this one involving a tractor, and a shoplifting incident.

"I saw Tyler Holmes here, with his father. Is he in trouble again?"

"No. I got the impression he's seen the light."

She sniffed. "That would be a welcome change. We don't need any more delinquency disrupting our community." She brushed an imaginary speck off her pristine black skirt. "You do know he's had a number of run-ins with the law."

"Yes."

"He gave Sheriff Blake fits for a while." She expelled a breath. "I hope he *has* seen the light."

"Based on the information he provided today, I'd say that's a safe bet. Unless he wants to start with a clean slate, why else would he admit he'd vandalized Grace Reilly's car?"

The woman's eyes widened. "Mercy! *He* was the culprit? Why on earth would he damage her car?"

"He claims someone paid him to do it."

Eleanor didn't attempt to hide her skepticism. "In light of his history, I'd take that with a grain of salt. But no matter *why* he did it, it was a crime."

"He offered to pay for the damage if Dr. Reilly agrees not to press charges."

"Hmph. Seems to me he's looking for an easy way out."

"Or a second chance to turn his life around."

"I suppose that's possible." Her dubious tone suggested otherwise. "On a different subject, would you mind if I leave half an hour early today? Tonight's my night to deliver meals through the church program, and I have an extra stop. The summer flu that's going around is felling volunteers left and right."

"No problem." He set the message slips down. "You ever run into Dr. Reilly during your work with the program?"

"No." She cocked her head. "Does she deliver too?"

"I think she's on the weekend cooking crew."

"The cooks and the drivers never see each other. But I commend her for volunteering. From what I've gathered during our conversations, she works long hours. She can't have much free time."

"That's my impression too." But she'd be squeezing fun into her schedule in the future if he had anything to say about it. "Go ahead and take off. I'll be here for a while."

"Thank you. Enjoy your evening."

She shut the door behind her as she left, and Nate swiveled toward the window. In the distant sky, a hawk soared in search of prey.

It was possible Eleanor's take on Tyler was sound. His history didn't provide much basis for trust. Perhaps he was letting the young man off too easy.

But he hadn't picked up one ounce of duplicity in him during their meeting.

Besides, the decision about whether to accept the restitution offer was Grace's, not his. From what he knew about her, though, she'd give Tyler a second chance. And it shouldn't be difficult to convince the attorney for Mavis Templeton to do the same.

However . . . there was still an unknown person out there who wanted Grace gone and who'd found another method to deliver increasingly upsetting messages.

Which brought him back to his earlier question.

Where did he go from here?

Nate had no idea.

At least the security cameras Grace was installing at her house would give her an additional layer of protection.

A good thing.

Because even if the Fred and Mavis investigations petered out, he had a gut-churning feeling the danger for Grace was ramping up.

17

AT THE KNOCK ON HER BACK DOOR, Grace set the kitchen knife on the counter, rinsed her sticky fingers, and twisted the knob.

"I'm ready to give you my recommendations, if you have a minute." The security company rep lifted his clipboard.

"Sure." She shaded her eyes against the sun, still high in the sky on this early Monday evening. "Come on in. It's too hot to talk out here."

He followed her into the kitchen. "If we're in agreement about where to place the cameras, I'll put together an estimate and email it to you tomorrow."

Her phone began to vibrate on the counter, but she ignored it. "That works. Have a seat." She motioned to the kitchen table, moving aside the vase of flowers from Kimberly.

She listened as he walked her through his rationale for the suggested placements.

"You also asked about interior cameras, but after assessing your existing setup and factoring in the visual surveillance I'm recommending"—the man indicated his diagram—"I think that would be overkill. If anyone tries to get in, we'll capture an image from one of the exterior cameras."

It was hard to argue with his conclusion, even if her inclination was to put a camera in every room and spring for full coverage of the yard.

"What you're proposing makes sense. How soon can you install?"

"By the end of the week."

Not as fast as she'd like, but she couldn't expect same-day service.

"That's fine. I'll watch my email tomorrow for the bid."

"I'll leave this with you, in case you want to study it further in the interim." He handed her a copy of the schematic, along with a card. "Anything else I can do for you today?"

"No. I appreciate you coming by so fast."

"If people have security concerns, there's often a reason for them. We may sell hardware and monitoring systems, but our real business is peace of mind." He stood and inclined his head toward the vase. "Pretty flowers. Are you a gardener?"

"No. They're from an acquaintance."

"Impressive bouquet." He fingered one spiky blue spray. "You don't see many delphiniums in Missouri. Climate's not conducive to them. Your friend must have a green thumb. I've never had any luck with these."

"You garden?"

"Every spare minute I can squeeze in. This"—he lifted the clipboard—"is my job. Gardening is my passion. And I appreciate people who don't settle for ordinary plants. Your friend grows quite a few flowers I don't see often, including several old-fashioned varieties. Like this one." He touched a stalk covered with purple, bell-shaped blossoms.

"What is that?"

"Foxglove. A spectacular plant, as long as you don't eat it." Grace froze. "It's poisonous?"

"Very. The whole shebang. Sap, flowers, seeds, stems, roots, and leaves. Doesn't take away from its beauty, though."

Her phone pinged on the counter, but she ignored the text alert as she wracked her brain trying to call up anything she could remember about plant poisons from med school.

Wait.

Wasn't foxglove the source of the common heart medication digitalis?

Yes.

And eating too much of it would be like taking a digitalis overdose—which could lead to potentially fatal cardiac arrhythmias.

The very cause of death she'd cited on her autopsy reports for Mavis and Fred.

She gripped the back of the chair beside her as she stared at the flower.

Sweet heaven.

Could she be looking at a murder weapon?

What, if anything, foxglove had to do with the sunflower seeds she'd found in the victims' stomachs was puzzling, but she did know one thing.

Digitalis poisoning didn't show up on a standard tox screen. It would go undetected unless a specific test for it was requested.

"You mind if I take a photo of this bouquet? I'd like to show it to my wife."

At the man's question, she tuned back in to the conversation. "No. Help yourself."

He pulled out his cell, snapped two shots, and walked toward the back door. "I'll have that estimate in your hands as early as possible tomorrow."

"Thanks." She followed him across the room, but as she said goodbye and locked the door by rote, one thought was front and center.

Dave Mullins had easy access to foxglove.

If she tested samples from Mavis and Fred, would toxic digitalis levels show up?

It was worth suggesting. The coroner's budget was tight, but it ought to be able to accommodate a specialized test once in a while.

She crossed to the counter, picked up the cell, and found a text waiting for her from Nate.

> Tried to phone. Have news. Heading home for a rehab evening. Call when you can.

Eyeing the baking pan on the counter, she tapped a finger against the screen. In view of what she'd just learned, an in-person discussion would be preferable—especially if he had news to share too.

Besides, a home delivery of her thank-you offering would be less conspicuous than stopping by his office with it tomorrow, where Eleanor would see her as she passed. While news about the sheriff dating the county pathologist wouldn't remain a secret for long in a small community like this, why spread the word sooner than necessary?

Grace typed in a return message.

> I have news too. You up for a visitor?

Thirty eternal seconds passed, the house silent except for the steadily worsening drip in the faucet that she ought to report to her landlord.

Way to go, Grace. You haven't even been out on a date yet, and you're already inviting yourself—

> Yes. When?

Relief coursed through her.

> Half an hour? I won't stay long.

> No need to rush. You have my address?

> No.

It appeared on her screen.

> Got it. See you soon.

As she tucked the phone into her pocket and pulled a plate from the cabinet, her spirits took an upswing. She had a possible lead on the two cases that troubled her, she'd have surveillance cameras in place in a handful of days, and she was about to see Nate.

Mondays didn't end much better than this.

She was here.

As his doorbell rang, Nate set the last of his supplies in the bedroom that was prepped and ready for painting—a chore he'd tackle as soon as Grace left.

Wiping his palms on his jeans, he strode down the hall toward the front door and pulled it open.

Grace gave his holey, paint-splattered jeans and threadbare T-shirt a once-over. "I can see you're deep in rehab mode. You sure you don't mind an impromptu visitor?"

"Depends on the visitor."

"I come bearing gifts." She lifted a foil-covered plate.

"If it's food, you're in." He grinned and pulled the door wide.

She eased past, her hair brushing his chin and leaving a sweet, spicy scent swirling around him that was far tastier than whatever treat she had on that covered plate.

To buy himself a moment to corral his unruly hormones, he fiddled with the lock on the door before turning to her.

The delay didn't help.

With the reddish strands in her hair glinting in a shaft of

light from the dipping sun, a soft knit shirt molding her curves, and legs that went on forever below her shorts, he'd need an hour—and a cold shower—to tamp down his libido.

"Where would you like this?" She lifted the plate again.

Focus, Cox.

"Um . . . in the kitchen?"

"Seems sensible. Can you point the way?"

"I'll show you. Follow me."

She fell in behind him as he led her toward the back of the house and flipped on the light.

Her jaw dropped as she scanned the seventies-style kitchen he hadn't yet touched, but she quickly snapped it shut and rearranged her features to mask her shock.

He hiked up one side of his mouth. "Don't worry about hurting my feelings. I had the exact same reaction the day I toured the house. It's like the kitchen got stuck in a time warp. Get a load of the avocado stovetop and dishwasher." He waved a hand toward the obnoxious duo. "Like I told you, the place needs major work. Whipping it into shape is a long-term project."

"It, uh, does have potential, though."

Her attempt to be polite only upped her cuteness factor.

Reining in his amusement, he tried for an earnest but clueless demeanor. "Do you think appliances in one of the primary colors would brighten up the room?"

Her eyes rounded, but again, she made a valiant effort to recover. "I agree the room could, uh, benefit from a few touches of color other than avocado, but why not add a bay window or put in a skylight? It's hard to beat natural light as a design element."

He gave up the attempt to restrain his mirth. "I'm kidding, Grace. I do have *some* taste. I'm saving this room until last, because if I ever share this house with a wife, I expect she'll want input into the kitchen décor. But I can visualize an island, granite countertops, stainless steel appliances. And that bay window you mentioned is a great idea."

She exhaled. "Can I say I'm relieved—and apologize for underestimating your decorating panache?"

"Apology accepted if you tell me what's on that plate. I scarfed down a fast-food burger for dinner, but I'm still hungry."

"This may not fill the gap in your stomach. It's more for your sweet tooth."

He bit back the flirty remark hovering on the tip of his tongue. Getting too pushy too fast with this woman could backfire.

"Dessert is always welcome. You can put it there." He indicated a spot on the counter, beside the coffeepot.

She set the plate on the chipped Formica and removed the aluminum foil.

"Is that baklava?" He leaned closer to peruse it.

"Yes. My specialty."

"You *made* this?" His mouth began to water as he gaped at the golden triangles oozing richness.

"From an old family recipe. In general it's reserved for special occasions, but after you listened to my story Saturday night, and held my hand—literally and figuratively—I wanted to thank you in a concrete way."

"I was just doing my job."

She arched an eyebrow at him. "You hold the hand of every woman at crime scenes you visit?"

Touché.

"Not as a rule. I made an exception for you." Without waiting for her to respond or ask questions, he waved a hand toward the plate. "Is that as complicated to make as it looks?"

"More time consuming than complicated."

He propped his hands on his hips. "As far as I can tell, you don't have a spare minute to call your own. How did you manage to work this in?"

"I carve out time for priorities."

"I'm flattered."

"You should be." She offered him a cheeky grin, then grew more serious. "I also have news."

"Me too. Want to exchange information over dessert and coffee?"

"I brought the baklava for *you*."

"I don't like to eat alone. Have a piece with me. Please."

Her lips flexed. "You're very persuasive, Sheriff Cox."

"Hold that thought. Let me put the coffee on. If you want to dish each of us up a piece or two, there are plates in the cabinet next to the sink."

She crossed the room and pulled them out. "Forks?"

"In the drawer on your right." He filled the filter with coffee. "I have to ask a question."

"Fire away."

"Why is a Greek pastry made from an old family recipe the specialty of someone with a name like Reilly?"

Grace set two pieces of dessert on one plate and a single piece on the other. "My mom was born in Athens."

"Ah. That would explain it."

"My sister Eve makes fabulous moussaka."

"What's Cate's specialty?"

"Eating."

He snorted out a laugh as he set two mugs by the coffeemaker. "I like her already. I assume your dad is Irish?"

"Yes. First generation."

"How did your parents meet?"

"In grad school in England. Mom was studying classical languages and literature, Dad was getting his degree in archaeology. Right now, he's doing a visiting professorship at Cambridge. But he stayed close to home during our younger days. You'll meet him at Cate's wedding, if you're still willing to subject yourself to a family event."

"It's written in ink on my calendar." He motioned to the hall. "Would you like a tour of the house while the coffee brews?"

"Sure."

She accompanied him through the rooms that were in various stages of completion.

"What drew you to this house?" Grace moved toward the large window in the master bedroom, skirting the king-sized bed that dominated the bare-bones, blank-walled space.

"The design will allow me to expand beyond three bedrooms if necessary, and I liked the big yard with the field behind it, where kids could play. The large kitchen was also a selling point. It reminded me of my growing-up years when we gathered for meals. A rare family occurrence these days, from everything I hear—more's the pity."

She smiled at him across the room. "I like how you think." A spark of electricity zipped between them, but before it could ignite, she cleared her throat and waved a hand over the walls. "I like the soft dove gray. It's restful."

"That's what the guy who recommended it at the paint store said." But as far as he was concerned, gray was gray. His decorating skills didn't extend to nuances like shades of color. "Let me show you my current project." He motioned toward the hall and led her to the room where he'd deposited his painting supplies.

After he told her the story about the claw marks, she entered to examine the repaired drywall up close. "Don't ever tell Eve I said this, but in a patching contest between the two of you, you'd win."

"My lips are sealed."

She perused his supplies, then bent down and picked up a jar, eyebrows peaking as she turned to him. "What's with the formalin?"

Whoops.

He'd forgotten all about that.

He rubbed the back of his neck. Shoved his hands in his pockets. May as well own up. "I asked Russ for a few jars. I've been putting them around the room while I work. The paint smell offsets the odor somewhat, and I'm hoping the diluted scent will help desensitize me."

"Is it working?"

"I haven't lost my dinner yet."

"Clever idea."

"The real test will be at an autopsy, when I have to inhale the stuff at full strength."

"You're welcome to sit in on any of mine and measure the success of your experiment."

"I'll keep that in mind. You ready for coffee?"

"Yes."

They returned to the kitchen, where baklava and business awaited them.

Too bad they couldn't chill out and talk about the subjects normal people discussed at the beginning of a relationship—movies, hobbies, sports, travel, childhood escapades.

But until the mysteries of the sunflower seeds and the terror campaign against Grace were solved, two troubling topics would continue to dominate their conversations.

Mayhem and murder.

───────────────

"You first." Grace picked up her fork, giving Nate the floor as they dived into their baklava. "Is your news about Dave?"

"No. It's about the other lead I received. I know who vandalized your car."

Grace's fork jolted to a stop halfway to her mouth. "I didn't know you had a lead on *my* case."

"I didn't either. It came as part of a package deal."

She set her fork back down and folded her hands. "You have my full attention."

Dessert forgotten, she listened without interrupting while he recounted the visit from Tyler Holmes and his attorney, concluding with the younger man's request that she accept restitution rather than press charges.

As he finished his story, Nate ate a bite of baklava, and an expression of pure bliss swept over his face. "Wow. This is incredible."

"My sisters and I agree, although I'm the only one who makes it."

"You have any other amazing recipes in your repertoire?" He gave her a hopeful look as he continued to chow down.

"A few. I like to experiment in the kitchen. Believe it or not, a lot of pathologists are foodies."

He stopped chewing. "For real?"

"Uh-huh. Go figure." She motioned to his plate. "Should we wait to continue our discussion until after you finish that?"

"No. I think I can give both their due attention. But I have to admit this is a major distraction." He ate another bite.

She leaned forward. "Do you think this Tyler Holmes is committed to cleaning up his act?"

"From what I can tell, yes."

"Did the Templeton attorney accept the offer of restitution?"

"Yes."

"Then I will too—and I won't press charges. I trust your judgment. But the information he passed on raises more questions."

"I know. And we still don't have a clue who's behind the campaign directed against you."

"Nor did he offer any leads on Fred and Mavis."

"It's possible there aren't any." He started on the second piece of baklava, brow wrinkling. "I don't put much credence in flukes, but maybe those seeds *were* a coincidence."

"Or not. I have news too." She told him the foxglove story.

He stopped eating again. "You're thinking Fred and Mavis were poisoned?"

"It's possible. Poison can be an effective murder weapon. Unless it's a common substance that shows up in a normal tox screen, you have to test for each element specifically. Without a clue suggesting which ones to target, it's like shooting blind. An expensive and time-consuming effort."

"I assume you have samples we could test from Fred and Mavis."

"Russ does, and I have a couple of samples from Mavis too. I'm thinking we may want to run a test for digitalis now that Dave is a suspect. Have you talked to him yet?"

"No. A visit to his office is my top priority tomorrow morning. I know he's on the road quite a bit visiting clients, so it could take a few attempts before we connect. But I don't want to set up an appointment. The element of surprise can be helpful." He finished off his baklava.

"What do you think about pursuing the foxglove angle?"

He set his fork on the table and took a swig of coffee. "Let's do this. I'll meet with Mullins. If red flags go up, I'll talk to Russ. He's tight-fisted with the budget, but I can exert pressure if necessary."

"I don't want to cause friction between the new kid on the block and someone who's been around forever."

"Let's cross that bridge if we come to it. In the end, the pursuit of justice and truth is what we're all after, even if it requires spending a few extra bucks. I think I can present a convincing case to Russ if necessary."

"I'd be happy to talk to him if that would be easier. I've worked with him longer than you have."

"Why don't we wait and see what comes out of my meeting with Mullins?"

She stabbed a bite of her baklava. "Waiting's not my style."

One side of his mouth rose. "Why am I not surprised?"

"I wouldn't insult your baklava maker if I were you." She pointed her fork at him.

"Duly noted." He lifted his mug in acknowledgment. "Where do your security cameras stand?"

"I should have the estimate tomorrow. They can be installed by the end of the week." She broke off another bite of the baklava with the edge of her fork.

"Good."

She watched him as she chewed. "You're worried my harasser isn't finished with me yet."

The twin grooves on his forehead answered her question before he spoke, validating her own concerns. "I don't think we should assume this person will disappear into the mist. I did try to track down the phone number Tyler gave me. It was a burner phone, as his attorney suspected."

"Bummer." She pressed the tines of her fork against a few flakes of phyllo dough and slid them into her mouth, but the honeyed sweetness didn't chase away the pungent taste of fear.

"Would you like another cup of coffee?"

She summoned up a smile and finished off her dessert. "No, thank you. I should leave and let you get back to rehabbing." She rose and picked up her plate and mug. Much as she'd like to stay, it wasn't fair to further disrupt his plans for the evening.

He followed her to the sink, his own crockery in hand. "You don't have to rush off. The painting will wait."

"But I don't want to be the one responsible for you living in a construction zone longer than you have to." She started to rinse the stickiness from her plate.

His strong, lean fingers touched the back of her hand, short-circuiting her respiration. "Leave it. I'll take care of the dishes later." A beat ticked by. "I wish you'd stay."

At his husky comment, she risked a peek at him. Inches away, his T-shirt stretched taut against his broad chest. His eyes were blue as a summer sky. His jaw sported the barest hint of late-day stubble.

Raw magnetism swirled around her, and she clutched the edge of the sink to steady herself.

"If I stay, you have to let me help you paint." The caveat tumbled out before she could stop it.

His eyebrows shot up. "Are you serious?"

No. Of course not. She *couldn't* be. Her whole life, she'd walked a wide circle around anything that could remotely be termed DIY.

However . . . she didn't want to leave. And since sitting on the sidelines watching him work wasn't an acceptable option, she'd have to pitch in if she stayed.

Yet strangely enough, much as she'd always disliked painting and sanding and sawing and stripping wallpaper and all the jobs Eve had done while rehabbing her house, the prospect of doing them side by side with Nate wasn't all that distasteful.

In fact, it held a certain tantalizing appeal.

Plus, she felt safe here. Protected. At home. As if she belonged in this house.

Odd, but comforting.

And painting a wall was a small price to pay to sustain that feeling as long as possible.

Because once she left . . . once she returned to her fortified house . . . she'd be alone.

Yes, her security should be adequate to keep her safe. But it didn't take the place of a living, breathing protector. In a dicey situation, she'd choose the man beside her over sophisticated surveillance cameras or alarms any day.

The ideal would be to have both.

For hard as she tried, she couldn't shake the feeling that whoever had left the doll with the dagger in its chest on her doorstep was still nearby, lurking in the shadows.

Planning another terror attack.

18

MR. MULLINS?"

At the summons from the unfamiliar voice, Dave pocketed his key and swiveled toward the foyer of the small commercial building where he kept an office for client meetings.

The uniformed man standing a few yards away wasn't his two o'clock appointment arriving twenty minutes early.

It was the sheriff.

And odds were he wasn't here to talk about insurance or investments.

Dave fisted his hand inside his pocket and fought back a suffocating wave of panic. Letting Cox pick up one iota of his fear could be disastrous. After all, there was a chance, however slim, the man was here on business unrelated to BK.

He pasted on a smile. "Good afternoon, Sheriff Cox. I don't believe we've ever been formally introduced, but I've seen you around." He pulled out his hand and extended it. "A pleasure to meet you."

"Likewise." The man's grip was firm. No nonsense. "Can you spare a few minutes to talk?"

"I have a two o'clock meeting. I'm free until my client arrives."

"This shouldn't take long."

"Then please, come in." He opened the door and motioned toward a round table with four chairs. "Make yourself comfortable."

The sheriff strolled over to the table and settled into a chair. Dave put his briefcase on the desk and joined him. "How can I help you?"

"I'm following up on an anonymous tip that came into our office. Are you acquainted with Mavis Templeton and Fred Wilson?"

Any hope that this visit was unrelated to BK's scheme evaporated.

Despite the surge in his pulse, he somehow managed to hang on to a neutral expression as he folded his hands on the table and debated how to respond.

It was possible the sheriff didn't know for certain he had a connection to either Mavis or Fred, but if Cox *had* linked them lying would be a mistake.

He'd have to tell the truth.

The bigger question was who had called in the tip. Since his access to the offshore account had been cut off, it could be BK. His tormentor's threat to create problems in his life hadn't been idle. And if Lee was BK, she had an ax to grind on more than one front.

Yet siccing law enforcement on him carried risk. Why would BK do that?

But if BK wasn't behind this visit, who was?

"Mr. Mullins?"

At the sheriff's prompt, he refocused. "Sorry. I don't usually answer questions like that. Financial matters are confidential and sensitive, and a certain amount of discretion is expected by my clients. Is this a crime-related query that would supersede privacy considerations?"

Cox leaned back in his chair, posture relaxed, manner

friendly—but his gaze was probing and razor sharp. "I don't think either Mavis or Fred would object to my inquiry. They're both dead."

The sheriff hadn't answered his question. And now he was waiting for a reaction to his comment about their deaths.

Stick with the truth as much as possible, Dave. There's no point in feigning ignorance about their fates.

"That's true." He maintained a mild tone. "As a matter of fact, I did business with both of them. In a rural area like this, the choices are limited for people in need of insurance or investment advice. I've carved out a niche in the market, thanks to my solid reputation. Most of my clients are referrals." It couldn't hurt to remind the sheriff he was a well-respected businessman.

"The anonymous caller suggested I talk to you about their deaths."

"Why?"

"I was hoping you could answer that question."

He tried to keep breathing. "Is this an insurance matter? If so, I could check my files."

"It could be. Or it may be more than that. The caller wasn't specific in terms of the information you might have." The sheriff crossed an ankle over a knee. "Both of the deaths have suspicious elements."

The word Kimberly hated ricocheted through his mind as the club sandwich he'd scarfed down at the Spotted Hen an hour ago churned in his stomach.

Hold it together. Stay calm. This has to be a fishing expedition. If Cox had any definite evidence, he'd be asking more pointed questions.

"I had no idea. I thought both died of natural causes."

"New information has come to light."

What did that mean?

Had law enforcement found a crack in BK's airtight murder weapon?

The sheriff continued to watch him, but he didn't ask any more questions. A common intimidation tactic, designed to get people to say more than they should. A staple in movies and TV crime shows.

He mashed his lips together and waited the man out.

"Do you have any enemies, Mr. Mullins?"

At Cox's unexpected question, an image of Lee flashed across his mind.

"No." The answer was knee-jerk—and too fast, based on the slight narrowing of Cox's eyes. "I mean, I'm sure I've ticked off a few people through the years, but I assume you're asking if I know of anyone who hates me enough to connect me to what sounds like a murder investigation."

"I am. You certain no one fits that category?"

"Yes." Even if his stomach was doing flip-flops and he was close to losing his lunch. What benefit would there be in sharing Lee's name? If she was BK, she could find a way to implicate him in the scheme without revealing her own involvement. If she wasn't, he'd be sending more grief her direction.

After a moment, the sheriff pulled out a card and set it on the table. "If any names or information you think could be helpful come to mind, give me a call. Day or night."

"I'll be happy to."

The sheriff rose. "I'll leave you with one thought. The courts are more favorably inclined toward guilty parties who cooperate. Have a nice day."

With that, Cox exited the office, closing the door behind him.

Dave swallowed.

The sheriff knew he was involved. Perhaps he didn't have details, but the man had picked up on his culpability. Realized he was privy to more information than he'd shared.

Raking his fingers through his hair, Dave stood, bracing his fingertips on the table as his legs quivered.

Now that law enforcement was on his scent, he had another incentive to come clean beyond saving Lorraine's life. Cox had a reputation for being as tenacious as the raccoons that burrowed for grubs in the mulch in Kimberly's garden. And he could leave as much chaos in his wake as those nocturnal mammals did.

Would it be smarter to take the initiative, as Cox had suggested, and throw himself on the mercy of the court?

With a life hanging in the balance, what choice did he have? Knowing what he knew now, could he live with himself if Lorraine died?

No, not if. When.

Because unless he acted fast, another victim would soon perish at the hand of a merciless killer.

Yes!

As Nate compared the bank statements provided by the attorneys for Mavis and Fred, another link between the two emerged.

Both had withdrawn $100,000, give or take a few thousand, several months before they died. About thirty days later, deposits began showing up in their accounts near the beginning of each month, continuing until they died. Always the same amount. Like interest payments.

He picked up the phone and punched in the number for Fred's attorney. Since the lawyers for both Fred and Mavis had been cooperative, it would be easier to ask them for additional information than to get a court order to drill deeper.

The man's secretary put him through at once.

"The banking information you provided was helpful." Nate positioned Fred's records in front of him. "I'd like more detail on the withdrawal made a few months prior to Mr. Wilson's death, as well as the monthly deposits that began thereafter.

As the executor of his estate, you can get that faster—and with far less hassle—than I can."

"I'll be glad to contact the bank. I noticed those entries myself. I wish I had more information about his finances, but Fred and I only talked on the rare occasions he needed legal services. I'll let you know what I find out."

Nate thanked him, called Mavis's attorney with the same request, and leaned back in his chair.

According to their legal representatives, neither Fred nor Mavis had much cash in reserve. A couple hundred thousand before the withdrawal. So money as a motive seemed a stretch . . . unless the perpetrator had targeted numerous people. A hundred thousand from one person wasn't a huge amount in the big scheme of things, but a hundred thousand from multiple sources could add up to a tidy sum.

And Grace had identified a number of deaths over the past two years of people who shared key characteristics with Mavis and Fred.

He picked up the phone again and punched in her number. For once it didn't roll to voicemail.

"How's my favorite painting partner?" Despite the serious nature of the call, he couldn't tamp down the smile that played at his lips as he greeted her—or erase the image of her from last night, wearing one of his old shirts while she painted, sleeves rolled up to the elbows, bottom lip caught between her teeth as she edged along the baseboards while he rolled the walls.

"Sore."

He winced. "Sorry about that."

"Don't be. It was a wake-up call. I've been too lax about adding more physical activity to my routine. What's up?"

He filled her in on the latest development and his visit with Mullins. "He knows more than he's telling."

"Shoot. I was hoping the tip had been a crank call and he wasn't involved."

"It's possible he isn't. I got the feeling he was trying to protect someone."

"But he didn't say who."

"No." He leaned back in his chair, watching clouds scuttle across the blue sky out his window. "However, I plan to pay him another visit later in the week. In the interim, I wanted to get the names of the people you identified while you were searching for deaths that were similar to Fred's and Mavis's."

"Are you going to run their financial records too?"

"If their attorneys cooperate—and I don't know why they wouldn't. Since one of your search criteria was little or no family, I'm assuming their lawyers are the executors."

"I don't have the list with me, but I can email you the names as soon as I get home."

"That works. I'll track down their attorneys tomorrow."

"Are you painting again tonight?"

"Unfortunately, no." He glanced at the folder on the side of his desk. Grimaced. "I'm speaking at an Elk's Club potluck dinner."

"Sounds like fun."

"Uh-huh."

"Your enthusiasm is underwhelming."

"Public speaking isn't my strength."

"You do fine in private. Pretend you're talking to me."

"If I said to them what I'd like to say to you, I might raise a few eyebrows."

Silence.

Uh-oh. Tactical error. Hadn't he told himself last night not to move too fast? That being flirty could backfire?

But Grace was easy to flirt with.

Too easy.

He straightened up in his chair. "Listen, I didn't mean to—"

"Hey. Don't apologize. I was just trying to imagine what it

223

is you'd like to say to me. Why don't you tell me in person on Saturday, at that romantic restaurant on the lake?"

The sultry undercurrent in her teasing tone goosed his pulse.

"I'll do that."

"While I'm waiting with bated breath, I'll round up those names and send them to you."

"What's the timing on your security cameras?"

"They'll be installed Friday afternoon. Good luck tonight."

"Thanks. I'd rather be sent on a mission behind enemy lines than face an audience or be forced to glad-hand. Schmoozing isn't my cup of tea."

"Every elected position has a PR component."

"I'm finding that out."

"You'll be fine."

"Yeah." He looked at his speaking notes for tonight. Sighed. "Much as I'd like to continue this conversation, I suppose I ought to prep a little more."

"Couldn't hurt. Watch for those names this evening. I think we're beginning to get closer to answers."

"I agree."

Yet as they said their goodbyes and he pulled the file closer, a niggle of unease rippled through him.

While they might be closing in, critical pieces of information about the deaths of Mavis and Fred and the attacks on Grace remained buried.

And unless they solved both soon, every instinct in his body told him that wasn't all that would be buried.

He had no choice. Kimberly had to be told.

Hands shaking, Dave filled the second glass with ice and added lemonade to both.

All these years, he'd done everything in his power to keep

the truth about his affair from his wife. To protect her, yes, but also for selfish reasons. Facing a future without the woman he loved was as daunting now as it had been after the accident, when the doctors in the ER had struggled to save her life.

But living a lie ate at his gut. And with people dying, he couldn't stay on the sidelines any longer. The visit from the sheriff today had been the kick in the pants he needed to shore up his resolve.

Maybe Cox wouldn't believe his story. He had no proof Mavis and Fred and the others had been killed. Nor could he access the offshore account anymore.

However, he could tell him about the investments and identify the people he'd sold them to. Torpedo BK's scheme. His tormentor would no longer have any control over him, nor would this nameless viper dare continue the scheme with law enforcement on the alert. And with the weight of the Feds behind him, it was possible Cox could track down who was reaping the benefits from the stolen money.

He picked up the two glasses, the ice clinking as he carried them to the screened porch attached to the back of the house where Kimberly waited.

With every step, he prayed for fortitude.

She smiled as he joined her. "Thanks, honey." She took the glass he held out and patted the cushion beside her on the wicker settee. "Sit by me."

"That was my plan." He attempted without success to force up the corners of his mouth.

"Are you feeling all right?" She studied him, forehead crimping.

"I had a rough day." More like a rough four years.

He watched a bead of sweat drip down the side of his glass. Set his lemonade on the small side table next to him.

"Want to tell me about it?"

No.

But it was time.

He tried to inflate his balking lungs. Failed. Drew in small puffs of air instead, hoping he didn't hyperventilate. "The story about my bad day starts not long after your accident."

A few taut moments passed, and she set her own lemonade down. "This sounds serious."

"It is."

Just do it, Dave. Make no excuses. Bare your soul and throw yourself on her mercy.

"You know you can talk to me about anything."

He forced himself to look at her, this kind, gentle woman he'd betrayed. He didn't deserve her love. And after tonight, he might not have it. But he couldn't continue the charade anymore. Not with people dying. "I have a confession to make."

Her frown deepened. "Is there an issue . . . with your job?"

"No. This is about us."

Her face crumpled. "I knew it. I'm too much of a burden, aren't I? I've watched you get . . . thinner and thinner . . . while you run yourself ragged trying to . . . take care of me and manage your business. It's not fair to you to—"

"No!" He took her hand, shock rippling through him. She thought the problem was *her*? "I love you, Kimberly. You're my life. You could never be a burden. The confession is about *my* failures."

She shook her head, tears brimming on her lower lashes. "You can't have anything to confess. You're a saint."

If only that were true.

A lump of ice formed in his stomach. "I'm not a saint. I'm a sinner. A bad sinner."

"I don't believe that."

"It's true." He twined his fingers with hers. Maybe for the last time. Once he confessed, he wouldn't blame her if she threw him out and never wanted to see him again. "While you were in the coma, everyone thought you were going to die."

226

"I know. I can't imagine how hard that was for you, coming on the heels of . . . losing Jeremy." Her voice broke, and she dug around in her pocket for a tissue.

"It *was* hard, Kimberly. Too hard."

She swiped at her nose. "What do you mean?"

"I made a very bad mistake." He hung his head, summoned up every ounce of his courage, and spoke. "I'd never felt that alone in my life. At my lowest point, when all hope for you seemed lost, I met someone who was willing to offer . . . comfort."

As she processed his comment, shock flattened her features and she sucked in a sharp breath. "You had an affair." The numb words were barely there. A mere whisper.

A cloak of misery settled over him, as suffocating as quicksand. "I didn't think of it in those terms. I didn't think, period. I just wanted someone to hold me, to let me vent, to help me wade through the darkness. I never thought you were coming back to me."

She eased her hand free of his, and his heart stumbled. It was what he'd expected, but the sudden loss of contact was as if someone had flipped his internal thermostat from heat to deep freeze.

"Are you still seeing her?"

"No!" Sweet heaven, how could she think that after his tender care during her recovery? "I only saw her five times. While I was with her, all I could think of was you. I wanted to be back at the hospital, willing you to live despite the grim picture the doctors painted. I realized that sitting by your bed, holding your hand, gave me more comfort than being with her. I never loved her, Kimberly. Never."

"I don't know . . . what to say, Dave." Her expression had gone from shocked to shattered.

"I don't expect you to say anything. I have no excuse for what I did. I knew it was wrong from the beginning, but I wasn't strong enough to deal with losing you while I was also grieving for Jeremy. Yet being with her didn't fill the empty place in my life. Only you could do that, even in a coma. Even if you couldn't communicate. Even if you were slipping away."

"After all these years . . . why are you telling me this now?" She searched his face, her shimmering eyes filled with hurt and bewilderment.

"Because there's more to the story."

Wrapping his fingers around the edge of the seat, he told her the rest. All of it.

By the time he ended, with his decision to talk to the sheriff, she was trembling and as pale as the moonflowers she planted every summer that wove through the trellis in the backyard.

But he didn't take her hand or pull her close. With his shameful secrets exposed at last, she would no longer welcome comfort from him or find it easier to fall asleep with him by her side.

Yet whether or not she wanted him in her life—or her bed— he wasn't going to desert her.

"I'm sorry, Kimberly. I've made a total mess of everything. If I could go back and change my decisions, I would. But all I can do at this stage is tell you the truth and try to stop the evil I've helped perpetuate."

"When are you going to . . . talk to the sheriff?"

"Tomorrow morning."

"Will he . . . arrest you?"

The mere thought of that turned his insides to ice. "I don't know. I imagine he'll want to check out my story first. But no matter what happens, I'll do everything in my power to continue helping you recover as fully as possible—if you'll let me. If necessary, I'll find a way to orchestrate the assistance from prison."

She rubbed her temples. "My head is hurting . . . too much to think. I'm going to . . . lie down."

He stood as she started to rise, but she waved him back down. "I can manage. I should be . . . more independent. I've been relying on you for . . . too much anyway. Good night."

Cane in hand, she shuffled into the house.

Shoulders slumping, Dave watched her disappear from sight—and quite possibly from his life. Kimberly hadn't cried, or asked many questions, or offered any hint she might consider forgiving him.

Perhaps she never would.

He'd done the right thing by telling her, though. And he'd do the right thing with the sheriff tomorrow too. He'd already been halfway to that decision prior to the man's visit. Now, with the clock ticking on the thirty-day opt-out period, Lorraine was living on borrowed time. He had to move before the deadline arrived and his newest customer demanded her refund.

And once the sheriff got involved, BK wouldn't dare touch her. If Cox agreed, he'd call BK after they talked. Share the news he'd gone to the police. That should keep Lorraine safe.

For now, he'd gather some bedding from the linen closet and make up the sleeper sofa in the family room. Not that he'd get much shut-eye tonight.

But at least he had a plan in place.

As for the old saying about confession being good for the soul?

He did feel a bit less burdened.

Yet the lightness in his soul was more than offset by the heaviness in his heart.

19

GRACE? SORRY FOR THE EARLY CALL, but we have a death scene that fits your parameters."

At Nate's grim greeting, Grace knuckled the sleep from her eyes, swung her feet to the floor, and peered at her watch. Six thirty in the morning wasn't *that* early—unless you'd spent half the night thinking about the man on the other end of the line and a painting party that had stretched past ten o'clock Monday night.

"Give me an address."

He recited it while she searched the nightstand in vain for a pen and piece of paper.

"I'll tell you what . . . could you text that to me?" She stood and shoved her hair back from her face. "Paper appears to be in short supply, and my brain's not quite awake yet. In the interest of full disclosure, I'm not a morning person."

"No problem. It's about a twenty-five-minute drive from your place."

"Look for me in forty minutes."

"Don't rush. The deceased isn't going anywhere."

Yawning, she padded over to the closet in her sleep shirt and pulled out a pair of slacks. "That's a riff on the old saying

in morgues at quitting time—they'll still be dead tomorrow."
She grabbed a shirt off a hanger. "Who's the victim?"

"I'm not certain yet she *is* a victim, but her name's Lorraine
Meyers. Ring any bells?"

"Nope. I'm hanging up so I can get dressed."

Dead silence.

Her lips twitched. "Erase those thoughts, Sheriff."

"You're a mind reader now?" Amusement lightened his
tone.

"Doesn't take telepathic abilities to decode the male mind."

"Is that a sexist remark?"

"Am I wrong?"

"No comment. I'll see you soon."

The line went dead.

Grinning, Grace threw on her clothes, ran a brush through
her hair, and slapped on lipstick and a touch of mascara. It
wasn't her best makeup job, but she'd pull out all the stops
on Saturday night.

Thirty-seven minutes later, she pulled in between Nate's
Jeep and Russ's truck, set the brake, and surveyed the farmhouse. The porch sagged in one section, the parched wood
cried out for a new coat of paint, and part of the gutter was
missing.

There wasn't any spare money to be had on this property.

Grace retrieved her bag from the trunk and walked up the
steps to the porch.

Nate opened the screen door from the inside as she approached. "You got here fast."

She sidled past him. "I pushed the speed limit a hair. But
if I'd gotten a ticket, I do have connections."

"Culling favors?"

"I was on official business."

"I suppose that could justify fixing a ticket."

"Didn't happen anyway. Tell me what we have here."

"The call came in about two hours ago. From Lorraine."

Grace frowned. "She was alive two hours ago?"

"Yes. And very sick. She asked for an ambulance. The dispatcher tried to keep her on the line, but she hung up. One of my deputies and the EMTs came. She was dead when they arrived. They called Russ, and after he got the lay of the land—she had no close family that he could tell, lived alone, didn't appear to be wealthy—he called me. I called you. As soon as we finish here, I'll track down her attorney. You're up to speed."

"Where is she?"

"In the den in back." He motioned toward the rear of the house and began walking that direction. "The deputy found her on the floor next to a puddle of vomit, a towel beside her. It appeared she was trying to clean up the mess."

Grace's step faltered.

Vomit?

She sniffed. Yep. The sour, acrid scent was faint but unmistakable. Thank goodness she hadn't scarfed down the bagel that had tempted her as she'd dashed out of the kitchen.

Nate paused. "You coming?"

"Uh-huh." She forced herself to resume walking.

Nate scrutinized her. "You're a little green around the gills."

She stopped again. The county sheriff had excellent observation skills. "You know how formalin affects you? I have a similar reaction to vomit. Not as bad as yours, but it's not my favorite aroma."

"You sure you want to go in there? The smell's worse."

"I'll be fine. I just had to psych myself up for it. Let's do this." She continued toward the back of the house.

The scene was exactly as Nate had described it—as was the smell, which activated her gag reflex.

Hold it together, Grace. You can handle this.

"Morning, Russ." Somehow she got the greeting out without choking.

"Grace." He dipped his head and slipped his cell back in his pocket.

"Have either of you spotted anything suspicious?" She moved closer to the woman.

"No." Nate answered for both of them. "If we hadn't been looking for similarities to the Fred and Mavis situations, only Russ would be here."

"Neither of them puked, though." Russ ambled over.

"That we know of." Grace knelt beside the woman. "Maybe they made it to the bathroom."

"Could be." Russ dropped to his haunches beside her. "But that summer flu bug is going around, and flu can be lethal for older folks."

"Or it could have been a heart issue again." Grace squinted at the vomit. Willed her stomach to behave as she bent closer.

Was that a seed?

"Spot something?" Nate dropped down beside her.

She pointed. "Check that out."

Both men leaned toward the foul-smelling stomach contents.

Nate transferred his attention to her. "It could be a seed."

"That's my take." She shifted toward Russ. "It's your call, but I'd recommend an autopsy."

The coroner scratched his bald spot. "I don't know. There's nothing here to suggest foul play, and we didn't find anything out of the ordinary—other than the seeds—in the autopsies for Mavis or Fred."

Grace swiveled back to Nate, angling her nose as far away as possible from the smell wafting up to her. "Did you tell him about the foxglove theory?"

"Not yet." He gave her a once-over and stood. "Let's talk about it in the living room or on the porch."

She telegraphed him a silent thank-you. "Let me get a sample first." After retrieving a screw-top bottle from her kit, she scooped up a portion of the vomit that contained the seed, dropped it in, and rose. If Russ didn't authorize an autopsy, at least she had this sample.

The two men followed her out, all the way to the porch.

Better.

Much better.

"You want me to fill him in?" Nate directed the question to her.

"Please." She stowed the sample in her kit. "I'll freeze this in case we need it later, Russ."

"Works for me."

As Nate told the coroner her theory about the foxglove while she sucked in fresh air, the man's expression grew more and more skeptical.

"I don't know." Russ shook his head as Nate concluded. "Seems farfetched to me."

"There are tests we can run to find out if foxglove could have precipitated the heart issues." Grace rejoined the conversation as her stomach settled down.

"We have a limited budget."

"We could test a sample from one of the victims to start."

"*If* they're victims." Russ shoved his fingers into his back pockets.

"Questions have also arisen about the finances of the victims, Russ." Nate kept his tone conversational, and Grace ceded the floor to him. "I'm going to review Lorraine's as well. I don't want to let someone get away with murder, if that's what we're dealing with. Do you?"

"No. Of course not. But I'm trying to be a responsible steward of taxpayer money." He exhaled. "I guess we can spring for one test." He turned to her. "I'll call the lab and see what samples they want me to send from Mavis's autopsy."

"What about an autopsy on Lorraine?"

"I'm not seeing anything here to warrant that."

"Why don't we try this." Nate rested his hand on his holster. "Let's keep her in the morgue until we round up her attorney or a family member. That will buy us time to send a sample from Mavis to the lab. We can regroup after we get the results. Is that acceptable?" He included them both in his question.

As far as Grace was concerned, they should do an autopsy ASAP.

But she wasn't the boss, and compromise was part of the job.

"I can live with that."

"Works for me." Russ motioned to the back of the house. "You okay if we transport?"

"Yes. I'll join you in a minute." Nate leaned a hip against the peeling paint on the porch railing.

"See you later, Grace." Russ disappeared back inside, the screen door slamming behind him.

"For the record, I think we should do an autopsy." Grace folded her arms. "Even if the test results don't show toxic levels of digitalis, these deaths are suspicious. We should have samples on hand in case we get a break later and want to test them."

"I agree. But let's give Russ a day or two to adjust to the idea, now that we've planted the seed. Pardon the pun."

"Cute." A smile played at her mouth. "And for a man who claims he doesn't like to schmooze, you handled Russ with aplomb."

"I'd classify my approach more as understanding the players than schmoozing. A handy skill in any job."

"I won't argue with that. How did the talk go last night?"

"No one fell asleep."

"I bet you were terrific."

"I didn't hear any complaints—but I prefer one-on-one communication." He leaned closer and dropped his voice to a husky whisper. "Like the kind we'll have Saturday night. I'm counting the days."

"Me too." Her response came out in a croak.

Oh, for pity's sake. She sounded like a lovestruck adolescent.

If Nate noticed, he was gallant enough to let it pass. "I'll ask Russ to request a fast turnaround from the lab."

"Thanks."

"Busy day?"

"Road trip. Two autopsies in different counties."

"In other words, *long* day."

"Longer than most, but I knew what I was signing up for with this job. Will you let me know what Lorraine's attorney has to say about her finances and next of kin?"

"Yes."

"I wish you didn't have to work tomorrow while everyone else celebrates Fourth of July with picnics and fireworks."

"Holidays are our busiest times. What are you going to do?"

"Veg at my house. I was going to go to St. Louis and hang out with my sisters, but Cate has to work too."

"You could use a veg day—and we'll make up for the missed fireworks on Saturday." His slow smile was far more potent than any pyrotechnics that would light up the sky tomorrow night. Then he squeezed her fingers and reentered the house.

Or crime scene, if her suspicions proved correct.

Grace returned to her car, slid behind the wheel, and drove down the gravel drive toward the main road.

Despite Russ's skepticism, with every day that passed she was more convinced that the older residents on their radar were victims. Too many pieces of the puzzle were missing to answer the critical who and why questions, but they were getting close to a resolution. She could feel it.

That was the good news.

The bad news?

Her intuition told her the person behind the scheme that was ruthlessly claiming lives knew they were closing in.

And just as the gray dust churned up by her tires followed her like a menacing specter, danger would continue to hover until the perpetrator was uncovered and put behind bars.

Another one out of the way.

BK locked the door, twisted the knob to verify it was secure, and walked away.

Too bad Lorraine had insisted on a refund. Back-to-back deaths weren't ideal, but as long as her demise didn't raise any red flags, what difference did it make?

And there was no basis for anyone to consider her death suspicious. She had heart issues, and she was close to eighty. The coroner wouldn't have any grounds to investigate.

Even if Grace Reilly got it into her head that he should.

Teeth clenched, BK mashed down the autolock button on the key fob.

The county pathologist was getting to be a royal pain in the butt. If the woman had any sense, she'd have paid attention to the warnings. She must have a stubborn—or stupid—streak a mile wide, despite all her academic credentials.

If she continued to make waves, she'd have to be dealt with.

But Lorraine would be the last victim for a while. With almost half a million in the offshore account, there was no urgency to find a new customer.

Besides, it wasn't easy running the show alone. With Tyler no longer available, sending warning messages was more difficult and riskier. And Dave appeared to be losing his effectiveness as a salesman along with his nerve. Taking control of the account had been prudent.

Unfortunately, he was still the best person to do the sell-in for future investments. His reputation and credentials gave him credibility that would be difficult to replicate. So when it came time to choose the next victim, he'd have to be pulled back into the scheme.

For now, though, best to leave him alone. Let him come to terms with how the plan had evolved—and stew about the havoc that could be wreaked in his life if he didn't cooperate.

Until their next contact, why not forget about him and Grace Reilly and enjoy this beautiful July day and the holiday to come? After all, despite a few glitches and a handful of vague suspicions, the sheriff and his cohorts were no closer to figuring out what had happened to Mavis and Fred than they had been two weeks ago.

And the odds of that changing were tiny. Without a clue pointing them in a very specific direction, they'd never be able to pinpoint the cause of death.

BK opened the door and slid behind the wheel of the car, mouth flexing. It took a smart person to outwit law enforcement, but it could be done if you planned the perfect crime.

Too bad the father who'd once said his sole offspring would never amount to a hill of beans . . . and the one true love who'd ended up being a two-timer . . . and the bosses who treated underlings like second-class citizens . . . would never know how wrong they'd been about the smarts in *this* brain.

BK inserted the key in the ignition.

None of that mattered, however. Proving to yourself you were worthy of respect was more important than proving it to the world—or the people who'd dissed you. If you got rich in the process, and added a bit of adventure and excitement to your life? That was a bonus.

Plus, pulling the wool over people's eyes had proven to be very entertaining. It was like a game. Challenging and fun.

As long as you kept on winning.

And BK intended to do exactly that.

20

MORNING, ELEANOR." Nate stifled a yawn as he passed the administrative assistant's desk.

She swiveled around in her chair. "Morning, Sheriff." She beckoned him closer and lowered her voice. "You have a visitor. I told him I didn't know how late you'd be, but he said he'd wait. It's Dave Mullins. He's sitting outside your office."

This day was full of unexpected turns.

"How long has he been here?"

"He was waiting when I arrived at eight."

Nate glanced at his watch. Nine forty-five. Still early—but after the pre-dawn wake-up call from Russ and a detour to a meth lab takedown en route to the office, it felt as if he'd already put in a full day.

"You want me to tell him to set up an appointment and come back?" Eleanor started to stand.

"No." He waved her back down. "I'll talk to him."

She dropped her volume again. "Do you think this has anything to do with the tip that came in about him having information on Mavis and Fred?"

"That would be my guess. I talked to him yesterday afternoon, but he didn't have much to say. Maybe he's had a change of heart."

"You think he really knows something about them?"

"Why else would he be here?"

She shook her head. "You can't trust anyone these days."

"I didn't say he was guilty of anything. But I'm hoping he can offer us a lead. As it stands, we're at a dead end—even though Dr. Reilly thinks we have another suspicious death."

"*Another* one?" The woman's eyes rounded.

"Lorraine Meyers. That's where I was early this morning. Do you happen to know her?"

"Not well, but our paths have crossed. What happened?"

"TBD. However, the circumstances are similar to those surrounding the deaths of Fred and Mavis."

"Will there be an autopsy?"

"Not yet. Dr. Reilly is pushing for it, but Russ isn't convinced. Whatever Mullins has to say may help us decide. Could you answer my phone while I talk to him?"

"Sure thing."

Nate continued down the hall. Mullins's head was tipped back against the wall, his eyes closed, face pale and gaunt. The man looked as if he'd aged ten years in the past twenty-four hours.

He stopped in front of his unexpected visitor. "Mr. Mullins?"

The man's eyelids flew open, and he stumbled to his feet. Tottered.

Nate grabbed his arm. Dark smudges hung under his lower lashes, and a spiderweb of red lines crisscrossed the white around his irises.

Either he'd been drinking, or he was exhausted and seriously stressed.

"Are you all right?" Nate kept a firm grip on him.

"Yes." He cleared the raspiness from his throat. Inhaled. "Actually, that's a lie. Just like my life's been for almost four years. If you have a few minutes, I'd like to talk to you."

"Come into my office. Could I get you a cup of coffee?"

"I'd appreciate that. An infusion of caffeine may help."

"Have a seat at the table. I'll be back in a minute."

Nate wasted no time filling a disposable cup with coffee in the break room. After gathering up a stir stick and packets of creamer and sugar, he rejoined Mullins and passed over the java.

"Thanks."

"No problem." While his visitor doctored up his coffee, Nate detoured to his desk for a pen and notebook, then took the chair at a right angle to the man. "I assume your visit is in reference to our conversation yesterday."

"Yes. I was on the verge of coming to see you anyway, but your talk gave me the push I needed." He took a sip of coffee, holding the cup with both hands as the liquid sloshed close to the rim. "Some of what I'm going to tell you is fact. Some is speculation. I don't know how to prove the speculative part, but if you believe me, you may have the resources to find the truth." He swallowed. "Why don't I give you the basics first? After I finish, I can answer your questions."

"That works."

Nate let the man talk, taking extensive notes as the sordid story unfolded. Infidelity, blackmail, fraud, murder—it was the stuff of dime novels. Of crime fiction.

Yet this man had lived it. Was living it now.

And while Mullins was guilty of multiple legal and moral offenses, Nate couldn't help but feel a twinge of compassion for him. The man had made a bad mistake in the midst of devastating grief and despair. While he'd regretted it almost at once, it had continued to plague him, and he'd found himself sinking deeper and deeper into the black morass of immorality as he tried to keep his life from shattering.

It was tragic.

But it didn't condone his involvement in the scheme to

scam innocent people. Worse yet, if his conclusions about this BK person were correct, he'd unwittingly aided and abetted murder.

Since Mullins's suspicions aligned with Grace's and his own, the veracity of the man's claims wasn't in question.

As Mullins wound down, Nate tapped the tip of his pen against the table. "I'll want the names of all your clients who bought the bogus investment."

"I brought them with me, along with their addresses and other vital information." He withdrew a multi-folded sheet of paper from his shirt pocket and set it on the table.

"How did you convince all these people to buy into your offering?"

"BK chose people who were barely getting by on fixed incomes and who were desperate to increase the return on their nest eggs. I offered a yield they couldn't get anywhere else, told them this was an exclusive deal available only by invitation, and asked them to keep the transaction confidential."

"Did BK know these people?"

"I don't think so. I asked once, and the response I got was, 'I have my sources.' Besides, if BK had talked to them about the investment, they could have mentioned the conversation to me. That would have been too risky, after all the effort BK has taken to stay anonymous."

That was true.

"You said that even before my visit to your office, you were on the verge of contacting me. Why?" Nate began unfolding the sheet of paper containing the names.

"Because I think someone else is about to die."

Nate looked up. "Who and why?"

"The woman I sold the last investment to. She elected to exercise the opt-out clause, and BK didn't want to return her money. When I tried to return it myself, I discovered the password and login on the offshore account had been changed."

"Is her name on this list?" Nate continued to unfold the sheet of paper.

"Yes. Lorraine Meyers."

Nate sucked in a breath.

"What's wrong?" The tension emanating from Mullins skyrocketed.

"You're too late. She died this morning."

Every vestige of color drained from the man's complexion, and beads of sweat popped out above his upper lip. "I can't believe BK moved that fast. The opt-out deadline wasn't for another two weeks."

Any doubt about the validity of Grace's suspicions vanished.

"How are these victims being killed?"

"I have no idea. But BK said the method was foolproof, and that there was never any evidence to suggest foul play."

Nate finished unfolding the sheet of paper Mullins had brought. Scanned the names of the six people who'd bought into the investment opportunity the man had presented. Mavis, Fred, and Lorraine were among them, as was one of the people Grace had culled from the list of deaths over the past two years.

He set the paper down and gave the man across from him his full attention. "Four of these people are dead. I expect the other two are as well."

The man's features contorted. "That's what I was afraid of."

"You didn't know about any of these deaths?"

"Not until recently. All I did was sell them the investment and deposit their checks. BK handled the monthly interest payments. The first death notice I saw was Fred's. It bothered me a little, since he'd bought the investment not long before, but it wasn't until I saw Mavis's two weeks ago that I began to suspect the scheme had taken a lethal turn." He twisted his hands together on the table. "I swear that's the truth."

"I'm not the one you'll have to convince of that." Nate set the paper aside. "Did you bring the cellphone that was provided to you?"

"Yes." He pulled it out and laid it on the table.

Definitely a burner phone.

And Mullins had said he couldn't tell whether this BK was a man or a woman.

An idea began to percolate in Nate's mind.

"Did the person who's calling the shots ever mention Grace Reilly, the county pathologist?"

"Not by name. But in one of our recent conversations, they said no one raised an eyebrow when old people die—except the county pathologist. They also said that could be dealt with."

Bingo.

Unless his deductive powers were failing him, Grace was being targeted by BK because she was viewed as a potential threat. Someone who, if she dug deep enough, could possibly uncover the truth behind what appeared to be perfect murders and expose Mullins's blackmailer.

Meaning the person who'd hired Tyler Holmes was also the person tormenting Mullins.

BK probably hadn't used the same burner phone for both men, but it was worth checking the incoming number against the one Tyler had provided.

"You said BK had threatened to expose you." Nate linked his fingers on the table. "Do you think that's who called in the tip about you to my office?"

"I considered that, but why would this person risk having me get involved with law enforcement?"

A logical question.

"It could have been a scare tactic. BK may have assumed a visit from the police would remind you of all you had to lose and persuade you to toe the line. If this person is convinced the murder weapon of choice is foolproof, he or she may view the anonymous tip more as a warning to you than a risk to the scheme."

"Maybe." But Mullins didn't appear convinced. "BK does know how much I want to protect Kimberly and preserve my marriage."

"Since you said you were discreet in your meetings during the affair, have you given any thought to the possibility that the woman you were seeing may be BK?"

"Yes." He stared down at his hands. "In fact, I went to see her a couple of weeks ago. I wanted to find out if she'd told anyone about us or had any inkling who might be blackmailing me. After I left, I did wonder if it could be her. But much as she hates me, I don't think she'd kill innocent people for money."

"Hate and greed are powerful motivators." Nate picked up his pen. "What's her name?"

Mullins raked his fingers through his hair, distress etching his features. "She's had more than her share of tough breaks. I hate to add any more trauma to her life."

"If she's killing people, she has to be stopped. If she's innocent, she has nothing to worry about."

He sighed. "Lee Jordan."

As Mullins recited the contact information, Nate jotted it down. "Anything else I should know?"

"I did tell Lee about Mavis and Fred. In fact, she asked for their names. So it's possible she called in the tip. Now you know everything I know." He swallowed. "Are you going to arrest me?"

"That depends." Nate sat back in his chair. "Are you a flight risk?"

"No. Kimberly needs me. I'd never desert her—by choice."

"Are you willing to cooperate with our investigation?"

"Yes."

"Then for the present, stick with your usual routine. Assuming our subject isn't Lee Jordan, let's not do anything to tip them off you've contacted law enforcement."

"I'm not certain I *can* continue with my usual routine."

"What do you mean?"

"Kimberly was asleep when I left this morning. I can't guarantee she'll be willing to let me stay at the house."

"Try to convince her. If you move out, our subject could put two and two together and realize they've lost their bargaining chip."

"I'll do my best. What if BK calls again?" He indicated the burner phone on the table.

Nate picked up the cell. Most basic burners weren't GPS equipped. If BK was using such a phone, cell tower triangulation would be the only way to target the source location of an incoming call—but that would give them no more than a general geographic area. Nothing precise enough to swoop in and nab the caller.

He scrolled through the phone log. The number had changed over the years. BK had switched burner phones on a regular basis. Smart move, if you wanted to stay one step ahead of the law. Although he jotted down the number for the most recent calls, there was no guarantee it was still active.

"If you get another call, answer—and contact me as soon as you hang up." Nate pushed the cell back across the table.

Mullins pocketed the phone, lines of weariness creasing his cheeks. "What will happen to me after this is over?"

"That will be up to the prosecuting attorney. The fact that you came forward will work in your favor."

"But I was too late to save Lorraine Meyers."

"Yes." Nate stood. "If I were you, I'd line up legal counsel."

Mullins pushed himself to his feet as if the weight of the world was pressing down on him. "There's no spare money for that."

"Did you benefit financially from this scheme with BK?"

"No. And the well is dry, after all of Kimberly's expenses. I can't sell the house and put her out on the street."

"Assuming this progresses to an arraignment, you can ask the judge for a court-appointed lawyer during that appearance."

"Thanks." He held out his hand. "I appreciate you treating me with respect despite everything I've done."

Nate took his hand. "I can sympathize with a man being caught between a rock and a hard place, even if I can't condone your choices. I'll be in touch."

He followed Mullins to the door, closed it behind him, and circled around to his desk chair.

First order of business? Call Grace to let her know her instincts had been spot-on and to alert her to work an autopsy on Lorraine into her schedule.

Second, brief Russ so the coroner could fill out the autopsy paperwork.

Third, check out the other two names on Dave's list to verify they were deceased.

Fourth, alert federal authorities about the fraud case.

Finally, see what he could find out about Lee Jordan and have a talk with her ASAP. If she hated the man who'd jilted her as much as he said she did, she could very well be the tipster.

The odds were slim she was BK, however, despite the rationale he'd offered to Mullins for that scenario. A methodical killer who left no traces had to know that tipping off the police about Mullins's connection to Fred and Mavis would put the entire scheme at risk if he cracked—as he had.

So while a follow-up with Lee Jordan was appropriate, Nate's gut told him that investigative trail wasn't going to lead him to BK.

It also told him the blackmailing, swindling murderer had

an ear to the ground. You didn't commit six flawless murders and amass a small fortune in stolen funds without doing due diligence. Sooner or later, BK would find out that the official cause of death for the victims was morphing from natural to homicide.

Whether they could ever prove that remained to be seen.

But he wasn't a quitter—and from what he knew about Grace, she wasn't, either. Between the two of them, they'd solve this case and bring BK to justice.

Or die trying.

A shiver raced through him as the old saying strobed through his mind, but he quashed that notion at once. Now that he was on to the scheme, no one else was going to die on his watch. Least of all himself or Grace.

Yet as he picked up his phone, he couldn't shake the feeling that despite all they'd learned and all the precautions they might take, someone who knew how to kill people without leaving evidence of murder was a formidable opponent who could attack without warning, wreak havoc, and vanish without a trace.

21

WAS THAT THE DOORBELL?

Grace stopped toweling her hair dry, opened the bathroom door, and poked her head out.

Ding dong.

Her ears hadn't been playing tricks on her.

Pulse picking up, she tossed the towel onto the bathroom vanity and finger-combed her hair.

Could Nate be paying an impromptu call? Yes, he was working on the holiday, but if he happened to be passing by, it was possible he'd decided to stop in and share a soda—or an iced tea.

A visit from her favorite sheriff would definitely add a touch of zing to an otherwise very low-key Fourth of July. The highlight of her day thus far had been catching up on laundry and giving the perennial gardens that rimmed the house a long-neglected weeding.

She jogged to the front door and peered through the peephole.

What on earth?

She unlocked the door and pulled it open.

"Surprise!" Eve grinned and held up a large bag with the logo of their favorite St. Louis barbecue place.

"I brought the drinks." Cate lifted a carrier containing four cans of soda and two mango iced teas.

"What are you guys doing here?"

"Melting in this heat." Eve fanned herself with her hand. "If you don't ask us in fast, we won't have to bother nuking our dinner."

"Enter." She stepped back.

Cate swept past her into the coolness and headed for the kitchen, Eve on her heels.

Grace padded barefoot after them. "I need answers."

"What? You aren't happy to see us?" Eve opened the fridge and slid the bag of barbecue in.

"You know I am. But I thought you"—she pointed at Eve—"were planning to spend the day with your new husband, and you"—she swung her index finger toward Cate—"were working."

"Change of plans. You want a bottle of your tea?" Cate filled a glass with ice and popped the tab on a Diet Sprite.

"In a minute. I'm waiting for answers."

"Pushy little thing, isn't she?" Eve directed the comment to their eldest sister, but the twinkle in her eyes took the sting out of her words. "And here I splurged on the best barbecue St. Louis has to offer to brighten up her Fourth of July."

"And I brought sparklers for later." Cate opened her tote bag and pulled out a handful of them.

Grace waited them out. Once her sisters were on a roll, there was no stopping them. They'd explain this spontaneous social call when they got good and ready.

Cate took a sip of soda. "Where's your sheriff?"

"Working—like I thought you were supposed to be."

"I ended up putting in twenty-four hours straight on a double homicide Monday. Sarge rearranged the schedule so I could get some shut-eye today."

"Instead, you came here."

She hiked up one shoulder. "I slept for five hours."

"Where's the fiancé?"

"Working. He got pulled in to help with a breaking case. Such is life in law enforcement."

"That's my story too. Get this—Brent got called in to cover for Cate." Eve raised her hands in a what-can-you-do gesture and pulled a soda out of the carrier.

Visit explained. Her sisters were at loose ends and had decided to liven up their Fourth with a road trip.

"Now that we have three law enforcement types in the family, I have a feeling unpredictable schedules will be the story of our lives going forward." Grace nabbed a tea and filled a glass with ice.

"Could be four law enforcement types, if your sheriff pans out." Eve nudged her aside to gain access to the ice dispenser.

"Aren't you being a tad premature?"

"Am I?" Eve arched an eyebrow at her.

"He checked out, by the way." This from Cate.

Grace pivoted and glared at her oldest sister. "You ran background on him after all."

Cate shrugged. "I had a few spare minutes one day. He appears to be the real deal, in case you're interested. It's hard to go wrong with a decorated former Green Beret. I can't wait to meet him at the wedding."

The decorated part was news, but she was *not* going to prolong this discussion by asking for details.

"Maybe I'll decide not to bring him."

Eve dismissed that with a flip of her hand. "An idle threat. You're besotted."

"Besotted?" Grace snorted. "Where did you dredge up *that* antiquated word?"

"Words are my business."

Cate began pouring the rest of her soda into the glass. "If you ask me, the fact she doesn't want to—crud." The Sprite overflowed the cup and dripped down her hand onto the counter.

Grace yanked open the cabinet door under the sink and reached for the dish towel.

It wasn't there.

"Sorry. The wash is in the laundry room, waiting to be folded."

"I'm on it." Eve bounded toward the small annex off the kitchen that doubled as a laundry/mud room.

When she returned, she was bearing not only a dish towel, which she tossed to Cate, but Nate's shirt.

The old one he'd loaned his unexpected helper to protect her clothes while she helped him paint.

The one she'd insisted on bringing home to launder.

"Since when are men's shirts in your laundry room?" Eve waved it like a flag.

Grace snatched it from her. "There's a simple explanation."

Without waiting to hear it, Cate sopped up the soda with the dish towel and strode toward the laundry room.

"What are you doing?" Grace wadded up the shirt.

"Searching for evidence."

"I already found plenty." Eve smirked and sipped her soda, perusing the shirt.

Grace tried not to squirm.

"There could be more clues." Cate's voice wafted from the recesses of the laundry room. "It's easy to overlook the . . . aha."

"What did you find?" Eve swung toward the doorway.

Cate reappeared a few seconds later holding one of Grace's sport shoes. "Get a load of this."

Eve leaned closer. "Is that paint?"

"I'd have to run it through the lab to be certain, but circumstantial evidence would suggest that's a reasonable conclusion."

"You were painting?" Eve gaped at her. "The woman who swore off DIY projects a decade ago, after Dad recruited all of us to help strip the window frames in the house after he decided we should restore all the woodwork?"

"I don't think she was doing this for herself. What do you want to bet that belongs to her date for the wedding?" Cate zeroed in on Nate's shirt.

Sometimes having an ace detective for a sister stunk.

"Does it?" Eve stepped closer to her.

Short of fleeing through the back door or lying, she was stuck.

"As a matter of fact, it does. I stopped by to, uh, discuss a case, and decided to lend a hand with the house he's rehabbing."

Cate began to prowl around the kitchen.

Of course she found the remaining baklava.

"Well, well, well. What have we here?" She lifted the plastic-wrap-covered plate with the remaining pieces and tilted it toward Eve.

"You made baklava? In the middle of the summer?" Eve scrutinized her. "I thought you were too busy to make that except at Christmas. At least that's what you told *us*."

"She did it for the sheriff." Cate set the plate down, dropped the shoe to the floor, and leaned back against the counter beside Eve, expression smug. "This guy must rate. I can't wait to meet him."

"You make baklava for him but not for us?" Eve folded her arms and sniffed. "I'm insulted."

"He did me a favor, okay? But you guys are welcome to what's left."

Eve nudged Cate. "Did you notice that? We get the leftovers."

"I noticed. However, I'm not too proud to help finish this off for dessert. No one makes baklava like Grace."

"You realize what this means, don't you? If Ms. I-Hate-DIY

helped him paint and carved time out of her schedule to make him baklava, this guy has serious walk-down-the-aisle potential." Eve gave her a once-over as she directed that comment to Cate.

"Uh-huh. Lucky he passed the facts and figures background test or we'd be having a heart-to-heart about now. We'll have to see how he does in person."

"Hey." Grace set the shirt on the kitchen table and planted her fists on her hips. "I'm thirty years old. I can handle my social life without input from my two nosey older sisters, thank you very much."

Eve ignored her and took another sip of soda. "So are we in the way here? Is he stopping by later?"

"No, he is not stopping by. And FYI, we haven't even been on a date yet."

"But painting parties can be very romantic." Eve swirled the ice in her glass, a slow smile bowing her lips. "I speak from experience on that topic."

"When *are* you going out with him?" Cate loosened the plastic wrap over the baklava and pressed her index finger against a crumb.

"Saturday."

"Where?" Eve edged in again.

"To a restaurant. For dinner. And speaking of food, why don't we eat now? I'm starving."

"I think she's done talking." Cate popped her finger into her mouth and sucked off the crumb.

"I think you're right." Eve strolled over to the refrigerator, opened the door, and pulled out the barbecue. "I'm fine with the eat-now plan. Cate?"

"I'm in."

Thankfully, Nate didn't come up again as they stuffed themselves with barbecue, played a killer game of Scrabble, and lit sparklers in the yard as night fell.

Only as her sisters were getting ready to leave did the conversation shift from lighthearted to serious.

While Eve detoured for a pit stop, Cate cornered her in the kitchen. "I noticed the bid for security cameras tucked beside your toaster. What's up with that?"

Naturally her detective sister had spotted that document.

"The car keying spooked me."

"That didn't happen here."

"No." May as well give her a bit more detail. Otherwise Cate would keep up the third degree until she got answers. Besides, if she hemmed and hawed, Eve would come back and begin tag-teaming questions. "But someone did break the buds off my lily plants. I also found a sort of voodoo doll on my back porch a week ago. I thought it was prudent to enhance my security setup."

Cate frowned. "Why am I just hearing about this?"

"You're in St. Louis. What would be the point of telling you every tiny detail about my life?"

"Threats aren't tiny details."

"They weren't overt threats." Even if the news Nate had passed on yesterday after his discussion with Dave Mullins gave credence to that possibility. Especially since the incoming phone number on Tyler's cell for the vandalism incidents had matched the latest one on Mullins's burner phone.

"I'm assuming your sheriff is on this?"

"Yes."

"Any idea who's behind it?"

"No." That was true, as far as it went. But she agreed with Nate that BK was probably responsible for the incidents—whoever BK was.

"Watch your back, and keep your Beretta handy."

"That's my plan."

"You ready to hit the road?" Eve appeared from the hallway.

"Yes." Cate squeezed Grace's arm. "Let me find my purse."

While their oldest sister went in search of her bag, Eve strolled over to Grace. "So do you think this sheriff of yours could be The One?"

Grace huffed out a breath. With her sister in the throes of honeymoonitis, it wasn't surprising she would circle back to that topic. "I met him less than a month ago."

"I knew Brent was special right away."

She'd felt the same about Nate. But in case she was wrong, it might be safest not to create expectations.

"For now, all I'll say is that at the very least, I think this is the beginning of a beautiful friendship."

"*Casablanca.*" Cate rejoined them.

"If we're going to play the classic-movie-lines game, I'll add this." Eve put her hand on Grace's shoulder. "May the Force be with you."

"*Star Wars.*" Cate chimed in again. "And remember—a good man is, to paraphrase, the stuff that dreams are made of."

"*The Maltese Falcon.*" Eve high-fived Cate. "Although I like your context better."

"You know what I think?" Grace took their arms and tugged them toward the door. "There's no place like home—and tomorrow is another day."

"*The Wizard of Oz.*" Cate jingled her car keys.

"*Gone With the Wind.*" Eve followed their sister out the door.

"You guys are nuts." Grace gave them each a hug. "But I love you anyway."

"Mutual, I'm sure." Cate squeezed her back.

"*White Christmas.*" Eve grinned.

"Go home. And drive safe." Grace shooed them out.

"We will. Lock up." Cate looked back at her, all levity gone.

"I will. Talk to you both soon."

"Count on it." Eve followed Cate down the walkway to the car.

Grace waved them off, then retreated into the house and

locked the door, a smile lingering on her lips. The holiday hadn't turned out half bad—or boring—after all. Reilly sisters get-togethers were always lively.

But tomorrow would be all business, beginning with Lorraine's autopsy.

And depending on what she found, along with the results of the digitalis test on the sample from Mavis that Russ had sent to the lab yesterday, another conversation with the botanist at the university could be in her future.

While foxglove might not be the culprit in the deaths, the whole notion of botanical poison was intriguing. There were a host of readily available toxins found in nature that would never show up on a tox screen. Russ would balk at ordering dozens of random tests that strained the budget, but a forensic botanist could be helpful in this situation. Maybe her contact at the university would be able to recommend someone.

If Russ wouldn't pay for that sort of speculative analysis?

She'd spring for the cost herself.

Because when murder was involved, there shouldn't be a price on uncovering the truth.

22

LEE JORDAN DIDN'T EXIST.

At least not the one Dave Mullins thought worked at the hair salon.

But Jordan Lee Thompson did.

Nate tapped a finger against the steering wheel of the patrol car and scanned the lower-middle-class enclave Mullins's former paramour called home.

The neighborhood fit with what he'd found out about her, but getting here had required more work than he'd expected after online and database searches yielded zilch. In the end, it had taken an early morning call to the owner of the salon—followed by an in-person visit to prove he was, indeed, the sheriff—to uncover Lee Jordan's real name and address.

According to her boss, Thompson was the ex-wife of Alan Waters and former girlfriend of Corey Grant, against whom she'd had a restraining order. Hence the alias. No one in town but her boss knew her real name or history. Had it not been for the tax documents she'd had to fill out for the stylist job, the salon owner was certain she'd have kept him in the dark too.

Mullins hadn't been exaggerating when he said the woman had had her share of tough breaks.

And they might not be over yet.

Nate slid out of the cruiser, locked it, and strode toward her apartment half a block away. Parking at a distance should minimize the link between his visit and the woman he'd come to see. Why complicate her life any more than necessary if she was innocent?

But if she happened to be BK, or had information that could be helpful to his investigation, he needed her cooperation. Six people had died, Grace could be in danger, and criminal fraud had been committed.

If she refused to answer his questions?

He'd play hardball.

At the door to her unit, he stopped and pressed the bell.

Thirty seconds passed.

He rang again.

Nothing.

But she was here.

Per the salon owner, whenever she had a late-afternoon/evening shift like today, she always slept in. Or so she'd told her boss.

Nate resorted to knocking. Not his first choice, since that would draw more attention to the presence of law enforcement, but if she wasn't going to answer the bell, he had no choice.

"Ms. Jordan, I know you're home. If necessary, I'm prepared to wait here until you leave for work."

After a brief delay, a lock flipped inside and the door opened.

The woman who answered didn't look anything like the photo on the driver's license he'd pulled up after the salon owner gave him her real name and other vital statistics. Her blond hair was uncombed, she wasn't wearing a speck of makeup, and oversized glasses gave her an owlish appearance.

"Sheriff Cox, ma'am. May I speak with you for a few minutes?"

"Why?"

"I believe you have information about a case we're working on."

She tucked a lank strand of hair behind her ear. "What kind of case?"

"I'll be happy to discuss it inside."

After a brief hesitation, she pulled the door wide and stepped back.

Nate entered and gave the space a quick sweep.

The unit was small. One bedroom, based on the two doors that opened off the short hall. Furnishings were sparse and utilitarian. No personal items were on display, nor any photos that would identify the occupant.

It was the sort of place inhabited by a person who preferred to remain anonymous and wanted to be ready to disappear at a moment's notice.

Given Thompson's history, the bland, bare-bones decor wasn't surprising.

She remained near the closed front door, tugging at the hem of the loose T-shirt she wore over a pair of leggings, tension radiating from her.

"For the record, I know your real name and a bit of your history, Ms. Thompson."

No reply. Nor did she invite him to sit.

Fine.

He pulled out his notebook and remained standing. "I understand you're acquainted with Dave Mullins."

The knuckles on the hand gripping the bottom of her T-shirt whitened. "He used to be a client."

"He says he was more than that."

Her nostrils flared. "He told you about us?"

"Among other things."

A muscle in her jaw clenched. "Why are you here? Our relationship ended years ago."

"But he came to see you recently. Told you about his dilemma."

She assessed him, as if gauging how much to reveal. "Yes."

"Did you call in the tip to us about his relationship with Mavis Templeton and Fred Wilson?"

"Why would I do that?"

"Payback."

Her eyes hardened. "If I did, he deserved it. Do you know what Dave Mullins is?"

She told him in terms that made his ears ring, bitterness rolling off her in waves.

Man.

Carrying around that much hate would cast a cloak of misery over a person so thick that no sunlight could ever penetrate.

It was a terrible way to live.

But Jordan Lee Thompson's attitude issue hadn't prompted today's visit.

"I'll repeat my question. Did you call in the tip? I'm asking because other than the murderer, only you know the connection between Dave, Mavis, and Fred."

She blanched. "I had nothing to do with their deaths."

"Then you were the tipster, not the murderer."

A few seconds passed as she mulled over the options he'd given her.

"Yes. It's not a crime to call in a tip to the police. In fact, it's encouraged." Her chin rose a hair, but the strain in her voice undermined her defiant body language.

"That's true—as long as the caller is innocent."

"I haven't done anything wrong. And I have no idea who's blackmailing Dave or running the scheme he's fronting. I just wanted to make his life miserable."

"It already was."

"Okay. *More* miserable. And don't bother trying to play the guilt card. He brought on his own problems."

There was no disputing that.

"What do you know about Lorraine Meyers?"

Her face went blank. "Who?"

Unless she was a stellar thespian, Lorraine was a stranger to her.

But some murderers were excellent actors.

"Where were you on Wednesday?"

She frowned. "What is this all about?"

"I'm looking for an alibi."

"For what?"

"Another murder."

She drew in a sharp breath and latched on to the back of a chair inside the front door. "I was visiting a friend in St. Louis for the holiday. I can give you her name and contact information."

He lifted his notebook. "Whenever you're ready."

Yet as he jotted down the information, he mentally crossed Thompson off the suspect list. If she had an alibi, Mullins was right. This woman wasn't a murderer.

However, intimidated subjects who wanted to avoid being labeled suspects often offered helpful information in the course of trying to prove their innocence.

He finished writing . . . and waited.

She filled in the silence.

"Listen, I called the tip in to spite Dave, okay?" She shoved her hair back, fingers trembling. "The first I heard of the scheme was the day he came to the shop to ask me if I had any idea about who could be behind the blackmail."

"Do you?"

"No. I told that to Dave. I never mentioned him by name to anyone while I was seeing him. I don't know who took the photos at the inn and the reservoir."

So much for gleaning a helpful lead or two from this visit.

Nate closed his notebook, pulled out a card, and passed it

to her. "If any information you think may be helpful comes to mind, I'd appreciate a call. Whatever your feelings toward Mr. Mullins, multiple people have died. They deserve justice."

He reached past her, opened the door, and let himself out. End of story.

The odds of Thompson contacting him were lower than the seasonal pond on his parents' farm during an August drought.

Striding back to his patrol car, he kept tabs on his surroundings as he dodged burnt-out remnants from the fireworks that had been set off by residents last night. Like the victims in the fraudulent investment scheme, the charred shells littering the street and sidewalk had perished in the night, leaving no trace behind of the hand that had destroyed them.

He kicked a spent rocket out of his path.

They were getting nowhere in their quest to identify the perpetrator of the deaths of older residents and the incidents with Grace. Even if the foxglove test came back positive and they solved the mystery of the "how," they still didn't know who was behind it.

One thing for certain.

Jordan Lee Thompson wasn't BK—and she didn't have a clue who was.

So unless Grace's autopsy on Lorraine unearthed new evidence this morning, they were no closer to solving this case than they'd been before Tyler and Dave had come forward with intriguing but minimally useful information about the perpetrator.

Meaning more havoc could be wreaked at any moment by the cold-blooded killer in their midst.

"Would you get me another sample container, Max?" Grace made a few snips with her scissors, then picked up Lorraine's stomach from the large cutting board and poured the contents into a measuring cup through the slit.

There wasn't much. Most had been vomited out.

"Coming right up." Her autopsy tech hustled over to the tool table and returned with a jar, lid off and ready for the sample. "Sorry. I thought I had you covered."

"You did." After only a few autopsies together, he'd learned to anticipate her every move. She never had to ask for the autopsy saw after she made the shoulder-to-shoulder Y incision that went all the way down the center of the chest. Max was always standing by with it—and whatever else she needed. "I'm taking a couple of extra samples with this one."

Russ wandered over but kept his distance since he'd elected not to suit up. "Find anything interesting?"

"Routine so far."

He grunted and returned to the counter on the side of the room to refill his coffee.

The door to the morgue opened, and Grace glanced over as Nate entered. "Morning."

"Morning."

"You want a cup of coffee?" Russ lifted his disposable cup from across the room.

"Maybe later. How's it going?" He stopped a few feet away from the autopsy table, as Russ had.

Grace eyed him. His color was normal, unlike during his first visit. But still . . . "We shouldn't be much longer. I can brief you after we're done if you want to wait in the hall or outside."

"I'll stick around."

Huh.

His sensitivity training with the formalin/paint combo must have helped.

"We've dissected most of the organs and taken our samples." She adjusted the splash shield over her face and motioned toward the colander, scale, and bucket on the table. "I'm doing gastric contents now."

"Anything unusual?"

"No."

"You going to examine the brain?" Russ called the question over his shoulder as he added cream to his coffee.

"Yes."

Factoring in everything they knew, and appearances aside, there wasn't anything natural about Lorraine's demise. It was wiser to dot all the i's and cross all the t's.

Max positioned the head block, elevating the head. "You want me to make the cut?"

That would be a typical assistant duty—and Max always offered. But she still liked to do this hands-on part of the job on a regular basis.

"Not today, thanks." She picked up the scalpel and carefully cut from behind one ear, around the back of the skull, to behind the other ear.

"Do you have a cause of death?"

As Nate spoke, she set the scalpel down and gave the sheriff a once-over. As far as she could tell, he'd licked his formalin-smell problem.

"Unless I find some indication in the brain to suggest otherwise, yes." She worked the skin flaps into position and took the saw from Max.

"What is it?" Russ sipped his coffee.

Instead of answering, she revved up the saw and cut into the skull.

Only after the noise died down did she respond, all the while continuing the rote steps to free the brain. "Cardiac arrhythmia due to atherosclerotic coronary artery disease."

"Same as Mavis." Russ finished off his coffee.

"Yes."

"Could the flu have been a contributing factor?"

"I can't rule that out, but I'd say it's doubtful—assuming she even had the flu."

"Sudden death from heart issues is prevalent in older folks."

"I know. Which makes it a perfect mask for murder." She finished prying off the skull cap. "Give me a few minutes to finish up here and we can chat."

Russ backed off, leaving her in peace as she removed and examined the brain.

There was no evidence of trauma.

"I'm done, Max. Will you close for me?"

"Of course." He took her place, and as she walked away, she began stripping off her disposable protective gear.

Russ was waiting with Nate on the far side of the room.

"You holding the body or releasing it?" Russ threw his empty cardboard cup into the waste bin.

"Releasing. I have all the samples we'll need." She tugged off her cap. "I assume you're going with natural as manner if all the tox screens come back negative."

"Yes. Unless you see any evidence of homicide?"

"We have Dave Mullins's statement." Nate propped a shoulder against the wall and folded his arms.

"But he can't prove his claim—and neither can we." Russ stuck his thumbs into his belt loops. "We can always revise the manner if we find definitive evidence of foul play later."

"Did you ask the lab to rush the foxglove analysis?" Grace tugged off the elastic ponytail band, releasing her hair from the messy bun she favored during autopsies.

"Yes. They said a single test is faster to run and they may be able to have it by Monday."

"Excellent. That's much quicker than their usual turn-around." She tucked the band in the pocket of her slacks and continued removing the protective gear.

"Are we done here?" Russ checked his watch. "I have to

meet with a family to arrange a funeral. Wearing two hats can be a challenge."

"I'm finished." Grace discarded the disposable garments.

"I am too." Nate pushed off from the wall.

"I'll let you know as soon as I hear from the lab, Grace." Russ pulled out his keys and hustled toward the exit.

"Thanks."

As he disappeared, Nate waved toward the door. "I have an update for you. Want to talk about it outside?"

"Smell finally getting to you?"

"No. I think I finally made my peace with it."

"I applaud your creative solution. Outside is fine." She shifted toward the autopsy table. "You want me to hang around for the next few minutes, Max?"

"Nope. I've got it under control." He waved her off.

"I'll be back for my kit." Grace followed Nate into the hall and indicated the rear door. "There's a bench around the side, if you aren't familiar with the facility."

"First visit—but I'm sure it won't be my last." He opened the outside door for her. "This setup beats the funeral home for autopsies any day."

"I agree. But we wouldn't be here if we hadn't thought we might have to hold the body longer than usual. It's helpful that one of the counties in my territory has an actual morgue and was willing to accommodate us." At the corner of the building, she motioned toward the bench tucked into a small, flower-filled planting area.

He followed her over, waited until she sat, and claimed the other end. "I spoke with Mullins's love interest this morning. It was a dead end. She's not BK, and she hasn't a clue who could be blackmailing him."

Grace blew out a breath. "That's not what I wanted to hear."

"Me neither. I didn't expect her to be the perpetrator, but I hoped she'd offer a lead that would help us track down BK."

"Where do we go from here?"

"I've reached out to Lorraine's attorney to see if her financial pattern is similar to the one we've identified for all the victims Mullins named. I'm assuming it will be. Other than that, we wait for the foxglove test to come back and cross our fingers."

Grace angled toward him, resting one arm along the back of the bench. "Or we could be more proactive."

"How so?"

"Have you ever heard of forensic botany?"

"No."

"It's a small field. Forensic botanists work at crime scenes or provide botanical insights that can help solve crimes. The most famous example is the Lindbergh kidnapping case in the 1930s. The testimony that secured a conviction was provided by an expert on wood anatomy and identification."

"Seriously?"

"Yes. It had to do with the wood in the ladder used by the kidnapper. But experts can also analyze botanical trace evidence from the plant cells found in gastric contents."

He squinted at her. "You're thinking we should send a sample of the stomach contents from one of our victims to a forensic botanist."

"Yes."

"It's not a bad idea, if your theory of botanical poison is correct. Can this type of analysis also be used for other kinds of poisons?"

"No. It has to be a food sample with a cell wall—like plants. It doesn't even work for identifying meat, because all skeletal muscles look alike."

"Any idea how much that sort of analysis would cost?"

"No. I can research the price, though. But in light of Russ's reaction to the expense of a foxglove screen, I imagine he'd consider any amount too much to spend to pursue such a speculative theory."

Nate crossed an ankle over a knee. "It may be a moot point, depending on the result of the foxglove test—and we could have that by Monday."

That was true. And if the result was positive, they had their manner of death. No further screening would be necessary.

If it was negative, however, Russ would be less inclined than ever to want to spring for what would be a much more expensive testing procedure.

Nate would go to bat for her if she pushed, but pitting him against the long-entrenched county coroner at this early stage of his career wouldn't be fair. Relationships mattered in this business.

The smart move would be to let this ride for now. With Nate, anyway.

"I can't argue with that, and Monday is only three days away." Though she didn't have all that much confidence the lab would send the results that fast, no matter what they'd told Russ.

"While you're waiting"—Nate leaned closer—"I promise to do my best to distract you with activities that don't involve tox screens. Think lakeside dining and dancing."

His slow smile and the warmth in his voice set her nerve endings aflutter.

"I have to admit those kinds of thoughts do tend to override other concerns."

"Then keep them front and center, and come tomorrow—" Twin furrows appeared on his brow, and he pulled out his cell. "It's Eleanor. Must be a call from dispatch she thinks needs my attention."

"Go ahead and take it. I should head out."

"I'll walk with you as far as the parking lot while I talk to her."

They returned to the back of the building as he conversed with the woman. He was still on the phone getting details about what sounded like a domestic violence incident as they parted.

Grace returned to the morgue for her kit, said goodbye to Max, and left the building again.

Nate was gone.

His promise about their date, however, lingered in her mind like the aromas wafting from a kitchen on Thanksgiving . . . a tantalizing hint of deliciousness to come.

And tomorrow night, she didn't intend to let any negative or unsettling concerns interfere with what boded to be an unforgettable evening.

In the interim, however, the fraud-related murders would remain top of mind. And she didn't have to wait for Russ's approval to pursue answers.

Maybe her theory was totally off base. Maybe every test they ran would come back benign. Maybe the murderer had, indeed, devised the perfect homicide.

But she wasn't about to cede victory to BK until every stone had been overturned.

The sooner the better.

23

KIMBERLY WAS HOME.

Stomach clenching, Dave closed the lid on his laptop as the front door opened, then shut. He'd offered to run her to and from work for her Saturday morning shift at the library, but she'd called a friend instead. Perhaps an omen of the new, independent life she seemed intent on creating.

A life that wasn't likely to include him.

The fact she'd agreed to let him stay in the house after he'd explained why that was important to law enforcement didn't mean she was anywhere close to letting him back into her heart. That would take forgiveness.

And while their minister had hopefully offered counseling based on the tenets of their faith during her meeting with him last night, forgiveness could be a long way down the road.

The tap of her cane on the hardwood floor in the hallway signaled her approach.

She stopped in his office doorway. "Do you have a few minutes?"

Pulse lurching, he straightened up. She must be ready to talk. "Yes." Somehow he choked out the assent.

"Let's go out to the screened porch." Without waiting for him to respond, she retreated.

Steeling himself for bad news, he followed her down the hall, through the family room, and into the bright space that overlooked her back garden. The sweet scent of honeysuckle wafted through the air, borne by a gentle breeze on this unusually temperate July afternoon, and he filled his lungs. But the pleasant fragrance didn't mitigate the sour taste of fear on his tongue.

She turned on the ceiling fan and sat on the settee.

"Can I get you a glass of lemonade?" He stopped in the doorway.

"I'm not thirsty."

"I made you a turkey sandwich for lunch. It's in the fridge. Would you like that?"

"Maybe later. After we talk."

The churning in his stomach increased. She'd come to a decision he probably didn't want to hear.

But there was no sense delaying the inevitable.

He crossed to the chair on the other side of the coffee table from the settee and lowered himself onto the cushion as his legs gave out.

"Reverend Patterson and I had a long . . . talk last night." Kimberly picked at a loose chip of paint on the wicker, brow knitted. "I didn't tell him anything about . . . the blackmail or fraud. Just . . . the affair."

The ugly word sickened him, and bile rose in his throat.

When he didn't speak, she continued. "I've also been thinking . . . and praying. And I've tried to put myself in your place. To wonder, if the situation had been reversed, whether I would have sought comfort in the arms of . . . another man." She lifted her chin and met his gaze. "I don't think I would have."

He already knew that. In their marriage, Kimberly had always been the glue. The strong one whose buoyant optimism, determination, and rock-solid values and faith had helped them weather countless storms—including the death of their son.

That's why he'd been lost after the accident. Without her steadying, loving presence, he'd floundered . . . and sought solace wherever he could.

He was, and had always been, the weak link in their relationship.

"I'm well aware of my character flaws, Kimberly." His shoulders sagged. "I've never had your grit and courage and fortitude, nor your unshakable values. I know I stumbled, and—"

"Dave." She leaned forward. "I didn't tell you that to . . . denigrate your character. I'm just saying it's been very hard for me to . . . understand how you could have done what you did." Her phrasing was more halting and choppy than usual, but she persisted. "The thing is, though . . . maybe I don't have to. Maybe I have to accept that no one is perfect and . . . and that people can cave under enough pressure. We all have our breaking point."

She sat back and twisted her hands together in her lap. "There's a lot I don't understand . . . but here's what I do know. During all the years of our marriage before the accident, you were a loving, devoted husband . . . who I trusted with all my heart and soul. As far as I know, you never betrayed that trust."

"I didn't." *God, please let her believe that!* "You were always the center of my world."

She searched his face . . . then continued. "I also know that since the day I woke up from the coma, you've done everything you can to help me recover. You work harder than any man I know. You've dedicated your life to making mine as . . . close to normal as possible. Nothing I ask you to do is too much trouble. Your tender care has touched my heart day after day . . . year after year. Bad as the accident was, good also came from it. It made me love you more than I already did."

Dave gripped the arms of his chair, bracing for the *but*.

It didn't come.

As the silence between them lengthened, he drew a shaky breath and tried to tamp down the tiny spark of hope that sprang to life in his soul. "What are you saying?"

A tear welled on her lower eyelid. "When you told me your story, my first instinct was to walk away. In fact, if someone had asked me . . . in the past what I would do in a situation like this, that's what I would have predicted. But I know you're sorry, and I can . . . imagine the despair and hopelessness you felt four years ago. I also realize that if you hadn't loved me as much as you did . . . your sense of loss wouldn't have been as overwhelming. You did what you did *because* you loved me so much, not because your love for me had faded."

That was a spin he'd never considered.

But it was true.

And while it didn't excuse what he'd done, it did help explain why his life had spiraled out of control after her bleak prognosis.

The question was, what did Kimberly's take on all this mean going forward?

"Are you saying you can forgive me?" Even as he broached the question, it seemed too much to hope for.

"I'm working on it. My mind has accepted everything I've told you . . . but my heart isn't quite there yet. I need time to absorb and adjust and . . . come to terms with the situation. I do know I'm not ready to walk away from everything we've had, or throw away the future we may still have. I love you too much." She pulled a tissue from her pocket and dabbed at a tear that rolled down her cheek.

He rose, circled the coffee table, and sat on the settee beside her—close but not touching, his own throat so tight he could hardly speak. "I love you too, Kimberly. I always have and always will. With all my heart. I'll do whatever I have to do to rebuild what we had. You set the ground rules, and I'll follow them."

"Are you willing to stay in the guest room for now?"

"For as long as it takes." He swallowed. "For as long as I'm here."

She scrutinized him. "You're thinking you'll end up in prison."

"I broke the law."

"The people who died . . . that wasn't your fault."

"A judge and jury may not agree."

"But you're cooperating with law enforcement."

"That may help, but there are no guarantees. I also stole a large amount of money."

"Not for yourself."

"Stealing is stealing. Prison is a very real possibility, Kimberly." He wasn't going to sugarcoat the truth.

She laid her cold fingers on his. "Whatever happens, I'll be here—waiting."

His vision misted. What had he done to deserve such a generous, forgiving, loving woman? "I don't know how to begin to thank you."

"Just keep loving me."

"Until the day I die."

She twined her fingers with his. "Do you want to sit out here together for a while?"

"I'd like that."

Silence fell, broken only by the chirp of a bird in the oak tree beside the screened porch and the muted laughter of children at play in a neighboring yard. The ordinary sounds of everyday, normal life.

But to him, they sounded like Handel's *Messiah*.

For despite all he'd done . . . despite his many faults and weaknesses and mistakes . . . the woman he adored still loved him.

And no matter how many years he might have to spend in prison paying for his crimes, she'd honor her promise to wait for him until he returned to her.

As far as he was concerned, that was a miracle—and as close as he'd ever get to heaven on earth.

Blast.

He was going to have to cancel their dinner date.

Bracing the heels of his hands on the bathroom vanity, Nate tried to will the roiling in his stomach into submission.

Didn't work.

He emptied the last of the leftover pizza he'd had for lunch into the toilet, then closed his eyes and leaned against the wall.

The flu had struck, and it was nasty. In the space of two hours, he'd progressed from chills to body aches to high fever to puking his guts out.

All he wanted to do was crawl back into bed, pull up the covers, and die.

His plans for a romantic evening of fine dining, witty repartee, and a slow dance under the twinkling lights on the deck at the lakeside restaurant were toast.

Double blast.

Pushing off from the wall, he dragged himself back to bed and crawled under the covers. Before he crashed, he ought to drink fluids and take aspirin—but he didn't have the energy to do either.

He hardly had the energy to phone Grace.

But he owed her a call. Otherwise she'd waste a lot of effort preparing for a date that wasn't going to happen. It was already after two.

He reached for his cell on the nightstand, a maneuver that took far more effort than it should have, and pressed her number.

As her phone began to ring, he eased back onto the pillow and stared at the ceiling.

"Well hello, Sheriff Cox. I didn't expect to hear from you until your Jeep pulled up in front of my house tonight."

Based on her upbeat, excited tone, she was going to be as disappointed in the change of plans for tonight as he was.

"About that." He turned on his side and pulled up his legs as the muscles in his stomach spasmed. Again.

"Uh-oh." A cautionary note crept into her voice. "Are you bailing on me?"

"Not by choice." He pressed a hand against his stomach. "I have the flu."

"Oh, Nate. I'm sorry."

"You and me both. It hit about noon. And I do mean hit. Within ninety minutes, I was flat on my back. Since then, I've been in bed or worshiping the porcelain goddess. I'm really sorry about having to cancel."

"Don't apologize. The flu can knock you flat. Are you drinking fluids and keeping the fever under control?"

"Yes." Or he would be, as soon as he mustered the energy to get up and take a few therapeutic measures.

"Can I do anything for you?"

"Yes. Keep your distance. I wouldn't wish these symptoms on my worst enemy." His midsection cramped again, and a wave of nausea swept over him. How on earth could there be anything left in his stomach?

"Are you certain I can't help? I could drop a care package at your door."

He swung his feet to the floor and waited a moment until the room stabilized. "No. I have everything I need." He stood, hanging on to the headboard for support as his stomach began to heave. "Listen, I have to go. I think the volcano is about to erupt again—and formalin isn't the culprit this go-round."

"Call me if I can do a grocery or pharmacy run."

"I will. Talk to you soon."

He ended the call and staggered to the bathroom. Barely got there in time.

Once he finished upchucking, he sat on the toilet seat and dropped his head into his hands.

Aspirin, clear soda, and rest. Those were his priorities.

Thank goodness he was off duty this weekend and the fraud/murder case was quiet at the moment. Since Mullins hadn't yet been instructed to sign up any new "customers," none of the county's older residents should be in imminent danger.

But the minute he was feeling halfway normal, he'd be back on this—regardless of the foxglove test results.

Because Grace was right.

Despite the manner noted on the official death certificates for the six people Mullins had identified as fraud victims, their demises were anything but natural. Every one of them had been murdered.

And he wasn't going to rest until he did everything in his power to identify the person who was targeting gullible seniors in desperate need of extra income, then sucking them into a scheme that promised to solve all their monetary problems.

Which it did.

After all, money problems vanished once you were dead.

———————

Grace Reilly had to go. Soon. While the window of opportunity remained open.

There had been too many autopsies.

BK knocked back a shot of scotch on the rocks and slammed the empty glass on the counter.

How to get rid of her wasn't an issue. That would be a piece of cake. And the flu epidemic provided the perfect cover.

The big question was when to do it.

A niggle of guilt raised its ugly head, but BK quashed it at once. Remorse had no place in this scheme. Yes, it was a shame the pathologist had to be stopped. Unlike the older folks who'd been targeted, who contributed nothing and were a drain on society, Grace Reilly had decades of productive life ahead of her.

But what other choice was there? The woman hadn't paid any attention to the warnings, and she kept raising red flags about unremarkable deaths that should have slipped under the radar of law enforcement.

It would be helpful to know what had aroused her suspicions . . . and it might still be possible to glean that information.

Not that it should matter much going forward. Without her in the picture, stirring the pot—and lacking any proof of foul play—the sheriff's hands would be tied and the coroner would be content with taking future deaths at face value.

That's why the pathologist had to be dealt with soon. Before it was time to enlist Dave to contact another candidate about his once-in-a-lifetime investment opportunity.

Before heart issues claimed the next victim.

BK rinsed out the glass, stashed the half-empty bottle of scotch under the sink, and strolled down the hall, pausing to straighten a nighttime photo of the illuminated Eiffel Tower. A bucket-list item that had already been crossed off. But there were others, and with the funding scheme in place, the rest were within reach.

Of course, being able to live the high life every day would be preferable to stealing away on occasion to play in the fast lane—but there was no way to do that without arousing suspicion, short of claiming to be the beneficiary of a windfall bequest from a long-lost relative.

A possibility that could be worth toying with if the game got old and the offshore account grew sufficiently to sustain a different full-time lifestyle far away from rural Missouri.

BK continued to the bedroom and released the latch on the hinged painting that hid the safe. How providential that the previous owner had been paranoid enough to install such a hiding place in a house located in a quiet, middle-class neighborhood populated by folks who tended to live paycheck to paycheck.

But unless he too had been leading a secret life, he'd never used it to store the kind of treasure now hidden inside.

BK worked the combination until the lock released, then pulled open the door and removed the box inside. Carried it over to the bed. Lifted the lid and fingered the contents.

Smiled.

In many ways, this tangible proof of success was more real than the online statements for the offshore account. This, you could touch. Feel. Weigh in your hand.

Even if you couldn't flaunt it, and no one in this rural setting would ever see it.

BK closed the lid, ran a finger along the edge, and replaced the box in the safe, completing what had become a satisfying nightly ritual.

There was no lingering tonight, however. Once the box was tucked away, there were strategies to devise and plans to make.

Eliminating Grace Reilly was the top priority, even though the threat she represented had to be minimal. No matter what had made her suspicious about Fred and Mavis and Lorraine, she couldn't have a clue about the actual cause of death. But with her dogged personality, she'd remain on high alert—and she'd keep raising questions in the mind of the sheriff and coroner. Plus, if she kept digging, it was possible she'd stumble across some piece of information that would lead her down a path that came uncomfortably close to the truth.

That wasn't acceptable.

As for Dave—his visit to the sheriff's office was a bit troubling, as was the tip that had been called in about him.

However, considering how much he loved his wife, he'd be a fool to admit anything to law enforcement. The sheriff had zero proof of his involvement in the scheme. And if Dave did tell him details, he'd also have to explain *why* he got involved. Meaning he'd have to spill his guts to both the sheriff and Kimberly.

In light of the lengths he'd gone to thus far to safeguard his marriage, an anonymous tip wouldn't convince him to fold. Why risk losing his wife and going to prison just to salve his conscience over the death of a few seniors who were probably going to die soon anyway?

He must have come up with some story to pass on to the sheriff as a follow-up to the man's visit.

BK flipped off the light in the bedroom and returned to the kitchen. Pulled a pad of paper and a pen from a drawer and sat at the table.

It was time to list next steps in the elimination plan, starting with a deadline and working backward.

After tapping the end of the pen against the blank sheet of paper, BK wrote in a date.

Saturday, July 13

By one week from today, Grace Reilly would be dead.

24

"**M**ORNING, GRACE. I don't usually see you in here on Sunday." Jolene stopped beside the window table at the Spotted Hen, order pad and pencil in hand.

"Hi, Jolene." Grace set the menu down. "I went to the early service and was in the mood for a splurge breakfast this morning." Especially after her much-anticipated date last night had failed to materialize.

"You came to the right place. If you want to indulge, go for the western skillet special with a side of biscuits. That'll hold you till dinner. Guaranteed."

"Sold."

Jolene picked up the menu and tucked it under her arm. "You're lucky you got a plum table. Usually we're packed on Sunday mornings, with a long line waiting to get in."

Grace surveyed the three-quarters-full restaurant. "What's going on?"

"One word—flu." The waitress shook her head. "Folks are dropping like flies. I understand our sheriff's the latest victim."

Was there anything this woman didn't know?

"How did you find out about that?"

"One of the deputies stopped in earlier for coffee. Nate must have passed the news on to his second-in-command,

and Deke shared it with the crew on weekend duty." The woman waved at a newly arrived family group and motioned toward an empty table.

"It's a bad bug, that's for sure."

"Must be, if it can fell someone as hale and hearty as Nate. That means none of us are safe." She pursed her lips. "Maybe I'll run a plate of food over to him after I get off duty."

"I applaud your charitable impulse, but I don't think he's in the mood to eat yet."

Jolene studied her. "How would you know that?"

Whoops. She'd walked straight into that one.

"I, uh, talked with him earlier by phone. About a case."

That was true. She *had* mentioned Friday's autopsy when she'd called him after church—but her main purpose had been to see how he was feeling.

"Must be a hot case, if you two spoke on a Sunday." Jolene continued to assess her.

"All cases are hot until they're solved."

"Uh-huh." Jolene stuck the pencil behind her ear, lips twitching. "I'm thinking that's not all that's hot around here—and I'm not talking about the weather." With a wink, she moved on to the table of new arrivals.

Grace rolled her eyes. So much for keeping her relationship with Nate under wraps. If Jolene had picked up on the electricity zipping between the two of them, the rest of the county wouldn't be far behind.

Her cell pinged, and she pulled it out of her purse.

A text from Eve.

At least she'd waited two hours longer than Cate had to ask about last night's date.

Grace scanned the message.

How was your dinner?

May as well answer their questions and be done with this.

She typed in a response.

Didn't happen. He's down for the count with the flu.

Bummer.

Yep.

Did he reschedule yet?

No. He's too sick to think about romance.

Guys are never too sick to think about romance.

I'm cutting him some slack until he recovers.

Take him soup.

The very offer she'd extended this morning. But Nate had extracted a promise that she'd keep her distance until he was certain he wasn't contagious anymore.

Thanks for the advice.

What are sisters for? I'll check back with you in a couple of days for an update.

Don't bother. I'll keep you in the loop.

Ha. I'll check back.

Fine. Brief Cate, okay? She texted this a.m. too.

Will do. Sorry about the date.

Me too. But we'll make up for it.

Hold that thought.

Grace stowed her phone as Jolene delivered a steaming cup of coffee and a glass of juice.

"Enjoy, honey. Too bad you have to eat alone, though."

"I'm used to it."

"More's the pity—but it may not be a permanent situation." Grinning, she bustled off to answer a summons from another customer.

Oh brother.

While small-town living had many charms, it appeared privacy wasn't one of them.

But an active grapevine and a modicum of nosiness were more than worth the aggravation for a payoff like Nate.

He felt like he'd been hit by a truck.

And he wasn't in the mood for company.

But if someone was ringing his doorbell on this Tuesday morning at—he squinted in the direction of the bedside clock—seven forty-five, they must have an urgent reason to see him.

After leveraging himself upright with considerable effort, he tugged on the jeans he'd dropped on the floor three days ago, pulled on a T-shirt, and padded barefoot to the front door.

Eleanor stood on the other side, holding a large Tupperware container.

"Sorry to come calling this early, but I'm on a mission of mercy." She sized him up and shook her head. "None too soon, either. You look like death warmed over."

"Good morning to you too—and keep your distance. I wouldn't wish this bug on my worst enemy."

"Do you still have a fever?"

"No."

"Then you're probably not contagious anymore."

"Let's not take that risk. You're leaving on your trip next weekend, and I don't want you to get sick."

Twin creases appeared on her forehead. "Maybe I should cancel. With you under the weather and half the department on vacation, someone has to keep the office running."

"Don't even think about it. I'll be back in fighting form in another day or so, and all your plans are made."

"I could go later in the summer. My cousin won't mind. It's not as if we have anything special planned. Just our usual traipsing around the backroads of Maine."

"No. Don't cancel. I'll be back up to speed before you leave."

"If you change your mind, let me know." She passed over the container. "I wanted to drop this off for you on my way to the office. It's homemade chicken-rice soup with vegetables. More healing than any medicine you could take."

She'd gone to the trouble to make him soup?

Pressure built in his throat at the act of kindness. "Thank you. I appreciate this more than I can say."

She shrugged, but a tiny blush crept over her cheeks. "It was my pleasure. Besides, I have to keep my mocha Monday provider healthy." One corner of her mouth twitched.

A positive sign.

It had taken five months, but perhaps his concerted effort to break down the barriers between employees at different levels in the department—and to win her over—was finally paying dividends.

"I'll enjoy every spoonful."

"Stay home until you get back on your feet. We'll keep the place running."

Without waiting for a reply, she descended the two steps from his front porch and hurried toward her car.

Nate closed the door and trudged into the kitchen, weighing the soup in his hand. Tangible proof that decent, kind people did exist despite the violence and hate and lawlessness he spent his days battling.

Not a bad start to this Tuesday.

And while soup wasn't a typical breakfast item, all of a sudden it seemed like the perfect meal to break his flu-induced fast. It was time to get real food into his stomach.

It was also time to give Grace a call, let her know he was returning to the land of the living, and get a new date on the calendar for their dinner at the romantic lakeside restaurant.

As soon as he downed a bowl of Eleanor's soup and took a much-needed shower.

———

The foxglove test done on the contents of Mavis's stomach had come back in the normal range. She hadn't been poisoned with digitalis.

Stifling her disappointment, Grace maneuvered her car around a slow-moving tractor as she responded to Russ's news. "I appreciate you letting me know the results as soon as you got them."

"I know you were hoping this would prove Mullins's claim that these people were murdered, but as far as I can tell, we're back to square one."

Not quite.

Yesterday, the forensic botanist had confirmed receipt of the sample she'd sent on Friday, promising to give it top priority after Grace filled her in on the multiple deaths under investigation.

Of course, if a non-botanical type of poison had been used, they really were back to square one.

"I'm still noodling on a few ideas, Russ. Have you passed this information on to Nate yet?"

"No. Next call. You know we don't have the budget to go chasing after a bunch of half-baked theories, right?"

"Yes."

Several silent seconds inched by.

292

"You aren't going to ask Nate to put pressure on me to do more tests, are you?"

She frowned and pressed harder on the accelerator, watching the tractor shrink in her rearview mirror. Pushing the speed limit wasn't wise, but she was already running late for this morning's autopsy in the next county. "Why would I do that?"

"I can tell you're not happy with this outcome, and I don't think you've given up on the theory that we're dealing with poison."

"That's true. But you and Nate can work out the particulars on further testing."

"You have his ear."

Sheesh. Even Russ was picking up on their budding relationship.

"Before we worry about next steps, give me a few days to think about the data we have and review the autopsy reports again."

"No hurry from my end. Now that Mullins has come forward and is working with us, I don't think we have to worry about any more victims."

"I agree." Down the road, the railroad gates began to descend as a train whistle wailed in the distance.

Well, crud. Another delay.

"You want to call Nate, or shall I?"

"I can call him. I'm stuck at a railroad crossing with nothing else to do." She applied the brakes and coasted to a stop.

"That works. Talk to you soon."

After turning on the engine, she called Nate.

He answered on the second ring. "Morning."

Her lips curved up. "You sound almost back to normal."

"I'm beginning to feel human again. Guess what I had for breakfast?"

The bells on the gate began clanging. "I don't know, but I guarantee it was tastier than my stale bagel."

"It was. Where are you?"

"En route to an autopsy, but I'm currently stuck at a railroad crossing. What did you have for breakfast?"

"Homemade soup, hand-delivered by Eleanor."

Her mouth began to water. "No kidding?"

"For real. She's all business at the office, but under that by-the-book exterior beats a heart of gold."

"How was it?"

"Delicious."

"Is it staying down?"

"Yep. I'm on the mend."

"That's great. I wish the news I have for you was as positive." She told him about the results of the foxglove test.

His sigh came over the line. "I was hoping we were on to something with that theory."

"I haven't given up on it yet."

"You have forensic botany on your mind, don't you?"

She tapped a finger against the steering wheel. Why not tell him about the initiative she'd taken? It wasn't as if she was asking taxpayers to foot the bill to satisfy her curiosity, after all.

"Guilty as charged. In fact, I called my contact at the university last week, got a recommendation for a forensic botanist, and sent off a sample Friday."

"Does Russ know about this?"

"No. It's on my dime."

"No one expects you to pay for forensic testing, Grace."

Russ might, since they had no solid evidence to suggest such analysis would lead anywhere, but she left that unsaid.

"If it produces any helpful information, I'll submit a bill for reimbursement."

"We need to discuss this."

"After you're back on your feet."

"I'm standing as we speak—and I'm planning to go back to work tomorrow."

"Don't rush the healing process." She glanced in her rear-view mirror as another car pulled up behind her.

"Eleanor is threatening to cancel her trip if I'm out of commission for too long."

"She is one dedicated employee."

"I think our county lucked out on the dedication front. We have a very committed forensic pathologist too."

Warmth filled her at his praise. "I'm just doing my job."

"Above and beyond."

"It takes one to know one."

"Let's switch gears."

A man who was more comfortable giving than receiving compliments and didn't require ego-stroking.

Nice.

"Okay." The train continued to rumble by. "I have nowhere to go and nothing else to do at the moment. My time is yours."

"I hope that will be true on Saturday night too."

Her pulse picked up. "You want to reschedule our dinner date?"

"Did you think I was going to forget about it?"

"No." Maybe. Until a date was on the calendar, it wasn't a date. "Do you think you'll be up to it?"

"It may not be a late night, but I'm game to give it a go if you are."

"Count me in." The end of the train came into sight in the distance. Thank goodness it had been a short one.

"I'll touch base with you to discuss details later in the week. Back to business for a minute. How soon do you expect to hear from the botanist?"

"Best case, end of week. After I told her how many people had died, she promised to bump my testing higher up in the queue and expedite the process as much as possible."

"So we may have answers by our date."

"About *how* the deed was done. The who remains a mystery."

"It won't forever. When BK calls Mullins with the next victim, I intend to have a serious conversation with said victim on the q.t. to see who they've talked with in the past few weeks. It's possible this BK has been in direct contact with them. All of the other victims were dead before we got to them."

"Excellent point." The gates began to rise, and she turned on the engine. "Gotta run. The train has passed. I'll have to pull out all the stops as it is to get to my autopsy."

"Understood, but drive safe. Expect to hear from me in a day or two."

"Take care of yourself."

"That's the plan."

As they said their goodbyes, she put the car in gear and rattled over the bone-jarring railroad tracks. Once clear of them, she pressed on the accelerator, sped toward the next county—and prayed the botany screen would provide answers.

Because if it didn't, they were at a stalemate.

Meaning someone could end up getting away with multiple murders.

25

"HAPPY WEDNESDAY, ELEANOR." Instead of passing by the woman's desk, Nate detoured her direction and set a lidded cardboard cup and the empty soup container in front of her.

"What's this?" She indicated the cup.

"Your mocha."

"Today's not Monday."

"It's a thank-you for this." He rested his fingers on the piece of Tupperware.

"That wasn't necessary."

"I disagree. I think your soup expedited my recovery. And my taste buds appreciated it too."

"I'm glad you enjoyed it." She picked up the empty container and moved it to the top of the filing cabinet behind her desk. "I have to say you do look more like yourself today."

"I'm *feeling* more like myself. Anything I should know before I plunge back in?"

"Nothing critical. Russ stopped in yesterday to see you, but as far as I know there haven't been any deaths that required him to wear his coroner's hat since Lorraine Meyers passed. Do you really think there was foul play involved in that one?"

"Yes."

"My." She expelled a breath. "Such goings-on can make a body paranoid. I've been watching over my shoulder ever since I heard about Fred and Mavis." She glanced around, leaned closer, and lowered her voice. "Not to be nosey, but how on earth did you figure out their deaths weren't natural?"

"I didn't. Dr. Reilly gets all the credit."

The woman gave a knowing nod. "I knew the first time I met her she was smart. Did she spot something suspicious during the autopsies?"

"Yep. Sunflower seeds."

Eleanor did a double take. "Sunflower seeds? You mean like the kind you plant in the garden?"

"Or eat."

"They aren't dangerous, are they? I've seen them on the shelf at the grocery store."

"Not that I know of, but—" His cell began to vibrate and he pulled it out. Skimmed the screen. "Speaking of the good doctor . . ." He lifted the phone. "After I take this call, I'll be playing catch-up in my office."

She waved him down the hall. "I'll try to divert anyone who comes by until your head's above water."

"Thanks." He put the phone to his ear and continued toward his office. "Morning. I was going to call you in an hour or two to talk about Saturday."

"You're never going to believe this."

He frowned as he entered his office and shut the door behind him. "What's wrong? You don't sound like yourself."

"I don't feel like myself. More like one of the zombies in *Night of the Living Dead*."

He halted. "You've got the flu."

"Bingo."

He expelled a breath and ran his fingers through his hair. "I'm really sorry. When did it hit?"

"About two o'clock yesterday afternoon, as I was finishing my second autopsy. I barely made it home."

"Tell me what I can do."

"Nothing. You know the drill. It has to run its course. I've got aspirin and fluids on hand. Did you go to work?"

"Yes." He dropped into his swivel chair and surveyed the stacks of documents waiting for his attention. Sighed. "And the state of my desk would suggest it's going to be a long day."

"Don't push yourself. Whatever you don't get to will be there tomorrow."

"Says the woman who works nights and weekends."

"No comment. And I won't be working *this* weekend—or doing much else."

"You know, at this rate that date of ours is never going to happen."

"Trust me, it'll happen. I'm nothing if not persistent about priorities. Our date qualifies." A rustle came over the line, like she'd turned over in bed or was getting up.

"Lay low until the worst passes, okay?"

"I couldn't lift a scalpel today if my life depended on it. I canceled the autopsies I had scheduled for the rest of the week and told the coroners to put the bodies on ice. I should be able to get to them by Monday."

"Don't count on it. Besides, you could still be contagious."

"Not a problem. In my line of work, I don't have to worry about exposing my customers to germs."

One side of his mouth quirked up. Despite being sick as a dog, Grace hadn't lost her sense of humor.

"I'm smiling here."

"I'm glad someone is." A small groan came over the line. "I have to go. Vesuvius is about to erupt again. Talk to you soon."

The line went dead.

His mouth flattened as he lowered the phone and pressed the off button. He knew exactly how she was feeling. Two hours into his own bout with the flu, dragging his body to the bathroom had required superhuman effort.

Maybe he ought to run over and—

Someone rapped on his door, and he swung toward it. "Come in."

Eleanor peeked inside. "Am I interrupting a call?"

"No. I just hung up. The flu's claimed another victim."

"Dr. Reilly's sick?" The woman tut-tutted. "Poor thing. And she doesn't have any family close by to take care of her, either."

No, but she had him—and despite their postponed date, he didn't have to be a stranger during her recuperation.

But Eleanor didn't need to know that.

"She seems very capable of taking care of herself."

"Yes, she does." Eleanor crossed to his desk. "But a bug like that can knock you flat, as you know. And it can be dangerous, even for younger people. I'll say a prayer for a fast recovery."

"I'm sure she'd appreciate that."

"I meant to give you these earlier, but the mocha distracted me." She handed him several message slips. "I passed on most of the calls to Deke, but there were a few I thought you'd want to address yourself."

He flipped through them. "I'll add them to my to-do list."

"You should take it easy your first day back."

Like that would happen.

"I'll try."

"You know . . . I never expected to say this, but you work harder than Sheriff Blake."

High praise coming from a woman who'd idolized her former boss.

"I appreciate the compliment. He left big shoes to fill."

She sniffed and adjusted the crisp cuff on her sleeve. "You're doing fine."

With that, she retreated, closing the door behind her.

How about that? Eleanor was finally accepting him and his new, more informal style.

That was one piece of positive news.

Now if he could get a handle on the fraud deaths and put away the person who'd committed multiple murders—and who had Grace in their sights—all would be well.

In the meantime, he wasn't about to let her suffer alone with the flu. If he could, he'd follow Eleanor's advice to cut the day short. And on his way home, he'd swing by Grace's house with a supply of her favorite iced tea and the biggest bouquet of roses he could find. Neither would cure the flu, but they might perk up her spirits.

Unfortunately, despite his best intentions, fate conspired against him. Not only did he end up working later than usual, but en route to the store to buy both items for Grace he got called by the responding deputy to a suspected arson scene.

As he switched gears and tried to shore up his flagging energy, he tapped in Grace's number.

The phone rolled to voicemail.

She must be sleeping. After multiple bouts of upchucking and a fever that kept spiking, she had to be as wiped out as he'd been. In fact, his call earlier in the afternoon had awakened her.

It was probably smarter to leave a message today and stop by tomorrow anyway. He wouldn't have wanted anyone showing up at *his* door during the first twenty-four hours.

Smothering a yawn, he waited for the beep.

"I hope the worst has passed, Grace, and that you're resting. I'll be working late and won't bother you again today in case you're trying to sleep. But if you need anything, call me." He hesitated . . . then threw caution to the wind. "I'll be thinking about you—day and night."

He ended the call and stowed the phone, already second-guessing his impulsiveness. Maybe being that up-front had been too much, too soon. After all, they'd met a mere month ago.

But he'd spoken the truth. She *was* dominating his thoughts. Had been almost from day one. And her assurance that their twice-canceled date would happen was solid evidence he was on her mind too.

At least they didn't have to worry about any imminent fraud-related deaths, now that Mullins had come forward. If BK contacted the man about a new victim, Mullins's next call would be to law enforcement. All should be quiet.

Unless BK decided to ratchet up the threats on Grace in the interim—or move beyond mere warnings.

Despite the hot sun piercing the windshield, a chill raced through him as he barreled down the two-lane road toward the fire.

Truth be told, he'd rather be barreling toward Grace.

Because quiet as the case was, deep in his bones it felt like the one and only tornado he'd experienced, when a sudden, eerie stillness had fallen over the land right before the full fury of the storm had hit, leaving in its wake destruction . . . and death.

A phone was ringing somewhere, nothing more than a faint echo in the recesses of her consciousness.

Grace pried open her eyes and peered at the bedside clock. Nine ten.

Morning or night?

She squinted at the window, where light was peeking around the edges of the blinds. Must be morning.

But what day was it?

Thursday. It had to be Thursday.

She groped for the cell resting beside her Beretta on the nightstand and put it to her ear. "Hello."

"Grace?" Nate's warm, mellow baritone came over the line.

What a great wake-up call.

"Hi."

"Were you asleep?"

"Um . . ." Clearing the fog from her brain was proving next to impossible.

"I'll take that as a yes. I'm sorry. I can call back later."

"No. That's okay. I'm waking up."

"How are you this morning?"

"Better." The mist began to lift.

"Better better, or improving?"

"Improving." She eased onto her back.

"Are you still throwing up?"

"No." She put a hand to her forehead. "I think my fever broke too. But I feel like a train hit me."

"I can relate. Is there anything I can bring you?"

"A pill that will cure me within the hour?"

"If it existed, I'd find it for you. Anything else?"

"No. I'm set. All I plan to do today is sleep."

"The best medicine. Don't forget fluids. Do you have anything like Gatorade in the house?"

The temptation to lie and say no was strong. Chatting with him for a few minutes if he swung by with provisions would be the bright spot of her day.

But in light of her disheveled state, she could scare him away forever if he showed up at her door.

Not worth the risk.

"No Gatorade, but I always have Diet Sprite on hand for Cate. Clear soda is about all my stomach can handle. Any news?"

"Lorraine's attorney finally sent me her banking records. The pattern fits with the others, as we expected."

"Now all we have to do is find the person behind the financial scam."

"We'll get there. Is your security system armed?"

Where had that come from?

"The door and window alarms, along with the exterior cameras, are on. The interior motion detectors are off. Why?"

"Until we find BK, I think it's wise to take as many precautions as possible."

Nate's tone was conversational, but she knew him well enough at this stage to pick up a subtle thread of tension.

"Are you certain there's not another reason for your concern? One you're keeping to yourself?"

"No." His reply was swift and definitive. "If there had been any new developments or threats, you'd have been the first to know. I just want to be certain we're covering all the bases. I'll let you get back to sleep, but if you're up for a visitor by tomorrow, I may swing by after work."

"As long as I'm not puking, you're welcome. But don't expect scintillating conversation."

"I'll settle for sitting next to you while you drink a Sprite."

"That, I can handle."

"We'll talk later. Until then, get some rest."

After they said their goodbyes, Grace set the phone on the nightstand and snuggled back under the covers. The more she slept, the faster she'd recover.

But it wasn't easy to rest, knowing BK remained at large and was planning who knew what as a follow-up to the voodoo doll.

Thank heavens she'd beefed up her security. And it was more than adequate. Despite Nate's touching concern and the flutter of nerves she couldn't quite squelch, she was safe. No one could get to her without tripping the alarm. If that happened, deputies would be dispatched instantly.

On top of that, her Beretta was close at hand.

And if anyone breached her defenses, she wouldn't hesitate to use it.

The timing was perfect.

Well, almost perfect.

Saturday would have been perfect, but you had to work with the circumstances you were given.

BK swung into a parking space. Set the brake. Pulled out the list of items to buy.

It was too bad the sheriff and Grace had taken a fancy to each other. The plan would have gone smoother if he wasn't hovering over her, as he no doubt would be during his off hours this weekend, especially with her being sick.

He did have a demanding job, however, so the troublesome pathologist would be alone during the hours he was on duty.

Like tomorrow.

An ideal day for a delivery.

A fatal delivery.

After the Grace glitch was taken care of, the focus could shift back to lining up new clients for Dave . . . and the scheme would continue.

Minus one much-too-diligent forensic pathologist.

BK slid out of the car and walked toward the entrance. Nothing on the buy list would arouse suspicion in anyone—the clerks, other shoppers, any acquaintances who happened to be in the store. They were all everyday items, found in many homes.

The most critical component was already stashed at the house.

But that wouldn't raise eyebrows, either, unless a person was looking for it—and knew what it could do. Even the brainy pathologist wouldn't realize it was a murder weapon if it was staring her in the face.

The automatic doors opened as BK approached, and a welcome surge of cool air mitigated the heat of this July afternoon.

Missouri in the summer could be a pizza oven.

One of these days, a permanent escape could be in order if all continued to hum along with the plan.

And why wouldn't it? With Grace gone and the sheriff busy learning the ropes of his new job, no one would waste time and county money delving into deaths that should slip under the radar screen—as the first three had.

BK entered the store and set about collecting the items on the list.

In less than ten minutes, they were stowed in the trunk and the car was pointed toward home. It would be a busy evening, with much to do, but in less than twenty-four hours the task would be finished.

And Grace Reilly would be dead.

26

ALL READY FOR YOUR TRIP, ELEANOR?" Nate
stopped beside her desk as he sipped his third cup
of coffee. Maybe the caffeine would jump-start his energy,
already flagging at only ten forty on this Friday morning.

The weekend couldn't get here fast enough.

"For the most part. I have a few odds and ends to pack
tonight."

"What time is your flight tomorrow?"

"One thirty."

"You need a ride to the airport?"

Her eyebrows peaked. "I'm flying out of St. Louis."

"That's what I assumed."

She squinted at him. "You're offering to drive me all the
way to St. Louis?"

He shrugged. "Isn't that what life's all about? Helping each
other?"

"Well . . ." She brushed a minuscule speck of dust off her
desk. "I must say, that's very kind of you. But I'm going to
drive in tomorrow morning and leave my car at a friend's
house. She'll take me to the airport."

"In that case, why don't you cut out at noon today? That
will give you a few hours to take care of any last-minute trip

details. We've already talked about procedures at the office in your absence, and as far as I can see, you've got everything squared away."

"I've never been one to leave early. It's frowned upon."

He smiled. "Not by me. New rules, remember?"

A flicker of indecision twitched in her features. "Are you certain?"

"Yes. Don't give it another—" His phone began to vibrate, and he pulled it off his belt. Scanned caller ID. "Hey, Deke. What's up?" As he listened, he finished off his coffee and pitched the empty disposable cup in the trash can beside Eleanor's desk. "I'm on my way." He ended the call.

"Crisis?"

"Messy domestic violence situation. Guy's barricaded inside a trailer with his wife. Deke thinks he's high and possibly armed. He's calling in backup."

"Be careful."

"Always. You have a great trip. Don't be here when I get back." He gave her a thumbs-up and hustled toward the door.

A tense standoff hadn't been in his plans for this post-flu Friday, but at least he wouldn't have to ingest any more caffeine to stay awake. Adrenaline would keep him plenty energized for the duration.

And later, if he had any pep left, he'd call Grace. Make good on his promise to pay her a visit tonight and share a quiet, uneventful couple of hours before they both called it a day and clocked a full night's sleep to recharge their flu-depleted batteries.

———

Ding dong.

Grace stopped halfway down the hall as the chime echoed through the house. Who would be stopping by in the middle of the day?

Could it be Nate?

Spirits picking up, she smoothed a hand down the oversized T-shirt and shorts she'd changed into after her shower. An improvement over the sleep shirt she'd been living in for the past three days, but there wasn't much she could do about her damp hair or makeup-free face. However, if he'd made the effort to stop by, she wasn't about to ignore the summons.

She passed up the bedroom and continued down the hall and through the living room, toward the front door.

Peering through the peephole, she furrowed her brow.

What was Eleanor Duncan doing here?

Grace deactivated the alarm and pulled the door open. "Hi, Eleanor. This is a surprise."

"I hope I'm not intruding, but the sheriff told me you were down with the flu, and I know you don't have any family in the area. So I brought you homemade soup." She lifted a small, lidded container. "I was going to run over with it on my lunch hour, but the sheriff said I could take the rest of the day off to get ready for my trip. So I stopped on my way home."

Wow. Nate was right. The woman did have a heart of gold.

"I can't believe you went to all this trouble. It was very kind of you to bother."

"It was no bother at all. As the sheriff said to me this morning, life should be all about helping each other."

That sounded like Nate.

"A wonderful philosophy."

"Why don't I put this in a bowl for you and you can heat it up for lunch? That will save you having to return my container later."

"Let me do that." She reached for the offering. "I hate to let you in and expose you to all my germs. I wouldn't want you to come down with this on your vacation."

"I have a hardy constitution—but if you insist." She handed over the container.

"Give me two minutes."

Eleanor retreated into the shade of the clematis vine on the porch as Grace shut the door and hurried toward the kitchen as fast as her shaky legs allowed. Her appetite had been nonexistent, but soup might tempt her—especially after Nate's glowing review.

She pulled a bowl from the cabinet and dumped in the generous serving. Chicken noodle, it appeared. Less hearty than what Eleanor had prepared for Nate, but probably perfect at this stage of her recovery. Rice and vegetables could be a bit too heavy for her stomach.

After stowing it in the fridge, she rinsed out Eleanor's container and returned to the front door.

"The soup smells delicious." Best not to mention Nate had told her how tasty his was, lest that further fuel the rumor mill about the two of them. "I can't wait to try it." She handed the container back to the woman.

"I hope you enjoy it. My mama always said chicken noodle soup could cure anything. Do you feel up to eating?"

"I didn't until I got a whiff of your soup. I'm going to take your advice and eat it for lunch as soon as you leave. I hope you have a wonderful trip."

"Thank you. I know I will. Take care of yourself." Eleanor pulled out her keys, descended the porch steps, and returned to her car.

Once the woman backed out of the driveway, Grace closed the door, rearmed the perimeter security system, and wandered back to the kitchen, where her laptop waited on the kitchen table.

Catch up on email, as had been her plan, or eat Eleanor's offering?

The smart choice was to take care of business while her energy lasted. If she ate first, she wouldn't want to do anything afterward except curl up in bed and sleep the afternoon away.

She crossed to the table and sat. Once her laptop was booted up, she checked her inbox. Groaned at the number of unread emails. How could so many have come in over the past seventy-two hours?

Eyeing the refrigerator again, she almost succumbed to temptation. Almost.

But you didn't get through medical school and residency and a grueling forensic pathology fellowship without a super-abundance of self-discipline.

She'd work first, then eat.

However . . . if Eleanor's chicken noodle soup was half as tasty as the chicken/rice/vegetable version Nate had raved about, the reward would be worth waiting for.

At the sound of splintering glass, Dave vaulted to his feet in his home office and dashed down the hall.

His wife was standing in front of the built-in desk in the kitchen, the Waterford vase they'd bought on their twentieth anniversary trip to Ireland in shards at her feet. The rose that had been inside lay in a widening pool of water.

Another casualty in their relationship.

But he was more concerned about the tears running down her cheeks.

"Are you hurt?" He moved closer and gave her a quick inspection.

"No. But I b-broke our vase."

"The memories are still intact, though. I'm more interested in repairing what the vase represents." Since their talk a week ago, he'd done everything he could to show her how much she meant to him and how sorry he was for all the distress he'd caused her. Fixing the damage would be a long-term project, but at least she was letting him make the attempt.

And it was his top priority going forward.

She met his gaze. "I know you're trying. Don't stop. And I'll keep praying."

"Fair enough. What happened in here?"

"My stupid drawer wouldn't open again." She indicated the middle one on the side of the desk that had always been reserved for her. The one that liked to stick. The one he'd been meaning to fix for months.

"Let me open it for you. And I'll take care of the sticking problem today. Why don't you sit and I'll get whatever you need?" He motioned toward the table, where the papers spread about suggested she was working on a church project.

As she complied, he gave the drawer his full attention. After two yanks, it opened with a screech.

"What can I get for you?" He surveyed the drawer, filled with neatly labeled hanging file folders. Kimberly had always been more organized than him. Without her managing his office these past four years, and with all the distraction and upheaval in his life, his own files had deteriorated to the point that every search took twice as long as it should.

"The file on the ladies' Christmas luncheon from . . . five years ago. I volunteered to help again, and . . . I wanted to review what I did before."

He bent down and flipped through the hanging folders. No doubt they'd once been perfectly alphabetized, but no longer. Several were out of order.

He'd have to start at the beginning.

Ten files back, he found the one she'd asked for and pulled it out. "Here you go." He set it on the table, next to a much larger file. "What's in that one?" He rested a hand on it.

"The meal program schedule. I ought to clean it out. We don't have . . . to keep the old assignment sheets. You can file it again for now, though, if you like."

He picked it up, but the sheets inside were askew, and a

number of them were sticking out. The folder wouldn't slide back in unless he straightened out the contents.

Back at the desk, he opened the file and took out the first few sheets of paper. After tapping them into a neat pile, he set them down and continued the process, building up a tidy stack.

As he lifted the fourth set of papers, two paired names caught his eye—one person he and Kimberly knew, the other someone he knew.

Small world.

Picking up the pace, he continued tapping and stacking the sheets into order. Kimberly hadn't been exaggerating. The ones in the back were from several years ago and ought to be discarded. They weren't—

He froze.

Two more paired names he recognized jumped out at him.

Coincidence . . . or something more?

"Everything all right, Dave?"

At Kimberly's question, he tried to tamp down his unease. "Yes. I was, uh, noticing how outdated these papers are. Why don't I go through the file for you and get rid of the old ones?"

"I don't want to take you away from your work. You have more important things to do."

Maybe not.

"I don't mind. It won't take long." He set the file on the desk and began to go through it page by page.

By the time he finished, his pulse was racing.

Maybe he was wrong. Maybe what he was seeing didn't mean what he thought it meant. Maybe he was overreacting.

But he wasn't going to make that call. If what he suspected was true, this was out of his league.

So as soon as he put the file back and escaped to his office, he was dumping this startling turn of events straight into the lap of Sheriff Cox.

———————

An hour after she dived into answering emails, five minutes after typing the last response, and several spoonfuls into Eleanor's delicious soup, a new message popped up on the screen beside her with a tiny ping.

Grace glanced over . . . and her heart missed a beat.

The email was from the forensic botanist.

God bless the woman for getting to the sample before the end of the week. Now she and Nate wouldn't have to wonder all weekend about the results.

Fingers trembling, Grace pushed the bowl of soup aside. This was it.

Bracing, she clicked on the email. All it said was "See attached report."

Grace opened the attachment and skimmed the clinical, botanical analysis.

Sucked in a breath as her suspicions were confirmed.

BK's victims had been poisoned—with *Taxus baccata*. Otherwise known as English yew. A beautiful conifer that happened to be toxic in very small doses.

Grace exhaled slowly, even as her pulse continued to hammer.

It was a near-perfect murder weapon. Unless a person was looking for the exact toxin contained in the plant material—or had taken a leap, as she had, and sought the help of a forensic botanist—the true cause of death would never be found.

Grace did a quick Google search. The yew was chock-full of taxine alkaloids—especially taxine B—that were potent cardiotoxins. The poison was absorbed through the digestive tract rapidly, with symptoms appearing in as little as thirty minutes. Nausea, vomiting, breathing difficulties, and irregular heart rate were among them, all leading to cardiac arrest. Ingesting as few as fifty grams of crushed needles or seeds, or drinking liquid in which that amount of plant material had been cooked, was fatal. There was no known antidote. Death often occurred within two hours of consumption.

Grace slowly let out a breath and leaned back in her chair.

Of course they'd test tissue samples from the autopsies to verify the presence of taxine B, but there was no question about how the deed had been done.

Wait until Nate heard this.

She picked up her cell and punched in his number. After four rings, it rolled to voicemail.

Drat.

At the message beep, she hesitated. This was news to be shared live, not left on a recorded line.

"Nate, it's Grace. I have an important update for you. Call me as soon as you can."

Setting the cell aside, she eyed the soup. Tasty as it was, her appetite had vanished. But she ought to begin reintroducing food to her stomach, and she had nothing else to do while she waited for Nate to return her call.

She picked up her spoon, pulled the bowl back in front of her, and ate a mouthful. Made a face. While she'd read the botanist's report and googled more information, it had grown tepid.

Sighing, she picked up the bowl, rose, and trekked over to the microwave. Perhaps while she was enjoying the rest of Eleanor's thoughtful delivery, Nate would call and she could share the news.

Now all they had to do was figure out who was responsible for the diabolically ingenious method of murder.

27

AFTER THREE AND A HALF TENSE HOURS, the guy had finally released his wife, laid down the hunting rifle he'd been brandishing, and surrendered.

No doubt intimidated by the sizable law enforcement presence.

Thank God the state patrol had sent reinforcements, as had the sheriff in the adjoining county.

"You want me to do the booking honors?" Deke swiped his uniform sleeve across his forehead as the early afternoon sun blistered down on them.

"Happened on your watch. He's all yours. I'll handle thank-yous." He motioned toward the troopers and deputies, who were preparing to leave the scene now that the situation was contained.

"That works." Deke glanced toward the guy's wife, who was hovering near the patrol car where her husband was secured, one of her eyes rapidly blackening. "Knowing this couple's history, I predict he'll convince her to take him back."

"Wouldn't surprise me." According to Deke, the wife called 911 whenever her husband got abusive—but in the end, she always refused to press charges.

A classic example of the never-ending cycle of domestic violence.

"We can prosecute without her permission." Deke kept tabs on the wife, who was inching closer to the patrol car.

"I know." And with their incidents escalating to include firearms, that would be a prudent strategy.

"We can also get him on other charges."

"Yeah." Like resisting arrest and unlawful use of a weapon. Both Class D felonies, each carrying up to a seven-year sentence. "He overstepped this go-round."

Nate's phone began to vibrate—again. Two other calls had come in during the final few minutes of the tense standoff, and three prior to that, all of which he'd let roll.

Too bad this couldn't have been a quiet Friday. What little stamina he had left was evaporating fast.

While he walked over to the troopers and deputies who were beginning to disperse, he pulled out his cell and skimmed the screen. The mayor's office from one of the towns in his jurisdiction was calling.

He let it roll too. The political two-step would be too taxing at the moment.

As he approached the reinforcements who'd come to assist, he began to scroll through the other calls, listening to Grace's brief, intriguing message from ten minutes ago before moving on. A return call to her zoomed to the top of his priority list.

Picking up his pace, he continued to skim his calls. Whoever else had phoned could—

He jolted to a stop.

Dave Mullins had called fifteen minutes ago.

Did that mean BK had contacted him about another victim?

Much as he wanted to give Grace priority, Dave had to come first.

He dispensed with his thank-you duties as fast as he could, lifted a hand in Deke's direction as the chief deputy slid behind the wheel of his patrol car, and strode toward his own vehicle while he placed a return call to Mullins.

The man answered on the first ring, as if he'd had his phone in hand, waiting to pass on whatever news he had.

"Mr. Mullins, has BK contacted you?" He had no patience for pleasantries today, not after dealing with an armed stand-off and battling the aftereffects of the flu.

"No. But I did come across what strikes me as a very odd coincidence. One that may identify BK."

"I'm listening."

"This is going to sound off-the-wall."

"Trust me, I've heard everything in this job—and I'm not a big believer in coincidences. Tell me what you found."

Nate cranked up the air in the sweltering car as Mullins launched into his story, struggling to keep his exasperation in check as the man provided irrelevant details about cleaning out his wife's file on the meal delivery program sponsored by area churches.

But his interest perked up at the name pairings.

"The same name showed up with every one of the victims of the fraud scheme—as the food courier. I never knew until today that all my clients were signed up for meal deliveries."

Nate's fingers began to tingle, as they used to overseas on high-stakes missions when his unit was on the cusp of enemy engagement.

If the victims had been poisoned, as Grace suspected, how better to do it than through a volunteer-run humanitarian meal program that would never arouse suspicion?

"Give me the name." He pulled out his notebook.

"This is the off-the-wall part."

"Like I said, nothing surprises me in this job."

"It's not someone you'd ever suspect."

"It often isn't."

Silence.

"Mr. Mullins?"

A sigh came over the line. "Remember, I'm just the messenger." Another pause. "It's Eleanor Duncan."

In the silence that followed, a cloud scuttled across the sun, dimming the daylight as Nate tried to wrap his mind around the name the man had passed on.

Eleanor Duncan?

The department's administrative assistant?

The woman who'd worked for the county for more than thirty years?

The kindhearted soul who'd brought him soup and did everything by the book?

Impossible.

"I told you it was off-the-wall."

As Mullins spoke again, Nate wiped a hand down his face and stared at the dilapidated trailer a hundred yards away that had appeared innocuous until the nastiness festering inside was exposed.

"I need a minute to process this."

"Maybe it's a coincidence, like I said."

Much as he'd like to believe that, Nate knew in his gut that wasn't the case. Bizarre as it was, they had their killer.

Why Eleanor had orchestrated such a lethal undertaking was beyond him, but all the pieces fit.

Proving it, however, could be a challenge. The woman had left no clues behind to tie her to the deaths. Or none they'd found.

But perhaps there was evidence in her house.

They had to get a search warrant ASAP.

"I don't think it's a coincidence." He forced the left side of his brain to engage. "Keep the papers you found until someone can come collect them. If your burner phone happens to ring, ignore it. I'll be in touch." He ended the call.

With Eleanor about to leave town, it was imperative to get the warrant in the works on the double.

Ironically enough, under normal circumstances he'd call their admin, have her fill out the form so it was ready for his signature, and ask her to alert the associate judge to meet him at the courthouse to sign the warrant.

The woman subbing for Eleanor ought to be able to handle the simple paperwork, but if he wanted to keep the identity of their suspect under wraps that wouldn't work.

He'd have to do this himself.

He put the car in gear, aimed it toward the office, and called the judge. Getting him briefed and onboard was imperative.

That task completed, he punched in Deke's number and brought him up to speed. "I'll want backup at Eleanor's house once I have the warrant in hand."

"Understood. After I book our shotgun-wielding charm-school dropout, I can join you." A beat ticked by. "You think this is on the level with Eleanor?"

"Sadly, yes. If we miss each other at the office, I'll text you en route to her house."

"Got it."

As soon as he ended the call, he phoned Grace. Her message about having news had been brief, but he was willing to bet whatever she had to tell him wasn't going to come anywhere close to his bombshell.

She answered two rings in as he barreled down the state highway.

"Sorry I had to let your call roll." He frowned at a slow-moving tractor lumbering down the road ahead. "We were in the midst of a tense standoff with an armed subject."

"No worries. That takes precedence over my news. You okay?"

"Yeah. No shots were fired. I have news too."

"Can I go first?"

"Sure."

"My suspicion was correct. Our victims were poisoned."

In light of what he'd learned about Eleanor, that wasn't surprising—but as Grace gave him the lowdown on the toxicity of English yew, the cunning choice of weapon blew him away.

"I'd never have guessed that in a million years." He whipped around the tractor.

"No one would. Not without anecdotal evidence pointing that direction."

"Or a smart pathologist who homed in on plant poisons and enlisted the help of a forensic botanist to prove her suspicions."

"I got lucky. If it hadn't been for those red-herring sunflower seeds, I would never have pursued that angle."

"More than luck was involved here." A muted ping came over the line. "What's that?"

"My lunch. This is my third attempt to eat it, but I keep getting interrupted. Hard as I've tried, I haven't made much headway."

"You want to get it while I share my news?"

"No. To tell you the truth, my stomach's queasy again. I'm not certain any food would stay down, even the soup Eleanor delivered earlier. You're not the only one who's in her favor, it seems."

For the second time in less than fifteen minutes, shock reverberated through him and his own stomach twisted into a hard knot.

Dear God.

If Eleanor was BK, she was also the one behind the attacks on Grace. She was the shadowy figure who'd hired Tyler Holmes. Who wanted the meticulous, persistent forensic pathologist out of the picture. Permanently.

Nate hit the siren, executed a U-turn, and floored the cruiser.

"Nate? What's going on?"

322

"We need to stay calm." The reminder was as much for himself as for her.

"I am calm. What's wrong?"

"In light of new information Mullins just passed on, Eleanor is our prime murder suspect. How much of the soup did you eat?"

Her sharp intake of breath sliced through him like a knife. Then nothing but silence from her end.

Blood pounding in his ears, he swerved around a car that didn't pull over fast enough. "Grace!"

"Yes. I-I'm here." Panic etched her choppy reply. "Nate . . . based on what I found in my Google search, there's . . . there's no antidote for yew poisoning."

He bit back a word he hadn't uttered since his Green Beret days, and then only in the thick of life-threatening situations. Like this one.

While there was no armed enemy taking aim at Grace, cardiac arrest was just as lethal a threat if what she'd shared moments ago from her research was true.

"How much did you eat and when did you eat it?"

"Maybe half. I started eating it about thirty minutes ago."

His brain clicked into high gear. "The quantity and timing have to be in our favor. I'm going to get paramedics dispatched and contact poison control. My ETA at your place is twelve minutes."

"I'll google emergency procedures." Her voice was shaking. "But I-I'm feeling sicker by the minute, Nate." The swish of movement came over the line.

"Hang in. We'll lick this." He managed to infuse his voice with far more confidence than he felt.

"I have to—" Her response was cut off by violent retching.

He gritted his teeth.

This was bad.

Really bad.

"Grace, I'm hanging up and calling for help."

No response.

He forced himself to press the end button and dial 911.

But as he relayed the information to the dispatcher in a clipped, no-nonsense tone honed from years under pressure in life-and-death situations, his heart was shattering.

He couldn't lose Grace. New as their acquaintance was, deep inside he already knew they were meant to be together.

So as he spoke with 911, contacted poison control, and mashed the gas pedal to the floor, he prayed.

Because at this point, nothing short of a miracle could snatch her from the jaws of death.

It was done.

Eleanor took a sip of her second scotch, set the tumbler on the dresser, and wiggled her finger, letting the facets of the diamonds and emeralds in her cocktail ring catch the sunlight streaming through the crack in the blinds.

Grace would be gone within hours, along with all of the problems she'd created.

It was a shame it had come to this, but the woman was too stubborn for her own good.

After fingering one of the designer cocktail dresses draped on the bed beside her suitcase, Eleanor crossed to the box she'd removed from the safe. Touched each bracelet, necklace, earring— all mementos of her fabulous trips these past few years.

Not to visit her cousin in rural Maine, as everyone thought, but to traipse through the glittering cities of Europe in style. First class all the way, treated like a person who mattered at every high-end hotel, restaurant, and shop she visited.

The way she deserved to be treated.

The way her critical father and deceitful boyfriend and every high-and-mighty boss should have treated her.

She closed the lid on the box and smoothed her palm over the satin finish of the wood.

Of course, there was one boss who'd treated her well. Sheriff Cox was the exception. His class and kindness and refreshing egalitarian attitude were commendable.

Too bad a man like him hadn't come along sooner. That could have made a difference in the choices she'd made.

Or not.

It was too late to know for certain.

What mattered was that she'd taken control of her life and found her own path to self-esteem and happiness.

Even if she'd had to do some bad deeds along the way.

She picked up the scotch and finished it off, examining the intricate pattern cut with painstaking precision into the fragile glass of the Waterford tumbler.

It was hard to feel much remorse about the old folks. They'd been on their last legs anyway. But the decision to end Grace's life had been more difficult.

Second thoughts were useless at this stage, however. A major relapse of flu should be setting in. How providential that she'd caught the bug at the perfect time. Sheriff Cox might suspect it was more than a virus, but he'd never be able to prove it. There would be no sunflower seeds lying around for anyone to find, nor any in Grace's stomach, to tie her death to the others under investigation.

Eleanor slipped the ring off her finger, opened the box again, and set the piece of jewelry in its designated spot. Replaced it on her finger with a ruby-and-diamond number.

Ironic—and aggravating—how those innocuous seeds had caught Grace's eye and fueled her suspicions. They had nothing to do with any of the deaths, other than acting as an additive to the salads she'd delivered so any of the highly toxic stray yew seeds among the greens wouldn't draw unnecessary attention.

Eleanor wandered back to the bed and began folding the cocktail dresses, layering them with tissue in the suitcase to prevent wrinkles, a tiny smile tugging at her lips.

Her plan really was masterful, thanks to everything she'd learned by watching the stupid criminals who passed through the sheriff's department every day and the inside knowledge she'd picked up about the workings of law enforcement.

Succeeding at crime was a simple matter. All you had to do was be smart, keep your ear to the ground, and watch for opportunities.

Like the day of the meal-delivery volunteers picnic at the reservoir, when she'd wandered away from the group and spotted Dave in a hot-and-heavy clinch while his comatose wife fought for her life.

A definite opportunity.

Thanks to those compromising photos—and the ones she'd taken after donning a disguise and following Dave and his lady friend to that inn, where her room offered a perfect line of sight to the gazebo—the whole idea for the fraud scheme had begun to percolate.

Dresses packed, she went in search of the Manolo Blahnik shoes that would go beautifully with the Dior dress she'd picked up on her last visit to Paris. The perfect outfit for her first dinner in Rome, her bucket-list city for this trip.

She found them in the closet and returned to the suitcase, spirits ticking up. This would be a grand adventure. One no one here in the heartland would ever know about.

Nor would they know about her other grand adventure— amassing a fortune under the radar by exploiting weaknesses.

Human nature was so predictable.

Dave had caved at the first threat and agreed to be her front man for the investment opportunity.

Tyler Holmes had been low-hanging fruit. After being kicked out of the house by his father, and after all his brushes with the law, it was a given that he'd jump at the chance to earn a few extra bucks under the table. He'd been the perfect person to do her initial dirty work with Grace.

As for all the poor seniors who'd been struggling to make ends meet, her volunteer gig with the meals program had provided her the ideal opportunity to screen candidates for her scheme. Befriending them and offering to do errands— like banking—had helped her choose clients for Dave who didn't frequent the same financial institutions . . . just in case anyone got suspicious about large withdrawals from more than one customer.

And once she decided to cease their monthly payments, all she'd had to do was supplement the dinner of the day with her special salad—crisp lettuce, assorted fruit, toasted nuts, cracked yew seeds, sunflower seeds, and poppy seed dressing laced with dried, ground yew leaves.

It had worked like a charm until Grace poked her nose in.

But soon the forensic pathologist would be history.

Eleanor strolled back to the dresser and picked up her glass again. Dare she have one more scotch? Two was usually her limit, but she had much to celebrate tonight. A trip to Italy, a hefty balance in the offshore account, and no more impediments to her scheme.

Why not indulge?

She was home free.

28

THE FAINT, WELCOME WAIL of a siren penetrated the bathroom walls as a wave of vertigo made the room spin, and Grace clutched the edge of the vanity beside the toilet, sagging in relief.

Thank God help was on the way!

Another shaft of pain knifed through her abdomen, doubling her over, and she emptied her stomach. Again.

It would almost be easier to die.

Almost.

But she wasn't going to let Eleanor win. Not if she could help it. She would *not* go gentle into this good night.

As the siren grew closer, she wiped her mouth on a towel and staggered to the front door. Despite her waning energy, she managed to unbolt the lock and twist the knob. Then, back against the wall, she slid down to the floor and dropped her forehead to her knees.

Three minutes later, a host of emergency personnel spilled into the house.

A paramedic knelt beside her. "Ma'am, we've already been briefed on the situation. Can you talk?"

"Yes." Barely.

"Where's the rest of the soup?"

"Microwave."

"Have you thrown up?"

"Yes. Three times." Violently.

They stopped asking questions and went to work, which was fine. It took too much effort to respond to questions.

After they lifted her onto a gurney, one paramedic prepped her for an ECG. Another started an IV. Someone took a blood sample. A bright light was aimed at her pupils.

More faces appeared above her. One paramedic had a cell pressed to his ear, relaying information back and forth between the medics attending to her and whoever was on the other end of the call.

Grace closed her eyes. The bustle and noise were exacerbating the pounding in her head. Yet a few words penetrated the fog that was sucking her down into a black vortex.

Mydriasis.

Tachycardia.

Hypotension.

Her MD-trained brain did the translation on autopilot.

Dilated pupils.

Fast heart rate.

Low blood pressure.

They were rattling off all the symptoms her Google search had indicated were signs of yew poisoning.

"Grace?"

At the familiar voice close to her ear, she forced her eyelids open. Nate was wedged between the paramedics, deep grooves etched beside his mouth and across his forehead.

"Hi." She tried to force up the corners of her lips, but they refused to cooperate.

He cocooned her hand in a warm, strong grip. "A medevac helicopter will be here shortly. The paramedics are on the line with poison control. We're flying you to Mercy in St. Louis."

"Okay." Taking her to a Level I trauma center was smart. She'd need every bit of expertise she could get to pull through this.

"I'm going with you."

"No." She summoned up the last vestiges of her waning strength. "Get Eleanor."

"There are other people who can do that."

"No." She gripped his fingers as tight as she could and did her best to focus on his face as it faded in and out. "You go. It's your job. Come afterward. And please call my sisters."

Someone nudged him aside, and he let go of her hand.

"I'm staying with you, Grace." Although he was out of sight, there was steel in his tone.

"Let's move." One of the paramedics motioned to his colleagues, and the gurney was raised.

"Nate." She squinted past the bodies surrounding her.

"I'm here."

He stepped into her field of vision again, staying close.

"Do your job. Come later. You know this case best."

He didn't respond.

"Nate. Please." She snaked a hand out, between the paramedics.

Once again, her fingers were engulfed in warmth. Despite her hazy vision, she could read the conflict in his features.

"I'd rather stay with you."

Coming from a former Green Beret who'd been trained to put duty above all else, that admission spoke volumes.

"Do your job. I'll see you later."

"Is that a promise?" His intent gaze bored into hers.

She understood what he was asking.

But they both knew that was a promise she couldn't make. Eleanor's concoctions had already killed six people. The odds were better for her because she'd eaten less and had gotten medical help early, but there were no guarantees.

"I'll do my best."

The paramedics hustled the gurney through the door and took off at a fast clip for the ambulance.

She didn't see Nate again.

But she prayed he'd honor her request. His presence in St. Louis wasn't going to determine whether she lived or died. That was in God's hands at this point.

His presence here, however, could make a huge difference in how the situation with Eleanor was handled.

And whether she survived or not, Grace wanted the woman who'd wreaked havoc on multiple lives to spend the rest of *her* life behind bars.

Who on earth would come calling in the middle of a Friday afternoon?

As the ding-dong of the doorbell echoed through the house, Eleanor set the sequined cocktail purse beside the open suitcase on her bed and went to find out. A solicitor, she could ignore—but if it was a neighbor, she'd have to answer. Several had seen her arrive home early from work.

She approached the door quietly and peeked through the peephole.

Froze.

Sheriff Cox and Deke were standing on her porch, and their grim demeanors said this wasn't a social call.

Something was up.

Eleanor backed off a few steps, palm pressed to her chest.

Could they be on to her?

Impossible.

She'd covered her tracks like a pro. Even if they were suspicious, they didn't have one iota of proof other than today's soup. But she'd left only a single serving, and that had to be long gone. More than two hours ago, Grace had said she was

332

going to eat it right away. Besides, they had no idea what to look for in her homemade offering, anyway.

And if you weren't looking for yew, you wouldn't find it.

The bell rang again, and her pulse ratcheted up.

Could she ignore the summons?

No. That wouldn't make the problem, whatever it was, go away.

She had to answer.

Just listen to what they have to say, Eleanor. Offer nothing. Feign ignorance if they ask questions. You can handle this.

Yes, she could. After masterfully executing her ingenious plan for all these years, she could win a game of dodgeball with the sheriff.

Squaring her shoulders, she returned to the door and pulled it open. "Sheriff . . . Deke. This is a surprise." She infused her tone with the appropriate amount of puzzlement. "What can I do for you?"

"We have a search warrant for your house, Eleanor." The sheriff held it up.

She widened her eyes, faking shock even as her stomach twisted into a hard knot. "Excuse me?"

"Let's not play games." Gone was the affable boss who brought her Monday mochas. This was the tough Nate Cox who'd fought shadowy adversaries in the Middle East. Who didn't give up until he'd routed the enemy. "Grace is being transported by helicopter to St. Louis as we speak. She only ate half the soup. We have the rest."

A word she'd never uttered flashed through her mind, but she managed to hold on to her bewildered expression. "What are you talking about?"

The sheriff shifted his attention to the hand she'd wrapped around the edge of the door. "Nice ring."

She was still wearing the ruby- and diamond-encrusted band.

The profanity she'd stifled almost tripped off her tongue.

Think, Eleanor!

Her brain began firing on all cylinders.

Lying would be a mistake. They had a search warrant. While it was unlikely they'd find her well-hidden stash of ground-up dried yew needles and seeds, they *would* find the rest of her jewelry. Not to mention her suitcases packed with designer clothes.

But she didn't have to talk to them or explain anything. Not without a lawyer present.

"What are you searching for?" Another cruiser pulled up in front of the house, and Beth—one of the deputies on duty today—slid from behind the wheel.

"Anything related to English yews or offshore accounts."

Her lungs locked, and she tightened her grip on the edge of the door.

How could they know about the yew? She'd left no clue to tip them off to the source of the poison, and the stupid sunflower seeds Grace had noticed that had led to this whole nightmare were of no relevance.

As for the offshore accounts—had Dave caved? Told the truth rather than fabricated a cover story that day he'd visited the sheriff?

She couldn't ask any of those questions without incriminating herself, however.

"Beth, keep Eleanor company in the living room while Deke and I do a walk-through." The sheriff motioned behind her. "Shall we go inside?"

It wasn't a request.

"I want to call my attorney."

"Fine. Beth will sit with you while you do that."

"My cell is in the kitchen."

"Beth will get it for you."

Slowly she loosened her grip on the edge of the door and

walked into the living room, her legs as stiff as they'd been after she'd overdone it at an exercise class in her younger days.

This wasn't how her plan was supposed to work.

And the catastrophe was all Grace Reilly's fault.

Panic morphing to anger, she fisted her hands at her sides until her nails bit into her palms. She was not going down without a fight. She could beat this. There was no challenge too difficult to overcome. Yes, the soup was an issue, but a smart lawyer could help her figure out how to deal with that complication.

The offshore account was less of a problem. It wouldn't be easy for US law enforcement to get access to that. Ensuring such accounts were inaccessible was a huge selling point for the companies that ran them.

She'd misjudged Dave, though. The man had more gumption than she'd given him credit for if he'd been willing to risk his marriage to approach law enforcement with what he knew.

Sometimes people just weren't what they seemed.

Eleanor sat and took the phone from Beth while the sheriff and Deke headed down the hall toward her bedroom. Scrolled through her contacts until she came to the name of the hotshot criminal defense lawyer she'd researched when this scheme began in case she ever needed him.

It paid to be prepared.

She twisted away from Beth and punched in his number.

There was no way she'd walk away from this untarnished. Not if they had the soup. But excellent attorneys could work wonders.

And she was about to secure the best.

The woman pacing inside the glass doors to the ER in St. Louis, her dark auburn hair pulled back into a ponytail, had to be Cate Reilly.

Nate jogged toward the building. Grace's oldest sister had done her best to keep him informed over the past several hours, but cellphone signals were spotty in ERs and it had been thirty minutes since his last update.

At least his call letting her know he was five minutes away had gone through and she'd agreed to wait for him at the entrance.

The instant the doors swished open, she spun toward him. "Nate?"

"Yes."

"Cate Reilly." She strode over and gave him a firm shake. "How is she?"

"Holding her own. I can fill you in while we walk back." She pivoted, and he fell in beside her as she launched into a rapid briefing. "The flu ended up being an advantage. With her stomach already queasy, it didn't take much to set off several bouts of throwing up. That got rid of a fair amount of the poison fast. Also, she didn't ingest a lethal quantity, from what they can tell, and it was caught early. The fact she's young and healthy and they knew what they were dealing with is a plus too. But the cardiac crew is keeping a close watch on her heart."

His own heart stumbled.

"Has that been an issue?"

"Not yet. But no one's had any direct experience with yew poisoning, so they're being extra cautious. If all her vitals remain stable, they'll move her to intensive care in a couple of hours for continued monitoring."

A woman with copper-colored hair slipped from behind the curtain of a treatment room as they approached.

"You must be Nate." She held out her hand, and he took it. "I'm Eve. The middle sister. We've heard a lot about you."

"Likewise. I'm sorry we didn't meet under less stressful conditions."

"We'll have plenty of opportunities to get acquainted. At the moment, Grace is waiting for you." She motioned to the room behind her. "But don't expect much privacy. It's like Grand Central in there."

"I'll be happy to stand in the corner, out of the way, and keep watch."

"Good man." Cate gave an approving nod, then nudged Eve. "Let's go raid the vending machines." She tugged her sister down the hall.

Nate pushed the curtain aside, slipped through—and tried to mask his shock. Grace's naturally fair complexion had lost any vestige of color. An off-putting amount of equipment was also staged around her bed. As he paused at the curtain, monitors beeped, IVs dripped, and an automatic blood pressure cuff inflated.

"That bad, huh?"

At her teasing question, he continued toward the bed and squeezed between two pieces of equipment.

She didn't look any better up close.

But she was alive and talking and getting the best of care.

"All this stuff is more than a little daunting." He waved a hand over the room.

"It's not as alarming as it seems. Most of it is routine monitoring equipment."

Not the crash cart parked in the corner . . . but he left that unsaid.

He took her hand and wove his fingers through hers. "I got here as fast as I could."

"I knew you would. Tell me what happened."

"Bottom line, Eleanor is in custody."

"Did she confess?"

"No, but we found a treasure trove in her house. Literally." He told her about the jewels and designer apparel and the first-class airline ticket to Rome that had been in plain view on her dresser.

"Wow." Grace stared at him. "It sounds like she's been living a double life."

"That's what the evidence suggests."

"Any sign of yew material?"

"Not yet, but the search is continuing as we speak. The remains of your soup are also being analyzed."

"What about the offshore account?"

He studied her. She appeared to be alert and resting comfortably, but after the ordeal she'd been through—was still going through—this might not be the time for heavy discussions. "You certain you're up to talking about all this now?"

"No, but it will keep my mind occupied on something other than my scary close call."

Made sense.

"The FBI will handle that part of the investigation. I have every confidence they'll crack whatever security she has on her computer. The trick will be getting the firm she used to turn over evidence. They don't tend to cooperate with law enforcement."

"That stinks."

"I agree, but I'm leaving that task in the hands of the Feds. I did find one other interesting item at Eleanor's house. A plaque on the wall in her bedroom that said Big Kahuna."

"BK."

"That's my take."

Grace's brow pleated. "I'm still trying to wrap my mind around Eleanor being the perpetrator. Why on earth would she get involved in such an evil scheme?"

"There could be any number of motives. Greed, wanting to prove she was smart, a misguided belief the world owed her a more upscale lifestyle than the one she had, a craving for an adrenaline rush to spice up her days. Or, as the plaque could suggest, a desire to be in charge. To have power and control. Your guess is as good as mine."

"I suppose that's one mystery we may never solve." Grace exhaled. "What happens to Dave?"

"TBD. Aiding and abetting fraud can carry serious criminal and civil consequences. However, he did come forward and offer to assist as soon as he realized the plan had turned deadly. That will work in his favor if he decides to plea bargain." He stroked a finger down her cheek. "But can we forget about murder and mayhem for a minute? I have a much more important topic to discuss."

"Like what?" The corners of her mouth tipped up.

"Us. But first . . ." He leaned down and—

The curtains swished aside, and he jerked up.

A nurse grinned at him. "Sorry to interrupt, but I have to get another blood sample. Give me a minute, and you can carry on."

Except that didn't happen. As the nurse exited, a parade of other ER personnel began to circulate through the room. And when the last one left, Cate and Eve returned.

Grace sent them a disgruntled scowl. "Can I go home now?"

"Not for three days. That's the word on the street." Cate glanced between the two of them. "Are we interrupting anything?"

"You and everyone else in the hospital." Grace arched an eyebrow at them. "Don't you two have places to go, jobs to do?"

"Nope." Eve plopped into a chair against the wall. "We're sticking close until they sound the all clear. Sorry, Nate."

"Don't be. I think it's great you three are so tight. Family should come first."

"Well said." Cate transferred her attention to her youngest sibling. "This one's a keeper, Grace."

A hint of pink tinted her cheeks. "You two are going to scare him off if you keep this up."

"Not a chance." Nate smiled at her. "I'm not going anywhere. We haven't had our dinner at the lake yet."

"You two also have my wedding to look forward to." Cate zeroed in on him. "You're coming, right?"

"Wouldn't miss it. I'll take any excuse I can get to hold Grace in my arms, even if she has to endure a few stepped-on toes on the dance floor."

"Definitely a keeper." Eve stood and grabbed Cate's arm. "Let's go outside and see if we can get a cell signal. I'm sure we both have messages we should respond to."

"Hey. We just got back. And you said you wanted to stick close."

"I'm not going to Alaska, Cate. Get with the program. These two need a few minutes alone to finish their . . . conversation." She winked at him, pulled Cate out of the treatment room, and swept the curtain back into place.

"Sorry about that." Grace gave him a rueful shrug.

"No apology necessary. I like your sisters." He strolled back to the bed and eased onto the edge. Took her hand.

After a few seconds, she cocked her head. "Don't we have some unfinished business, from before the parade started?"

"I'm rethinking my impulsive move." Especially with a crash cart within reaching distance. "I don't want to strain your heart."

"Trust me, I can handle a kiss—if that's what you had in mind. I'm a doctor, remember? I can assess my own medical condition."

"This isn't the most romantic setting for a first kiss."

"But it will be memorable." Her features softened, and she lifted a hand to play with a button on his shirt. "Besides, anywhere with you would be romantic."

"You're putting a major strain on my self-discipline, you know. If you keep this up, it's going to crumble."

"Good." She slid a finger between the buttons and tugged on the edge of his shirt.

He gave her a slow smile. "I like a woman who knows what she wants."

"Prove it."

"Happy to oblige." He leaned closer, until their noses were inches apart and her beautiful hazel eyes filled his vision. "But let's take this slow and easy, okay?"

"I'll follow your lead."

He checked the heart monitor. Her pulse had picked up, but it was strong and steady.

His own was off the charts.

Because almost from the day they'd met, he'd known Grace Reilly was special—and that this moment would come.

And as he at last lowered his lips to hers, all the unromantic hospital sounds faded into the background.

For Grace was right.

Anywhere would be romantic as long as they were together. For always.

An outcome he intended to pursue with singular focus from this day forward.

EPILOGUE

WELCOME HOME, MRS. COX."

As Nate carried her across the threshold of his house—their house now—in a swirl of snow flurries, Grace snuggled into the white faux-fur stole Eve had rounded up for her and tucked the long lace skirt of her wedding gown against her legs.

"None too soon. Much as I love this dress, it was *not* designed to be worn outdoors in February."

Nate shut the door with his shoulder but didn't set her down. "I still can't believe you wanted to spend our wedding night here. You deserve a suite at the Ritz."

"The Hawaiian honeymoon you've planned is extravagant enough. Besides, what better place to begin our marriage than in the home where, God willing, we'll raise our family and grow old together? Where the best is yet to be?"

His eyes warmed . . . softened—and a rush of tenderness tightened her throat as his husky words filled her heart with joy. "I love you, Grace Reilly Cox."

"I love you too, Nathaniel Joseph Cox." Looping both arms around his neck, she lifted her face toward him.

He responded with a most satisfying kiss that lasted far longer than the polite smooch at church after the pastor pronounced them husband and wife.

"Mmm." She gave a contented sigh as he at last drew back. "That was delicious."

"But it was only the appetizer. Get ready for the main course—and dessert."

A tingle of anticipation zipped through her. "Promises, promises."

"Soon to be fulfilled." He started toward the hall.

"You can put me down, you know. We've done the threshold thing."

"Not yet."

Fine. She was in no rush to leave his arms.

At the closed door of the master bedroom, he stopped. "Want to turn the knob for me? I'd do it myself, but my hands are occupied."

"What's it worth to you?" She waggled her eyebrows and snuggled closer.

"Turn the knob and I'll show you." He waggled right back, his deep baritone teasingly roguish as he angled sideways so she could reach it.

She twisted the handle, and he pushed the door open with his hip. Stepped inside.

"Oh!" Her exclamation came out in a hush of amazement as she took in the setting.

Candle groupings of various heights were placed around the room, the flickering flames casting a glow over the new comforter and linens she'd purchased while decorating the space. A vintage recording of Nat King Cole singing "Our Love Is Here to Stay" played softly in the background. The comforter had been folded back, and rose petals were sprinkled across the sheet and pillows. An overflowing vase of red roses and baby's breath stood on the nightstand, the sweet scent permeating the air.

It was magic.

"How in the world . . . When did you . . . I can't believe . . ." She exhaled and looked up at her new husband.

"I recruited Kathleen to help. My most excellent sister-in-law snuck away from the reception early to take care of this, watched for us from inside, and slipped out the back door when we arrived."

"I wondered why I didn't see her before we left. Your excuse that she must be on the deck enjoying the view of the lake seemed a bit lame, given the cold weather."

"I don't know. We went out to stand under the twinkle lights for a minute and watch the reflection of the moon on the water—for old times' sake. As first dates went, ours definitely fell into the memorable category."

"Making the lakeside restaurant a perfect choice for our reception." She waved a hand around the room as she continued. "This is perfect too."

"If you wouldn't let me take you to the Ritz for the night, I wanted to replicate the experience as best I could. I'm happy to see Kathleen followed my instructions to a T—and added a touch of her own." He nodded to a small, linen-draped table with a bottle chilling in a cooler, two stemmed glasses, and a plate of chocolate-covered strawberries.

"For the record, the Ritz would pale in comparison. This is every woman's fantasy of how to launch a honeymoon." Or hers, at least.

"I'm glad you like it." Slowly he lowered her feet to the floor. Lifted the stole from her shoulders and set it aside. "I'm glad you're *here* to like it. I still wake up once in a while in a cold sweat, thinking how close I came to losing you."

At his hoarse admission, she traced along the edge of his

chin, her fingertip grazing the faint hint of evening stubble that was beginning to darken his jaw. "But you didn't, and all's well that ends well. I'm fine—no thanks to Eleanor."

A muscle in his cheek ticced. "She'll pay for what she did. I don't care how high-priced her lawyer is."

"I know. That soup alone is hard evidence of intent to kill."

"The autopsy samples that tested positive for yew from the suspicious deaths will also work against her, even if we never did find any traces of English yew in her house."

"But we know she had access to it, thanks to the English yew on the grounds of her church—where, as you discovered, she used to do volunteer gardening."

"True. Plus, the FBI did identify her as the owner of the offshore account that funneled the so-called interest payments to her victims via a New York address. If this goes to a jury, I don't think there's any question that the prosecutor will convince them she's guilty beyond a reasonable doubt, even if some of the evidence is circumstantial."

"I hope so." Grace shivered, despite the cozy warmth of the room. "It creeps me out how she methodically eliminated people without any apparent remorse."

"Unlike Mullins, who was eaten up by guilt."

"I'm glad the courts didn't treat him harshly." She crossed to the bouquet of roses and bent down to inhale the heady fragrance.

"They tend to be lenient with people who cooperate and admit their guilt. Setting up the offshore account for Eleanor and sucking in the clients she selected was the least of the evils committed in this scheme. That doesn't condone what he did, but the blackmail threat hanging over his head was powerful."

She fingered a velvety petal. "He's lucky his wife stuck with him and that the congregation at church rallied around to watch out for her while he serves his one-year sentence."

"He'll be paying off the money to the charities that were supposed to get it for a long while, though."

"Unless the FBI manages to pry the funds loose from the offshore account." She turned back to Nate. The mellow light warmed his skin, giving him a golden glow.

Appropriate.

For the man who had stolen her heart over these past months with his tenderness and kindness and caring was pure gold.

"I hope that happens—but I'm not in the mood to think about Mullins tonight. I only have one person on my mind at the moment." Nate joined her by the roses and pulled her into the circle of his arms. "Have I told you how beautiful you look today?"

"About a dozen times." She fingered his bow tie. "Have I told you how handsome you look in a tux?"

"Mmm-hmm. But I'm not a tux kind of guy. I'm ready to ditch this noose of a tie."

She tugged one side until the knot came loose and the two ends hung down the front of his shirt. "Done."

His eyes darkened. "The top button on my shirt is tight too."

She worked it open. "Better?"

"Uh-huh." He motioned to the fancy upsweep her stylist had created. "Are you going to leave your hair up all night?"

"You don't like my do?"

"Very much. But you may be more comfortable sleeping if you let it down."

"I won't argue with that. However . . . there are dozens of pins that will have to come out, and I can't see them all. I may need assistance."

"That can be arranged." He began slowly removing them one by one.

Her pulse fluttered as his fingers brushed her neck. "You know something?"

"What?" He kept taking out pins but stopped when she didn't respond. "What's wrong?"

"Not a thing. In fact, everything's right. I just wanted to tell you how incredibly blessed I feel to be your wife. You're everything I ever dreamed of, Nate." She swallowed past the lump in her throat and smoothed out the twin lines above his nose with her index finger. "Handsome, smart, compassionate, principled, trustworthy. A man of faith and values. I feel like the luckiest person in the world."

One side of his mouth hitched up. "Mutual, I'm sure."

A soft laugh bubbled up inside her. "I see my sisters have let you in on our little game."

"Yep. They even gave me the answer—*White Christmas*."

"That makes it official. You're now part of the family."

"We should celebrate." He resumed his pin-removal mission.

"I agree. Especially since my sisters were convinced a woman who spent her days around dead people didn't have much chance of meeting a living, breathing man to date, let alone marry."

"I'm very much alive. Want me to prove it?"

"By all means."

He quickly dispensed with the rest of the pins.

Once her hair was tumbled around her shoulders, he framed her face with his hands, his gentle touch bordering on reverent. "I love you more than words can say, Grace. And I'll spend the rest of my life proving it."

"You've already made an excellent start on that." She put her arms around his waist and moved in close, until there was no space between them. Then she rose on tiptoe.

He met her halfway as Nat King Cole launched into "Unforgettable."

How appropriate.

For this man . . . this day . . . this moment . . . were indeed unforgettable.

And as his lips closed over hers—tender, ardent, filled with the promise of passion to come—Grace gave thanks.

Maybe her sisters had found their real-life heroes first, but as far as she was concerned, God had saved the best one for last.

Loved this book from
Irene Hannon? Read on
for a sneak peek of
the next installment in
the Hope Harbor series,
Windswept Way.

COMING IN 2023

MAYBE BUYING A HAUNTED HOUSE wasn't her best idea.

Stomach churning, Ashley Scott braked as Windswept Way dead-ended at two open but imposing iron gates bookended by a tall, overgrown hedge. Surveyed the large, faded "Private Property—Keep Out" and "Trespassers Will Be Prosecuted" signs posted at the entrance. Read the word carved into the weathered stone block on the left.

Edgecliff.

Also known as Fitzgerald's Folly, according to local lore. A place with a storied past filled with triumph and tragedy. Where nocturnal sightings of a woman in white and ethereal music seeping from the house fed the rumors that the estate was haunted.

Ashley massaged her forehead and blew out a breath.

No wonder her mother thought she'd gone off the deep end.

But after forking over the money for a cross-country trek to Hope Harbor, Oregon, it would be even crazier to turn tail and run without keeping the appointment she'd made last week with the owner.

Besides, after all the times she and her father had driven by these then-closed gates during summer vacations and speculated about what lay on the other side, she owed it to both of them to check the place out.

Especially since the money that might or might not be used to buy a stake in Edgecliff had come from the inheritance Dad had left her.

Tightening her grip on the wheel, Ashley transferred her foot to the gas and—

Sweet mercy!

Gasping, she mashed the brake to the floor again as a tall, muscular man emerged from behind the hedge, brandishing a chain saw and wearing a black, Covid-style mask that covered his nose and the bottom half of his face. The brim of a baseball cap pulled low over his forehead shadowed the rest of his features.

Ashley groped for her autolocks and secured the doors as he stopped in the center of the driveway, blocking the entrance.

Now what?

Before she could decide, he began walking toward her.

Pulse skyrocketing, she raised her window. Scanned both sides of the shoulderless narrow lane.

No room for a U-turn.

All she could do was put the car in reverse and back away. Fast.

As she fumbled with the gears, the man picked up his pace, heading straight for the hood.

Heart galloping, she tried to engage the left side of her brain.

Did she have a weapon?

No. Not unless a nail file or spike heel counted. But both were in her luggage in the trunk, anyway. And her keychain pepper gel was languishing in a bin of confiscated items at the airport back in Tennessee.

Ruing the day she'd decided to embark on this uncharacteristic adventure, she tried to coax the unfamiliar gearshift into reverse with one hand and lifted the other to the horn, prepared to press and hold on the off chance someone would—

All at once, the intimidating stranger veered toward the passenger side of the car, brushed past the door, and strode away.

What?

For a long moment . . . or two . . . or three . . . Ashley remained frozen in place.

Only after the thundering in her chest subsided did she peek in the rearview mirror.

The guy had vanished.

Meaning he hadn't had any nefarious intent after all.

Sagging in her seat, she lowered her forehead to the steering wheel and faced the truth.

She'd overreacted. Big time. Jumped to the wrong conclusion, thanks to every nerve-wracking headline she'd ever read about lone women in isolated places meeting untimely and gruesome ends.

No wonder Jason had preferred someone who was more daring and exciting and bold.

Maybe she ought to eat the cost of this trip, can her half-baked idea, and slink home. Like she'd done the day their so-called relationship had crashed and burned.

As all the emotions she'd felt in those first moments— hurt, resentment, anger, shock— swept over her again, Ashley clamped her lips together and straightened up.

No.

She was *not* going to run at the first little glitch. She would see this through, even if the trip ended up being a bust.

Taking her foot off the brake, she eased through the gates and into a tunnel of dense foliage that put the brambles and thorns Sleeping Beauty's prince had battled to shame.

Thank goodness a passageway had been cleared for vehicles.

But if the rest of the grounds were as overgrown as this, and if maintenance on the house had also been allowed to slide, she was out of here. She may have let herself get carried away with the fanciful notion of owning a piece of a historic property, but she wasn't about to get lured into a bank breaker.

Blue sky appeared around a bend in the gravel drive, and she pressed harder on the accelerator. The house should be—

Whoa!

Ashley jammed on her brakes yet again as she exited the warren of tangled greenery. Stared at the house, situated across a wide expanse of lawn dotted with stately evergreens and deciduous trees and backed by the bright June sky.

Double whoa.

The pictures supplied by the owner hadn't lied. Nor had they done this place justice.

Edgecliff wasn't crumbling. Or overgrown with vegetation. Or missing any vital parts.

It was beautiful. Stunning. Exactly what a classic 1910 Queen Anne Victorian–style house should be.

And the setting?

Breathtaking.

Surrounded on three sides by the sea, the house had a commanding view from its perch on the ten-acre promontory it had claimed as its own long ago.

Easing back in her seat, she studied the details of the ornate three-story home. The wide wraparound front porch, with a rounded, domed-roof extension on the right and decorative railings, posts, and spindles. The asymmetry of the façade, with a section bumped out beside the front door. An octagonal turret on the left, its roof steeply pitched. A multitude of windows, all different shapes and sizes.

The brick exterior also gave it a sense of permanence and stability often lacking in shingled Queen Anne houses—but unusual for this part of the country, particularly in that era.

Even more unusual given that a lumber baron had built it.

But perhaps the solid construction was why it had held up despite its exposure to the Oregon coast's notorious fall and winter storms, when powerful winds and the raging waters of the Pacific put on quite a show.

Or so she'd read while researching the location.

If this trip panned out, however, she'd find out firsthand what—

Her phone began to vibrate, and she picked it up off the seat beside her. Skimmed the screen. Grimaced.

She did *not* need any more negativity undermining her confidence. Especially on the heels of her unsettling encounter at the gate.

AUTHOR'S NOTE

ONE OF THE QUESTIONS I'M OFTEN ASKED during interviews and speaking engagements is how much research I do for my books. The simple answer: a ton. By the time I finish a suspense novel, I generally have more than one hundred pages of single-spaced typed research notes and citations. Only a tiny portion of that material ends up in the book, but in order to write credibly about often complex subjects, I have to do extensive homework. Yes, my stories are fiction, but the protocols for the various law enforcement agencies and organizations I write about are real. Likewise for the professions of my characters. And I'm a stickler for accuracy.

In addition to my online research, I consult with experts throughout the process to add a final polish of authenticity to my work. When the book is finished, they often also read not only the pertinent sections, but the entire novel. For this book, I owe a huge debt of gratitude to former Monroe County, Missouri, sheriff David Hoffman and to board certified forensic pathologist Dr. Mark Peters, who regularly testifies in homicide cases and teaches at the university level in addition to his autopsy work. These two gentlemen went above and beyond, answering my many questions promptly and thoroughly. Thank you both so much.

As always, special thanks to my husband, Tom, who has encouraged me every step of the way in my writing career, and to my wonderful parents, James and Dorothy Hannon, who are both cheering me on from heaven now. While the absence of their physical presence will always leave a huge void in my life, the sweet memory of their unconditional love and support continues to sustain me each and every day.

Looking ahead, in April 2023 I'll take you back to my charming Oregon seaside town of Hope Harbor, where hearts heal . . . and love blooms. You'll find an excerpt for *Windswept Way* in this book. And next October, I'll be launching a brand-new suspense series featuring three foster siblings. It promises to be a thrilling ride!

Until next time, I wish you good health and happy reading.

Irene Hannon is the bestselling, award-winning author of more than sixty contemporary romance and romantic suspense novels. She is also a three-time winner of the RITA award—the "Oscar" of romance fiction—from Romance Writers of America and is a member of that organization's elite Hall of Fame.

Her many other awards include National Readers' Choice, Daphne du Maurier, Retailers' Choice, Booksellers' Best, Carol, and Reviewers' Choice from RT *Book Reviews* magazine, which also honored her with a Career Achievement award for her entire body of work. In addition, she is a two-time Christy award finalist.

Millions of her books have been sold worldwide, and her novels have been translated into multiple languages.

Irene, who holds a BA in psychology and an MA in journalism, juggled two careers for many years until she gave up her executive corporate communications position with a Fortune 500 company to write full-time. She is happy to say she has no regrets.

A trained vocalist, Irene has sung the leading role in numerous community musical theater productions and is also a soloist at her church. She and her husband enjoy traveling, long hikes, gardening, impromptu dates, and spending time with family. They make their home in Missouri.

To learn more about Irene and her books, visit www.irene hannon.com. She posts on Twitter and Instagram but is most active on Facebook, where she loves to chat with readers.

Love Irene's Romantic Suspense Books? Don't Miss the **TRIPLE THREAT** Series!

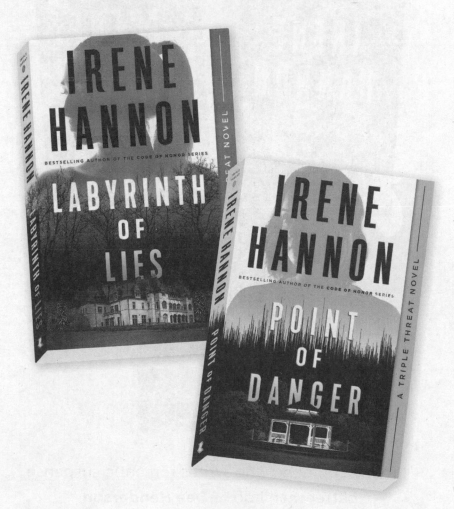

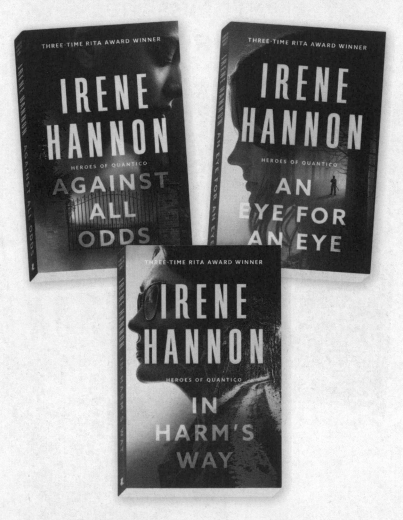

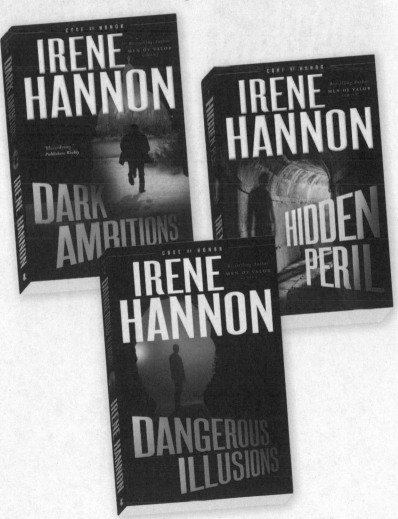

DANGER LURKS AROUND
EVERY CORNER

Come home to Hope Harbor—
where hearts heal . . .
and love blooms.

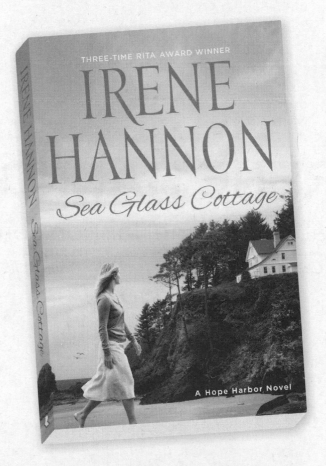

Christi Reece is desperate. The onetime golden girl's life has tarnished,
and a cascade of setbacks has left her reeling. She needs help,
and she's certain Jack Colby is in a position to provide it.
Can these two hurting souls open their hearts to a new beginning?

Meet
IRENE HANNON
at www.IreneHannon.com

Learn news, sign up for her mailing list,
and more!

Find her on